TALION

JIMMY L. CULLORS
JOSEPH SZEWEZYK
FIRST EDITION

LITTERATEUR PUBLICATIONS, INC.

 LAS VEGAS, NEVADA

LPI® is a registered trademark of Litterateur Publications, Inc.
Cullors, Jimmy L. /Szewezyk, Joseph
Talion
Fiction
Edited by Sean Hoade, Mishawaka, Indiana
Library of Congress Control Number: 2002092666
San: 253-6668
ISBN 0-9707914-0-2
Cover Design by Create Space Charleston, SC

ABOUT THE AUTHORS

Jimmy L. Cullors was born and raised in the city of Detroit, Michigan. When he reached adulthood he became a Detroit Police Officer and served for 15 years. He achieved mediocre accomplishments in his short life, but is happiest with the accomplishments he made with his children.

With the autumn years of his life slowly approaching, Mr. Cullors has decided to spend that time putting his past life's experiences into writing.

Over the years he has gained the ability to push his imagination to the limits and create remarkable stories, which will hit on every emotion of human existence. He takes his abilities and unites them with Joseph Szewczyk and together they have created a remarkable story. A story that will give you the opportunity to use your imagination

Mr. Cullors is overflowing with experience in the field of entertainment and has taken his experience in that field to create Litterateur Publications, Inc. Mr. Cullors is not only an author, but also the founder and President of Litterateur Publications, Inc.

Joseph Michael Szewczyk has won academic and athletic awards in the quarter century he has been alive. Being active in all formats of the entertainment fields, Joseph has excelled at his first love, writing, as well as movies and sports. He is an accomplished entertainer, teacher, storyteller and martial artist.

While working with Mr. Cullors, Joseph seems to be continuing his successful ways, but when asked what he wanted to be the best at, Joseph only replied, "Being a human being."

DEDICATION

To the all mighty God, my mother, all of my family members and the friends who stood by me and supported me in my endeavors.
Jimmy L. Cullors

"Hatred is what stirs up contentions, but love covers over even all transgressions."
Proverbs 10:12

To God, my Mom and Dad, my Aunt, my Family and Friends; all of those that helped me get to this point where I am now.

Those that the gods love grow young; those that God really loves receive His Grace.
To Nanci, whose name and Soul mean just that.
Joseph Szewczyk

TALION

<u>Acknowledgments</u>

"No man is an island"
Thanks to those who trusted and supported us.

Alderman, Aunt Sharon- WI.	Johnson, Wade & Lois- MI.
Allen, Cecil & Ola- MI.	Johnson, Wanda- MI.
Bolden, Art- NV.	Jones, Williams A.- MI.
Brittenham, Don- NV.	Kuczmarski's, The- WI.
Coleman, Gerry- WI.	Levandowski, Allan- IL.
Cullors, Christie- NV.	Levandowski, Andy – WI.
Cullors Jr, Jimmy- NV.	Levandowski, Barbara- IL.
Diorio, Cherie- WI.	Levandowski, Jackie- WI.
Doolin, Brian- WI.	Levandowski, Jerry- WI.
Elmore, Patsy- MI.	Levandowski, Norman- WI.
Fried, Mrs. Stanley- NV.	Levandowski, Wayne- KY
Green, Theresa- MI.	McVay, William- MI.
Halada, Crystal- WI.	Montgomery, Adrienne- MI.
Medina, Trina- NV.	Paramore, Alton- MI.
Nanci –NV.	Sailor- NV.
Hicks, Edna- MI.	Szewczyk, Joseph- NV.
Higgins, Eileen- MI.	Turner, Harold Keith- MI.
Jennings, Beverly Ann- MI.	West, Dorothy- MI.

Table of Contents

chapter

1

THE FINISH

The silence was broken by the loud, commanding voices outside the shabby motel room and the thunderous noise of the door as it separates from its hinges and crashes to the floor. The voices and the sound of destruction are loud and frightening, causing the two men who were sleeping in the dark room to jump up and violently attack the six figures rushing into the tiny room. Groggy and still full of the tequila they consumed the night before, the two men try valiantly, but in vain, to defend themselves. They gather courage and strength from the fear that consumes their bodies. The figures, which appear as sinister silhouettes, meet a resistance that is unimaginable from two men who were supposedly drunk.

The first man attacks one of the intruders, yelling obscenities as he elbows the intruder in the nose and knocks him against a wall.

"Ah…Ah…Ah…Goddammit! I'm gonna to fuck you up!" he bellows at the intruder.

As the man searches in the darkness for another victim, the butt of a 12-gauge shotgun meets him. He falls back on the bed, absorbing the pain as he grabs his face and feels it to be a bloody mess. He attempts to retaliate, but is met by a second blow to his back and a kick to his ribs.

The pain is so intense that the man can do nothing but yell to his partner as he rolls onto the floor.

"Get them motherfuckers, McCulley! Fuck 'em up!" he screams, as he lies there writhing in pain.

On the other side of the room McCulley has little problem dealing with the silhouettes. One by one, they are hurled across the room. And one by one, they return to cause as much damage to this hulk of a human frame as they can. With a single blow, McCulley knocks one of the intruders unconscious, and in the same motion, he grabs another and throws him out through the window.

As the body flies out the window, McCulley yells for his partner to help him. "I got rid of two of 'em, Jamie…get your ass over here! There's only three left".

Jamie attempts to get up, but is knocked unconscious by two more blows to his head. McCulley, realizing he is alone, continues to fight for his life as the three remaining men converged on him. Blow after blow lands on his exhausted body, but with each blow, he seems to become stronger…stronger, that is, until the wooden butt of that same shotgun crashes across his lower jaw, sending him into oblivion.

The silhouettes stand back, admiring their trophies, and turn to the commanding voice speaking in the darkness that orders them to clean up their mess.

"You two check the bodies and see if they're alive. You, go outside and make sure we don't have any uninvited guests. Hector, are you all right?"

"¡Chingada madre! I'm all right, Pheellips," Hector, replies in a distinct Hispanic accent. You deedn' tell me that we would run into tanta violencia. ¡Puta, cabron! I thought it was going to be two tired men who would geeve themselves up. Who the hell are they and what are they so afraid of?"

"Well Hector, you live and learn," Phillips replies cynically.

Hector gives Phillips a hard, cold stare and rolls his eyes as he turns away looking for his cousin. "Oye, Frankie. ¿Cómo estás?"

"Puta madre, Hector! Qué divertido! I was ready to get down 'n kick ass, 'mano, until Phillips came con esa pinche escopeta. Man, you are so brutal with that thing? I thought you say we no gonna kill these men?"

"Yeah, I did say that, I don't think I killed them. Just gave them a little 'in service training.' They'll remember me from this day forward. I made my statement. Frankie, get some water and throw it on them. We need them awake. Hector, you and Smith sit them up in a chair and 'cuff 'em."

The two unconscious men are placed in chairs and handcuffed with their hands behind them. Frankie returns with the water and douses the two men. He steps back and smiles as the shock of the cold water begins to revive the men. The chill surges through their bodies and they grimace in pain as they stir back into consciousness.

McCulley moves a little, but he remains semi-conscious. Jamie opens his eyes, looks around the room, and realizes he's finally caught. He knows his life was over now, and he begins to drift back to the time when all of his problems began...

Jamie's mind begins to block out the sights and sounds of the present. His mind goes back to another time, another place. The warm familiarity of unconsciousness starts to tug at Jamie. Like a prisoner that can't escape his physical bonds, Jamie's mind takes him someplace else. Most prisoners dream of the future, or of things they loved in the past, Jamie dreams of the events that lead up to this moment, to everything in his life that brought him to this point.

He came too suddenly, fully awake with the instant recognition that he was someplace unfamiliar, but his mind resisted the memory of where he was and why he was there. He remained motionless except for his eyes, which stared at the yellow ribbon that hung from the rear-view mirror. A smile creased his face at the memory of his nine-year old daughter lying there.

The sun, just rising over the distant horizon, shone through the windshield. The strands of the cheerful ribbons cast parallel shadows that fell across a picture lying on the passenger seat–shadows that appeared like prison bars across the faces of his sons– and he remembered. And then he remembered where he was and why he was there.

Then cold, hard anger replaced the warm memory of his daughter, anger and something else–something unfamiliar and unwelcome. It was there at the edge of his consciousness, where it reached out to him begging to be heard–pleading to be heeded before it was too late. He felt it as a weight in the pit of his stomach, a heaviness on his chest, a rolling mass of fear, of guilt, dread, of remorse and misgivings, and uncertainty.

For a moment, his resolution wavered, and then he saw again in his mind's eye, the picture of the two handsome young men. The camera had captured them in a moment of shared laughter during a time of celebration. When had they last had occasion to laugh? When had they last had cause to celebrate? He had done everything he could to protect them from the perjurious testimony of a crooked cop, but to no avail. Their only hope lay in this dangerous plan that carried no guarantee–or even a remote chance–of succeeding. He knew it was a crazy scheme, but it was a   plan born of a father's desperation to prove his sons innocent of the crime that resulted in their imprisonment.

The rumbling of an approaching truck interrupted his thoughts, and his eyes flicked to the rear-view mirror. A 1954 blue Chevy pickup was rattling down the driveway.

Reflexively, he slid further down in the seat of his parked Nissan as he watches the truck approach in the mirror. The sun reflecting off the pickup's windshield prevents him from seeing the occupants, but his mind's eye fills in the missing details as he watches them bounce up and down in a cracked, blue, vinyl seat. Each time the old truck found another of the potholes in the road; it disturbed the dust that settled on the seats of the old vehicle. He watches warily, as the truck rolls to a tired stop in front of the squat, dingy building from which hung a sagging sign reading "U-Store-IT."

The truck sits quietly and motionless while the dust it raised behind silently settles back on to the earth. Then the passenger door swings open as its hinges groan their objection.

He turns and looks through the rear window at the dirty, blue pickup truck. It seems as though an eternity has elapsed, before an elderly lady dressed in a red, dotted duster and tennis shoes exits the vehicle. Her gray-blond hair is still in rollers haphazardly placed about her head. The movement of her body causes the rollers to fall into her face, which she brushes away as she turns, and reaches for the picnic basket she prepared the night before.

The basket, covered with a red and white-checkered cloth, seems heavy, but she deals with the gravity acting against it as though she was lifting a basket of flowers. She handles all of her problems in one swoop, preventing the basket from hitting the ground, moving her hair, and closing the door of the truck simultaneously. Flinging her hand woven shawl over her shoulder, she walks toward the weather beaten building.

From her slow pace, it appears as though she was waiting for the driver to get out of the vehicle. Like smoke flowing through the air, the mass of human flesh begins to emerge from the truck. With a pipe set firmly between his teeth, the man grunts and hawks up a wad of phlegm from deep in his throat and spit it at a grasshopper shading in the shadow of the truck.

The man cloaks his brown tweed coat around him, as though it was ten below zero–or maybe it is to conceal the dingy, white T-shirt and blue coveralls he's wearing.

As he walks toward the building, he kicks at the grasshopper he missed with his phlegm and became more irritated because he misses again. He thinks of the days when that grasshopper and a few more would have been caught and hung on fish hooks in the time it took him to get out the truck and walk the few feet to the entrance of the building.

Satisfied with the fact that, that grasshopper is one of the lucky ones to survive to his age, the man, also carrying a basket, follows the elderly lady into the building.

After a few moments of contorting his body and rubbing his eyes, Jamie realizes there was not enough room to stretch out his legs; they demanded space. His toes wiggled around in his shoes and the pricks of a thousand needles raced through his feet. With no room for comfort, it was time for his fifty-year-old body to get out of the truck and stretch. His stretching and his groan of relief keep his body under control for a few seconds, and as he begins to relax, the red flat-topped mountains grab his attention.

He arrived at the storage facility in the middle of the night while the darkness covered the landscape, not revealing the mountainous range he had driven through. He had felt his way in the darkness, and luckily enough for him, there were no cliffs or other dangerous obstacles to cause him any injury. Sleeping in his truck was not in his plans; a motel room with a soft bed and television were his preference.

Now all the kinks were worked out of his body and it was time to move forward and continue with the business at hand. After first locating his glasses, Jamie walks to the door of the building, grabbing the knob and turning it. Resenting his harsh handling, the door refuses to budge. After regrouping, he delivers a more aggressive twist and harder push, which forces the door to give way much to the surprise of the old man and his wife inside.

As he enters the lobby, the brilliance of the sun races across the room and encroaches on its dimness strips, accentuating the silhouettes of the two clerks in the background. The clerks stare at the large frame of the light complexioned, black man who stumbled into their lobby.

"That's a helluva way to come into a building scaring the hell out of everybody," the old clerk blurted out as Jamie adjusted his eyes to the darkness of the room. "If'n ya couldn't open th' doe, ya shoulda knocked!"

Jamie, dressed in blue jeans, a pull over jacket and with his head adorned by the hat of his favorite baseball team, which shouts "The Detroit Tigers" to the world–walks slowly across the room and looks observantly at the artifacts that lay around the room. They seem to be waiting for time to restore them.

After several seconds, Jamie turns and looks at the clerk and mumbles through his thick beard, "Do you ever open the doors in this place? It smells like hell in here.

Mold, mildew, or whatever it is. This place needs some air."

"Fer a city boy, ya gotta heap t'say 'bout smells," the old man retorted. "Seems t'me anything'd smell better'n where y'all come from. That smell enterin' yore lungs is th'sweet smell o'fresh country air–fresh outdoe air. Somethin' y'all caint get in th' city."

For a moment there is complete silence as they stare at each other across the room. Jamie looks around and notices that no major effort has been put into decorating the place. The beams on the ceiling are exposed, and in three places there are unconcealed light cables with dangling light bulbs.

Several windows are covered by sunburned drapes; the color was unrecognizable. The dust on the windowsill reveals the tracks of every insect that had walked over the area.

As Jamie scans the room, other items grab his attention, reminding him of his earlier days, such as the blue speckled metal coffeepot and cups.

The silverware, which is used to stir coffee, is sitting on the table; it is tarnished to the point where it could be mistaken for gold. The chairs are of good quality, manufactured probably at the turn of the century, and looks as though they could withstand another 50 years.

As he walks across the room, the floor gives under the pressure of his body. By it's squeaking it seems to be protesting that every step was causing it pain. The roll-top desk sitting in the corner would demand top dollar at any antique shop. The counter on which they served their customers was put together haphazardly, probably by the neighborhood handy man, who may have intended it to serve no real function.

"Okay, young feller," the old man demanded, now annoyed, now that we done cleared th' air...whatcha want?"

"I don't know if I want to deal with you. You act as though you woke up in a bad mood. The reason I came here is to store my vehicle. So, I need a storage unit."

"Well, we got plenty o' them. What size d'ya want?" the old man replied, ignoring Jamie's quip.

"I'm looking for something large enough for my pickup. It's parked right outside. That one...the red pickup."

"Why d'ya wanna put yore truck in a stowage bin?"

"If you must know, I've had a stroke of bad luck in this god-forsaken town. Things aren't going right for me here, and I need a change of pace. So I decided to check out Las Vegas and I don't want to leave my vehicle out on the street."

The old man looked at Jamie as if a bug just landed on his face. "If'n ya ain't workin', how th' hell y'gonna pay fer th'stowage?"

"I don't think that'll be a problem. As a matter of fact, I'm paying for a month's worth of storage now just so you won't have a cow. I'll be back in a few days to get my truck. At that time I'll want the difference of the money due to me. Speaking of money, what's the cost and size of this unit?"

"Well, if'n ya want one big enough t'stow yore truck, it's gonna cost ya a hunnert fer the bin an' twenny-five deposit fer damage-due today."

"Okay, give me the paperwork I have to sign and point me in the direction of the unit. You have taken up enough of my time."

The old man looked around the room and then back at Jamie, a poorly concealed look of disgust on his face, "Young'n, yore jes' like any common city boy allus in a hurry. That's th' problem with ya city slickers today. Y'all'r allus in a hurry. Why don' ya go'n set down over yonder? Set a spell an' enjoy a nice cuppa cawffee while I git th' papahwork together. Anna jes' made it fresh, an' she'd be quite upset, if'n ya don't have some."

"Okay," Jamie conceded, "but hurry, I have a plane to catch."

Jamie walks towards the wobbly table in the corner, which was home to the blue-speckled coffeepot and its cups. He pours himself a cup of coffee and was very anxious to taste it because of the enticing aroma, which encircled the room. He picks up the coffee creamer and begins to pour cream into his coffee, when a clump of cream falls into the cup.

"Damn! Anna will have to be mad because I'm not going to drink this shit."

He places the cup on the table, and walks away mumbling to himself.

"I have to get out of here...this place is the pits. Sugar clumped in the spoon as though it's been there forever...not to mention, the hundreds of flies calling this place home..." Jamie cut himself off when he sees the old man motioning to him.

"Hey youngster... c'mere. I need some information from ya!
What's yore name?"

"It's Jamie Collins."

"And yo address?"

"I have none at the present."

The old timer looks up from his contract form long enough to give Jamie a stern gaze, "Well, ah gotta put somethin' down here."

"Okay, how about my son's address? That's where I am going anyway."

"That'll do. What is it?"

"It's 618 W. Washington Ave. Las Vegas, NV 89106."

"Y' got a phone number?"

"Yea... it's 702-555-5555"

Satisfied with Jamie's answers, the man went over to explain how the unit worked.

"Okay, Mista' Collins, that'll be a hunnert and twenny-five dollars. Here's th' code t' th' gate. When ya'll punch in th' code, ya'll hafta punch in foe other numbers ya like. Got that?"

"Yeah... okay."

"Now, when ya go through the gate, drive down t' th' end 'n turn left, then go down two moe rolls an' turn left agin. Yo storage bin is number 2344."

JIMMY CULLORS/JOSEPH SZEWEZYK

"Okay, thanks a lot," Jamie said on his way out, then he stops to add, "Oh… by the way, while I'm in the back, would you please call me a cab. I need a ride to the airport."

The old man chuckled, "Y'all forgot where ya is, young'un? Ain't no damn cabs be comin' out here. Either ya gonna hitch a ride or come up with some mo money t' take ya."

"Okay, I will give you ten dollars to take me to the airport."

The man's face reddened, "Ten dollars! Ya outta yer mind? That ain't even a dollar a mile. If'n ya gonna catch that thar plane ya better git t' walkin'."

"How far is the airport anyway?"

"Bout twenny miles…an' that means ya gonna pay me more'n ten measly bucks."

"Okay, how much do you want?" asked Jamie trying to save time.

"Least fifty dollars!"

"Fifty dollars! You must be crazy."

"Ain't me who got t' git t' th' airport." the old man replied, looking every bit like a man who knows he is about to win.

"Shit man, I don't have that much money. All the money I have I need in Las Vegas."

The old man smiles at Jamie, "Mista' Collins, y'all got a problem with yer hearin'? I don't need t' go t' no airport."

"Okay, here's your money and no more, I need to leave as soon as I get back."

Jamie leaves the lobby and climbs into his truck, thinking about the fare that he has to pay. He had only brought a certain amount of money with him and felt that would be enough. But now he realizes he has to allow for mistakes and eventualities if he was going to go through with his plans.

"Let's see," he muttered to himself. "First punch in this code-234986 and a four-digit number. I'll try this

'7272'. That should do it. Okay, the gate is opening. Down the aisle, left, then left again."

The storage bins are situated on ten acres of land and arranged like a maze. Each building resembled the others in every way: built of wood and painted over many times in red, but it has been at least two years since a new coat had been applied. Large pieces of paint chips lay on the ground covering entrances to homes of field mice, rabbits and anything else that crawls and needs a burrow.

The storage bins are configured four together, then four more going in the opposite direction, and continuing thus around the entire site.

Jamie finally reaches his assigned bin, only to find that the elements would have no problem getting into his vehicle. The seams between each board were at least an inch apart and the roof and the walls had enough space between them that a small person could crawl through. Keeping out the sun would be impossible.

After pulling his vehicle into the bin, Jamie steps back and stares at the structure and mumbles to himself.

"My problem now is...hoping this place holds up until I return...I wonder if there is anything living in there. I'm glad there is a cover over the bed of my truck or all my belongings would be ruined.

"Now, where is that damned lock? Oh, I remember–I put it in the glove box. But I don't know what I'll accomplish by locking this door...I just hope my truck is here when I get back."

With some reservation Jamie walks away, following his fresh tire tracks back to the lobby. When he reaches the front, the old man was sitting patiently in his truck. Jamie couldn't help but interrogate him when he reached the vehicle.

"Is it safe to leave my truck in this dump? Have you ever had anything stolen from your units?"

The old man turns toward Jamie with a hint of anger on his face as he grabs the pipe from his mouth and begins to tell this man from another world how he felt about his intrusion into their lives of peace and tranquility.

"Ah–lived in these here parts fer th' better part o' mah life. Fought in Ko'reeah…187ᵗʰ Regimental Combat Team…made a combat jump at Pyongyang, an' ah been all over th' world.

"Everywhere I been thar was some kinda problem. Ah look at that dam thing y'all call a telly-vision fer so-called ennertainment, an' ah sees and hears is problems.

"Ain't nobody livin' in dese here parts is gonna do nuthin' t' me or mah propity. It jes' plain pisses me off thet you big-city folks come out here 'n' think yore problems is here, too.

"Ah'll tell yo' what–yo' get that piece o' shit foreign truck off'n mah propity, an' kiss me whar th' sun don't shine. This so-called dump, as ya calls it, is mine, an' it takes care o' me an' mah wife. No, it ain't like what y'all got in Las Vegas, but it pay th' bills. Now, get out of mah way afore I spit on ya."

Suddenly at a lost for words and desperately needing a ride, Jamie begins to grovel. "Wait a minute old man. I'm sorry if I offended you. It's just that I have so many things on my mind. I didn't mean to insult you or your property. To show you I am sincere, here, take an extra ten dollars. Okay?"

The man looks Jamie in the eyes, " Well, let me put it thisa way young'n if'n I'm gonna take y'all t' th' airport–an' y'say one moe thing bout mah town, mah propity, mah wife or mah biz'ness, ah'm gonna pull out dis here gun an'make ya git out an' walk. Y' hear me, young'n?"

"Yeah. Okay, I will be nice," Jamie starts apologetically, "now can we go, I got a plane to catch."

Jamie and the old man traveled down the road and headed for Tucson International Airport in silence for most of the way. As he looks out of the window, Jamie marvels at the breathtaking sight of the mountains.

These mountains are unique, he thought. There is something about the mountains in Arizona…most of them are flat topped, and the colors seem to be more evident than on other mountains elsewhere. Sometimes you can pass a certain mountain and it's red–but on your return that same mountain is purple. As far as you can see, there are mountains on both sides of the road. Big flat tops, tall flat tops, and long continuous flat tops. In between the mountains is nothing but flat land with creosote bush and cactus growing in all shapes and sizes. Occasionally, you see a jackrabbit running across the road and fields. One rabbit running in a field stirs up what you thought were cactus, but turns out to be a few more jackrabbits all scattering in different directions.

Jamie is so lost in his thoughts that he forgot about the man and the ride to the airport. *What a shame, that people and events in life can make a person resort to such measures.*

He wishes he was back in Detroit on the Police Department, just living the life he was used to. But now here he was involved in something, which could put him in jail for the rest of his life–or even worse, on death row.

How and why do I continually involve myself in bullshit? How come I can't have a life like everyone else? Jamie ponders self-pityingly in his mind.

Deep in his thoughts, Jamie is abruptly awakened by a rough, familiar voice, "Hey young'n! We're here. Hey! What's wrong wit'ya? Are ya dead? Hey, wake up."

"Yeah…Yeah…I'm awake."

"Y'all' coulda fool' me. Ah thought you was dead' cuz, yore eyes was open."

"I was just deep in my thoughts. That's all."

"Boy, I hope ya don't go there too ofin…somethin' could happen t' ya."

"Yeah, you're right old man. At any rate, thanks for the ride. I got to go."

"Yeah, but where is mah money? Plus the extre ten?"

"I paid you, old man. Thanks again, I'll see you in a few days." As Jamie walks away he mumbles, "Loi du Talion."

Jamie enters the airport and finds he is early and has a couple of hours remaining before the plane's departure. So he decides to sit down and rest.

The thoughts of his sons come easy. They had spent so many good times together. In Detroit, when other fathers didn't have enough time for their children, Jamie not only had taken time with his kids; he also involved other children with them. When his youngest child, Jamie Jr., was eight years old, he came to his father and asked if he could play baseball. So Jamie and his two sons tried to find a team.

After searching unsuccessfully, Jamie decided to start a team of his own. He had to create two teams because of the age difference of his sons. Jamie Jr. was eight and Marvin was ten. The two teams then grew to four, because of regulations of the league. Before he knew it, Jamie was coaching sixty children. They were all playing and enjoying themselves even though they didn't win a game that year.

At the end of the season, he gave them a banquet and awarded trophies and Certificates of Appreciation and bided the children farewell. But it wasn't that easy. The children wanted to play football. Jamie, not knowing enough about football to coach, convinced several of his friends to assist him.

Little did Jamie know he bit off more then he could chew. In order for his teams to play football, he had to buy equipment. He searched the community for donors, but no one was willing to put up the money necessary for the children's uniforms and equipment. Jamie was then faced with the task of telling the children they couldn't play.

On the day he decided to give the children the bad news, he was explaining the situation to a police officer. The officer asked Jamie if he really needed the money and Jamie said he was sincere and serious. The cop advised Jamie to go to the horse races and bet on a certain horse who was going to win that day. Jamie stared in disbelief at the officer, who assured him it was on the level. Jamie went to the races very reluctantly and bet two hundred dollars on "Choice" to win, at twenty-to-one odds.

Jamie walked away with four thousand dollars that day. For the next month, Jamie got tips on the winners and raised enough money to purchase the necessary equipment to outfit one hundred and fifty children, who also played a losing season.

The screeching brakes of an approaching car startled Jamie back to reality as he began to gaze around the city. Tucson is a lovely city. All the trees, grass, and birds seem to bring some order to it, nothing like Las Vegas. People here don't seem to be in a hurry, and if they were, the way to get where they are going was well laid out. People had alternate routes–a complex skein of alleys and through streets–to wherever they wanted to go.

Jamie settles back on a bench and stares into space, engrossed in a deep conversation with himself.

Now, this is a beautiful town; I wish I had moved here from Detroit, instead of to Las Vegas. Hell! I wished I had done a lot of things, but there is no use in crying about something that I have no control over. The future lies ahead…I don't like this feeling that comes over me. I know what's going to happen in the very near future–the lives of a few hundred people will be altered, for the good of some and for much the worse of others.

I hope my love ones forgive me, if my plan doesn't work. I hope they can look into my heart and know why this tragedy had to happen. I know that in my heart I am not a bad person, but I also know that what is about to happen has to take place.

Shit, Jamie! Just listen to yourself. Who the hell do you think you are? You're not God, and you're not the President. You're just a man caught up in worldly matters. You need to turn your head away from these worldly problems and let God take over your life. You can't right a wrong, you can't bring back the past, and you most certainly can't change man's way of thinking. Jamie, stop now! Stop before it is too late. There are so many people who need you, who won't be able to go on without you. Think of your daughter and the other children in your life. You always speak of how people don't think, how can you speak of people that way when you are just like them. Jamie stop now–you don't want to die."

Lost in his thoughts, time slips away and the noise from a baby crying brings Jamie suddenly back to reality.

Jamie looks at his watch and realizes he has only twenty minutes to make his plane. Not knowing where to go, he looks around frantically to find an airline information board. Jamie spies one of the boards and scans for his flight Southwest Airlines 286. Finally, he finds it on the screen and immediately starts running for gate C-23.

The run through the airport was an amazing feat for Jamie because the days of his running have been over since he left the police force fifteen years previously.

People stop and watch him pass; he even runs through the moving walkway. But age would have its way and he is forced to stop and catch his breath; the long line at the metal detector is a convenient spot. His labored breathing confirmed that smoking is not good for the lungs. He needs more room in his chest for oxygen, but because of his approaching project, to quit smoking is out of the question. So, not only does this over-aged youth look ridiculous running through the airport, he also embarrasses himself by breathing like he has asthma. Not wanting to direct too much attention to himself, Jamie quickly recovers as though nothing is happening and continues through the metal detector toward the awaiting plane.

When he arrives at the gate, there was no one waiting to board. However, the door is still open, so he approaches the door and is greeted by the flight attendant, who stated he was just in the nick of time. Jamie walks down the passageway to the awaiting plane and finds his seat.

The plane is full of happy, excited people who are on their way to Las Vegas. The incessant mumbles of anticipated wealth fill the plane with cacophony. Several people have money they know they are going to lose; others have money they are going to double. These hopes and doubts are overshadowed by the thought of going to Las Vegas itself–away from routine and drudgery. It is enough to be away from the crying babies and the tension of menacing friends. Now is the time to enjoy oneself and be together with their loving partner just for the fun of it.

After settling in his seat, Jamie blocks out the sounds and concentrates on the very near future. He knows that what he is about to do can result in is imprisonment but he also knows, he has to do something, to right a grievous wrong. He could not; with a clear conscience simply do nothing, to save his sons. Every step he takes closer to Las Vegas puts him closer to the inevitable, to the demise of Jamie, as he knew him.

The vision of his sons crying for him as they were being escorted off to prison still rings through his head. The tears begin to flow; his heart begins to beat faster and his anger becomes more intense than ever. He drifts off into a deep sleep. He awakes as the plane is making its final approach into Las Vegas.

The rolling mountains beneath seem like anthills until a large metropolis appears over the horizon. The view of the Valley Auto Mall from the sky gave an exact location as to where he would be if he were on the ground. Following the long dark line running adjacent to the mall was Sunset Boulevard, and on either side were beautiful new homes most with swimming pools and/or Jacuzzis. Sprawling lawns and parks were a welcome sight for first time viewers and the traffic was flowing as though the person watching was controlling it.

The runway was in sight and Jamie is startled by the loud voice of the pilot; he begins to look around and prepare himself for the landing.

Final thoughts go through his mind. *My that was a quick trip; the plane is getting ready to land. I must have really slept hard or was it deserved sleep?*

Let me see. Is everything covered so far? I have my belongings packed away in my pickup in Tucson; nobody knows me there, and I didn't make any dumb mistakes as far as people remembering or recognizing me. Maybe I should keep this beard and glasses on until I leave the airport in Vegas. That way, when and if a picture of me is seen on TV, it won't jog anyone's memories.

Yes, I think everything is covered on that end, now to get into Vegas and start everything rolling there. This plane lands at 10:45 a.m. That gives me an hour and fifteen minutes to get to my next location and make sure everything is all set there.

I wonder how my boys are doing. I hope they are not having any problems. If they can just hold on a little while longer, everything will be okay. God, how I love them! I hope they understand why I am doing this. I can't let them rot in prison without trying to do something to help them.

As the plane touches down, the palms of Jamie's hands begin to sweat and his stomach churns. His contrived and complicated plan is finally becoming a reality.

The wheels of the landing gear scream as they touch the ground, as Jamie leans back in his seat and stares at the overhead. The plane finally parks and the loud passengers begin to deplane. Jamie stands up, his legs so wobbly and weak that he could barely make them move. His heart is racing and fear consumes his entire body. It was a long, slow walk through the plane; after reaching the exit, Jamie's adrenaline begins to flow and the rush starts again.

The first order of the day is to find a restroom to change clothes and relieve the pressure on his bladder. This was an easy accomplishment; after entering the airport, Jamie notices the restroom. He enters, finds the room empty, and then quickly dashes into a stall. Off come the beard, mustache, and hairpiece, which he places in a plastic bag. After removing all facial hair, he goes to the sink and begins washing his face. He washes again and again, but nothing could get rid of the fear, which has set in hard. While his face is completely covered with soap and immersed in water, several men walk in talking–then total silence. It is not unusual for this to happen in the men's restroom. Men, for some reason, don't hold conversations in the restroom.

Jamie wipes his face and watches the other men as they finish their business, exit the restroom and resume talking. He laughs to himself, decides to change clothes—and goes back into a stall and replaces the facial hair and hairpiece. His conversations to himself begin again.

As he exits the restroom he murmurs under his breath, "Now I know how Superman feels."

With no baggage to claim, he rushes through the airport and outside to the waiting line of cabs.

"Taxi…Taxi!"

A black and white cab pulls up and Jamie gets in. The driver is a stout Caucasian male with a beard and sunglasses. His stomach was holding on to the steering wheel as though it were doing the steering.

"Where to," the cabby demanded in a heavy New York accent.

Jamie looks at the man, thinking how good it would be to be in New York.

"I want to go to Valley View and Spring Mountain."

"Okay mister, you new in town?" The cabby asked, attempting to make conversation.

"No, I just got back from LA. I had to take care of some business. It's nice to be back in the land of sunshine. Anything been happening in the last few days I should be concerned about?"

"Nah, just the same old stuff…all of it, is just a bunch of shit. I try not to even look at the news…it's all depressing to me. They should change the news programs and just put on good news and sports. What did you do in LA, if you don't mind me asking?"

Yeah, he doesn't look at the news or, for that matter, anything else on TV, Jamie thought, looking at the man. *Too much time is taken up filling up that body.*

"I was looking for a place to live. I'll be leaving Las Vegas in a couple of days. I need a change of pace," Jamie continues. He looks at the clock on the cab's radio, "Go up Paradise to Twain and travel so you can avoid traffic. I have to be at my location at a certain time. Someone is meeting me there.

"Okay. You got it pal."

"Jamie."

"What's that?"

"Jamie–Jamie is my name."

"Okay Jamie; got you."

The cab circles the airport and arrives at Paradise Road where they approach the skyline of Las Vegas. The first hotel he sees is the MGM Grand off to the left, then the pyramid-shaped Luxor Hotel, the colorful Excalibur and finally the Mirage Resorts.

Jamie reflects back to the day when he and his children were enjoying life. Life, as they knew it then, was being awakened by the smell of bacon cooking, fried potatoes, eggs and brewing coffee. As the delectable aroma lingered through the house, Jamie could visualize his children tossing in their beds.

After the breakfast is cooked and placed on the table, Jamie turned on the component set and looked through large stacks of LPs to find his favorite album "Harold Melvin and the Bluenotes". He placed the album on the turntable and turned up the volume and blasted the tune "Wake Up Everybody."

Jamie sat down and watched as his half-asleep, half-awake children flowed slowly down the steps. First, it's Jamie Jr., then his daughter, Deborah, Marvin and finally, his wife.

Loud explosions interrupt Jamie's deep thoughts. He turns his head to the left and sees the firing of cannons from the ships at the Treasure Island.

Ugh, my place of employment. I guess they must be testing the cannons, because it is too early for the Pirate Show. Jamie moans as they pass the building. He doesn't want to be reminded of going to work to deal cards. That's the last thing on his mind.

They approach the intersection of Spring Mountain and Valley View, and it's just another day of business. A few people are walking around in a hurry, trying to make a quick buck, while others want to fill the empty space in their stomachs at the Chinese Restaurant. Jamie has the driver pull into the parking lot of the bank building and he exits the vehicle. He slowly pans the area checking to see if everything is the same.

On the southwest corner is the mini mall. People are going in and out of the Chinese restaurant, and the print shop is doing as much business as ever. A man and woman are standing on the corner arguing. The man becomes upset when the woman pushes him and demands money. The man walks away, with the woman close behind yelling and pointing her finger.

The northwest corner stood a Firestone Dealer, and as usual, they're busy. Cars are lined up waiting for service and the workers are frantically running around trying to please everyone.

On the northeast corner, it's quiet and peaceful, as people stand around waiting for the bus under a big shade tree. Just behind the tree, two men share a bottle of beer before the approaching bus arrives. A man is running down the street towards the bus stop, waving his arms hoping that the approaching bus sees him.

Then there is the southeast corner where the bank sits. The parking lot is in front of the building and there are seven cars parked, probably belonging to the employees. No one is in the lot except for Jamie, who decides to walk inside the bank and wait for the armored truck to arrive. As he enters the bank, he surveys the vestibule and notices how a wall obscures the view from the inside. He thinks to himself, this is a perfect spot to stop the guard and engage him in conversation.

Inside the bank are five people. The bank manager is trying to look busy by having a phone conversation, probably with his girlfriend, while simultaneously watching Jamie walk into the bank.

A woman is sitting at the first desk, making the calculator sing to the rhythm of her fingers and two tellers are conducting transactions with customers, while another bank officer is on the phone–again, probably trying to look busy.

Jamie takes a seat and looks at his watch. It's 11:57 a.m. – he wonders if the guard is going to be on time. Like clockwork, however, the red armored truck pulls up precisely on time and a large human frame dismounts.

The guard is quite overweight, with the pinkest complexion Jamie could ever remember seeing, and sporting a pencil-thin mustache and a dimple in his chin. The guard's belt buckle points toward the ground, beneath his bulging stomach. The worn black shoes he is wearing needs to be replaced, but serves the purpose of covering his feet. His pants are about three inches above his ankles and reveal his incongruent white socks.

The guard waddles slowly into the bank, and passes by Jamie, who is sitting against the wall, pretending not to see him. Just as he had done on previous occasions, the guard greets the first woman and follows the manager who heads toward the vault. The manager and the guard disappear into the vault, emerging after some five minutes had passed. The guard smiles and says good-bye.

Jamie waits until the guard is almost into the vestibule; then he follows as the guard pushes the door open. Looking back, Jamie can see no one inside the bank and realizes that no one inside can see him. He seizes this opportunity to say a few words to the guard–just to see the man's reaction and to get familiar with him.

"How are you doing? Can you give me change for a quarter?" Jamie laughs, and continues talking to the guard, "I just couldn't resist it," he says sheepishly. "I always wanted to say that to a bank guard."

Without even so much as a flinch, the guard mumbles, "Yeah, I get that all day…bad joke, bro'."

"Well, you know how people are. Just need something to do or say to help pass the time. By the way, my name is Jamie Collins what's yours?" Jamie says while extending his hand in a gesture of friendship.

"Clyde-Clyde Figson," the guard replies, looking at Jamie's outstretched hand. "I'm not allowed to shake hands with anyone when carrying money. You know... security."

"Yeah, I understand. Well Clyde, I know how busy you are. You enjoy your day and watch out for the thieves."

Jamie then walks out past the guard, who shouts at him while holding on to his sidearm, "Don't worry, I can take care of myself with the help of my glock."

Jamie walks away shaking his head and thinking to himself, *He's just like most of these security guards. They place too much weight on his gun...never taking into consideration that the gun won't get them out of everything.*

As Jamie walks off, he looks at the other security guard who had remained in the truck, reading a magazine and completely unaware of his environment.

Jamie shakes his head and mumbles, "Well, do I have a lesson for the both of them?"

Everything checks out at the bank just as Jamie hoped it would. It is now noontime–time to check on the next step of the plan and make sure everything is the same. But first, Jamie needs a car to proceed with phase two of his operation.

He walks to the tree next to the bus stop and leans on it as he tries to think of someone who would loan him a car. About thirty seconds later, a thought comes to him. *Rena...*the name flashes through his head; the problem is he hasn't seen her for sometime, and she will probably be mad at him because he also owes her money. Jamie discards the thought of Rena being mad and decides to call her anyway.

He looks around, sees a phone booth about a block away and walks toward it. As he walks, he tries to think of what he is going to say to her. The one-block walk gives Jamie the opportunity to absorb the clean air and collect his thoughts. He still had time to reconsider, his plan, but is totally committed to freeing his sons. Nothing at this point will stop him from attaining that goal. He reaches the phone, picks up the receiver and begins to dial, knowing he is going to encounter an irate person on the other end.

"Hello," a female voice echoes through the phone.

"Yes, hello, is Rena home?"

"What's wrong with you?" The voice shouted back, "You can't recognize my voice?"

"Oh, I'm sorry baby; I can hardly hear you. What are you doing?"

"What do you mean, what am I doing? Why the hell are you calling me? I haven't seen or heard from you in months and you call me with that, I'm sorry baby-shit. If you don't get off this phone I will come through these wires and kick your ass." There was a hint of anger in the voice this time, but even more of a hint of hurt.

"Look Rena, calm down. I know you're mad at me, but give me a break. Let me explain."

"I'm not going to let you do anything with me. You are one sorry sucker, and I swore that if I ever saw or heard from you again, I would kill your monkey-ass! And by the way, where is my goddamn money?"

"Why don't you relax a bit and give me an opportunity to talk? I know you are pissed at me and I know you probably don't want to see me again, but right now I need your help."

"I have heard it all now. You just up and disappeared on me. I haven't seen you in a month of Sundays, and you want me to help you? You can kiss my ass!"

Jamie is at a loss for words, but he has to conjure up something to persuade her to help him. Before he could say anything else the voice sharply said, "If it's money you want, I don't have any."

"Don't worry. That's not why I'm calling. You see, I want to borrow your car, and I also need you to pick me up."

When he delivered this statement, he stands back and waits for the screaming to begin. But the voice came back, this time a little softer, "Shit Jamie, I'm relaxing and don't have any clothes on."

"Look Rena," Jamie begins in a reasonable tone, "if you let me use your car, I will fill up the tank, plus give you a hundred dollars."

"Well, I do need some gas and that two hundred dollars will come in handy."

"What do you mean two hundred dollars? I said I would give you a hundred."

"That's right, plus you owe me a hundred. If I don't get two hundred, you can stay your ass right where you are."

Considering the bind he is in, Jamie agrees, "Okay! Okay!"

"Where are you?"

"How about picking me up on the corner of Sahara and Valley View at the 7-11?"

"Okay, I'll be there in about thirty minutes."

"Okay baby, try and hurry. See you in a few."

Jamie looks up the street and realizes it would be quite a walk to meet Rena. But he had little choice since one bus has already gone by. He begins to walk and thinks about Rena and how much he really cared for her. He knew why she gave in so easily; he knew she thought about him... only if things could have been different...

They met in a cozy neighborhood bar. Both were there because the bar was convenient. Jamie had come from a meeting and Rena had just finished jogging.

Jamie was on one side of the bar while Rena was on the other. It was karaoke night and several people were on stage trying to sing. Jamie noticed Rena sitting and singing to herself, and he shouted across the bar trying to get her go up front and sing. But she refused. Jamie asked her to find a duet in the song book so they could sing together and she came up with Marvin Gaye and Tammy Terrell's "Ain't No Mountain High Enough".

They both went on the stage made fools of themselves, but it was fun. After that night, they continued to see each other, and the inevitable happened, they fell in love. They kept score on the number times they made love in one day...then how many times in a month. They even hoped for years, but things faded on Jamie's part. Rena wanted marriage and Jamie did not.

Jamie had gotten to a point in his life where he didn't have to share his life and was enjoying it. He felt his new found freedom was being intruded upon.

He began the breakup by decreasing his contact with Rena. When Rena began experiencing personal problems in her life, Jamie backed off even further, knowing this would piss her off. The more he backed away, the more he knew it hurt her. He lost twenty pounds and began to increase his drinking in an attempt to ease the guilt.

When he decided to separate permanently, he invited her to his home and made love to her one last time. He wanted to make sure that she remembered him. When she left that day, he gave her the impression that he would see her later that evening, but days turned into weeks, and weeks turned into months. He could no longer live with himself; so for a month, he was totally immersed in alcohol. He could not get over the fact that Rena was always there, and now would no longer exist in his life. He knew she truly loved and trusted him.

Despite the time that had passed, he knew he hurt her badly and didn't know how to make it up to her. At least, he has the chance to see her and tell her face-to-face why he did what he did. He knew that's the only reason she agreed to come and pick him up.

He finally reaches the corner of Valley View and Sahara and saw the yellow, four-door Mercedes. As he approaches the car, Rena steps out of the vehicle wearing a tightly fitting, red dress (she knew Jamie was partial to red), which accentuated the natural curves of her body and excited every man passing that corner. Horns honk and a few whistles are heard as Rena flings her long, auburn, braided hair back behind her bare shoulders. She reaches for her sunglasses to take them off as her pretty smile begins to widen revealing her stunning pearly whites.

Jamie approaches her, expecting a hug and reaches out for her, when from nowhere, five fingers slam across his face. The impact is so powerful that it makes Jamie's nose bleed. The slap is quickly followed by...

"That's what you made me do, you bastard! You made my heart bleed. It's still bleeding because I loved you, and you screwed me. You treated me like I was a total stranger. I will never forgive you. You hurt me, and you hurt me badly." Rena then gets back in her car and begins crying uncontrollably. Jamie looks around for something to wipe his bleeding face with, only to notice several people standing around, looking at what just transpired.

One guy is overheard whispering to another, "Man he must have pissed her off." The other guy looks at the first and says, "Whatever it was, it wasn't worth losing that fox." Jamie goes to the passenger's side of the car and climbs in. Rena hands him a towel to wipe his bloody mouth and chin.

Jamie looks up at her, "I was going to ask for a kiss, but I guess that was out of the question?"

Jamie proceeds to wipe the blood off his face and Rena turns and stares at him as though she is trying to turn back the hands of time.

"Jamie, I'm sorry I hit you. I didn't want that to happen. I didn't know what came over me. Are you all right?"

"No, my face is going to be swollen for awhile. I sort of figured you may do something like that, but my imagination did not realize the pain. Are you finished inflicting pain on my body?" Remorseful now... Rena tries to make it up to him. "I'm not going to hit you any more. I really shouldn't have done that. I am sorry."

"Apology accepted. Now let's get down to why you are here."

Rena puts the car in gear and drives off. Even though she promised not to hit Jamie again, that didn't mean she wasn't going to pour out the contents of her heart.

"Aren't you about nothing? I haven't seen you in about eight months; then you call wanting something from me. Where do you want to go and where is your truck?"

"I have some business to take care of and my truck is in the shop for a tune up. Why are you so full of questions anyway? Aren't you glad to see me?"

"You know I used to always be happy to see you. You also know I am a bitch, so leave me alone. What kind of business you got to take care of and why can't I tag along with you?"

Jamie wonders how much he should tell her–how much she should know, and how much he knows himself. "Well, what I have to do is go and watch someone and I know you don't want to just sit around with me."

"I don't have anything else to do. As a matter of fact, you can take me out to that dinner you promised me." Rena says with a friendlier tone coming back to her voice.

"Well okay, I guess it doesn't matter. Just don't ask me any questions and be patient. It would be nice to spend a little time with you. I need you to drive to Radcliff and Alta. I will direct you from there."

Rena drives in the direction Jamie indicated, frequently glancing at him and smiling as though she is saying," I have him now".

The area changed from commercial businesses to tree-lined streets and homes valued in nineties to the low hundred thousands. Children are playing on the street and several people pass them on bikes as they cruise slowly by. Soon they reach the area where Jamie wants to be, and Rena pulls in the parking space next to a tree. When the car is parked, Jamie takes out a pair of binoculars and pans the area focusing on one house in particular.

Rena's curiosity gets the best of her. "What are you doing with those binoculars?"

"I told you not to ask any questions. The less you know the better off you'll be."

Jamie continues to survey the house. It was colored beige, with one small tree in the center of the front yard, encircled by white bricks and flowers. The lawn is well manicured with small lanterns lined alone the walkway. The front window is bare, allowing Jamie to see into the house. As of yet, he saw no movement inside.

Seeing Rena's curiosity, Jamie decides to change the subject, "Well, Rena, how have you been? How's your son doing...the one in prison?"

"He's doing just fine. We talked to him yesterday. He needs some money, so we packed him a care package and sent it off this morning. I really do hope time passes fast. I can't wait until my baby gets home again," Rena stares off unfocused at the house, "I really miss him," she said.

Jamie tries to pull himself together and continues with his attempts at a bit of small talk, "How is Shirley doing? Is she still living on Carey or has she moved in with her boyfriend...Uh, uh...I can't remember his name, but you know who I'm talking about."

"Yeah, you mean Larry. They're doing all right. They bought a house and the kids moved in with them...all except her oldest son. He has two kids now and trying to make it."

Rena is about to continue the meaningless conversation when she finally decides to stop beating around the bush. "Jamie, will you stop all the bullshit! Where have you been, and why did you screw me?

"Jamie, you took my heart. I gave you all of me. What's up? Jamie, I love you...and on top of that, where in the hell is my two hundred dollars?"

"Rena relax, everything will be all right. There are things I am involved in and I need your help. Stop with the bullshit and do as I ask you. If you are tired of the way I am treating you, then leave me alone! I will get out, and you can go on about your business. But understand one thing. You are part of my life, and I do love you. I want you to know the things I have done against you were not intentional, but necessary. If nothing else, you will be taken care of and if that's not enough, I will try and compensate you above that. Now please shut up!"

The moment the words leave his mouth, Jamie knows he has gone too far. Bracing himself for the emotional outburst that he knows is coming, Jamie tries to act busy watching the house."

"Who do you think you are?" Rena yells at him. "Don't do me like this! Don't use me, and don't cast me off, Jamie. I love you!" She cries out at Jamie, knowing very well that she might just be setting herself up to be hurt again.

Jamie sighs and tries to console her. "Rena, I know this, just give me some time. I will make amends...Look!"

A figure in the house begins to move around. Then the front door opens and a red headed woman with rollers, fills the doorway dressed in a red flowered robe and pink house slippers. She stands in the doorway for a few seconds and stretches. She re-enters the house and closes the door.

"Okay, I'm finished, but I have one more favor to ask of you. I need to rent a car, and I want you to take me. Will you do it?"

"I guess so. Since you have turned me into a peeping-tom, I may as well go all the way."

When he hears this, Jamie knows that Rena would do anything for him. She still loved him very much. It was at this moment that Jamie realized he could not endanger her any further, "No...no further. You've done enough. After we are finished with the car, we will go to that dinner I promised you, and whatever you want to talk about, I'm all ears. Give me a kiss, I do love you baby, I do!"

chapter

2

THE REASON

The next morning broke sooner than Jamie expected. Today is the day that will change his life forever. He rises from a deep sleep, thinks about showering and brushing his teeth, but decides not to. His nerves are tight with anxiety, causing his stomach to churn, impeding his ability to stand. He looks at his hands–they're shaking uncontrollably. He can't even collect his thoughts regarding what to wear.

Oh God, I have to pull myself together. I have to get out of here. It's 7:30 in the morning. My buddy, Clyde will be leaving at 8:15. Just grab anything and put it on and get out of here…No! I'm supposed to wear the gas company uniform. The time is here and now, I can't be making mistakes. Slow down and think.

After hurriedly dressing, Jamie stands before the mirror to inspect himself. He dashes out of the apartment and jumps into his rented gray Mercury Sedan. He drives to the area of Radcliff and Alta and sits under the same tree he and Rena had been beneath the day before. Only this time, his mission is to watch the security guard leave for work. He looks at his watch, 8:15 a.m. The front door opens and the portly security guard emerges, followed closely by his wife, now dressed in a waitress's uniform.

Boy is this guy predictable, he thinks. *On time, nice kiss, a hug, walk to the car, and drive away.*

The security guard drives off and Jamie exits his vehicle. He is now so nervous he can hardly walk. He stops, leans on his car, and lights a cigarette in an attempt to gain a little courage. Taking a long drag from the cigarette, he exhales the smoke into the air. Before taking another, he hesitates and then begins walking slowly toward the house. The short walk to the house becomes excruciatingly longer with every step. Jamie feels like he will never get there. He walks with his head down as if he were going to his death.

Finally, the lawn lanterns appear at his feet. He looks up and finds himself a few feet from the front door.

Then a change comes over Jamie's body and he begins to stride with confidence. Before he realizes it, he is knocking at the door. After a short wait, the door opens and the redheaded woman appears in the doorway. Her hair is half in rollers, and she is adorned in a red robe and pink house slippers.

"Excuse me ma'am," he says, "my name is Jamie Collins. I'm from Southwest Gas. We're experiencing some problems with our gas lines in the area and I need to come in and check the meter connection in your house."

The woman looks at him a bit suspiciously, "Can I see your ID please?"

It is now too late to turn back–too late to think of something else to do. Despite all of his planning, Jamie has forgotten the ID card. So, instead of making excuses he pushes his way into the house. The erstwhile gasman's sudden movement stuns the woman, but before she can even yell out, Jamie has his hands around her mouth and pushes her back, while shutting the door behind him. Then he walks the woman forcefully to the sofa.

"Calm down...calm down! I said, calm down!" Jamie commands, while holding the struggling woman down against the sofa.

The words seem to have the opposite effect, and the woman struggles and screams silently against Jamie's hands smothering her mouth. Looking around the room, Jamie spots a throw pillow on the couch. Holding her down with the hand that is muffling her screams, Jamie manages to replace his hand with the throw pillow.

"Now, scream all you want. Nobody can hear with this pillow over your face. Look lady, I don't want to hurt you, but if you keep screaming, you're going to end up suffocating yourself... just calm down. I'm not going to hurt you."

The captive woman starts to settle down and gradually ceases her kicking and silent screaming. Quiet envelops the room.

"Now, I'm going to take this pillow off of your face so that you can breath, okay? But if you scream again, so help me there won't be enough pieces left of you to make a jigsaw puzzle. Got it?"

The woman nods and Jamie slowly removes the pillow from her face. Fearing for her life, the woman put up very little resistance and does everything she is told.

"What...what do you want from me? Please, we don't have much money here"

"Listen lady, I don't want your money..."Jamie begins, but the woman won't let him finish.

"Please, no! Not that! Don't rape me! Maybe we do have some money. Just don't rape me," she begs hysterically.

Sensing his time window closing, Jamie tries to comfort his prisoner as quickly as possible so he can get on with his job.

"Listen! I'm not gonna to rape you or hurt you in any way! All I want you to do is, relax and do as I say, or I will be forced to kick your ass! Now sit on the floor. Lie flat on your back. Roll over, and pull your arms behind you."

The terrified woman complies and lies down on her stomach. Her rollers are scattered over the floor from her struggles and she adjusts herself a bit to avoid lying on one. Jamie goes for his belt and the woman begins to sob.

"Now, don't you worry lady. I'm not going to hurt you. I'm just reaching for my handcuffs." Jamie tries to keep the woman calm as he applies the handcuffs to her wrists.

"Okay. Now, you have cuffs on. Come on, stand up. I'll help you," Jamie says as he drags the woman to her feet. "Here, sit in this chair and open your eyes. What you see here is a Smith and Wesson 357 Model 19. If you screw up, your head will be in several pieces. All I want you to do is talk into this little tape recorder. We will practice first okay?"

The woman nods in slow recognition of her predicament and Jamie begins to recite the lines he has rehearsed interminably. "Now, repeat after me," he said, "Please baby, do as he says. I love you. Can you remember that?"

"Please baby, do as he...as he..." the woman trails off in a flood of tears.

Jamie sits down next to her, looking into her eyes. She catches his gaze for a second and begins bawling again. Losing his patience, Jamie grabs the woman forcefully by the face.

"Hey, stop it! Stop crying! Try and relax. This shit will be over soon. Now, repeat after me."

The woman is trembling with fear and can barely get a word out between the spasms of her body and her crying. Jamie ignores the crying as one would an infant who needs a nap.

"Ready? Just say everything after me and you'll be okay."

The woman looks up at Jamie and stops crying enough to blink understanding.

"Please," Jamie starts.

"Please," the woman mimicks him.

"Baby."

"Baby."

"Do as he says."

"Do as he says."

"I love you."

"I love you."

"Don't let me die."

"Don't let me die."

"Okay, that was good. The recorder is on. Now it's your turn," Jamie says. "Here we go." He clicks on the tape recorder as the woman recites her lines.

"Baby, I'm tied up...Please baby, do as he says. I don't want to die! Don't let me die. I love you. I love you very much. Please come home."

The recorder clicks off and Jamie smiles a bit relieved. Easing his gun back into his pants, he arises and takes a few steps away from the chair.

"That was better than I thought you could do. I thought you would have to rehearse a bit more. You are a natural. Now, let's do a playback."

Jamie clicks the recorder to 'play' and the room is filled with the woman's monologue.

"Baby, I'm tied up. Please baby, do as he says. I don't want to die! Don't let me die. I love you; I love you very much. Please come home."

Once again, Jamie shuts off the recorder, happy with his work, "That was beautiful! Now, if you relax and do as I say, the next person you will see is your husband.

Get up! I'm gonna take off the cuffs. Have you ever watched a TV program or the news and wondered how those captives could function without going to the bathroom? Well, I'm gonna do you a favor. We're going into the bathroom. You're going to sit on the toilet and relax. Take off your panties, and get comfortable...I'm not looking."

Embarrassment does not over come fear as the woman strips her panties off in front of Jamie. Catching a glimpse of herself in the bathroom mirror,   she sees her tortured body and face reflect their haunted gaze. This is not how she saw herself in this morning...not how her day was supposed to go.

"I'm   done," she   says,   grateful   for   his accommodation of her modesty. "You can turn around again"

"Okay, give me your right hand. I am going to 'cuff you to the sink. You should be comfortable for awhile. I doubt if you get hungry...but the main thing is you are able to use the toilet. I know it will be quite embarrassing when the cops get here, but you can deal with it. Now, how much do you love your husband?"

The woman thinks of her husband–her loving husband who has never abused her–a husband that may not have been the "best catch", as her friends often said, but he never let her want for anything, either. Sometimes one never knows what they have until that thing's very existence is threatened. She knows what she has now.

"A lot," are the only words she could choke out.

"I sort of figured that. What I want you to do is read your magazines or whatever, until help arrives. If anything goes wrong, your husband will die. I don't have anything against you or him. Just cooperate and everything will be all right." Jamie says as he hands his victim a stack of magazines.

"You are connected to the main pipe," he continues. "Unless you are really strong, it's going to take a lot for you to get free. If you should happen to get free, don't call the police. They'll arrive soon. If you call the police, your husband will die, and you will carry that guilt for the rest of your life,"

Jamie starts towards the bathroom door, "I'm gonna be here for a while, and while I'm here you need to stay calm. I am not going to do anything against you. Before you know it, I'll be gone.

"I know you use this time of day to take a nap and so does everyone else in the neighborhood, so there won't be any phone calls or any visitors."

"You see, I have been watching you for some time. I suggest that when this is over, you should change your life a little. Do something different everyday. Change your routine, don't live in a rut."

After trying to console the lady, Jamie begins walking through the house. He notices the mantle where there are several family pictures. One is a picture of Clyde when he was younger and a hundred pounds lighter. There is also a high school prom photo of Clyde and his wife.

It is quite evident that they were high school sweethearts. There are also pictures of four children: two boys and two girls. Around the mantle are pictures of smaller children, more than likely their grandchildren.

The house is well kept and the furniture is a combination of French Provincial and Modern American.

Three comfortable recliners surround the fireplace and in the den is another recliner, which seems to be well broken in, with a 32-inch TV in the corner. Sports magazines are stacked adjacent to the recliner and the room is wood paneled, which makes it easy to tell who owns the room.

Jamie spots the liquor cabinet and decides to peep inside–nothing but whiskey, rum, gin, and vodka...no cognac. But because his nerves are frayed, Jamie decides to indulge in some vodka–no ice and no water. The burning fire trickles down his throat, making goose bumps rush all over his body.

After consuming a couple of shots of vodka, Jamie settles down into an easy chair just to gather his thoughts.

The fear has subsided and now he is just impatient. He now knows that no matter what, he has to complete the plan. He is at the point of no return. He is now facing a long term in prison–unlawful detention–his first crime.

If he gets caught now, it will be all over for all those concerned, so everything has to be just right. No mistakes are allowed.

His next move is to go back to the bank on Spring Mountain and Valley View. Jamie looks at his watch. It's 9:45a.m. and decides it's time to go, but only after he checks on his prisoner.

As he walks back towards the bathroom, carrying a small TV he picked up in the hallway, Jamie can hear the woman's quiet sobbing. He enters the bathroom to see his prisoner where he left her, soaking up the tears coming down her face with a wad of tissue paper.

In her robe and tattered hair, she looked more like a beggar than the middle-class wife she is.

"Ma'am, I'm sorry we had to meet under these circumstances, but if you do as I say, everything will be all right and you and your husband will be together again. Now sit back and relax; watch a little TV."

Jamie positions the television set as best he could for the woman to watch while waiting for the police. After he is satisfied, he surveys the house again then walks back to the hallway and yells to his prisoner, "You have a nice home and I'm quite sure you want to continue living together. So follow my instructions. Wait until 2:00 p.m. If the police are not here, you can call them. If you're not able to call at that time, I will. So, enjoy. Okay?"

The woman looks a bit stunned. *Enjoy?* After all of the hell that Jamie has put her through, he tells her to "enjoy" herself and "relax" like this was some weekend spa get–away. Instead of saying her true feelings, the woman responds with a meek, "Okay."

"Good, just remember, do what I say and nothing bad will happen."

"I'll do as you say, but please don't hurt Clyde. Please don't take him away from me..."

"I want you to understand that you have nothing I want and neither does your husband. Just cooperate, and everything will be all right."

Jamie gently closes the door; the woman ponders the phase he softly speaks, "Loi du Talion."

Jamie then disconnects all of the telephones, turns off the lights and stands in the living room and looks around. The front door opens and he scans the neighborhood. It seems to be safe, so he walks out to his car.

As Jamie drives off he begins talking to himself, "Boy, am I glad that's over. Holding captives is not my bag, but I guess I have to get used to it. What's ahead is going to take a lot of concentration, now that the first part is over."

He checks his watch and heads towards Spring Mountain and Valley View. While he is driving south on Jones Boulevard, he thinks of how nice it is to be free and have no worry in the world. He passes the Skipco Print Shop on Charleston and Jones and remembers what it used to look like and how they have grown to be one of the largest printing companies in the valley.

The area between Charleston and Oakey is still empty until you reach the Las Vegas Academy, which has not changed over the years...then the busy intersection of Jones and Sahara. All of the businesses in the area are thriving and busy: doctors' offices, The Bra shop, Real Estate office, and so forth, and of course the Taco Bell–the only fast food restaurant on the corner.

Because of his situation, Jamie is paying more attention to these locations, not daring to take their state of being and the status quo for granted. He knows the smallest slip up could land him in prison, and he also knows that not one piece of his plan can be neglected.

He makes a left turn through the busy traffic onto Spring Mountain and reaches the intersection of Valley View and Spring Mountain. He turns right on Valley View then a right again into the parking lot of Chun King's Restaurant.

While walking to the restaurant, he glances at the bank directly across the street. He then enters the restaurant. He requests a window seat, which faces the bank and orders coffee and peruses the menu.

In a matter of minutes, the coffee arrives and Jamie orders, "I'll have the Chicken Lo Mein and Lo Mein Noodles please and some water."

"Yes sir, will there be anything else?"

"No, that's all."

He looks through the window and can see the front of the bank and the location where he will park his vehicle. Right now someone is parked in that space, but he knows they should be gone by the time he is ready.

The intersection is quite busy and he feels sure his entire operation will go down without attracting undue attention.

The bus stop on the Northeast corner has its usual customers who will shortly be gone. The parking lot of the mini mall and the restaurant also has their share of customers. There is a couple sitting in the restaurant with two children who seem to be learning how to eat in public. The parents, who are in their mid-twenties don't seem to have anything under control. The cries of the children and the loud demands of the parents, disturb the peace and quiet of the dimly lit room.

"Joey, sit down and eat your food. Stop throwing your food in his plate."

"Mommy, Joey hit me. Stop it. Leave me alone!"

The frustrated mother runs her fingers through her hair, brushing it from her face.

"Look Lester, if you don't do something with these kids, I'm gonna kill'em."

"Okay kids, I said stop playing around and eat. If I have to say one more thing to either of you, I will take you in the bathroom and spank your bottoms."

"No you won't Lester," the young mother said. "You better not lay a hand on my kids."

Bewildered, the husband becomes defensive, "What do you mean your kids? They're mine too. If you would stop pampering them and beat their butts every now and then, we wouldn't be having these problems. You told me to do something and that's what I'm going to do...and don't you ever contradict me in front of them again!"

"What if I do? Are you gonna hit me too?"

With an angry glare, the husband throws his napkin on the table, gets up and stomps over to the bar. The children, observing what just transpired, start to cry.

"See what you've done? Now they are upset," the woman snaps at her husband.

Seeing all this, Jamie remembers when his own kids were younger. There would not have been an argument at all. The children would have been in the restroom at a drop of a hat, getting their butts whipped, and his wife wouldn't have said a thing.

The attention of everyone in the restaurant is directed toward the lady and her two kids. The husband calms his nerves with a shot of brandy at the bar, and Jamie starts to relax. This unforeseen little incident has taken a lot of pressure off of him.

With that family acting like they are, I shouldn't have any problems keeping out of these folks' memory, he thinks to himself.

The waiter brings Jamie his food; "Here's your order sir. I'm sorry for the disturbance. We're going to try and quiet them down."

Jamie looks up, "Oh that's all right," he says, "they're not bothering me, it's sort of entertaining. The food looks great. Thank you."

He looks at his food. Even though it looks delectable, he has no appetite. He tastes several morsels, but mostly just plays in the plate and stares out the window, counting the customers going in and out of the bank.

A lady in a wheelchair rolls herself slowly into the bank and captures Jamie's attention, mainly because she could cause a problem.

She would have to be out of the bank before anything happens. She may be leaving just when the armored truck arrives, and that could pose a real problem. A hundred such "could of's" are flowing through Jamie's mind. He looks at his watch and realizes he has plenty of time before the truck arrives.

A sudden crash breaks Jamie's concentration and he jerks his head in the direction of the noise. The two unruly children have pulled the tablecloth off the table along with their food. The husband runs across the restaurant and proceeds to whip the children, prompting the wife to yell and cry at the same time. The manager and several waiters try to appease the young wife, but to no avail. Customers begin loudly demanding their checks.

Jamie leans back in his chair and begins laughing uncontrollably. He turns towards the front door and sees two Metro Police Officers enter. The laughter stops abruptly and suddenly real panic set in.

What am I going to do now? I have one hour before the armored truck arrives and those jokers come in here to eat, Jamie thinks to himself. Jamie is very observant of his surroundings, but the same can't be said for the father of the two kids. He doesn't see his wife reaching for him and slapping him. The husband, embarrassed and angry, takes a wild swing at his wife, striking her in the jaw and sending her flying onto the table behind her. The officers don't see the husband get hit, but sees the roundhouse blow take effect on the woman. They rush across the room and grab the husband, throw him to the floor and attempt to handcuff him.

Meanwhile, several less than honest customers take advantage of the disturbance and leave the restaurant without paying.

The wife lies unconscious on the table, and the children are crying inconsolably. The police call for backup, and an EMT wagon.

By this time Jamie is nearly out of his mind. He squirms in his chair, trying to figure out what to do next.

In just a few moments, there are five squad cars outside the restaurant and police are trying to disperse the gathering crowd.

The EMT's examine the woman, put her on a gurney and wheel her out to the waiting ambulance. The handcuffed husband is placed in one scout car and the children in another.

After several more minutes, everyone drives away simultaneously and the disturbance is over as quickly as it had begun.

Jamie feels that everything that happened is a blessing; the cops may have sat down and lunched there, except for this unruly family.

The manager comes to Jamie's table and apologizes to him for the commotion. He tells him that his meal is free, but that he will have to leave the restaurant.

Jamie looks at his watch. Forty minutes before the truck arrives. He goes outside to his vehicle, drives across the street and parks in the now vacant spot he had staked out for himself.

He walks around to the front entrance of the bank, carrying an empty duffel bag, and looks across the street to make sure the crowd had dispersed before he enters the bank. He approaches the desk of one of the bank officers.

His adrenaline is flowing heavily and beads sweat covers his forehead. He is thankful that many of the customers in the bank are also sweating heavily.

Unfortunately, not a lot of them are trembling, he thinks, trying to calm himself.

Mistaking the look on Jamie's face for confusion, one of the bank workers starts to come towards him. Jamie catches the clerk's movement and begins thinking about what to do next.

What am I to do? Relax Jamie...remember how you use to handle it on the police department. Take everything slow. Don't move too fast, and watch out for the unusual. Stay on your toes and always keep an eye out. This woman probably only wants to know if I need help picking the right interest rated account or something, Jamie reassures himself as he coolly meets the woman's gaze.

The eye contact elicits a smile from the young bank worker and Jamie wonders if she can sense his nervousness, or if his feigned cool attitude is enough to allay any suspicions she might have.

"Can I help you sir?" Her smile restores Jamie's confidence.

"Oh, yes, thanks. I need some information on your checking accounts."

"Okay sir, would you step over to my desk, please?"

"This won't take long, will it?"

"No sir. Here are some brochures on our bank policies. This one explains the three types of checking accounts we have, and this one explains our savings accounts."

As he talks with the lady, Jamie looks at his watch. It is 11:57 a.m. He then looks at the front door just as Clyde walks in, waving at a few of the bank tellers with his usual casual demeanor.

Right on time...my little fat boy is here. Okay, I have the tape recorder and it's all set. Another couple of minutes and fat boy will head into the back. There he goes. Now, it's time for me to start fading away from this clerk.

"Okay, ma'am, I'll take these brochures and read them." Jamie leaves the bank officer at her desk, taking a few of the pamphlets with him. He goes over to the windows as if he is reading the brochures and waits for the guard to exit the vault.

"Now, you take it easy." Jamie says out loud and finishes with, "Here comes the fat boy," under his breath. With a glance at the clock, Jamie makes his way towards the door as Clyde exchanges brief good-byes with one of the younger clerks. As Clyde is leaving, Jamie approaches him and tries to initiate some friendly conversation.

"Hey Clyde, how are you doing? Remember me from yesterday?"

"Oh yeah I remember. How are you doing?"

"Okay, I guess. Look, I have something I want you to listen to. Listen to this."

As they entered the vestibule, Jamie hands Clyde the tape recorder. They stop as Clyde listens to the recording. "Baby, I'm tied up...Please baby, do as he says. I don't want to die! I love you; I love you very much. Please come home."

Clyde's face turns red, as though he had been struck a physical blow. As the total realization of what is going down sinks in, Clyde reaches for his glock.

"You son of a bitch..." Clyde begins as his hands race towards his weapon.

"Calm down son," Jamie says reassuringly. "Remember, I have her and she is safe...for now. But you go for that gun, and I don't make it out of here, then my partner will have no other choice but to... well I don't need to paint you a picture." Clyde's hands freeze and he breathes toward Jamie, "Okay, just don't hurt her. What do you want from me?"

"Okay Clyde, do as I say if you want to see your wife again. Give me the bag and you stand here in this hallway." Jamie takes the bank bag from Clyde and puts it inside his duffel bag. "Okay, now hand me back my tape recorder." Jamie puts that into the duffel bag, as well.

"I have a walkie-talkie with me to reach my partner. If he doesn't hear from me, your wife dies. Don't move from this hallway until you count to one hundred. If I see your face outside of this door before then, your wife dies. Don't look so dumbfounded. Face outside and start counting...slowly! Remember, if I don't get word back to your house that I am okay, your wife dies."

Jamie looks at Clyde again, smiles and walks out the door–right past the armored truck. As always, the driver is engrossed in a magazine. Jamie checks the time– 12:01p.m. He casually looks back and continues walking until he reaches his vehicle. He gets in and drives east on Spring Mountain without attracting any attention.

The guard reaches the count of one hundred, and then runs outside to the truck.

"I've been robbed!" he yells, beating frantically on the side of the vehicle.

His two partners inside the armored truck immediately exit the vehicle, trying to both obtain and give information, but no one knows what to say or do since the guards outside the bank have seen nothing go down.

Meanwhile, Jamie drives to the I-15 expressway and heads north and exits westbound Charleston Boulevard. He then drives to a mini storage place across the street from U.M.C. Hospital, which he had previously reserved.

He punches in his code and enters and drives to unit 386. When he arrives at his unit, he waits a moment and looks around. Seeing no one in the area, he gets out, unlocks the unit and opens the door. He then drives the vehicle into the unit.

After a final check to make sure he has everything, he locks the storage unit, leaves and walks north on Shadow Lane, then east on Alta and waits on Martin Luther King Boulevard for a bus.

Some time passes before the bus arrives, giving Jamie ample opportunity to think about what just happened. In formulating his plans for this wave of terror, Jamie has also provided sufficient time to think about what has gone down and what is about to happen. It also gives him time to look at the things around him and to appreciate being free. He wanted to absorb and enjoy as much freedom as possible, just in case his plan goes awry.

Riding on the bus, he observes a group of young men getting on with an "I don't care attitude." Jamie positions himself where he has a comprehensive view of things, just in case something should happen. Not thirty seconds into their bus ride, the young thugs initiate their mischief.

First, they turn up their boombox, knowing they are not supposed to have it on. The bus driver stops the bus and announces that he won't continue driving unless they turn it off. The young men decided to wait the driver out and continued to play their music full blast.

The bus stands for five minutes and the passengers begin trying to reason with the teenagers. The passengers, complaints go unheeded and the music continues to blare. Jamie looks at his watch and then back at the teenagers. He knows he can't do too much, but is worried about the time and knows the police will surely be summoned if the kids continue their raucous behavior.

He finally decides to intervene. He leaves his seat, walks toward the youngster carrying the boom box and whispers in his ear.

"I know who you are. I know your mother. If she were to find out you were being such an asshole, she would beat the shit out of you."

He then backs away from the kid, winks at him, and returns to his seat. By the time Jamie sits down again, the music has been turned off and the bus proceeds on its' way once more. Finally, it pulls up to the corner of Washington Avenue and Martin Luther King Boulevard, where Jamie exits the bus. He walks east on Washington to his sons' apartment.

The area Jamie is in is considered the poor side of town. It isn't all that bad though, when compared to similar neighborhoods in other cities.

The streets are clean and there are no abandoned cars with missing wheels or motors. Every house has a lawn and there are no crowds of people assembled at every corner. The homes are mostly single level and unlike the more affluent communities, every house looks different. There are some two-story and single level housing projects, on one side of the street. From the exterior, they all look clean, but just like every urban area; there are crack dealers, pimps, prostitutes, and junkies.

There are six single-level apartments at 618 Washington Avenue, distinguished by letters, apartments A, B, C, D, E, and F.

Jamie's sons occupied apartment A, which faced Washington Ave. It was a large, two-bedroom apartment with enough room to satisfy anyone. It was furnished just the way it was when his sons lived there. Jamie has continued to pay the rent and kept the apartment, hoping that one-day they would return.

A brown, sectional couch smothers the corner to the right as you walk in the front door. Another long brown couch runs down the center of the living room. A 32" TV stands to the left of the front door and a stereo on the wall faces the front door.

The kitchen, which has a table and four chairs, can be seen off to the right. Straight ahead, empty bottles of every type of alcohol they had ever drank, stand over the kitchen cabinets.

The house itself is neat and well kept, mainly due to the older son, who is obsessively neat and meticulous. The younger son–a slob–is quite the opposite. Pictures of their relatives are scattered throughout the living room in frames on the walls and on the tables. There is also a drawing created by Jamie's grandson in the mist of everything.

Jamie lies back on the couch and turns on the TV just as the news comes on with a special bulletin.

"Good afternoon," the anchorman announces. *"We have a breaking news story to report. A daring robbery took place at the People's Savings and Loan on Valley View and Spring Mountain. Details are sketchy at this time, but we do have a description of the perpetrator: a Black male,*

about six feet tall, two hundred pounds, light complexion, medium length hair, and dimples. He was wearing a blue jacket, blue jeans, and glasses. We have no information as to how the suspect made his escape, but the police think an accomplice may be involved, possibly driving the get away vehicle.

"No weapon was seen, but the police think the subject may be armed and dangerous. We will update you as the information comes in. Stay tuned to Channel 7 News."

Jamie sits up and realizes that he had succeeded in stealing the money from the armored car. No one saw him drive away–at least no one has come forward...now its time to execute the second phase of his plan...call the police and get two of Las Vegas finest here.

Jamie knows this part of his plan is not the most dangerous, but danger and death will be raising its ugly head very soon. He sits on the couch and stares into space– and for some unknown reason, begins to tremble and tears stream down his face.

Never in his entire life has he been so afraid and never before had he ever been in such a predicament. He rolls off the couch onto the floor on his knees and calls out loud to God.

"Oh, God...Oh, God...Please help me! Please find it in your heart, God to help me through this. Dear God, you know from all your mighty wisdom that the things I am doing and am about to do are to help my kids. I know you don't condone these things, but God, I know of no other way to handle it. I am supposed to wait for you to do your will. But God, what is your will? How long will my children be locked up? What am I to do? Please help me to decide. If I continue, please watch over me and make sure everything comes out right. These things I ask in the name of your son, Jesus Christ, Amen."

Jamie finishes his prayer and remains on the floor for a bit, trying to collect his emotions.

Finally pulling himself together, Jamie sits down on the couch and picks up the phone. He stares at it and hesitates for a moment, then dials that magic number: 911.

"911, what is the emergency?"

"Yes, could you please send the police? I want to report a prowler, "Jamie replies in a hurried anxious tone.

"What is your address?"

"618 Washington Avenue... at the corner of H Street."

"Okay, just remain calm and don't go outside. Stay away from your windows and draw your blinds. We will have a unit out right away."

"Okay, hurry up. Please!" Jamie hangs up.

As time passes by, Jamie begins thinking to himself again, and again, he takes this time to talk with God, "This waiting is going to kill me," he prays aloud. "Now my head is full of 'what ifs'. God, I know you don't condone anything I am doing, but please don't let anything go wrong. I don't want anyone to die and I don't want to die either. I have to help my kids. I have to do something to right the wrong done to them. I can't let them remain in that hellhole. Please God, watch over me and make sure nothing goes wrong. I ask in the name of your son, Jesus Christ, Amen."

Time passes and Jamie falls into a fitful sleep. He is soon awakened by a loud knock on the door. It is now 4:32 p.m.

"Who is it?"

"It's the police. Did you call?"

"Yes. Yes, Just a minute."

Jamie has no time to think about what to do. He just reacts and does what he has practiced so many times in his head. As if in slow motion, he puts his thoughts into action.

Next to the door is a twelve-gauge shotgun. Jamie picks it up, stands behind the door, opens it and invites the officers in. The
Officers enter the house and proceed to the living room. Jamie pulls out the shotgun and aims it at the officers.

"All right, boys and girls," he snarls, "don't you even as much as sneeze."

The two officers immediately freeze in their footsteps, and turn and look at each other to ascertain what the other one is thinking. Long-time police partners can generally tell what each other is thinking by body language; and if they were partners long enough, sometimes not even body language is needed. Unfortunately for them, these two officers, are not such partners.

"What the hell," the male officer gasps.

Jamie cuts him off sharply. "I said shut up! Get on your knees and put your hands on top of your heads.

"Now you, young lady, reach over very slowly and take your partner's gun out of his holster and throw it on the couch. Use your left hand. Then do the same with your weapon. Take out your handcuffs and 'cuff your partner's hands behind his back, and I want the 'cuffs as tight as you can get them."

The officers are slow to move, but Jamie convinces them with the shotgun to hurry up. Complying with Jamie's command, the female officer disarms her partner and then herself. Then she takes out her handcuffs and locks them over her partner's wrists.

"I said tightly! Don't pull any crap with me... now do it!"

The female officer glares at Jamie and bites her tongue. She tightens the handcuffs to the point where they make the skin around her partner's wrists turn white with pressure.

"Push him over on the floor. Now, or I will blow your brains out! Take your partner's 'cuffs out and lay them on the floor next to you. Now lie down!"

"Who do you think you are? We are cops, you jerk!" shouts the man on the floor.

Jamie points the shotgun directly at the man's head, "You ever see what a shotgun can do to a man's head this close? If you don't shut up, they're going to have better luck finding eggs at Easter than pieces of your brain– you got it?"

The man remains silent, and the woman quietly complies with Jamie's demands.

"Put your hands behind your back," Jamie orders her. "Here, 'cuff yourself–tightly! Now both of you roll over to the wall and sit up."

The female complies with speed of a professional officer. Jamie is not fooled by her swift compliance. He had been a cop for too long to not know the difference between giving up and analyzing the situation. *She may be doing what I say, but if I don't keep an eye on her, she will be the most trouble*, Jamie reflects.

"What are you doing, fool? We're the police. You're looking at some heavy-duty prison time," her partner injects.

This guy, on the other hand, Jamie thinks...then addresses the male officer directly.

"Okay Officer McCulley, I expected you to be a mouthy sucker, so I'm going to warn you; shut up and do not speak unless I tell you to. Otherwise, I will bust your jaw with the butt of this shotgun. Are you both comfortable? I hope so, because it's going to get worse. I have another surprise for you on this table here. I want you to take your medicine like two little children and you will feel positively shitty in the morning."

Jamie goes into his bag and pulls out a small brown bottle with a white lid, the kind of non-descript vial one might have seen in chemistry class as a child or in a grandparents' bedroom to keep change in.

The white and yellow label announces that the bottle contains Ketaset®, 100mg/mL, 10mL. Below that, in smaller letters, is the brand name: Ketamine HCl, INJ and USP. Jamie then reaches inside his medical bag and produces a 10-cc syringe. Uncapping the bottle and the needle, he sticks the needle of the syringe through the rubber gasket and carefully fills the tube with the clear liquid.

This powerful drug, which is related to phencyclidine or PCP, is commonly used recreationally to induce heavy psychedelic out-of-body and subjective near death experiences. But it is also used to rapidly induce surgical coma in both humans and animals, and Jamie knows that it is reasonably safe to administer in high enough doses to produce unconsciousness. It is the only agent capable of inducing a rapid coma that does not depress the breathing centers, and therefore does not require incubation and artificial ventilation to prevent death.

Jamie's purpose for the medication is more sinister. He has devoted most of his adult life to stopping sinister things in the world, but he also knows that he will do anything for his sons–even if it means losing his own soul.

"What's that?" ask the woman.

"If you must know, this is a drug called ketamine. I'm going to knock you both out with it. You'll sleep like babies and wake up in twenty minutes to an hour and a half or so. Don't worry, it's perfectly safe and you'll both be fine. You may have some serious hallucinations as you come out of the drug, and you won't be able to walk or stand very well for a while. And you'll have a hangover from hell for a couple of days. Now, it's your turn, Officer Ramirez. Before I do this, do you want to say anything?"

"Yes, why are you doing this? And who the hell are you? You are going to be in some real serious trouble. On top of everything else, you are also going to be charged with kidnapping,

"Her eyes widen with fear as Jamie approaches her with the syringe." Oh, no…please don't!" she pleads.

"Don't move!" Jamie commands her, "or this needle will break off in your leg."

Jamie then plunges the needle right through her pants into her thigh and injects four cc of the solution into her quadriceps muscle. It takes about five seconds to administer the shot. The last thing Ramirez hears is, "Because I have a purpose and my name is Jamie Collins, goodnight, Loi du Talion."

Jamie repeats the process with McCulley, but he ups the dose to five cc. About forty-five seconds later he, too, is unconscious.

Jamie begins to go through the pockets of the comatose officers, looking for keys to their cars. Then he looks outside and notices the approach of dusk.

Unlike some other cities, police officers in Las Vegas ride in separate cars, even though they are partners. And in this case, the partners also work in separate units. McCulley is on the Tactical Unit, which is comprised of officers deployed throughout the city.

All these officers carry standard riot equipment in the trunks of their vehicles.

Jamie locates their keys to both vehicles, goes outside and drives Ramirez's vehicle to the rear of the apartment complex. He returns to the front of the apartment and opens the rear door to McCulley's squad car.

Then he goes back into the apartment and tries to pick McCulley up. He finds this to be a real task, so he drags the officer's inert form to the vehicle and places him into the car as far as he can. He then goes around and opens the driver's side rear door, crawls inside and pulls McCulley into the car through the rear door.

"Damn, you are one heavy sucker," he mutters to himself. "I'll put you on the bottom and let your partner rest on top of you."

He returns to the apartment, picks Ramirez up and throws her over his shoulder. Then he carries her to the squad car and lays her on top of McCulley. This accomplished; he rushes back into the apartment for the duffel bag containing various items he will need at his next destination. He then turns off all the lights, locks the door, gets into the squad car, and drives away with his captives.

Police procedures require each officer to make an entry on their log sheet at least every half-hour, and when out of service; they must contact the dispatcher every fifteen minutes. Aware of this, Jamie knows that his time is limited and he has to get off the street quickly and hide the squad car. So he heads back to the storage unit across the street from U.M.C. Hospital. He removes the rental car from the storage room and quickly replaces it with the scout car.

Jamie picks up Ramirez and carries her to the rental car and places her in the back seat. Next he places McCulley in the rental car's front seat. He removes the 'cuffs from McCulley's hands and places the officer's left hand into the handle of the door and presses his hand and fingers to leave prints. He does it several times on the door, windows and on the dashboard, and then repeats this process with McCulley's right hand.

Finally, he encircles the steering wheel with McCulley's hands as though he has been driving.

After putting McCulley's prints all over the front of the vehicle, Jamie then places the 'cuffs back on the unconscious officer's wrists and lays him down in the front seat.

Jamie then removes the riot gear from the trunk of the squad car. It consists of a black tactical uniform, kevlar helmet, flack vest, a twelve-gauge shotgun with twenty rounds of double-aught buckshot, smoke bombs and stun grenades, and one M-16A2 rifle with one hundred and four rounds of 5.56 mm Nato 65-grain ball ammunition in eight fifteen-round magazines.

Each magazine contains just thirteen rounds to prevent excessive compression of the follower spring. This is to ensure adequate feeding into the chamber and avoid a malfunction—which could be disastrous in a serious social encounter.

That's done; Jamie locks the door and closes the trunk. Then he is off to another location on the Northwest side of town. Luckily enough for Jamie, the darkness has concealed his criminal deeds. Now, he can travel across town without fearing any interference from police officers on patrol. He drives cautiously to the 95 expressway and heads north to Jones Boulevard.

He exits on Jones, makes a right turn past a 7-11 and a Smith's Shopping Center, and then turns left onto Fawn Circle and backs into the driveway of number 6116.

This is a nice location because of a large aloe Vera plant and a tree in front of the house, which blocks the view of others. Jamie carries all of the bags and supplies into the house.

The house is not fully furnished—just enough to fulfill his needs. In the center of the living room is a steel pole attached to the floor and ceiling. Dangling from the pole is two five-foot chains—one on either side, with handcuffs welded to the ends of the chains.

Next to the pole and on either side are two recliners. One chair has a bucket next to it and on the other side there is a three-sided wall unit, approximately four feet high. Inside, also, is a bucket for the private use of Ramirez.

The recliners face a 27-inch TV and a table. To the right of the table is yet another recliner for Jamie. The house contains no other furniture. All the windows are covered with aluminum roll-down shutters.

In the kitchen is a pot of chili, which was cooked the day before, a large box of crackers to go along with the meal and two fifths of cognac and coffee serves as refreshments.

Stacked in a neat pile are four plates, four bowls, four spoons and a bag of plastic cups.

Jamie returns to the car, picks up Ramirez and carries her into the house. He sits her in her designated seat, props her up and inclines the chair, and then handcuffs her to the pole.

He returns to the vehicle to retrieve McCulley. He is not as easy because of his height and weight: six foot five inches and about two hundred and sixty pounds. Jamie has to drag him from the car and it takes everything he has to pick him up and sling him over his shoulders.

With heroic effort, Jamie gets McCulley inside the house and into the recliner. He tries to set him gently in the chair, but the officer's body lands in the chair with a slam. Jamie is worried that he might have injured McCulley's neck, but he will have to wait until he awakens to find out.

Once McCulley is secured in his chair, Jamie chains him to the pole as he did Ramirez. Then he rests a moment while he wipes off the sweat that has accumulated on his brow.

I should have started working out more before I did this, Jamie thinks to himself. *This McCulley is one heavy guy. I hope these guys don't puke and aspirate their vomit. I don't need any additional trouble...I don't want these guys to croak on me.*

Almost as if God were giving him an answer to his question, Jamie notices that both officers are breathing normally and easily. The shots had taken effect within a minute or so and had rendered both officers completely comatose and helpless. Jamie had designed it this way to eliminate any attempt to escape. Jamie reclines in his easy chair, waiting for his two captives to awaken. Soon he falls asleep.

chapter

3 The Reason

In the maximum-security prison, at Indian Springs, the loud speakers shout out two names.

"Marvin Collins, cell P34, and Jamie Collins, Q23, you have a visitor."

The prisoners could barely conceal their excitement as they prepare to leave their cells to see their visitor. They walk down the hall, which seem longer as they take each step.

Finally, they reach the doors blocking their exit; a bell rings and the doors slowly open and both men eagerly rush to the visitors' room. They peek in and survey the room until they see the familiar face of their father. A smile breaks out on their faces and their jaunt gait turns into a fast shuffle until they reach the window that prevents them from touching their father.

Their broad smiles indicate they were glad to see him. Jamie Jr. picks up the phone and speaks first.

"Hi Daddy, it's so good to see you."

"How are you doing son? Is everything all right?"

"Yeah, Daddy, we're all right. We're close to one another and we're watching out for each other. We've gotten to know a few people in here and they have shown us the ropes."

"How are you doing Marvin? Are you all right?"

The second young man pipes up close to the phone, "Yeah, Daddy, I'm fine. I just don't know how long I can stay in here. But like Jamie Jr. said, we have friends and we can make the best of it. Have you seen any of my kids?" How are they doing?"

"They all are doing fine. You will be able to see them again; just give me a little time," Jamie paused for a moment, and then continues, "In a few days, you're going to hear a few things about me. I just want you to relax and not worry. Everything you hear about me is designed to help you get out of here. I need you both to be patient and don't let the guards here harass you too much. Don't let anything they say get you down." Jamie looks at his sons, and then went on, his voice an almost hoarse whisper, "I need you both to have faith in me and believe that everything I am doing is going to get you out of here."

The brothers look at each other and then back at their father through the window, "Daddy, what are you going to do?"

"Jamie, don't worry about what's going to happen; the less you know, the less they can hurt you." Jamie Sr. looks at his sons through the thick window, "Jamie, share the phone with Marvin," he said. "I want you both to hear this," He then begins speaking in a low tone of voice, "There are other men in here that have been railroaded by that pig McCulley. I want you to try and locate them. Tell them to stick together with you because all of you going to get out of here."

"Daddy, what are you going to do?" Marvin asks his father.

"Just like I told your brother, it's none of your business right now."

"I can't help it; I just need some kind of hope. I need to know that this shit is going to end."

"I promise you both, it won't be long. But if things don't work out right, then you will have something to worry about. I will be dead!"

"Now, you really have me worried Daddy," Jamie Jr. said, upset by this unpleasant surprise.

The father looks at the son, his heart filled with love and sadness.

"Jamie, how well do you know your father? Have I ever let you down? Have I ever let you linger in pain and misery?"

"No," was all Jamie Jr. could get out.

"I am not going to start now," Jamie Sr. reassures his son.

"Daddy, you need to send us some money. The only things we can get for free are what they give us and that ain't much," Marvin interjects.

"Don't worry; I put thirty dollars apiece for you in your bank account. I will send more every time you run low. I need you both to look really hard and find those other guys. Do either of you have a pencil or pen?"

"Yes, Daddy, I have one." Jamie Jr. responds.

"I want you to write down these names. Are you ready?"

"Yeah, Daddy, go ahead."

"Okay, the first one is, Terry White, got it?"

"Yeah."

"Lawrence Wilson, Joseph Phillips, Jesus Mendoza, Lumas Taylor, James Doolittle, Kenneth Patrick, and James Willie Nelson. Got 'em all?"

Jamie Jr. looks up from his writing, "Yeah, Daddy, I got them."

A voice calls out from the back, "Collins, you both have five minutes."

"Okay kids, now remember what I said. Be cool. You'll be out of here before you know it."

"Okay Daddy, I love you."

"I love you too, Marvin. Y'all be good."

****

A moan from McCulley shakes Jamie from his sleep, "Ooh-ooh, my head, ooh-ooh." mutters McCulley.

Jamie watches McCulley as he tries to recover... it *looks like somebody else is trying to wake up. A few minutes more and I will have some company. Let me brew some coffee. I know they will want something to drink when they come out of this, or maybe they won't. I can't wait until they are awake and see how messed up they are. This is gonna be good.*

Returning from the kitchen, Jamie sees a groggy, semi-conscious McCulley struggling to talk and trying to figure out where he is.

"So, you're finally coming around," Jamie observes to the dazed McCulley.

"What the hell did you do to me," McCulley whispers. "Where am I? I feel like hell. I can't feel anything. I feel like my legs are cut off and I can't move them. What's wrong with me? Shit! I feel like I'm floating outa my body. What the hell did you do to me? I can't remember anything. Christ, I think I'm gonna puke."

"Oh, just relax McCulley, you will be all right. Go ahead and puke if you have to. It won't bother me any."

Looking up at Jamie through half closed eyes, McCulley whispers, "You black ass nigger, when I get to you, I'm going to jack you up good." Jamie bites his lip, but his emotions get to him nonetheless. "You really like that word, don't you, you honkie-prick? How many times have you used it in your short thirty-odd years of life?"

"Don't worry about it sucker, you got a lot more problems to deal with. What did you do to me? I can't feel anything."

"Oh, a little shot of Ketalar did the trick on you, cracker. You see, right now all I want to deal with is your ugly mouth, and on top of it, I may want to get a little sleep. So try and enjoy being 'high' you white piece of shit. You probably won't ever experience anything like this again."

Jamie looks over at Ramirez. *Nice looking lady*, he thinks, it's a *shame to treat her like this.*

"Look, shithead, your partner is waking up. Help her out a little—do you want some coffee?"

"How in the hell do you expect me to drink anything in the condition I'm in?"

"Don't worry McCulley. Actually, I don't give a shit about you. I just as soon kill you as look at your ugly face. Talk to Ramirez while I fix you both a cup."

McCulley gradually begins to gains a little strength and the timbre slowly returned to his voice. He calls to his partner, pathetically, it seems to Jamie.

"Ramirez! Ramirez, wake up! Wake up dammit!"

Ramirez finally answers in a groggy voice, "¡Aye, Dios mio. ¿Qué me ha pasado? ¡Chingagda madre! No siento mi cuerpo...Socorro...¡Por Dios, ayúdame!" as she gradually shakes off some of the effects of the drug,

She continues in English, "Help me! Jesus, I can't move!" McCulley tries to arouse his partner with his voice, but only whispers emerge.

"Ramirez! Hey woman, wake up. This nigger has us drugged up and tied to this post."

"What's wrong with my arms and legs? I can't feel them. Where are we and why am I chained up?" Ramirez cries out loud as her mind starts to slowly shake the cobwebs.

McCulley is getting angrier by the minute. "You stupid broad! This is your fault. You shoulda tried something! Now look at us. I can't move my arms either. That nigger drugged us...he said some shit about a drug I never heard of. His black ass is going to need a drug when I am done with him." McCulley finally realizes he is trapped and tries to reassure his partner.

"Just lay back and relax, Ramirez. It looks like we're going to be here for a while. That friggin' nigger kidnapped us and brought us here and chained us up. Where here is, I don't know. But I guaran-damn-tee ya, we're gonna get the hell out of here!"

"Why don't you button your filthy mouth, you racist pig," protests Ramirez who is disgusted by her partner's bigoted epithets.

"Cause I'm going to pay that sucker back! I want to see his black face when the judge takes his mallet hits the gavel and sentences him to life in prison! But you can count on one thing...he will either go limping or minus an eye. I'm going to screw over that sucker big time!"

Jamie re-enters McCulley's line of sight and his very presence sends McCulley over the edge, "Let me out of here, you son of a bitch! Let me loose and fight me like a man, you sorry piece of shit!"

Jamie walks over to his prisoners carrying a coffeepot on a tray with three cups and wearing a big smile on his face, "Calm down dumb ass, the coyotes may hear you. All that yelling won't get you out of those cuffs. So, sit your sorry ass there and shut up."

McCulley is drooling heavily from the ketamine he was given. He tries to spit on Jamie but is unable to control his spittle, which just runs down his chin and onto his throat and chest. He becomes momentarily quiet and tries to assess his circumstances. But each thought causes him to feel pain in his head, and the pain only adds to McCulley's anger.

"Why are you doing this to us?" Ramirez complains. "Why are you screwing with us... we're cops, for Christ-sake! We never did anything to you. Just let us go, before you get yourself into more trouble!"

"Listen lady, I don't want to do this anymore than you want to be here," Jamie replies, "but sometimes things have to be done to get results. If this is the only way, then this is the only way."

"The only way? The only way for what? Tell me, and why can't I move? I can't feel anything!"

"Look, you'll know what you need to know and nothing more."

McCulley snaps out of his trance, "Please, both of you shut up! My head is about to split wide open! And you sucker, tell me what the hell are your intentions and why am I feeling like a talking piece of shit! My arms and legs won't move. They actually feel like they're not there."

Jamie looks over at McCulley, "McCulley, you feel like a talking piece of shit, because you are. Now shut the hell up before I give you a permanent vacation from breathing."

"You wouldn't dare, nigger."

Jamie turns around at this remark and goes over to McCulley's limp body. Taking advantage of the fact that neither captive could move at this point, he presses his weight against McCulley's left knee.

"Wouldn't dare do what, butt brain?" Jamie demanded. "You see here, you may not be able to feel all this pressure on your knee, but I assure you that I am putting pressure on it. You might not be able to feel the ligaments and tendons stretch with tension, but if I adjusted my foot a little more, you might just hear those ligaments snap. Funny thing is, you have no way of knowing if I really am putting that much pressure on your leg, or if I am just full of shit; but do you want to chance it?"

McCulley's head sinks to his chest in defeat.

"I didn't think so...cracker," Jamie said as he walks in victory back over to the coffee, leaving McCulley alone.

"Why couldn't he feel his legs, and why the hell can't I move mine?" Ramirez asks Jamie.

"Don't worry Officer Ramirez; you just had a few shots of a drug. It will wear off soon. I just didn't need the aggravation of you two trying to escape." Jamie bends down and places the coffee tray near his two prisoners. "Now, here is your coffee. I guess you will have to wait until your limbs come back before you can drink it, so sit back and relax."

Ramirez looks over at the coffee then at her silent partner. Trying to gather information she can use to possibly escape, Ramirez continues with her questions with a friendlier tone.

"What was the drug? How did you measure everything out so fast? Or did you know that we were the ones coming? I am sorry if you feel slighted somehow; maybe if we just talked I could help you out?"

Jamie gives Ramirez an interested look, "Help me out, huh? I see you are the levelheaded part of the team. McCulley sure could learn a thing or two from you."

"You still haven't answered my questions. When are we going to get to that?" Ramirez persists.

"Okay, you win. I just had to wait until everything was in place and we were comfortable before we got to the matters at hand," Jamie pauses for a second as if he is trying to formulate how to express his plan without giving too much away, "it's going to be like this. We are going to spend several days here until I get some answers. As far as what the questions are, that also will come with time.

"In the meantime, I want to explain your surroundings to you. This long pipe you are handcuffed to is bolted to the beams in the ceiling and the floor. Notice the holes. Four-foot six-inch lag bolts hold in the top and bottom, trying to pull the pipe out is impossible so don't waste your energy.

"Next, notice the two large buckets next to you. Those are your toilets. Ramirez, you have your bucket behind that wall so you can have a little privacy. Mind you, the use is for "number one" only. If the need for anything else should overcome you, hold it in, unless you plan on sitting on those buckets.

"And last, but not least, your beds are beneath you. Your chairs are recliners. You watch TV, listen to the radio, and we are going to talk, and I mean talk. You see there are lots of things I want to talk about. There are a lot of answers I want, and my source of information is you two. Because of you two, two lives have been shattered and because their lives are shattered, it creates a domino affect and hundreds of lives are affected; and so on down the line.

"There could be thousands of other lives, which will be shattered. But I'm not going to let that happen even if I have to kill the two of you in this very room. I want you both to know, and to understand I do mean business. I have gone too far to stop now, and believe me I will kill you. I'm very nervous and I don't need either of you to get out of line. So that's why you're tied up and why you'll sit until I'm satisfied."

Officer McCulley looks at Jamie and rolls his eyes and again bursts out, "You can't do this. You cannot just hold people against their will. And as an officer of the law, I demand you to release my partner and me."

Jamie looks at McCulley with a smirk on his face, "McCulley, it appears to me that you are not in the position to demand anything. If I were you, I would follow

Officer Ramirez example and change your tone; or better yet, just shut up."

"Shut up? Kiss my ass nigger, you release my bonds and we'll see who 'shuts up,' but only it will be permanent for you sucker."

"Okay, McCulley, go ahead, run your mouth; that's just what I want you to do. I have a few questions just for you, but first I am going to ask your partner. Ramirez! Are you together yet? Are you a part of this world, or are you still in la-la land?"

Ramirez answers coherently, but has her head back in disbelief. She stares at her captor and wonders where she had seen him before. She normally doesn't forget a face and knows she has seen this one before. The thoughts are scrambled in her mind and she knows sooner or later it will come to her, but the image of this man seems to stand out.

She stops grilling herself and decides to deal with the matters at hand. "I'm here," she said "but I need you to explain one thing to me. My legs and arms are numb as hell, and now, I have to take a leak. Are you going to stand me up and hold me over your bucket?"

"To answer to your question Ramirez, don't pee in your bed. You better hold it until you can stand on your own, now, both of you quiet. I want to hear the news."

Having little choice, both officers lie back in their recliners as Jamie turns on the television.

"In today's daring hold-up at the First State Bank, the authorities have no leads and don't know whether the robber, who is described as a light complexion black man of medium build, with short hair and thin mustache, and wearing a baseball hat, blue jacket, blue jeans, and glasses; worked alone or had one or more accomplices. The method and route of his escape is also not known at this time. The armored truck guard reported that the lone male approached him and held a gun to his head. He had a tape recorder with his wife's voice on it telling him to do as the robber said or she would be killed.

"Authorities raced to the guard's home, where they found the wife tied up in the bathroom, unharmed.

"She stated that the robber seemed to be very caring and concerned about her welfare. The amount of money stolen is unknown at this time, but inside sources state it's in the range of $750,000. The bank is offering a $10,000 reward for information
leading to the arrest and conviction of the robber, who is considered to be armed and dangerous.

"If you have any information, please contact the Secret Witness Program at 555-8889.

McCulley breaks out in a grin and comments sarcastically, "My-my-my, we have been busy, haven't we. What the hell are you trying to do? Get in the Guinness Book of World Records for the most felonies committed in one day?"

Jamie leans back in his chair like a proud rooster and smiles. McCulley continues with his verbal assault, "Sucker, you are now wanted for four kidnappings and bank robbery. Boy, your balls are bigger than Adolph Hitler's, and on top of it, you got the nerve to sit and smile about it. When they catch up with you, you are never going to get out of prison. Your ass is going to have a permanent spot in Indian Springs. I just can't get over this. You're one, bad, stupid sucker."

"Okay, McCulley, you had your laugh, but don't count your chickens yet; there are going to be more charges. And one of the charges may get me the death penalty...murder. I have the feeling that one, or even both of you are going to die. But, it won't be my doing. To determine which one of you it will be depends on what goes on here."

Ramirez turns her head to Jamie. "Look, what is your name anyway? You may as well tell us because it's going to come out sooner or later."

"My name is Jamie, Jamie Collins."

"Okay, Jamie, Jamie Collins, I want you to explain to me how in the hell did you pull a $750,000 bank robbery by yourself? Where is the money and why did you do it?"

"My, my, Ramirez, you're a very inquisitive soul aren't you? First off, I'm the one who's going to be asking the questions. Second, you are going to know everything you want to know about the hold-up, your kidnapping and about me; but in my time."

Jamie has no sooner finishes his statement when, the police prep radio crackles.

"Three-Victor-thirty-four, Three-Victor-thirty-six," the police radio crackles.

"What time did you get your police run to the Washington address?"

McCulley, being the officer that he is, continues antagonizing Jamie.

"What do you care punk? As a matter of fact, it's none of your business!"

Jamie remains calm, "Well, I have been listening to your radio and I do know your car call signs, Three-Victor-thirty-four and thirty-six. I was just wondering how much time would pass before they would miss you. By my calculations, you've been missing for about an hour and a half. I would imagine that they have been by the Washington address and located an empty squad car."

"Victor-thirty-four, Victor-thirty-six please respond."

The veins in McCulley's face protrude as he again fire questions at Jamie, "What do you mean an empty squad car? There are two vehicles. What did you do with the other one, and how did you do it?"

Ignoring McCulley, Jamie addresses his captives, "My-my," he said mockingly, "the little kiddies are bubbling with questions. Let me begin this session by telling you what I know about both of you. That way we will all be on even ground and it will begin the process of deciding which one of you is going to die."

"Ramirez, I will start with you. Your first name is Dolores. You were born in Idaho on a little farm outside of Twin Falls. You have two sisters and one brother. Your father died in Vietnam and your mother raised the four of you by herself until you were sixteen, at which time, she remarried and your stepfather moved in.

"You were an honor student in high school and went to college at University of Idaho. You majored in Criminal Justice and watched all the 'cop' shows. You eventually moved to Las Vegas and joined the Police Department at the ripe old age of twenty-one.

"You have been on the job for two years and as of yet; you are without any type of awards. You were teamed up with McCulley a year ago; since then, you have been involved in several questionable arrests."

"You live alone at 1117 N. Jones and you drive an Escort 1999, license number 432-555. Your phone number is 258-0063.

"You're not a born leader, but if forced into a position, you would do well. You have a boyfriend by the name of Willis and you have been dating each other for over two years.

"You have yet to show any racial bias against the community, even though you work in a mostly black community."

"Three-Victor-thirty-four, Three-Victor-thirty-six, ten-sixteen," the urgency in the dispatcher's voice is obvious.

"I have noticed that you continue to stare at me. I can't help but wonder if you remember me."

Ramirez tries to clear her mind of the spacey feeling induced by the drug, and focuses her mind through the haze as best she can.

All the people she has met, all the places she has been, and it's all going through her mind now. Slowly, names and faces come to her as she searches for this man's identity. *Why does Jamie look so familiar to her?*

"Yes, that did cross my mind. I usually don't forget a face, especially one like yours. You have that kind of face that stands out. From what I remember, you were a friendly sort of person. You didn't cause me to raise my defenses."

Still searching though a sea of faces in her mind, Ramirez does her best to probe her memory for a reference to "Jamie Collins" but comes up empty handed.

Seeing the struggle on her face, Jamie helps her out, "You met me at the Las Vegas Health Club, where you do your daily exercise. I went to the club a half-hour everyday before you arrived. I purposely arrived early to make sure you were going to be there and so not to give you the impression I was following you.

"After a few weeks of this, I finally decided it was time that you met me.

"One day when you were leaving, I accidentally, on purpose dropped my gym bag and spilled all of its content in front of you.

"You were gracious enough to assist me in retrieving my property. I enjoyed your helpfulness and you were so pleasant. I knew at that point you were incapable of doing the things I had suspected you of doing.

"After that encounter, I continued to watch you and on one other occasion I spoke to you while you were out to dinner with your boyfriend Willis, at the Peppermill on Las Vegas Blvd.

"I was lucky enough to get a table right behind yours and after an hour or so; I came to your table and spoke to you reminding you of where we met. Is any of this coming back to you?"

The gym—yes, she has seen him at the gym. He was just an acquaintance then, not even someone she could pick out in a crowd. This man was watching her, stalking her, all this time without her even knowing it. The cop in Ramirez was disappointed.

"Well, yes now that you mentioned it, but you were so kind and attentive. I remembered thinking at that time that if I didn't already have a boyfriend you would make a handsome candidate; but now I wished I never had that thought."

"Ah, come on Ramirez, I am not that bad. You still have to get to know me. I may yet become the man of your dreams. Don't knock it until you try it. Now, my question to you is; how well do you know your partner? And what do you have to say about yourself?"

Ramirez sits back, looking dumbfounded. She's shocked at the amount of information Jamie has revealed about her. How could she have missed someone stalking her and cataloguing her every movement? No, it had to be something else; her mind tried to reason. It had to be some sort of a trick.

"How did you get that information on me?"

Jamie smiles, as if he expected this question, "Thanks to friends at the DMV and the Social Security Office, I can get information on anybody. Also, with the help of your friends in Idaho, I found out all I needed to know."

"You see, I spent several months looking into both your backgrounds. I also spent approximately $2,500.00 traveling around the country to complete that background check. You were a really dull person. I guess moving to the big city helped you to gain a little confidence in yourself."

Ramirez falls quiet, becoming lost in her own thoughts, trying to retrace every moment she saw Jamie's face or had spoken to him.

Everything was starting to come down on her. She is just beginning to truly realize that this wasn't a random thing, that this man really did have something in store for them.

"Cut out all of this bullshit, what do our backgrounds have to do with you kidnapping us and tying us up?" McCulley demanded, breaking the silence.

Jamie turned to face McCulley with a slight grin, "Okay, McCulley, it's your turn."

"Your first name is Clarence. Boy did your parents misname you. You were born in Winnfield, Louisiana on July 3, 1970.

"The population is 7,311. I guess you spent a lot of time playing in the Dugdemona River!

"The area was totally white, and if I am correct, the only non-whites were seen on TV, if you had a TV.

"You graduated from high school; your class consisted of sixty-four students.

"Immediately after high school, you joined the Army, where you were in the Military Police.

"At the end of four years, you came to Las Vegas on the advice of a friend, James Witherspoon, who talked you into joining the police department.

"You worked patrol, then the bike squad. You were eventually transferred back to patrol because of your aggressive nature.

"Again, you received no citations, no commendations, only complaints from citizens. You have a problem with your mouth. You think you are God. You think you are invincible. You have no girlfriend and you hang out with James Witherspoon and his cronies.

"You occasionally send money home to your mother who is single and on welfare and raising your three sister and four brothers.

"Your father died when you were sixteen years of age. He drowned in the Dugdemona River when his boat tipped over.

"You took the death of your father pretty hard, because you were really close to him. He always wanted you to take care of the family if and when he died.

"You fell short of that goal and are probably blaming yourself for your shortcomings.

"You spend a lot of time drinking and getting high on weed, which you and your friends take from people on the streets.

"You live alone in an apartment at 2405 Rampart and drive a bright red 1998 Chevrolet truck; license plate number 876-ABC. Your phone number is 555-6534."

Jamie stares hard at McCulley, "Do you have any questions, and what do you think of your partner?"

McCulley stared blankly at Jamie. Jamie's rundown of his life was too much for McCulley's mind to handle for the moment. Feeling his self-control returning, he brings himself back into the moment.

"Understand sucker, I am the police officer. I am the one who asks questions. Now, I demand that you release me!"

Jamie laughs at this; "You are joking right, McCulley? What part of 'you're not in the position to demand shit' did you not understand?"

McCulley lashed back at Jamie, "Understand? You damned nigger, just understand this you son of a whore…understand that your black ass is dead as soon as I get loose."

"Hey Ramirez, this stupid sucker just can't come to the fact that he is a prisoner. I just can't believe it. He doesn't even think his shit stinks."

"You are the only thing stinking here, you piece of shit. You are nothing but a common hood, stalking us and shit. Just street trash like the rest of your kind," McCulley hissed.

Now angered by McCulley's outburst, Jamie walks around his chair and stops in front of the captive officer, and leans down to his face and attempts to instill fear into him.

"Look punk, I'm not shitting with you! Now, for the last time, shut your goddamn mouth or I will stick the butt of this shotgun down your throat!

"I just can't believe you, stuck in a chair, unable to move anything on your body except your upper torso, talking shit like this!

"I want everything to come out about you. I want to see the expression on your face when you are exposed! Then and only then will I look into your face, smile and spit in your eye!"

Next, he focuses his attention on Ramirez, who is sitting back staring into space. "Ramirez, how well do you know this piece of shit? Start talking now!"

Ramirez sees the danger lurking in Jamie's eyes and starts to talk, "Well, I don't know too much about McCulley, other than on the job. I don't hang out with him after work. He seems to be a good cop. That's about all I can say about him. We haven't been working together that much…I think about twelve months."

"Yes, but what do you think of him? Twelve months is a long time to be partners with someone without even having an opinion of him."

"I said he is a good cop!" Ramirez forces out.

"Don't give me that shit! What do you think of him, besides being a good cop?"

"I don't know. We really never talk beyond work."

Jamie decides to be more direct with Ramirez, "Has he ever invited you to the Web Inn!"

"Yeah he has on several occasions."

McCulley starts to stir again, "So what if I did, there are plenty of cops who hang out there."

McCulley seems to be a bit defensive on his reply. Jamie tries to look at Ramirez' eyes but she turns away, avoiding him.

Seeing that McCulley thinks he needs to talk, Jamie walks over to him and looks him over again, "And I guess they are all like you, eager to clean up the streets of Las Vegas!"

"Yeah, we're all cool and understand one another. So, what does that have to do with shit?"

"Sorry, I don't remember addressing you with a question, McCulley. Do you always have an answer for your partners, or don't you think they can talk for themselves. Or maybe you have something to hide?"

"Hey, we hung out there. You asked a question, and I was tired of hearing your mouth move."

Jamie ignores McCulley's comments and turns back to Ramirez, "Ramirez, have you ever been with your partner after work? Have you ever gone anywhere with your partner after work?"

"No, no I haven't."

"What are his politics?"

"Well, I think he is a republican, I'm not sure. I would say he is a conservative."

"Has he ever discussed with you how he feels about other races or has he ever used any racial slurs!"

Ramirez stalls for a second before she answering, "Yes, but no more then any other cop I've talked to."

"Are most of the cops you associate with really close to your partner?"

"Yeah, it's a group of about twelve. We manage to run into each other on a daily basis," Ramirez begins in a confused voice. "But what does this all have to do with us being tied up? Did something go wrong at the bar? How are we involved? Talk to me!"

Jamie thinks about telling Ramirez more than he intended to, but McCulley cuts him off before he can begin, "Hey Ramirez, why don't you just shut up. You act like you have to answer those damn questions."

Ramirez looks at McCulley with the patience one might have with a child, "McCulley, we are handcuffed to a steel pole, which we can't move under any circumstances. Even if we could, we can barely make our arms and legs work. I feel like a piece of shit because I can't move. This guy has a .357 and a shotgun. He has already said he is going to kill one of us, and I don't want to be the second one."

Ramirez' matter-of-factness enrages McCulley. Using his head to whip himself around, McCulley starts in on Ramirez, "What the hell are you talking about; you don't want to be the second one! What makes you think he wants me dead!"

"Haven't you been listening to the conversation? It seems to me that you have already been chosen!"

Jamie watches the two bickering. Just what he wanted, divide and conquer. Not that Jamie actually had to try too hard to separate the two partners; it appears that the twelve months they were together had in itself generated enough reasons for a fallout.

"Ah woman, you're full of shit. That sucker is not going to do anything. This is the United States; this shit can't go on here, especially to police officers. You dumb broad! Can't you see he is just using us? He isn't going to do shit with us...he doesn't have the balls. He's just bluffing, but when I get out of here, your ass is mine too Ramirez."

Ramirez has heard all she can stand from McCulley. "Shut up McCulley!" she screams.

Jamie cuts McCulley off from any response, "Ramirez, these cops I assume are all white?"

Ramirez' face lights up with the look of sudden insight, "Right!" she replies.

"When you say they use racial slurs and talk about other races, what was said?"

They are interrupted by the prep radios.

"Three Victor seven-forty, would you check the area of 618 W. Washington? We can't raise Victor thirty-four or thirty-six."

"Ten-four, Radio. Victor seven-forty, ten-seventeen."

"Victor seven-forty, check. Those units were responding to a four-o-three report. Exercise caution".

"Any unit, ten-thirty-two, 618 West Washington."

"Victor four responding."

"Victor three-two responding."

"Victor three-two and Victor four, your call is Code Two."

"Okay, guys, your buddies are out looking for you, and they're upset. So we must continue."

McCulley turns his face away from the radio and looks up at Jamie. Trying not to get too far out of line with his words, McCulley tries to be reasonable. "Where are we anyway?" he asks.

"McCulley you are in Las Vegas, NV, and that's about all you're going to know until I am ready to tell you more," Jamie responds, turning his attention back to Ramirez, "Now Ramirez, back to the questions. When other races were mentioned, what was said?"

Ramirez looks at Jamie as she responds, "Look Jamie...you don't mind if I call you Jamie, do you?"

"No, go ahead."

"Okay, Jamie, remember these aren't my words. I don't care for those people or their language. Blacks were referred to as 'nigger', Asians were 'gooks', Italians were called 'wops' and Mexicans were 'wetbacks' and 'greasers'. They also mentioned that nobody should be living other than white people."

"And you sat around listening to this bullshit?"

"That's the main reason I wasn't involved with them after work. I didn't like how they felt about other races. I am not that type of person. I love life and I love people. For someone to dislike a person because of their race or nationality is totally against everything I was taught in life."

"Did you ever report your findings about your partner to your supervisors?"

McCulley looks at Ramirez as if to give her a silent command to remain quiet. If Ramirez saw the glance, she chose to ignore it. This outburst by Ramirez has been bubbling up for quite some time now.

"Jamie, when I moved here, I was totally excited about becoming a police officer. Since I have been on the force, the things I have seen and what I have heard has turned my stomach. We are supposed to be the protectors of liberty. We are here to serve the public, but what I have seen is a very harsh and aggressive posture against the public. Everyday, I watch how my partner abuses and uses individuals just to gain rank in the department or recognition among his peers.

"Justice just does not exist. These cops will lie to put people in jail to satisfy their needs. I am pissed off and sorry sometimes to even wear this uniform, but I stick with this job hoping that sooner or later, things will change.

"This town is so far behind every other city in so many areas; it seems to me they will never catch up."

Again, the conversation is interrupted by the police radio, and greater fear consumes Jamie. He knows death is near. He can't afford any mistakes and he has to really watch himself and how he handles the unfolding situation. Not only is Jamie beginning to get jumpy; now, the ears of all the police officers in Las Vegas are standing on end.

McCulley and Ramirez are suppose to contact their dispatcher every 15 minutes while involved in a police run and make an entry on their log sheet every thirty minutes and they haven't executed either of these duties.

It is department policy; any violation could result in disciplinary action. Since these rules were violated, the officers in charge will assume there is a real problem.

Now, they have an empty squad car and another car is missing, the higher echelons of command in the department will most certainly get involved.

Jamie is now totally consumed by fear, to the point that he begins pacing the floor and tossing his .357 Magnum from hand to hand and listening intently to the police radio. Then he breaks out in a smile and turns to his captives, but is interrupted by McCulley once again.

"Well, people, it looks like the search is on. Let's listen and watch them run around this city like chickens with their heads cut off..."

"Look Jamie."

"Hold on McCulley, I gave Ramirez permission to call me by my first name, not you. When you want to address me, use my last name, which is Collins spelled C-O-L-L-I-N-S."

"Okay, Collins, I have a lot of friends out there, and they will find me even if they have to tear the city down."

Again, Jamie leans back in his chair aggravated by McCulley's comments. But he ignores him.

"Ramirez, you want to finish?"

"Well, that's all I have to say right now."

"Okay, McCulley, do you have anything to say?"

"Yes, yes I do. Ramirez, why are you giving in so soon? Why are you talking all that shit? You sound like someone out of the sixties. I didn't know you felt like that about the force. Why the hell am I stuck with Ms Goodie Two Shoes?

"Look, you stupid broad, when we get out of this, your ass is going to be drummed right off the job. I don't need to be working with an ass like you, Ms Bleeding Heart."

McCulley does his best to get a rise out of Ramirez. He doesn't even know exactly why he is saying what he is. He won't get advantage from making Ramirez more upset at him, but for some deep psychological reason, it makes McCulley feel better. Bullying people, physically or verbally, always made McCulley feel better.

"Go ahead McCulley, say what you please, I'm going to live for another day and God is not going to look down on me. He knows I'm good at heart. He knows I am not going to screw anyone, but you, I have questions about."

Ramirez was already familiar with her partner insatiable need to make himself feel superior whenever he could. She was not about to let the things he was saying get in the way of her thinking. He is tied up and she is tied up. As far as she was concerned, they are equals in every way now, even in their helplessness.

Seeing that his words weren't touching Ramirez yet, McCulley tries to push it, "Yeah, you and the rest of those bleeding heart liberals. You're going to suck out the asses of all those other people who don't belong in this country. This country was made for the white people. The white people deserve all the riches this country can provide. Everyone else needs to go back to where they came from: Africa, China, Japan, Mexico, or wherever. We don't need any of those people, including you Ramirez. Mexico is still open.

Ramirez knows that McCulley only wants her to get upset. She sees it strictly as a childish game. McCulley can't order Jamie around and is taking his frustrations out on Ramirez. Jamie watches most of the conversation but has decided to teach McCulley a bit of a history lesson.

"McCulley, you haven't even thought of what every other race has done to make this country what it is today! You probably don't know what contributions they have made or how their contributions were stolen from them and claimed by the whites!

"Simple little things that make our lives easier, such as, traffic lights, the ironing board, the by products from peanuts and grapes, ranching, irrigation, the first open heart surgery, and lots more!

"We owe people like Dr. Daniel Hale Williams, Lewis Howard Latimer, George Washington Carver, Geronimo, Tecumseh, Crazy Horse, Chief Joseph, Juan Bautista de Anza, and Juan Ponce de Leon!

"All of these people contributed in a way that made the United States think and behave the way it does today! All of them are from races of people you deal with everyday! Mexicans, Africans, and Native Americans!

"I suggest that before you form any opinion about who deserves this country, you should do a little research and get your facts straight."

Ramirez stifles a cry of admiration when she hears Jamie put McCulley in his place. McCulley turns his attention from Ramirez to Jamie. It seems that his words were affecting someone, not just Ramirez.

McCulley begins thinking that perhaps Jamie isn't in as much control as he thinks he is.

"Look Collins, I don't need to do any type of research. If you're not white, you're not right…it's that simple," McCulley says trying to push the issue.

Jamie picks up the shotgun lying next to his chair and walks around the room trying to calm down. But McCulley continues his remarks and the more McCulley runs his mouth the angrier Jamie becomes.

"Just face it; you guys have always been a slave race. Hell, you wanted a history lesson, Mister Collins? Did you know that niggers always been selling other niggers out? White men didn't make them slaves they made themselves slaves. They still are making themselves slaves today. How is that for a history lesson, Mister Collins?"

Jamie finally stops in front of McCulley and stares him in the face. And then loses it. Jamie raises his voice so that the blood rushes to his eyes and rattles off at McCulley all in one breath, "What makes white people any better than anyone else! You have ten toes, so does everyone else! You have two legs and two arms; a brain, which is the same size as everyone else, nose, eyes, and a mouth with thirty-two teeth...and if someone were to take this shotgun and hit me in the mouth like this, I would bleed the same red blood you are going to be bleeding in a minute!"

McCulley starts to rebut Jamie's words with more slurs, but not before Jamie smashes him in the face with the butt of the shotgun.

McCulley's head flies back as though it were trying to leave his body and then, bounces back as blood gushes from his mangled mouth onto his upper body.

Fearing for her partner's life, Ramirez begs Jamie not to hit him any more as she turns her head from side to side, unable to do anything.

"Jamie stop! That's enough; don't hit him any more! Plee-ease stop!"

Jamie walks back to his seat, gazing in the air and halfway sorry he reacted the way he did. He puts his head in his hands and mumbles to Ramirez, "I needed him to know how that felt! Let me get some water."

Jamie leaves the room to retrieve some water for McCulley's face. This gives the two officers time to talk by themselves.

"McCulley, McCulley, are you all right!" asked a worried Ramirez.

Bleeding from the mouth, McCulley tries to answer his partner, "Yeah that son-of-a-bitch broke my nose and loosened my teeth! Shit, he jacked me up! Just wait until I get my hands on that sucker, he won't make it to court!"

Jamie walks into the bathroom and returns with a cloth and water. He pours the water on McCulley's head and then hands him the bowl with the cloth, "Here, McCulley, this water will cool you off."

The water runs down McCulley's head and mingles with the blood from his face. His crimson mask starts to fade in lines, like a drying riverbed. The lines from drying blood makes McCulley look like a clown or an actor in some Japanese theatre.

"Why do you have to pour it on me? Why are you screwing with me?" McCulley snaps at Jamie in frustration.

Jamie walks calmly towards McCulley, holding out a bowl and a towel. "Here, take this, and clean out your mouth. I'm glad you asked that question because I am tired of beating around the bush."

JIMMY CULLORS/JOSEPH SZEWEZYK

chapter

4

THE REUNION

"Excuse me Sheriff, but you have a call on line one."

"Okay, Sharon, I got it." The sheriff stretches out in his chair and lets out a moan as he rubs his large beer belly. The day has been long and he is ready to go home. He rubs his mustache and then reluctantly reaches for the phone while pushing his glasses up on his face. "This is Sheriff Kerns. Can I help you?"

The voice on the other end seems professional yet edgy, "Yes, sir, this is Lieutenant George. We have a serious problem on the Westside, sir. Two of our units were sent to an address on West Washington Avenue at 4:15 p.m. and we haven't heard from either of them since."

The sheriff stares at the phone receiver and squeezes the phone so tight his knuckles began to turn white. Did he hear correctly? Two of his units are out and missing? Impossible!

"Did you get a supervisor out to the location?"

"Yes sir. Three 700-units are on the scene now, sir. They've located one scout car, but both of the officers are still missing."

"What was the nature of the run?"

"It was a four-o-three report, sir."

"A prowler? Look, Lieutenant, get more help out there and keep me abreast of the situation. What's the address?"

"618 West Washington"

"I'm on my way. I'll meet you there." The sheriff barely stayed on the phone long enough to make his last sentence audible.

Filled with shock, the sheriff moves quickly through his office on the way to the scene. He is utterly overwhelmed that someone would actually have the unmitigated gall to kidnap one of his officers, let alone two of them.

Knowing that the police are now aware of the fact that two of their officers are missing, Jamie continues to question his captives. "Do you recognize me at all sucker? It's been several hours and you have never said anything about recognizing me at all...and you call yourself a cop. Look at me, sucker!"

McCulley tries to look at Jamie, but between the haze of the resent blow to the head and the overall shock of the situation he's in, he has a hard time making out Jamie's identity. Someone from his past, he is sure–but whom?

"You look familiar, but I don't know where from." McCulley admits.

"All us niggers look alike, eh cracker?" Jamie retorted sarcastically. "Well, let me refresh your memory," Jamie said as he closes in on the helpless officer.

McCulley tries to focus his attention on Jamie, while Ramirez listens intently to what Jamie is about to say.

One of the officers has witnessed everything Jamie is about to relate, but neither of them could have recalled the story that he is about to tell.

One of the officers had not been present; the other had been there, but what transpired is such a common occurrence for him that he would be equally at a loss to recall the events. It would be like trying to describe the carpet at his house–he might walk over it everyday, but his lack of attention to its detail would preclude his giving an adequate description.

"On the evening of August 28, 1998," Jamie begins, "two young men were having a party to celebrate the first year anniversary of living on their own.

"There were approximately sixteen people in their apartment– a mixture of Blacks, Whites, and Mexicans–

drinking, dancing, eating, playing cards and having a good time.

"The oldest in the house was a young man by the name of Marvin–he was the only one who was of age.

"Marvin shared the apartment with his brother Jamie who was eighteen years old.

"At one time, during the evening, Marvin decided to go to the store–that's when you decided to show up, McCulley.

"Some of the partygoers were outside. Two of them were white females just enjoying the evening air. While they were outside, you drove up in your squad car, and saw these young people standing around. You slowed down as you passed and noticed the two white girls.

"Then you drove about two blocks away, parked and called for your partner to meet you at your location. A few minutes passed before your partner showed up and the two of you discussed what you had just seen.

"You were angry because of the white girls partying in a black neighborhood and decided to teach them a lesson. You and your partner, James Witherspoon, returned to the party and decided to roust everybody.

"The two of you parked in front of the house, got out of your cars and began to harass the young girls. When you found out the girls were only seventeen years old, you decided to arrest them for violation of curfew.

"In your own unique and inimitable way, McCulley, you impressed upon them that they shouldn't be hanging around with a bunch of niggers. Do you remember any of this, cracker?"

McCulley shook his head dully.

"What a piece of work you are, you bigoted prick. You do this shit so much you can't even keep track of it.

"Jamie, being the renter of the apartment, saw you outside, and he decided to go out and see what the problem was.

"He approached you and asked why you had the girls in the car. You told him it was none of his business. Then you reached into your pocket and pulled out a rock of cocaine and threw on the ground next to his feet. You told him, 'You see what I can do to you, boy?'

"Then you picked up the cocaine and returned it to your pocket and ordered Jamie back into the house and followed him inside.

"When the two of you got into the house, you asked who was twenty-one and no one answered. You and your partner then took it upon yourselves to walk through the house, rummaging through everything.

"You spotted a bathtub full of beer and ice, and ordered the partygoers to take out all the beer cans and crush them on the floor.

"Both of you then went in to kitchen, where there are several bottles of liquor. You took each bottle and poured it on the carpet. After soaking the carpet with alcohol and beer, the two of you laughed and left with the two young girls.

"The next day, the boys called their father and the three of them went to the police station and filed a complaint. From that time on, you and your partner continually came by the boys' apartment and harassed them.

"You followed them and ticketed them for every inconsequential violation they made, and the father and his sons continued to file complaints.

"By December of that same year, you and Witherspoon had gotten tired of the complaints being filed against you and decided to do something about it.

"The two of you forced several people in the neighborhood to file complaints alleging that drugs were being sold at the kids' apartment.

"The Narcotics Unit made plans to raid the boy's apartment and, of course, since it was the area where you and Witherspoon worked, you had to be present during the raid.

"No drugs were found until you emerged from a bedroom with a pound of cocaine, which you said came from under one of the mattresses.

"In reality, McCulley, you planted the drugs in the apartment and lied about finding it there.

"The father and his sons fought the system for eight months, trying to keep them out of jail, but they failed, and the boys were found guilty of possession with intent to sell cocaine. They were sentenced to ten to twenty years in state prison.

"Officer McCulley, thirty thousand dollars was spent trying to keep those young men out of prison. Their father assisted them in filing one complaint after another against you. He was in court with them everyday, watching your ass grinning, laughing, and lying in court.

"He watched his sons break down and cry as they were being led off to prison, while you laughed and chuckled with your friends.

"Those two young men you framed are my sons! Young men I raised and taught to be good citizens!

"These young men never used drugs, much less sold them!

"My sons have never been in trouble their entire lives–up until the time they ran into you! We had a unique relationship–I was at their home practically every day–we could discuss anything! If anything unusual had been going on in their lives, you better believe I would have known!"

Jamie looks up from the anguish of his story-telling frenzy, momentarily lost and unclear of his surroundings.

Still defiant, McCulley rolls his eyes upward in his head and turns to Jamie as though he heard the story many times before. Jamie stares into the officer's eyes, almost as if he could see right through him.

"You got a problem with that, McCulley?"

"Man, you sound like all the rest of the black people whose children get arrested. 'Not my baby, my baby didn't do anything wrong.' I'm sick of that shit! I didn't set up your sons! I am a police officer! Now get off my back!

"Your sons were found guilty in a court of law because the evidence point to their guilt and a jury of their peers found them guilty," McCulley shot back.

Jamie's face turns red at this comment and his hand clench into a fist so tight; his nails start to dig into his flesh, making his palms bleed.

Now is not the time for Jamie to lose control, to let McCulley, and all the others like him win because he can't keep the reins on his emotions. Now, more than ever, he needs to maintain tight control and a cool composure, even if it was a bit forced. It is still Jamie's ace for the moment.

Jamie clears his mind and focuses his anger in words instead of physical violence, "Based on your perjured testimony, you renegade cop!

"First off, the evidence was planted! Second, I don't know if you're blind, deaf, or just plain dumb, but all the jurors were white and over fifty! How in the hell were they my sons' peers. My kids were twenty-one, eighteen and black!

"I am really tired of your shit, but I won't lose control with you–that would be defeating my purpose.

"Yes, McCulley, those are my children and you screwed them up!"

Jamie paused and then added in a sinister voice, "And now I'm gonna screw you up."

"Ramirez, I'm telling you now; you have a messed-up partner, and today you will find out how messed up he really is!"

Now tired of McCulley's denials, Jamie grabs a stack of papers from the table, the contents of which are hidden to all but him.

Ramirez tries to get a peek at them to see what Jamie might be leading into, but to no avail. Jamie keeps the papers well hidden.

"McCulley, are you or are you not a member of the Aryan Nation?" Jamie asks flatly.

McCulley looks at Jamie as if he was speaking in tongue, "Sucker, please–I'm a cop!"

Jamie responds to McCulley as one would with a child who is lying to avoid punishment,   "One more chance, McCulley. Are you a member of the Aryan Nation or are you affiliated with them in any way?"

As Jamie continues to push for answers, McCulley begins to turn red. Spittle is hanging from the corners of his mouth, whether from anger or the effect of the ketamine, Jamie isn't sure.

"I said no, so don't try and hang that kind of crap on me!"

The conversation is interrupted once again by the crackling of the prep radios.

"Victor seven-forty..."

"Go ahead Victor seven-forty..."

"Radio, we've located one squad car, but still no sign of the officers or the other car. William three-twenty is ten-twenty-three. I called the senior one-hundred on the landline and he is en route."

"Ten-four, Victor seven-forty. The senior one hundred is ten-seventeen. Do you need a sky unit?"

"Ten-four Radio. Also, a K-nine unit".

"Roger, Victor seven-forty. All responding units go to channel eight..."

Hearing all this, Jamie knows that there is no time out or opportunity to turn around.

From his experience as a police officer, he is well aware there will be a major manhunt for the missing officers. His heart is pounding and he's very shaky, but he tries to play it off and directs his attention back to McCulley.

"Now a major search party is underway for you two. You should be on the Eleven O'clock News...we will see soon enough.

"McCulley, as I was beginning to say, I spent a lot of time researching you both. I want you both to know I followed you, Ramirez for one month, and you, McCulley for four months."

"Ramirez, I kind of like you. You're no phony. You're a real down to earth person. But McCulley, you're the type of person every one loves to hate. And as far as I know, there are at least ten people who are in prison because of your lying and manipulations. If everything goes right, they should all receive new trials."

JIMMY CULLORS/JOSEPH SZEWEZYK

Jamie pauses to let his words sink in, and then continues in an even voice.

"I asked you a question, McCulley: have you ever seen me before? I told you about one time that our paths have crossed, and yet you still can't seem to remember me. Now I will tell you about another time we were together. Maybe this time it will rattle your brain."

As Jamie starts to relate another time and place their paths had crossed–McCulley begins to stir uneasily in his chair; a look of uncertainty clouds on his face. He questions himself as to where he had previously seen this man and begins listening carefully to what Jamie has to say.

Jamie ignores the change in McCulley's expression and continues with his story. "I use to counsel pregnant teenagers and their boyfriends or husbands. My main purpose was to teach the men how to be responsible husbands, boyfriends, and fathers.

"My counseling took me away from my personal life and I became a part of their lives. I would go to court with them and try to convince the judges that my clients were on a road to becoming responsible citizens of society.

"I got them in to see doctors, into drug rehabs, and even sent them away for months at a time to get the streets out of their systems.

"After they showed some sign of rehabilitation, I would get them started in a career of their own choosing."

One couple, Donald and Rachel, was more or less a favorite of Jamie's. He got Donald started in an apprenticeship program at the Las Vegas Sun in the field of photography.

Donald was doing well, except for one problem–he was involved with methamphetamines and Jamie felt he had to do something to help Donald kick the habit.

Jamie also told Donald about the trouble he was having with his children, and Donald offered to help.

Donald knew McCulley, and offered to take Jamie to the bar where McCulley hung out–the same place where Donald got his drugs.

Jamie figured it was strange that a cop would be hanging out in a place where drugs are sold. He also figured the information could be used to his advantage.

So Donald, Rachel, and Jamie decided to visit the bar, meet the supplier, and see McCulley at his best.

As Jamie continues to relate the details of their meeting, the officer squirms more and more anxiously in his seat.

The three of them left the school and went to a bar on Boulder Highway. 'The Mosquito'...a few blocks north of the Boulder Station Casino.

From the outside, the building was quite different from the rest of the buildings in the area. It had several steers' horns on the eaves of the building. The doors and outside walls were made of logs. The windows were small–a person would have to place their face against the glass in order to see inside.

Opening the door was a chore itself. It was heavy and squeaked when it was opened. The three figures entered into total darkness, aided by the dim light coming from behind the bar.

Jamie took off his sunglasses, so he could adjust to the darkness and finally made his way to a barstool. When he sat down, Donald and Rachel went to the rear of the bar looking for the dealer.

Little did Jamie know that, while he was adjusting to the darkness, the rest of the patrons, in the bar, had stopped drinking and talking.

Just as Jamie ordered a Cognac, someone walked up behind him and slapped him on the back of his head. Since he was in a strange environment, Jamie took his time before he reacted.

He looked up at the mirror behind the bar and saw a big, burly, white man with a beard, wearing a straw, cowboy hat, with a white dingy tee shirt.

Before he could turn around, the man yelled out, "What the hell are you doing here, nigger!"

Jamie is now lost in his reverie of the event. He slowly turned around on the stool, and six more clones of the first man appeared out of the darkness.

Jamie realized that he was in a very precarious situation and tried to remain calm, "I came in with friends to meet someone, and decided to have a drink," he replied, trying to defuse the situation.

The first man looked at Jamie, and reached out and began adjusting Jamie's collar and tie.

"Yeah, I saw you come in here with that nigger-loving Donnie boy and his old lady. Said you come in here to meet somebody? Well there ain't nobody here that wants to meet you! So, I advise you to finish your drink, and get the hell out before me and my boys wipe this place up with your ass."

Jamie turns back for his glass, and the big man grabs him by the nape of his neck. But before the assailant could pull him from his seat, a voice yells from the back, "Leave him alone!"

Jamie didn't know who his guardian angel was, but he surely wanted to meet him.

The big guy releases Jamie's neck, as Jamie looked around, and saw a man dressed in leather pants, a white long sleeve shirt with a black leather vest. He had dirty-blond, shoulder-length hair and a mustache that grew beyond his chin. He could have been a cowboy, or a rock n'roll star.

As Jamie looked the man over, he realized that he was under examination as well–and by the very man he was looking over.

A sneer came across the man's face. "You got a lot of balls coming in here! What the hell do you want?"

Just then Donald emerges out of the darkness. "This is Jamie Collins. He is the one I told you about."

"You didn't tell me he was god dam nigger!"

"You didn't ask. And I didn't think it really mattered!"

"This ass will probably run to Metro. What have ya told this son-of-a-bitch!"

"Nothing–he just wanted to meet you."

"I don't believe your stupid ass. You brought this ass here to meet me?"

Jamie interrupts before the conversation got too loud, and out of control.

"Excuse me. I think I can answer your questions, if we can talk alone, how about at the end of the bar?"

So Jamie and the man, who seemed to be in charge, walk to the end of the bar and took two seats. Jamie explained who he was and why he was there. When Jamie asked him not to sell any more drugs to Donald and Rachel, loud laughter erupted from the man.

"As you know, asshole, that's how I make my living. And now you're asking me not to sell to my favorite customers? You have to come better than that!"

As the man continued to laugh raucously, loud talking and laughter from another quarter distracted Jamie. He looked in the direction of the noise and saw someone very familiar to him–Officer McCulley.

McCulley was not in the condition expected of police officers. He and several other men were placing bets on who could drink the most boilermakers.

Jamie continued watching McCulley and his crew, no longer paying any attention to what the drug dealer was saying to him. His concentration was shattered by a loud slam on the bar.

"Look sucker, I thought you said you wanted to talk to me! All you been doing is sitting here staring at those cops. If you don't have anything else to say, I suggest you get the hell out of here!"

Jamie snaps back with his focus on the man, "Wait! Wait a minute! You said that Donald and Rachel are your best customers. What if you didn't sell to them anymore, and let me purchase what they would normally buy? Would you then agree not to sell to them?   "Look, you can keep the shit and sell it again to someone else. I don't want it, but I'll pay you for it. What do you say?"

The dirty-blonde dealer looked at Jamie as if he were just asked where the capitol of Brazil was. Placing one hand on his chin, the other on his drink, the drug dealer thought Jamie's offer over. What seemed like an eternity to the sweating Jamie only lasted ten seconds in real time? The man put down his drink and smiled at Jamie.

"Well, I guess I can do that. But what if I decide to sell it to them anyway?"

"I do believe that if anyone were to give their word, they should stick to it. Do you give your word?"

The dealer's eyes twinkled with this statement. A word? A handshake? What is a word or a handshake among thieves? The man almost laughed in Jamie's face, but then he saw how serious the black man was. A word may not mean much to dealers and junkies, but to Jamie it was everything, and this much the man could read in Jamie's face.

"Man, if you miss even one week, I will sell it to them. Get my drift," the dealer, says as he agrees to Jamie's request.

A brief wave of relief passed over Jamie. "No problem, brother. By the way, how much were they buying?"

"One hundred bucks a week!" the dealer sneered.

One hundred bucks a week! All of the jobs, all of the personal attention Jamie had given Donald-gone! All of the money Jamie had loaned them just so they could eat, gone. Clearly now, Jamie could see everything was going to drugs.

Sometimes people have to take a step back from the situation to see how bad things are. Jamie had to get into the lion's den to realize what sort of empty life the drugs his clients were using had produced.

Jamie sat back, dumbfounded about the deal he had just made, but it had given him an opportunity to see what McCulley was about. Before leaving he wanted to find out more about McCulley.

Feigning concerns, Jamie asks the dealer, "If you don't mind telling me, how often does that group of cops come in here? I don't want to get busted."

With a laugh, the dealer replied, "You don't have to worry... they're with me. They're more or less my enforcers. If you are thinking of screwing me, they will be the last people you will ever see! Now don't ask any more stupid questions, and take care of your students. Hey Joe, give this nigger another drink on me."

The bartender goes over to Jamie, holding a dirty rag in one hand and a glass in the other. He wiped the clean glass with the filthy rag and poured Jamie a drink, not bothering to ask what was his preference.

The dealer started to get up to attend to other business, but Jamie grabbed him before he could leave, "Wait a minute. What's your name, and where are Donald and Rachel?"

The dealer stopped and looked Jamie dead in the eyes, "First of all, never touch me! Second, my name is no concern of yours. When you want the shit, just walk in, I will know you're here. As for your students, they are finishing up their last blast."

The dealer shoved Jamie's hand off of his shoulder. Now, for the first time, Jamie saw something he had missed before in the dealer's eyes: danger–as if he were confronting a rattlesnake.

This man standing before Jamie may look like a harmless dealer that might be hooked on his own stuff, but his eyes–his eyes were fathomless and empty. They were completely devoid of any trace of warmth, light, or even a soul that Jamie could detect. They were dark, cold and dead. The dealer had the eyes of someone that had seen far too much and had too much happen to him to care about anything anymore. The most dangerous man in the world, Jamie reflects, is a man that doesn't care about anything.

Jamie broke away from the dealer's gaze, "Tell them to get their asses out here so we can leave," he demanded. The man gave Jamie a long, hard stare, then turned and walked away.

As he finished his drink, Jamie continued to watch McCulley, who was now the loudest person there. This is just the place, he thought, for him to get more information about this cop.

As the drinking continued, he noticed the other men calling McCulley "Chew", and was urging him to do something.

"Chew...Chew...Chew...Chew..." they began chanting.

Jamie watched in disbelief, as McCulley begins to chew on a shot glass until it is reduced to pieces on the table. At the same time, Donald and Rachel return to the bar area.

Their eyes were glazed and they mumbled incoherently as they stumbled towards Jamie. Rachel giggled nervously as she bumped into a barstool left out on the floor. Their noses were running and their eyes were puffy, they frequently jerked their heads around to get a better look at the fleeting images in the corner of their eyes...only whenever they looked at the object, it was gone.

Jamie shook his head in disappointment.

"Hey man, did you finish your business?" Donald asked.

Jamie looked at the young couple with their long, scraggly hair and their glassy eyes and begins to reprimand them, "I hope you got a good fix, because there won't be any more!"

Before they could respond, Jamie stood up, and walked over to McCulley and stood over him, "You are a very unusual person and I commend you on your feat," he said, reaching out to shake the officer's hand.

His mouth bloody, McCulley looked at Jamie as if he had crawled out of a sewer to bother him with insane questions.

"Get away from me, nigger!" he snarled. "I know you don't want me to touch you?"

Jamie laughed, and called to Donald and Rachel, and the trio quickly left the bar.

As Jamie finishes recounting his story McCulley looks up at him in drawing recognition. Everything was coming back to him now. That was him. That was that nigger that he ran into in that bar so long ago. How could he have forgotten? He was drunk that night, but you don't just forget a black man walking into that particular bar and walking out alive.

Now things were starting to drop into place for the groggy, McCulley.

Jamie looks at McCulley sensing that things are starting to come back to him.

"So, your name is 'Chew' when you're not on the job? You earned that name by chewing on your drinking glass. Speaking of drinking, how about a drink? Aw, gee, I'm sorry 'Chew'; I don't have any Jack Daniel's or a glass for you to chew on."

McCulley realizes he is in for a long day, "It doesn't matter sucker, just give me a drink!"

Jamie turns to Ramirez, "Ramirez, do you want a drink? Never mind, I'll give you one anyway. It's Cognac...It's good for your blood."

Ramirez looks up with a weak smile, "I'll take the drink, but nothing alcoholic my stomach won't take it."

"Okay, drinks are coming up; one Cognac and one virgin."

While McCulley and Ramirez engage in conversation, Jamie mixes the drinks for himself and McCulley. He then, takes another glass; pours in some soda, drops in a small pill and fills it with water.

"Look Ramirez," McCulley whispers to his partner so that Jamie cannot overhear, "while that sucker is busy making the drinks, we have to make plans to get out of here. We have to work together. Forget what I said earlier...we're partners. We got to stick together."

Ramirez half snorts at this statement. "McCulley, this conversation is getting good. I want to know what else he has to say. By the way, how in the hell are we supposed to get away? Crawl?"

"I don't care how we do it! I just want to get out of here. It seems to me a lot of drinking is going to take place, and if he drinks enough, he'll fall asleep, and then we can try and get out."

Jamie enters the room and catches the end of McCulley's statement. "Okay, numb nuts, how do you propose to break your chains? Oh, I forgot–they call you 'Chew.' Here is the ice, water, soda, Cognac and one virgin." Jamie sets the drinks down, and then turns back to McCulley as if in an afterthought.

"Oh, by the way McCulley, I have been known to drink an entire fifth and still control myself, and if you think I am going to pass out without being secure, you're crazy. I didn't go through all of this just for you or me to blow it. Well, McCulley, what do you have to say now?"

McCulley considers his situation. He remembers Jamie now, but he can't let Ramirez in on anything, other than the fact that Jamie might have met him at a bar. McCulley needs Ramirez in order to escape and this really disturbs him.

"Look," he says defiantly, "I can hang out anywhere I want. As matter of fact, I do remember that night and your friends. As for the drugs, I don't know anything about it. I don't deal in drugs, and I don't know anyone who does…other than the criminals I bust."

"Well McCulley, I bought five hits the next night."

McCulley is taken back by this statement. *What was this guy talking about…the next night? There was no way Jamie came back there the next night!* But before McCulley can complete another thought, the floodgates suddenly open up in his brain. He now remembers exactly who Jamie is.

It is well established that people will be more likely to remember things in the state they learned them in: 'state-dependent learning,' they call it.

McCulley was drunk when he first encountered Jamie, and now that he is drinking again, everything about the situation is coming back to him.

"Wait a minute, you mean to tell me that you are that fat guy with beard and glasses?"

Jamie glances at McCulley with a proud smirk. "The very same person...yessiree that was me. Now, I hope you can remember the many other nights I just happened to come by."

"You were there quite often. I remember you now. But you still don't have anything on me. It's not against the law to hang out in a bar!"

"Yeah I know, but do you remember your oath, you do don't you? I think somewhere in there you promised not to hang with unscrupulous people. From what I saw, your buddies fit that mold.

"What really surprised me is that I also counted ten cops there, and I have their names and addresses.

"On all my visits to your hangout, I recorded the dates and what exactly what was going on. Not only is it written down in detail, I also have it on tape. So, what you said to me and the person who sold me the drugs is forever held by me to do with as I please."

Jamie looks over at Ramirez who is sipping her drink. "Hey Ramirez, ask your partner what they do with the drug money."

McCulley immediately realizes that things might be getting out of control. If he were to lose Ramirez completely to Jamie, then there would be no chance of him escaping. He needs a way to change the subject.

Just how much did this old nigger know about him anyway? Almost as important, how did this guy that kidnapped him, know all this about him?

"Look sucker..." McCulley starts in his usual threatening tone.

Jamie is quick to cut McCulley off, "Just a minute McCulley, you and your partner need another drink. Y'all are drinking too slow." Jamie walks over to Ramirez, "Go ahead Ramirez, throw that down your throat, the caffeine will help you." After the officer slams her drink, Jamie offers another, "Now here, have another one."

Jamie looks over to McCulley, and sees him a bit nervous, "What about you, McCulley? It will help you stop shaking."

McCulley grits his teeth and forces himself to stop trembling by the sheer effort of his will. "To hell with you sucker, and give me another drink, because this is going to be the last time you booze it up like this.

"I can see it now, your ass in chains, struggling to walk into the courtroom. I can't wait–your ass is grass and I'm gonna be the lawnmower."

Jamie smiles at McCulley's ranting and continues his conversation with him as though the latter had said nothing. "Okay, McCulley, tell your partner what happens to the drug money?"

"I don't know what the hell you are talking about! I don't know anything about drugs or what happens to drug money! But, I am going to bet my life you know...but how could you know? Nothing was discussed about money in the bar, and I know you didn't meet with anyone who did discuss it!"

"You're right, McCulley. I wasn't invited to meet anyone, but I may as well have been. You see, next to the bar is a motel. And in that motel, meetings are held. I watched the motel for a week before I was able to get the room next door. Then two days before another meeting, your so call headquarters was empty. I installed a miniature listening device, which went through the wall.

"None of you, drunken jerks, ever noticed it. If you're wondering McCulley, I tape recorded conversations in that room for a whole month. Yeah sucker, I have everything that was said in that room for one month. I left my room only when your headquarters was empty. As long as someone was there, I was there. So now, do you want to tell your partner the rest of the story or shall I?"

McCulley stares blankly at Jamie. *The tape recorder from the other room? This guy was serious. He really thought things out. Maybe he didn't hear everything though–it could all be a bluff.*

"I don't have a thing to say; you don't have a thing on me. You can't prove I was even in that room."

"My God, you are the dumbest cop I have ever met. I am quite sure you have heard of voiceprints, and on top of that, I have dozens of photos of you and your ten other cronies going in and out of that room. If nothing else, you are guilty by association."

McCulley's temper boils over, "Guilty of what sucker! Tell me what the hell you are talking about and stop this bullshitting!"

Jamie laughs at him. "Okay, McCulley, I will do just that. Ramirez, are you ready?"

Ramirez sits and swivels in her chair like a restless child. Her speech is now slurred as she becomes more intoxicated with the drugs; the Spanish dialect flows out, intermixed with English. Her head is lulling from side to side as if her neck had been broken and could no longer support itself.

"Si, estoy lista. Esta mierda is getting better by the minute. I have been riding with you, patrón, hace un año," Ramirez mumbles, rocking in her seat like a child. "But I didn't know all the things I have found out in these last few hours. Eres un bruto. Ya sabía que eras pendejo because of the many cosas estúpidas you have done...pero no sabía todo esto. Qué cabrón sin vergüenza! I'm tied up...en una silla with my legs and arms numb as hell...tomando Cognac con este pinche negro who threatens to kill us! I can't wait for the punch line. This will make un buen cuento policiaco! Oye, tú-negro-dáme otro trago...y porque somos prisioneros aqui, ¿hay música para sazonar este cuarto."

McCulley, now rolling his eyes again, looks at Ramirez and blurts out one of his racial comments, "Ramirez, you need to shut the hell up or speak English. You're not in Mexico any longer.

"All of you foreigners come over and think you can take over and throw your lingo around and expect everybody to understand you! To hell with you!"

Ramirez snaps out of her delusions for a second to respond, "Oh kiss my ass McCulley! This is turning out to be an interesting kidnapping. Can you understand that? Oh, and by the way–I'm not from Mexico, asshole. I was born and raised in the United States."

JIMMY CULLORS/JOSEPH SZEWEZYK

chapter

5
THE NIGHTMARE

Jamie is now in his world of glory; he feels he has an ally in Ramirez. So, he strolls, smiling across the room to the radio and Ramirez makes an attempt at a joke, "In the words of the famous Ricky Ricardo, McCulley you got some 'splaining' to do."

"To hell with you, Ramirez! I'm not explaining anything to you or that asshole! I'm going to get out of here and Mr. Wise Guy will have to "splain" to a jury!"

"Okay, guys, you mustn't fight amongst each other; we have some unfinished business to take care of." Jamie goes on with his story, "Ramirez, your partner here and about twelve other assholes are about to commit a crime that will make the Oklahoma Bombing look like a fireworks show."

"You see, the money they make from selling their illegal drugs is used not only to purchase an arsenal of weapons, but also enough explosives to level four hotels during the New Year's celebration for the year 2002."

"Also, Ramirez, they are a bunch of thieves. Let me read this news article to you. The title is: *AGENTS PROBE ARIZONA EXPLOSIVES THEFT*

Federal agents combed the rugged mountains of northern Arizona on Friday, looking for evidence in the theft of some 1,000 pounds of explosive materials.

Authorities said about 750 pounds of ammonium nitrate, 225 pounds of dynamite, 6,000 feet of detonation cord and roughly 20 blasting caps were stolen from a rock quarry either Monday or Tuesday.

The materials are common mining equipment but could also be used to make a bomb, authorities said. Ammonium nitrate was the main ingredient in the 4,800 pound device used to blow up the Alfred P. Murrah Federal Building in Oklahoma City in 1995; 168 people were killed.

If someone knew what they were doing, they could do a lot of damage," said Lawrence Wilson, a spokesman for the Federal Bureau of Alcohol, Tobacco and Firearms.

He said the amount stolen from the flagstone quarry owned by Riverside, Calif. based 40 Loss Mining Co. was unusual but that the theft itself was not.

"This kind of thing happens across the country all the time," Wilson said.

From 1993 through 1997, about 3,900 pounds of explosives were stolen in Arizona, according to the ATF. Nationwide, it was almost 50,000 pounds for the same period.

The ATF, which regulates explosives and firearms, has 11 agents investigation the theft in a remote, rocky canyon west of Flagstaff near Drake. Wilson said it was not clear whether the theft was part of a New Year's plot or if the timing was a coincidence. A recent FBI report warned of potential violence around January 1.

"We don't know what their intention is, that's part of our concern," Wilson said.

Coconino County Sheriff Jesse Richman said authorities were aware of no threats related to the theft and no suspects had immediately been identified.

Authorities said the materials had been inside two locked steel plated boxes beside a dirt road on the quarry property. They would not discuss how the thieves opened them.

"Ramirez, this article was taken from Saturdays', December 18, 1999 issue of the Las Vegas Review Journal. By doing this theft a couple of years early more or less, the perpetrators hoped to throw the federal government off their trail."

"So, what do you think of that!" Jamie exclaims thrusting the paper towards McCulley's face.

Ramirez turns her body sharply and looks angrily at Jamie, forgetting she is chained to a pole, almost causing injury to her arm, "¿Que? What the hell are you talking about?"

Jamie turns his attention back to Ramirez, who just rebounded against her chains, "You better watch yourself there, don't get too jumpy or you'll liable to hurt yourself."

Ramirez ceases her bouncing around and addresses Jamie again, "Bomb? What the hell, are you talking about?"

Jamie offers Ramirez something to ease her pain, "Here, have another drink! Have a smidge of Cognac this time." Jamie hands the drink over to Ramirez, who gulps it down greedily, "You see, they're waiting for one of the busiest nights of the year in Las Vegas, to blow up four hotels–a night when there will be over a million people in town, filling all the hotels to capacity."

Jamie is interrupted by a news flash on the television. He turns off the radio and turns up the volume on the TV, "Hold on, just a minute, the news is coming on."

"Today in Las Vegas," the anchorman intones, "it appears that two of Metro's police officers were kidnapped. The details are sketchy, but Metro states that the officers were sent to an address on the six hundred block of West Washington in response to a prowler report. After an hour of trying to raise the officers on the radio, a squad car was sent to the scene and they located one of the patrol cars; but neither of the officers or the other squad car has been located.

Metro does not know if the officers were taken by force or that they left on their own. At this time, the names of the officers are not going to be released pending notification family and relatives.

If anyone has seen anything-unusual happening in the area pertaining to the officers, you are asked to call the Secret Witness Program at the number on your screen.

Stay tuned to Channel 7 News for further details on the missing officers.

In other news tonight, using an unknown vehicle, a kidnapping scheme and information likely gathered from extensive surveillance, a man carried out a bank robbery at the First State Bank earlier today.

While there have been several armored car heists in Southern Nevada that have yielded more than $727,000.00 in cash–the amount taken today. This is the most sophisticated job against a bank or armored car. FBI Special Agent, Tom Moss said, '"The people or the person who did this, gave it quite a bit of planning. That leads us to think that the perpetrator or perpetrators were residents of Las Vegas. We are confident we will be able to solve this crime eventually'.

It all started at noon, when the armored car security officer was leaving the bank with the money from the bank's vault.

A lone, black male approached him and held a gun to his back. He then produced a tape recorder, handed it to the guard and demanded that he listen to a recorded message of the guard's wife, who was crying and telling the guard to do as he is told or he wouldn't see her alive again.

The perpetrator took the bag containing the money and walked pass the waiting armored truck and left the scene. No vehicle was seen leaving the scene, but when the police went to the guard's home, they found the wife tied up and badly frightened, although unharmed.

Federal authorities believe, at least two people were involved. The investigation is also focusing on how the perpetrators knew the guard's schedule, and the business operations of the bank.

Somehow, the perpetrators knew about the guard's family schedule and took advantage of this when they imprisoned the woman.

The armored car guards are trained to look for suspicious people and vehicles in the area. Seeing nothing, they were not unduly concerned.

When asked if the assailants are believed to have ties to either the bank or the armored Car Company, the police spokes person said this was being explored as a possibility".

After the news broadcast ends, Jamie immediately resumed his conversation, but was interrupted by Ramirez, "Okay, that's enough," she said, "Now let's go back to our business at hand. Hombre, why did you take the dinero? Why did you put so many people in jeopardy?"

"Well Ramirez, number one, I decided to sue the citizens of Las Vegas for allowing so many assholes to be employed as police officers.

"I have been in this city for ten years and I have never seen so many flagrant violations of people's rights in my life. The police department here is a travesty of what effective law enforcement is supposed to be about.

"One guy is awakened by six cops standing over his bed and is killed by them because he struggled with them. Police routinely intimidate partygoers on the strip during New Year's Eve Celebrations.

"Police walking through a black neighborhood dressed in riot gear, telling people they were supposed to be rioting because of Rodney King."

"Police shoot a man fifteen times in front of 7-11 because he pulled a knife. They again shot at another man thirty eight times because he had a knife.

"And that's not to mention, cops doing drive by shooting themselves.

"These cops remind me of how the cops used to be in the early sixties in Detroit.

"People got so tired of them, they started rioting. As years passed, cops began to die at the hands of the citizens. If the cops continue to react to situations the way they are now, pretty soon, there're going to be riots here in Las Vegas, and people will also begin killing Metro officers! Mark my words.

"I also decided to sue for all the money and time I spent on investigating the case against my sons and on their attorney's fees. Not to mention all the traveling I did investigating you two."

Jamie pauses for a drink before giving Ramirez the answer she waiting for.

"Included in this lawsuit, is the fee I'm charging the city and the casinos for uncovering the plot to blow up the hotels and all the mental anguish I suffered from having my sons locked up and for having to follow this asshole McCulley around.

"I was going to sue for Ten Million, but instead, I decided to settle out of court for $727,000."

Jamie looks over at Ramirez, who has a bit of a grin on her face. "So, that's the reason I took the money. As far as putting people in jeopardy, I took a lot of extra steps to make sure no one got hurt, including me. I don't know if anyone is going to get hurt, before this is over, but if that happens, it happens. It will be out of my control.

"I want you to know, I went through all of this to make sure that justice was done and luckily enough, I think I found the right person who will make sure that happens.

"You see Ramirez, with all the evidence I have against your partner and his friends, it would do me no good. As far as I am concerned, I would have as much chance as a snowball in hell, to make it through this without going to jail. I am black and they, the white authorities, would never believe me.

"They'd say that all evidence was obtained illegally and they'd throw everything out. My sons would remain in jail and so would the others.

"The plan to blow-up the hotels would be called off and the mastermind behind this plot would live to plot again.

"I need someone who is intelligent and believes in fair play. I need someone who will take all this evidence and help free my sons and the others who were framed by this asshole. The person I need is you, Ramirez. You can help right a wrong, plus put these assholes behind bars, where they belong.

"I have at least three hundred tapes covering my investigation. The tapes expose the illegal arrest of nine black males, one Mexican, my sons, and the plot to blow up the hotels on New Year's Eve.

TALION

"I am quite sure you have seen the strip on New Year's Eve; there's going to be over one million people in the area. The damage that would be done would be astronomical.

"You have to set up a sting in order to bust them all in the act. You have to get some help, someone you can trust, and you also have to get the FBI involved.

"I plan on being out of the country; somewhere I can't be extradited."

Jamie leans closer to Ramirez, "On my departure, I will supply you with all the information necessary to bust those shits, but first, you have to muster up some serious courage."

McCulley, tired of listening to Jamie, jumps in, "And what am I to be doing while you two save the world. I'm not going to be sitting and keeping my mouth shut while you two plot my fate." He laughs at Jamie, "When I get out of here, I'm going to run my mouth non-stop. You're not going to screw my friends with some drummed up shit you created.

"All these so-called tapes of yours are fake, and you know it. Why would I want people dead, especially people I don't know? The only sucker I want dead is you, sucker, and one day soon; I'll watch you die."

McCulley then directs his attention towards Ramirez; "The big joke is you're trying to use this little Mexican whore to do your dirty work. This wimp is going to shit all over herself when it comes down to it. She can't handle my friends. My friends will jack her up good and then come and get your ass.

"This is all bullshit, you're not going to get away with this crap, and you're not going to get out of town, much less out of the country. You'll be just another black ass nigger on the run."

Jamie's anger is now nearly uncontrollable. He walks around in front of McCulley's chair, stops in front of him and waves his fist in McCulley's face. "One thing, I will guarantee, is the fact that you won't live to see anything you have described. When you die, you will die by the hands of your overzealous police buddies. You will see first hand how quick the police officers in this town will shoot and ask questions later."

Backing off somewhat, Jamie adds gruffly, "I think it's only fitting that you die by the hands of your colleagues. I want to see you try and convince them not to shoot you forty or fifty times like they have done to people in this town. Yes, my man, you will die at the hands of those who are supposed to be protecting you. You will die in disbelief, and mark my words–I will be the last person you see before you die. I want that, and I want that more than anything else in this world!

"You are one cold-blooded, calculated murderer. You care for no one but yourself, and everyone in authority is turning their backs, allowing you to continue ruining innocent people's lives.

"It's going to stop, and it's going to stop now. I plan on opening the eyes of this community and the police department. I want Metro to realize and acknowledge that they are here to protect and serve, not imprison and intimidate. You are not God! Someone has to stop you and your buddies.

"I think I was chosen to do just that. You went out of your way to bring me into this bullshit. All you had to do was leave my kids alone, but no, you had to persist.

"You wanted to lock up some more innocent niggers. Well Mister McCulley, you locked up the wrong ones. That's when you got me involved, and you don't know me. You don't know what I'm capable of doing, but you're gonna find out. You got me pissed, so now you're going to suffer. You're going to suffer...

"I hate your ass and watching you die will be nothing but shear pleasure. I'm tired of you and other people like you screwing me. I'm tired of letting the courts handle it.

"You white racist chums are causing too much pain and anguish among peace and fun loving people.

"There is a lot to do in this world to occupy your mind, without clouding it with hate. Learn from other races and cultures and use what you learn to make your life brighter, but no that's not easy for you to comprehend. Your mind is stuck in a valley and all you see, hear, and smell is stupidity and ignorance."

McCulley, feeling as if he as nothing to lose after being hit in the face with a shotgun and being threatened with extermination, retorts with the same level of rage.

"Who you calling stupid, sucker! If you didn't have me chained, I'd kick your ass! Let me out of here.... let me out!"

Jamie watches McCulley struggle against his bonds, "But I do have you chained up don't I, cracker? Go ahead McCulley, and holler. Nobody can hear you, and if they could, they wouldn't give a damn!"

Jamie backs away from McCulley, grabs the officer's drink and takes a gulp, then hands it to McCulley, "Here calm down. Have another drink you cocksucker."

Jamie glances at Ramirez and sees that she is about to fall asleep and thinks to himself. *Damn, can't have her nodding off just yet. Need to have everything sink in before I am done with her.*

He walks over to Ramirez with another drink in his hand, "Hey, Ramirez. Don't nod out, have another soda."

Ramirez looks up at Jamie, more coherent than he thought she would be, "I'm not nodding out, I'm just thinking about myself and what has been going on here. I don't know how to get nasty. I don't know how to screw over people. Maybe, McCulley is right; I'm a wimp of a cop.

"People have run over me all my life. I felt that if I joined the police department it would help me. Help me to relate to people on their level, but since I been here in Las Vegas, I don't like what I see.

"People are such scums; they hate each other. They will screw you at a drop of a hat. I don't want to be like that. I wasn't raised like that.

"Now you drop something on me that I know, my partner knows, and even you know I can't handle. I'm not worth shit. I will tell you, if you're relying on me to handle the problem of a terrorist group blowing up four hotels, you got the wrong person.

"I'm not going to do a thing but screw it up. I can't do it. Get someone else. I'm the wrong person."

Laughing now, McCulley agrees with Ramirez, realizing that this is his chance. *Finally, we have a weakness in this asshole's plans. Let's see the bastard work his way out of this one. Maybe I can use this to my advantage.*

McCulley looks over to Jamie and gestures towards Ramirez, "I told you, you got a punk. That little bitch will screw up everything.

"Look, I could help you; I could turn state's evidence and help you bust these guys. That way, I don't go to jail and you get out of the country. That twit is going to screw you up."

Jamie looks over at Ramirez and sees the self-doubt in her face. *Damn it, I need that girl to stick together. If she falls apart on me now, what good will any of this be? I need to bolster her confidence, and I need to shut this McCulley up.*

Jamie snatches the momentum from McCulley and bashes him in front of Ramirez.

"Hey wait a minute, Ramirez do I have any rings around my neck? Does my head screw on and off?"

"McCulley, am I supposed to trust you after all the things you've said to me? Look McCulley, kiss my ass, nothing changes."

And then, to help boost Ramirez's deflated ego, "Ramirez, I have been in your shoes before, believe you me, partners come and partners go, more bad ones than good ones." McCulley is thinking hard on this one. *Partners? What the hell does this piece of trash know about partners? Making himself sound like a cop now.*

And then everything clicks in McCulley's mind; the call in, the observations, the handcuffs and the shots– maybe Jamie is a cop?

McCulley immediately dismisses the thought–*he's just one lucky ass nigger whose luck is about to run out.*

"What the hell do you know about partners?" he rages at Jamie. "What do you know about being a police officer? You have been watching too much TV. Wherever you got your ideas, they ain't gonna work in the real world. You don't have the slightest idea what it's like being a cop, or how much trouble you're in."

Jamie angrily snaps back, "Again, you opened your big ass mouth without thinking. Have you ever looked at the time and care that I took in setting all this shit up? Did you hear how the bank was robbed? Do you see how I got you two here? Do you think some Joe Blow off the street could do all the things I have done? Next question; have you ever heard the expression, 'cops make the best criminals'?"

Ramirez looks at Jamie with a puzzled look on her face then sits up in her chair.

"Are you saying you are a cop?"

Jamie looks at Ramirez and lets out a remorseful sigh, "No Ramirez, I'm saying, I was a cop…a cop in a city, where you have to use your wit, brains, tact, and intelligence.

"I worked the streets of Detroit for fifteen years, and believe you me–I have had my share of partners. Your partner, McCulley, fits right in the category of asshole partners."

"I'm going to turn on some music, as you requested a little while ago…'to season the room,' as you put it."

Then answering her quizzical look, "Oh, yes, I understand some Spanish. Anyway, I have this little thing I can't seem to shake and it's been bothering me ever since I left the force."

Jamie looks over at the CD player, "When I'm drinking, I listen to certain songs and just reminisce about my past. There are so many things that trouble me about my past and I never had the opportunity to talk about it, so I kept it to myself and think about where I went wrong.

JIMMY CULLORS/JOSEPH SZEWEZYK

"Partners come and go as I said, and you can believe I had my share of 'em."

Jamie places his glass of tea on the table and walks over to the CD player and starts playing The Gap Band's "Early in the Morning". He then makes himself a large drink and sits back in his recliner and starts to reminisce about the days he was with the Detroit Police Department, and the partners he had. He begins by telling them about his third partner, Abe Lawrence.

Abe had just graduated from the Police Academy and was assigned to the 12th precinct. Jamie had already been on the force for six months and he and Abe were assigned to work as partners.

They walked a beat on W. Eight Mile Road, which was crowded with prostitutes, pimps, and pushers. They both were green and were dependent on each other to help make it through the transition.

During their time together, they got to know quite a few people on their beat. A lot of the people were seedy, low lives, but friendly.

Case in point... the prostitutes...two in particular confided in Jamie and Abe and also helped them bust several drug dealers.

These two women were on the streets to provide money for their families. They didn't do drugs nor did they have a pimp.

One day, they approached Jamie and Abe and told them they didn't like turning tricks, but the money was good and they had no other skills. So Jamie and Abe devised a plan where they didn't have to have sex, but still earn money.

The girls would pick up the johns and bring them to a certain location in an alley. When the time was right, Jamie and Abe would walk up on them just before the sex act was to happen, but after the money was collected.

They would have both parties exit the vehicle and pat down the john; the girl would in turn run trying to get away. Abe would chase her running out of sight of the john. In turn, Abe would collect half the money and let the girl go and return without her. They would tell the john, the girl got away and because of it, they had to let him go– only if he promised not to return.

They did this quite often, and the money they made was distributed among the homeless people Jamie and Abe knew on their beat or used it to buy information. Because of the two young cops' contribution, the community helped them bust even more drug dealers. One day Jamie and Abe got a tip about a big drug buy that was going down.

They were led to a known drug dealer's vehicle that was parked on Eight Mile Road right where they were told the exchange would occur. Jamie approached on the driver's side while Abe approached on the passenger's side. Jamie asked the driver for his driver's license, registration and proof of insurance. While he was waiting for the documents, the right front passenger, who was a female, pulled out a .38 Special and began to point it at him. Luckily, Abe saw this and reacted quickly by yelling for Jamie to step back saving Jamie's life. Abe drew his weapon, ordered everyone out of the car and to lie face down on the sidewalk and called for backup.

After the scene was secured and backup arrived at their location, the vehicle was searched and three other guns along with the .38 and five pounds of cocaine were found. A computer check later revealed that the two passengers in the back seat were wanted for murder.

After that episode, Jamie felt he owed Abe his life and they became even closer friends on and off duty. Their friendship continued to grow, but Jamie began to develop bad feelings about the relationship due to incidents that occurred afterwards.

One night, while they were on patrol, walking through an alley, they were approached by a drunken prostitute.

Abe had a few words with her, and then escorted her into a back yard garden, where he raped her.

Jamie stood in the alley in utter disbelief. When he finally grasped what his partner had done, Jamie rushed Abe and began to beat him about the face as he cussed him.

The rest of the evening they worked in total silence. Over the next few days, Jamie was terrified about going to work because he didn't know whether the woman was an undercover cop or if she had reported the incident.

Time passed and they heard nothing about the incident. Jamie was disturbed because he didn't report Abe. But as the code stated, we were to protect each other–plus Jamie felt he owed Abe for his life.

Thereafter, Jamie spent a lot of his time keeping Abe out of trouble. They were eventually transferred from foot patrol, to a patrol car as the problems with Abe worsened. It got to the point where Jamie no longer covered for Abe.

The straw that broke the camel's back was when they had to make an arrest for domestic violence.

The man involved was intoxicated and placed in the back seat of the patrol car. While on the way to the station, Abe began to argue with the man.

Jamie thought nothing of the argument because the man was in the back seat while Abe was in the front, but things changed when Jamie stopped for a red light.

Abe, uncontrollably angry, exited the vehicle and opened the rear door, grabbing the handcuffed man and pulling him out and throwing him to the ground. The man lay defenseless on the ground as Abe began beating and kicking him about the body.

A woman, standing on her front porch, saw what was happening, began yelling at Abe to stop. Like a wild animal thirsty for more blood–Abe peered at the woman. The now lifeless body was no longer of importance to him–the yelling and cursing seemed more tantalizing and demanded his attention.

Just as fast as he jumped from the vehicle, Abe ran on the porch and pushed the lady into her home and slammed the door.

By this time Jamie was behind Abe grabbing him and forcing him back to the squad car. Jamie insisted that Abe drive as he put the prisoner back into the car.

On his arrival to the precinct, Jamie immediately reported the entire incident and put in a request to be assigned to another shift. Abe was extremely upset at Jamie for a while because of the discipline he had to face but, as time went on, he got over it.

Eventually, they worked together again, only this time in another capacity.

Abe became the Head Coach of one of three football teams Jamie owned. Coaching didn't calm Abe's temper any. He eventually got into trouble again. This time, he pistol-whipped a man because of a traffic accident and was sent to jail for six months. He was also fired from the police department.

While Abe was in jail, Jamie helped his family as much as he could by buying groceries and paying their rent. Jamie sent Abe money while he was incarcerated and even gave him more money when he was released.

Abe's way of repaying for Jamie's generosity was by pulling a gun on him and threatening to shoot him, after Jamie learned that Abe was having an affair with his wife.

Needless to say, that ended their relationship, and to this day, Jamie has had harsh feelings toward his former partner.

As Jamie finishes his story, McCulley interjects a sarcastic remark, "Yeah, yeah, so you had a jerk for a partner; that doesn't mean you're an authority on partners. That doesn't mean you can pass judgment on me."

McCulley tries to go in a bit deeper, "You have this one little incident all wrapped up in your mind, and you think you have the right to turn Ramirez against me. Just who the hell do you think you are, sucker?"

Jamie rises from his chair, walks away, smiles and faces the wall. "I'm the sucker who has your ass tied up and your body in the Ozone! I'm the sucker who is going to put all the things you've done out in the open. I'm the sucker who's going to let mama and daddy know they raised an asshole. If nothing else, before this shit is over, I'm the sucker who's going to make you wish you were never born!

"An asshole like you, who sits and preys on innocent unsuspecting people, needs to feel the fear of death!

"That's one advantage you have over the people that you planned to kill; you'll know it's going to happen; you'll see it coming.

"Those people who are going to be partying on New Year's Eve don't expect to die that night; they expect to return home to their loved ones."

Jamie's voice fades a bit on the last part of the sentence, but then continues, "But you, you piece of dog shit, you plan to put a stop to all their hopes and dreams for some stupid reason. You are going to kill innocent, women, and children just because they want to try and live together in racial harmony."

Jamie, now in a fit of rage, grabs the shotgun and heads toward McCulley, then stops short, "You make me so mad sucker, I should just take this shotgun and stick it in your mouth and blow your stupid ass head off right now!"

Tired of threats and filled with liquid courage, McCulley tries to edge Jamie on.

"Then do it nigger, if you think you can! I don't think you have the balls. Shit, I don't even think you can use that thing, you dumb ass monkey!"

The words send Jamie over the edge. He gets close to McCulley, shotgun in his hand, "Open up, McCulley. Yeah, open your mouth, I know it isn't a shot glass, but maybe you can try chewing through this steel before I shoot the back of your head off!"

Jamie shoves the shotgun in McCulley's face, trying to get the barrel into his mouth.

Ramirez starts to panic, "Jamie! Jamie, stop! Don't do it! Don't do it! You'll be adding murder to your list of crimes! Stop, Jamie, stop!"

Jamie shoots a look over at her and then looks at the gun in hand. Then he looks back at McCulley's sweat–covered face, his eyes closed and his mouth fitting over the barrel of the shotgun.

Ramirez is right, if I kill him now that makes me no better than he is. Then all the planning would have been for nothing. This asshole is just trying to rile me up. Damn it Jamie, you should know better than this. Get your shit together!

Jamie takes the gun out of the mouth of McCulley and heads back towards his drink,   "Okay Ramirez, you win this time, but McCulley, if you don't shut your trap up, you're going to wish you had!"

Jamie looks straight into McCulley's eyes, "Now, sit there and drink, shit or do anything, just don't speak until I tell you so!"

Turning his attention from the two, Jamie feels the need for something to calm his nerves, "Where is the alcohol?" he mutters, "my glass is empty! I need another drink!"

Jamie heads off towards the kitchen. His nerves are getting close to being shot. He is sweating heavily through his clothing now, and the drink glass starts to slip in his palms.

The cold from the ice in the glass feels great against his forehead. Trying to maneuver the cap off of the bottle, Jamie's hands start to shake.

"Get a hold of yourself, Jamie," he says almost inaudibility to himself.

It takes a few seconds before his hand is steady enough to pour the drink, but Jamie finally gets the glass filled. Slamming down half of the glass, Jamie refills the drinking glass before he starts to head back out towards his hostages. Stopping short of the entrance way, Jamie drains the rest of his drink to try to calm the queasy feeling in his stomach. The butterflies are moving up to his throat, but everything is drowned by another shot of alcohol.

With that last shot, Jamie feels ready enough to go back and face the officers. He is back in control of his mind and emotions… for the time being.

While Jamie is dealing with his fear, Ramirez is worried about her partner, afraid that he putting himself in danger. "McCulley, I don't know what you're trying to do, but whatever it is, you're going about it the wrong way."

"Right now, I'm going to try anything... even if I have to piss him off enough to take advantage of him!"

Ramirez is shocked by McCulley's last statement. "How in the hell do you plan on doing that?" She asks him. "We're still handcuffed and our bodies are still screwed up."

McCulley moves his arms around, "Look stupid! The stuff is wearing off! Maybe he will forget to shoot us up again!"

Jamie walks back into the room just in time to catch McCulley scheming, "Fat chance about that, McCulley. When I feel like I want to sleep or whatever, you'll get your shot all right. Oh, by the way, it will only be one more time. I figure we will spend about another twelve to twenty hours together, and then everything will be over. But until then, we're going to sit here and talk. We still have a lot of ground to cover."

Jamie settles back into his chair and again begins talking about his partners again. He leans back and smiles–those were the good times of his life.

As the years went by, Jamie prospered and became well known in the community. He founded an athletic club for children from ages 8 to 16 interested in sports.

He became president of his block club and won two Community Service Awards, seven citations, and five commendations from his department.

He was at the pinnacle of his life and had the pleasure of being partnered with quite a few people.

The times were changing and women were now allowed to work on the streets as patrol officers. Jamie took this opportunity to be one of the firsts to volunteer to work with female partners. He taught them a lot and he, in turn, learned a lot from them.

He felt he had reached the peak of true professionalism through their efforts. His partnership with women lasted a few years.

Following his time working with the women, Jamie decided to relinquish his duties as senior man on his squad car to work with veteran police officers.

He was paired with a police officer whose name was Richard Perkins, who was also known as "Perk". Jamie didn't know what to expect working with Perk, but he was more than willing to pursue the experience because of the things Perk had been through–or perhaps he was just attracted to the fact that Perk was a rebel.

Jamie knew how to be a true, down-to-earth police officer, but now he needed to know the ins and outs of being a good cop.

Perk was assigned to the 10th precinct and he became more or less the Serpico of the precinct. He and several other officers had been involved in reporting a number of other officers for drug violations.

Perk was ostracized for his role in the raid on the precinct, but it didn't matter to him, until he received a police run to meet a narcotics unit and prepare for another raid.

Perk got suited up with his flack vest and met the unit. They were going to raid a house, and because Perk was in uniform, he had to go through the door first.

Everything was as planned, but when they hit the door Perk was shot seven times by the drug dealers, who seemed to be anticipating his entry. Not one shot was fired by the police officers.

Perk was rushed to the hospital and, amazingly, lived through the whole ordeal. After recuperating for over a year, he returned to work, much to everyone's surprise, only at a different precinct.

He reported to the 12th precinct and Jamie was assigned to be his partner. Another veteran, Lawrence Jackson from the 6th Precinct, also joined them.

With the two veterans now assigned to work with him, Jamie became the low man on the totem pole.

The three men worked together beautifully, because they enjoyed a similar outlook on life–including the city government.

None of them liked the Mayor of Detroit. Because of their dislikes for the Mayor, they followed him on his midnight tryst to spy on him. They knew all about his many girlfriends in the 12th precinct, but didn't know what to do with the information. So they kept it to themselves just in case they might need it at some future time.

Jamie's first encounter with the Mayor came unexpectedly.

Both of his partners were off and Jamie was assigned to work with Cheryl Hype. They received a run to a high-rise apartment complex on a disturbance.

When Jamie and his partner arrived, a few residents of the complex told them there was a woman throwing trash down the steps met them.

After walking up five flights of steps, they heard a commotion and observed trash on the stairs.

A black woman was yelling obscenities and was behaving as though she were intoxicated.

As Cheryl approached the woman, she removed one of her high-heeled shoes and swung it at the officer. Cheryl dodged, but not soon enough. The heel of the shoe hit Cheryl in the ear, rupturing her eardrum.

Cheryl fell to the floor squealing in pain, and disoriented because of the loss of her equilibrium. The woman then ran toward Jamie, and while he was trying to fight her off, two other women joined in the melee.

Cheryl put out an "officer in trouble" call over the prep radio, and within five minutes, help arrived and the women were arrested.

While they were being put in patrol car, the women continually yelled, "You're going to pay for locking us up."

When the officers arrived at the precinct with the prisoners, the phones began to ring incessantly: the three arrested women were the niece and sisters of the Mayor.

The watch commander, who had been at home with the flu, was eventually fired for failing to control his men.

Something negative happened to all the officers who had been at the scene; they were all transferred, suspended, or terminated.

Everyone, that is, except Jamie. But little did he know there was a more severe punishment in store for him.

Jamie stops, pausing in his story, because his attention has been drawn to McCulley, who is blowing cigarette smoke rings and rolling his eyes in an exaggerated gesture of disbelief.

"Am I boring you two with my story?"

"No! I have no where to go," McCulley begins sarcastically, "especially since I can't feel my leg. I guess I will just sit here and listen to you ramble on about your exploits as a cop.

"You know my grandfather used to bore me like this when he told me about the Korean War."

"McCulley, if I were you, I would listen. At least when I finish you will know why I am doing the things I am. In the meantime, your glass is getting a little short. You may as well eat, drink, and be merry."

"Yeah, yeah, cause tomorrow I may die. I know that shit. Give me another drink."

"Jamie, speaking of eating, where is the food?" Ramirez asks.

"I have a pot of chili. If you don't like chili you're up the creek because that's all I made." Jamie replies.

Ramirez immediately jumps on the chance to eat, "Sure that will do... I am starved."

McCulley looks at Ramirez, astonished. "Ramirez, how in the hell can you eat anything? My stomach is in knots."

"Well McCulley, between not eating all day and drinking, I can't help but be hungry."

"Look, both of you may as well eat something. We're going to be here a while."

Jamie stands up and walks into the kitchen and pours himself another glass of tea. He takes out three bowls, fills them with chili, places the bowls on a tray along with spoons and crackers, and returns to the living room. He places a bowl in front of each of his prisoners and resumes his story.

"At any rate, back to where I left off, and McCulley you better listen very carefully...

"Cheryl's eardrum was badly torn and she spent several years off the job. Jamie continued working with Perk and Lawrence Jackson.

From that day on, they seem to run into one relative or another of the Mayor–at least once a month.

These chains of events didn't seem to go well with Hiz Honor and Jamie began to worry. For some unknown reason, their squad car became a felony car.

They were sent to the most dangerous runs, such as armed robbery in progress, family trouble, man with gun and bomb threats.

It became a standing joke to them, but deep inside they were worried. Their deep concern was manifested in their drinking habits.

They would consume a fifth a day and they even smoked marijuana. They often said if they got shot, they didn't want to feel the bullet.

On Sundays, there was always a special attention read off at roll call about a certain area of the precinct where the people who attended the local church were blocking driveways.

Since it was slow on Sundays, Jamie, Perk, and Jackson would always go there and write parking tickets.

On one particular Sunday, the parking situation was worse than ever. It was difficult for even a single car to drive down a two-way street, and the parking was like this for a three-block radius around the church.

Jamie and Lawrence Jackson were patrolling the area and writing tickets when they saw large columns of smoke shooting into the air.

They rode around for several minutes until they located a burning house.

Their car had to be parked a half block away so they had to run the rest of the way to the house. When they arrived, the family was standing out front, screaming and yelling for another family member to jump.

Jamie looked up at the roof of the house and saw an eight-year old boy standing in a window on the second floor, crying.

Just as he noticed the boy, he heard the sirens of the fire truck, which was stopped even further away then their squad car.

Jamie ran to the truck and explained the situation and ordered the fire truck to drive on the sidewalk if necessary, because they needed to get their ladder to the kid.

They tried to pull the fire truck onto the sidewalk but could not get by the double-parked vehicles.

Then, Jamie saw a man running toward him yelling for them to hurry. The driver of the fire truck took it upon himself to ram the cars to get through, and Jamie jumped on the truck as it passed.

As the truck pulled up in front of the house, Jamie saw the child disappears in a ball of flames as the roof-caved in.   The entire house was engulfed in flames and the child was presumed dead.

The crowd, which was standing around, became enraged and began stoning and breaking windows of every car that was illegally parked in the neighborhood. Jamie and Lawrence stood by and watched the people go mad without intervening.

Ten minutes later, Jamie called the dispatcher and informed him of what was occurring.

Other patrol cars arrived at the scene only to find people lying on the ground or supporting each other, crying about the little boy who lost his life because of the illegally parked cars.

It took sometime to disperse the crowd, and the sergeant felt that it would be necessary for the police to stay in the area until the church service was over.

The people in the church were unaware of what was going on outside. When they did come out no one was on the street, but every illegally parked car was damaged to the point where they could not be driven. All the tires were flat and all the windows were broken.

The many towing companies that were called made a lot of money that day, but the damage and the death did not stop the people from continuing to park illegally.

For the next three weeks, Jamie and the other police officers on his shift spent the hours from 10:00 a.m.–2:30 p.m. writing tickets and towing cars.

When the Mayor became aware of their activities, he ordered every police officer in the 12th Precinct to discontinue writing tickets in that area on Sundays.

All the officers felt if they couldn't write tickets in the area of the church, they were not going to write tickets anywhere else in the precinct either.

This ticket stoppage lasted for several months; until one day just after roll call, Jamie was ordered to report to the Lieutenant's Office. On this day both of Jamie's partners were off again and Jamie was assigned to work with a female officer.

He reported as ordered and had a discussion about ticket writing. The Lieutenant told Jamie that if he were to start writing citations again, the others would probably follow.

So Jamie agreed and returned to the church and began writing tickets. Jamie and his partner reached the area of the church and found the traffic to be just as horrible as ever.

The church service was over and the traffic began to flow again. Jamie sat in the squad car catching up on his run sheet while his partner was out directing traffic.

From his periphery, Jamie could see a flash of red darting across the tops of cars. Looking up, he saw a man wearing a red suit, diving onto the back of his partner.

Jamie exited his vehicle and rushed to his partner's aid. When he reached her the man had beaten her to the ground and her nose was bleeding.

At this point, Jamie grabbed the man and began struggling with him. He told his partner to get to the car and start it up.

Jamie's partner did as she was directed, quickly, while he fought with the man, attempting to get him closer to the squad car.

Finally, Jamie got the man to the car, but now the people coming out of the church were upset because they saw one of their own being beaten and forced into a police vehicle.

Jamie got the man into the rear of the squad car and yelled at his partner to get moving. He grappled with the man for the three miles he had to travel to the station. When they arrived, other officers helped to subdue the man and took him into the lock-up.

When Jamie emerged from the vehicle, his shirt was practically torn off and both he and his partner were bleeding about the face and body.

They entered the station to book their prisoner and to their surprise, the station was filled with the churchgoers, demanding the release of their deacon. But the deacon could not be released until he was taken to the hospital and received medical attention.

Within minutes, the pastor of the church entered the station demanding to speak to the arresting officer.

Jamie approached the pastor and they exchanged a few harsh words, as the pastor's ultimate mission was, of course, the deacon's release. Jamie refused and continued booking the prisoner.

After a half-hour, the station commander arrived and had the same discussion with Jamie about the prisoner's release. Still, Jamie refused to release the prisoner.

The next morning when Jamie returned to work, there was no evidence of the arrest and his run sheet was missing. From that time on, Jamie and his partners were followed by Internal Affairs, who had no problem in making their presence known.

It reached the point they were even being followed while off duty. Jamie and his partners knew that IA's prime objective was to find negligent or dereliction in their duty in some way–but it was to no avail.

Following these events, Jamie, Perk, and Lawrence continued working together until Jamie decided to give Abe a benefit cabaret to raise money for Abe's family.

It was a large turn out and Jamie raised $2,700.00 for Abe. The following day, while counting the door receipts, Jamie discovered that $2,100.00 of additional funds was missing.

Lawrence Jackson and Perk had been working the door and Perk's wife told Jamie that they had taken the money. Of course, that incident ended their partnership.

Jamie transferred to the 12th Precinct Detectives Bureau where he worked several areas in plain clothes. But he missed working the streets in a squad car, so he transferred back to patrol and worked with several different partners and continued to encounter the wrong people.

These people complained so much that Jamie was ordered to report to the mayor's office. It was a total surprise and shock to Jamie. He felt he was really in trouble now, as he wondered why he was the only one ordered to appear before the Mayor.

When Jamie arrived at the Mayor's office, no one was there to receive him. He thought that was unusual and began to look around.

In a moment, Hiz Honor appeared and directed Jamie to come into his office.

Jamie walked a little unsteady and when he entered the office, the door slammed and Jamie was thrown against the wall.

The Mayor yelled and cursed Jamie, and asked him who the hell he thought he was intimidating his family, friends, and other officials in town.

Jamie tried to explain that he didn't purposely pursue anyone and if the people he arrested had not violated the law; they wouldn't have had any trouble with him.

The mayor told Jamie if he attempted to arrest, or cites anyone related to him or associated with him in anyway, he would see to it that Jamie wouldn't see daylight for quite some time.

The Mayor then released Jamie, who stood there in shock. He couldn't believe the Mayor had really grabbed him and threw him against the wall and threatened him.

The mayor looked at Jamie and said if his name came across his desk one more time, the last thing he will do is put him away. He also told Jamie that if he divulged what transpired, he would pay dearly for it. He then threw Jamie out of his office.

Jamie walked out in disbelief, and asked himself what the hell had he created. If he thought he was afraid before he entered his office, he was terrified now.

Jamie didn't return to work that day, and he called in sick for the next three days. He didn't know what to say or do, so he kept his mouth shut.

When he returned to work, Jamie was assigned to another squad car. For about a year, all he did was fight and took down anything that got in his way. To hide what he really felt hostility towards the mayor as well as fear.

The crews from other squad car were happy when Jamie and his partner arrived on their runs because they knew they would fight, if necessary.

After some time, Billie Davies and Albert Smith approached Jamie. They wanted him to work on their squad car. He agreed, mainly because he would be senior man.

They worked pretty well together, or more accurately, they didn't work at all. They just answered the police runs and wrote an occasional ticket if it were necessary.

During this assignment, Jamie began consuming alcohol heavily, using what happened to him as an excuse. Some days he and his partners would drink two fifths of hard liquor.

Between the three of them several squad cars were destroyed, and no disciplinary action was ever taken. They were getting lackadaisical on the job and really no longer cared what happened to them.

As time went by, Jamie and his partners heard rumors that Internal Affairs was looking for police officers who were responding to felonies only and ripping off the complainants. They weren't worried because they knew they were not targets of these investigations.

But one day they accidentally ran into the officers who were committing the crimes.

Jamie and Albert received a police run to a Caldean supermarket and they knew, as did every cop, there were night receipts in the store.

When they arrived at the store, there was an unmarked car outside and the officers were in the store.

Thinking little of this, they went inside where they saw Officers Roy Trees and Dale Taurus stuffing money in their shirts.

They yelled to Jamie and Billie that everything was okay and that they would handle the run.

Jamie and Albert didn't think the officers knew that they had seen their illicit actions. Following that day, Jamie and Billie tried to respond to as many of those officers' runs as possible–mainly just to be nosy.

They knew they weren't going to do anything with the information they had, but they did want to know how far Roy and Dale would actually go.

In keeping with tradition of police silence, they kept their mouths shut, but they knew that one day Roy and Dale would get busted.

At 6:00 a.m., on March 27, 1983, Jamie and Billie were on patrol, bored to death and talking about needing money.

They were heading east on West 7 Mile Road from Schaefer when they saw a silhouette dart and run into the shadows of the alley.

At this time in the morning, neither one of them wanted to do any police work, so they did not pursue the figure. Instead, they checked out the location where the figure had run from–the front of a dry cleaning shop.

As they approached the building they could see the front glass was broken.

Jamie and Billie called dispatch and reported that they had just chased an unknown individual away from the dry-cleaners, and that the glass was broken and they were going in.

To Jamie and Billie, the perpetrator saw them and ran off–that was their interpretation of chasing away.

They casually walked through the building and found no evidence of the perpetrator having been inside. After checking out the building, they played around for a few minutes and even made faces in the 24-hour surveillance camera.

Then Jamie called the station and spoke with the lieutenant in charge to see if there was a listing for the owner. He told Jamie there was no listing and hung up.

Immediately after, the phone rang. It was the alarm company calling and Jamie told them who he was and requested that they send a guard over until the owner arrived.

Jamie notified the dispatcher and advised him that the building was open and needed special attention. Then he and his partner left the scene.

Around 7:00 a.m., they received a radio run to go back to the dry-cleaners and meet the owner.

As soon as they entered the cleaners, the owner yelled at Jamie, "You broke into my cleaners". Jamie looked at the owner and explained to him that if he had a complaint, he needed to contact Internal Affairs.

In the meantime, a report was made and if he noticed anything missing, he should contact the detectives at the precinct and they left.

In August of the same year, Jamie and Billie were off duty and their third partner; Albert was assigned to work with another officer, Lisa Marks.

They were sent to investigate a breaking and entering report at a shoe store.

While Albert was checking out the storeroom of the shoe store, his partner had taken several pairs of shoes out of the store and placed them in the trunk of the squad car.

When Albert came out, they got into the car and drove away. Unknown to them, they were being watched by Internal Affairs, who pulled them over and arrested them.

Jamie and Billie learned from the dispatcher, a good friend of theirs, that the run was meant for them.

The dispatcher explained to them that while he was working, Internal Affairs come to his board and ordered him to send their car to the shoe store.

The dispatcher informed Internal Affairs that he could not do that because Jamie and Billie were off that night. So, after a few minutes of arguing, they ordered him to send Albert since he was their partner. They said they already had enough on Jamie and Billie.

Albert and Lisa were tried and found guilty and sent to the Detroit House of Correction.

Billie and Jamie were worried, but not too much because they knew they hadn't done anything wrong.

In September, Jamie took a two-week vacation, and on his return, he went to the football field to watch his teams' practice.

Billie approached Jamie and told him there was a warrant out for his arrest, and that he should turn himself in.

The following day, Jamie went to headquarters where they arrested him, booked him and released him on his own recognizance.

He was charged with breaking into the dry-cleaner establishment and stealing $185.00–a felony in the State of Michigan.

Lying back in his chair and yawning, McCulley interrupts Jamie, "So, you became a thief and lost your job because of your sticky fingers. Just like thieving, ass nigger. You and the rest of your race were born thieves, whores, drug pushers and junkies."

Jamie shakes his head at his antagonizer. "McCulley, if I weren't so melancholy, I'd kick your ass. But you have my permission to say whatever you want to. Right now, I am getting pissed because of the way we treat each other. I know I didn't do a lot of things right in my life, but for someone to come and screw me because they felt like it–really gets to me!"

Like a child, McCulley attacks Jamie by means of insults. "Yeah! You're another one of those crybabies, bleeding heart liberals. You think everything should be perfect.

"Well sucker, wake up! This is the real world! Whenever someone sees an opportunity to screw you, they are going to take advantage of the situation and get what they can out of you.

"From what I've heard so far, you were a prick! You didn't know how to follow orders, and you wanted everything your way. You kicked people's ass and just like the rest of the world, you took advantage of people and screwed them."

McCulley starts to laugh sarcastically, "Now, you're telling us this so–called story of your life, and I guess you want us to feel sorry for you. You got screwed because it was your turn. So, get over it, release us, and get ready to spend the rest of your miserable life behind bars."

Jamie stares at McCulley without saying a word. *Is this asshole for real? Nobody can be this dumb without a reason. The boy wants me to tell him why everything was happening, I try to explain it and all he can do is shoot back with childish insults. I should have thought twice about letting this sucker live when Ramirez begged me not to kill him. The world would be a better place without this jerk.*

Jamie's brain finally sends the correct words to his mouth; "You're the slowest, red-necked asshole I have ever met in my life. Most people who are in your predicament want answers to questions. That's what I am providing for you. You don't have the foggiest idea what you're about to face and yet you want to talk shit."

Jamie shakes his head at McCulley again before he continues, "Well Mr. McCulley, I am going to continue my story and you will listen!"

McCulley isn't fazed by Jamie's words. "Hey! Jamie, I still have a few things to say."

Jamie gets up and goes back behind the kitchen counter. On that counter is a tape recorder. He checks the tape and sees it is time to turn it over, while he listens to McCulley.

chapter

6

THE NIGHTMARE
CONTINUES

"Well, go ahead McCulley. There are a few things I have to do around here anyway." Jamie says as he walks across the room.

"Thank you," McCulley says sarcastically. "First off, all of you so called Americans, be you Afro, Chinese, Mexican, Jewish, or whatever, you need to understand this is not your country. God made this country for the white man. We are superior in every way over all you assholes and you need to get that through your head. We have the technology to wipe your asses clean off the face of the earth, and the right to do it because none of you, suckers contribute a thing to a good, decent society."

McCulley pauses for any retribution, but gets none. "You niggers are the main ones who are born into a family that don't have shit, don't want shit, and ain't gonna get shit. You're all into stealing and rioting. When things don't go your way, rather than get a job, you'd sell drugs to your own people and screw them up even more.

"Then you got your black woman; she's nothing but a whore. She never gets enough dick, always wanting to screw somebody. Do you know I can go out and screw as many black women I want and they will be crying for more."

Ramirez, after a long period of silence, decides to interject, "Yeah, you're right McCulley. Your dick is too small...just like your brain."

"Go to hell, Ramirez! And listen; another thing about niggers–when you see them in big cars–the car is owned by more than one person. They parade around the community with gold around their necks and on their fingers living in a barn with ten other niggers."

McCulley looks at Ramirez. "And as for the Mexicans; they are just trying to populate the world. Everywhere I look in Las Vegas; there is a pregnant, Mexican woman with another one in her arms one barely walking and three or four stair steps, the oldest being four years old."

Feeling he has ragged Ramirez enough, he goes back to Jamie. "And again, just like those stupid niggers, ten or twenty of them are living in the same house. And these Asian gooks are even worse..."

Ramirez, sick of McCulley's comments, jumps in the conversation.

"McCulley, shut up! I don't want to hear another damn thing about what you think about people and other races. You are one of the most ridiculous people I have ever met. I've only heard about white people like you and seen them on television. But never in my life would I think I would be putting my life into the hands of anyone like you. Just because of you and your ideas, I'm chained to this god dam chair!" Ramirez tugs on her chains to demonstrate her point.

"So, just shut up, before I kick your ass myself. You are one sorry son of a bitch!"

McCulley's mental game seems to be working. With nothing left to lose, he lashes out the only way he can, trying to inflict as much emotional and psychological damage as he can before Jamie silences him permanently. All the words, all the slings and insults are starting to build up against Ramirez and Jamie like water against the dam. What McCulley doesn't realize is what would happen if that dam were to burst.

"Give me another damn drink so I can calm down! One day you people will realize that we are in a war against all other races. We want you gone, back to your homelands!"

Ramirez looks at McCulley like someone who can see for the very first time in her life. *How the hell did I put up with this shit? Was I this blind that this prejudice asshole, was this bad and I never knew about it? This sorry piece of shit isn't a cop. He may have a uniform, but that doesn't mean he is worth his weight in shit. I can't believe I was this blind.*

"Jamie, I want this shit over and done with. So, if you have something to say, get on with it?" Ramirez demands. "I can't wait to get away from this jerk who calls himself a cop! Screw this stupid-ass redneck pig."

Jamie hides a slight smile by turning his back to the others. This is just what he wants. Everything is going according to plan. He needs Ramirez on his side, and most importantly, he needs her to be tough enough to be useful. This sudden show in courage and contempt for McCulley from her was encouraging. She isn't what he needs her to be quite yet, but with a few more pounds of the hammer, Jamie will have the tool he needs in her.

"Ok, I'll get back to my story and McCulley, listen well. There may be something in it for you."

Jamie settles himself with another sip of his drink. The alcohol has taken a bit of an effect on him, but nothing to make him worry. Jamie does an internal check to make sure everything in his body is still performing up to par. Feeling still in his hands and legs, his face isn't going numb and his head is still clear; the alcohol is just killing the edge, and nothing more. Turning back to his captive audience, Jamie resumes his reminiscing.

During the summer of that same year, Jamie participated in the Police Field Day. It was fun, and Jamie felt good being one of Detroit's Finest, marching around Tiger Stadium with 30,000 people looking on.

But when the Field Day was over and Jamie was leaving, he was approached by the chief of police. Jamie saluted him, but the chief looked at Jamie with a broad smile on his face without returning his salute. "Ha!" he said, "we got you now, and you won't get out of this."

Jamie stopped in his tracks and watched as the chief walked away grinning. He didn't know what to say or do; he just stood there dumbfounded with a knot in his stomach and a strong urge to relief himself.

As time went on, Jamie could no longer concentrate on his job or his private life. He even stopped entertaining, and just sat around and sulked.

The day after Jamie turned himself in, pictures of Billie and him was all over the front page of the newspaper. Jamie was hurt, embarrassed, and mortified. He didn't leave the house and didn't know what to do. One thing he didn't want was to see anyone. So, he turned to his good friend, "Remy Martin" and drank himself to sleep.

However, it seemed like something or someone wanted Jamie to face all the things that were going to happen to him sober, because he didn't drink anymore for a while. And then the first blow came.

His wife divorced him, he lost all his vehicles, and his daughter came to him and told him she was pregnant. Jamie was two months behind in his house payments and he still was facing a possible jail sentence. He didn't know what to do and had no one to talk to.

Everyone who used to come by and eat his food and drink his liquor was now non-existent. So, he sent his three kids to their grandmother's home and for a month sat and drank himself into a stupor.

One night, a few close female friends invited Jamie out to party to help him forget his troubles. It took serious convincing, but Jamie agreed to meet them at Jimmy D's Lounge.

Needing transportation, Jamie called another female friend, who allows him to use her car, but he had to go and pick it up. So, he rode the bus to her home and picked up her car and returned home.

Jamie showered and shaved, got himself looking really good. Starting to actually feel better then he has in months; Jamie gave himself a few last touches. He went out to the car; ready to go, turned the key, but nothing happened. He turned the key again and nothing happened—a third time, and again nothing happened. He tried it yet once more—still nothing. The starter was out. The tears began to roll down Jamie's face and he screamed out his rage.

He jumped from the car, ran back into the house and upstairs to his room. He grabbed his .357 magnum and began to run back down the stairs. As he cocked the weapon to put in his mouth, he tripped and fell down the steps and lay on the floor and cried like a baby.

After coming to his senses, he realized he needed someone to talk to. No one came to mind except his first girlfriend, Patricia "Candy" Heard. He knew she wouldn't criticize him and that she would listen. So, he called her and soon she was there with her husband, daughter, and another close friend. They sat and talked to Jamie for hours until he regained his equilibrium.

He went to bed that night and prayed for help and guidance from God, and finally fell asleep. The next morning, he woke up, determined not to wallow in self-pity and decided to go job hunting, since he was still suspended from the police department.

His prayers were answered that day; he found a job at General Motors.

Gradually as he began to put his life back together; the time came for him to hire an attorney. He found all his assets, had been frozen by the police department. There was no money available at the Credit Union, even though he had over five thousand dollars in his account. All assets in his children's organization account were also frozen. He tried to borrow the necessary money to defend himself, but all friends and relatives turned their back on him. So, he had to settle for the attorney provided by the police union.

The time finally arrived for Jamie and Billy's pre-trial; and the tension was mounting. Jamie had originally joined the police department to protect himself from the adversities of his environment, which he believed would land him in jail. But, ironically, being a police officer itself seemed to be helping to put him in bars.

Jamie and Billy arrived at court and met their attorneys for the first time. No, there was no meeting before the actual court date. The attorneys introduced themselves and told Jamie and Billy that the case seemed to be open and shut. Before any proceedings could begin, there was an adjournment, so they had to return the following week. In the meantime, their attorneys, William Goldberg and Fred Minch, assured them they would be back to work soon because they knew Jamie and Billy had been set up.

Monday arrived and the pre-trail was held. They really felt confident, because Jamie knew the judge. The judge told Billy and Jamie, they had nothing to worry about because he could see that the prosecution was on a witch-hunt.

That weekend, Jamie and Billy felt good because of what the judge had said. They returned the following Monday knowing that all their problems were over.

While sitting in the hallway waiting to be called, the Judge's clerk came out looking for Jamie and Billy. She pulled them to the side to deliver a message from the judge. She said the judge was deeply sorry, but he had to bind them over for trial. Something happened over the weekend and she was ordered not to discuss it. What the clerk said, hit the like a ton of bricks.

Jamie arrived home to find a police car waiting for him. When he pulled into the driveway, his old boss approached him. George Wilson and Jamie didn't get along very well; Jamie could feel George laughing inside because of what was about to happen. They went into the house and that's when Jamie saw that his conceptions were wrong. George truly felt bad. Jamie let down his guard and put trust in George. He waited about thirty seconds and looked into George's face and proceeded to deny all the accusations.

"I didn't do it!" he simply said.

George looked back at Jamie and said with a heart felt respond that surprised Jamie, "Jamie, I know it!"

George, then resumed his official demeanor, and ordered Jamie to turn over his badge, ID card, and his weapon.

Jamie sat in silence upon reaching this moment in his life. His words stop flowing and he found himself beginning to tear up. The tears forming in his eye is just enough to blur his vision, but he can still see McCulley making the same yawning motion over in the corner.

How can this chump be so stupid? This man must be dumber than the glass he chews on. He asks question and when I try to tell him something, the moron barely pays attention. I'm not just avenging my sons when this sucker dies; I'm doing the entire world a favor.

Jamie gets up from his seat and goes over to McCulley, drags a chair and places it backward in from of him and straddles it. Jamie stares into McCulley's eyes in total silence. Then he begins to speak, "Try and image your self committed to a purpose as I was...I really wanted to help people–people of all walks of life. I wanted to be an asset to my community! I chose to involve myself with children. I felt if I were going to have any future at all, I might as well start with the future. I was assertive, and I did a lot for the children of my community!"

Jamie gets up from the chair and flings it behind him as he points a finger in McCulley's face; "I instilled the same values in other children as I did with my own kids. They enjoyed living, they cried when they hurt, and they played with vigor without the fear of death, drugs, or disappointment because they knew I was their protector, their father and their friend!"

Jamie turns and walks away from McCulley, as he wipes away the now freely flowing tears. He continues to voice his opinion and tries to put his captive officer in the same frame of mind.

"Let's look at your job, McCulley. I suppose you are totally comfortable with it. And you are looking at retiring from the force.

"You actually, love your job. Suppose you had a family. You feel it in your heart that you will be a family forever. You have several vehicles or you can purchase a new vehicle whenever your heart desires. You have good friends around you constantly, you own your home for a number of years, you have credibility in the community, and your future is mapped out to the point of reality!

"Then, in one day everything comes crashing down. No money! No kids! No family! No car! No friends–neighbors wanting you to move! And No future! Now take that small amount of grief, depression, and anger that you would be feeling and multiply it ten thousand times. That's how I felt when my pride and dignity walked out the door! And on top of everything, I also faced the possibility of going to prison!"

"My boss knew I was innocent when he walked out my door. He knew I was being set up and could do nothing but feel sorry for me. He paused at the door and wished me good luck. I went back into my home and drank myself into a frenzy." Jamie finishes as he looks at the glass in his hand.

Returning to his seat Jamie resumes his story, as McCulley and Ramirez listen intently. Jamie's mind searches through his past. It is like a window–you can see most things through the minds eye, sometimes things are hidden, other times you might notice things that you missed while living that part of your life.

A flood of emotion surges back into him back from the time of the trial. Jamie's eyes start to stare out into space, as if he wasn't even in the room at all. To Jamie the room didn't exist, the two officers aren't in their chair; to him time had reversed itself. But instead of being able to change the past, Jamie is a prisoner of it. Just like Ramirez and McCulley have their chains, Jamie has his too.

That week went by rather quickly for Jamie and Monday was upon him before he knew it. It was time for the trial.

Jamie felt like he was going on a canoe ride upstream without a paddle. The fear was indescribable and was suddenly double when the judge walked in. It was not Jamie's friend; it was a judge from another jurisdiction.

No money for a decent attorney, and now Jamie had to deal with an unfamiliar judge. He may have been placed there to ensure a conviction; by the end of the trial,

Jamie knew he was right. The trial turned out to be a hoax. Just something to document that Jamie was given a trial.

The main evidence at the trial was the twenty-four hour video film, which recorded everything that had taken place in the dry-cleaning shop, but there was one fatal flaw. It had been in the possession of the shop owner from the time it was recorded, to the day of the trial.

When the film was viewed, it was distorted and in some frames, it was hard to tell who was there, because it had been played so much. It was brought up in cursory-cross examination that the owner played it for his friends and relatives every opportunity he had.

In the entire time with the police department, Jamie has never known anyone to hold on to evidence and bring it to a trial with them.

What supposedly convicted Jamie and Billy were four seconds of videotape showing that Billy had at one point leaned over the locked box, which was supposed to contain the money. The video also showed that the security guard had removed his coat and placed it over the camera monitoring the box for over five minutes.

The prosecution's conclusion was that the security guard, which made less than eight dollars per hour and had no high school education, had no reason to steal the money, but Jamie and Billy did.

The attorneys representing Jamie and Billie rushed through the trial without providing anything approaching a proper defense. They raised the issue of a possible set-up with Jamie and Billy, but it was never brought out in the trial.

Jamie and Billie felt that their attorneys didn't really give a damn about getting to the truth. Billy's attorney didn't even appear during the last few sessions, leaving Jamie's attorney to handle the remainder of the trial himself.

When the prosecution completed its case, Jamie and Billie were almost convinced they were guilty. Nothing was left but the verdict, and the verdict was, of course, "Guilty of Larceny from a Building".

A few months elapsed before they were sentenced. So Jamie spent that time organizing his life in preparation for sentencing.

Finally, it was time for Jamie's sentencing. As the months passed, his attorney and other counselors informed him that the probability was slim to none that he would go to prison.

On the day of his sentencing, Jamie left work believing he would return. He felt good at heart and was confident everything would turn out right. But at the sentencing, Jamie stood in front of the judge shaking as he listened to the things the latter was saying. Jamie was so dumbfounded and shock that the words were permanently emblazoned in his brain: "Being found guilty of the crime of Larceny from a building," the judge intoned, "I hereby sentence you each to one year and one day to four years at the Michigan State Prison in Jackson, Michigan.

You are now remanded to the custody of the Department of Corrections. Bailiff, take them away."

Jamie leans back in his chair and stares at the ceiling, blinking away the tears. But that doesn't stop McCulley, who is now sitting up in his chair, from taking another cheap shot at him. "Man, you're about to bore me silly. Do we have to listen to what the judge had to say about the poor little innocent boy? He's so hurt and lonely; he doesn't know what to do with himself. I don't give a damn what he had to say! I don't give a damn about your life! I just want to get the hell out of here!"

Jamie snaps back into the present and looks at McCulley. *Just like a child, this stupid ass can't seem to sit still for more than three seconds, he thinks. I am glad I'm not taking his ass out shopping; he would be the type of child to want everything and cry for the moon when he doesn't get the world.*

Jamie shakes his head and addresses the problem, "What makes you so mean and vicious, McCulley? What kind of person were you anyway? I bet you spent half of your life screwing the farm animals."

Jamie's barbs were ineffective. There comes a point in everyone's life when one meets someone so blind to the rest of the world that no matter what you say or do to them, he will always think he's in the right and you are nothing but a moron.

That time in Jamie's life is now and McCulley is the blind man. No matter what degree of reasoning Jamie tries with him, no matter what kind of slings he may throw; McCulley brushes them all off as if he has no idea what language Jamie is speaking. Jamie will have to find another way to control this man, because his usual tactics were proving unproductive.

"No, I never screw any of the animals, but my life was free of niggers. I never even saw one of you jungle-bunnies in person until I was on my way out West... and he was on the road ducking and hiding in the brush."

McCulley then looks at Jamie. "Hey Jamie, tell me something. Why after three hundred years, you niggers are still mad at white people? We're not holding you in slavery. You can work anywhere you want. Hell! They even let you become cops! Why don't you all get a country of your own? Some place like Africa?"

Now lost in emotion, Jamie sniffs and wipes the tears running down his face, sits up in his chair and stares at McCulley in disbelief.

After several seconds, he finally blurts out, "Boy that alcohol is really talking for you now. That's just the way you were talking the first night I met you. Tell me something–have you gotten anything out of what I have told you yet?

"In case you haven't noticed, the people who screwed me were all black. I haven't begun to get into what the white man has done to me, and right now, that's not important. Right now, I am speaking of injustices brought on by a man, whether he's black or white. None of the damage to me was brought on by prejudice, but what you did to my kids was.

"I'm trying to point out to you that people can hate no matter what the color. I hate your ass because you are an asshole, not because you're white. I hate you because you have taken my children's life because of their color! I want you to hear what I have to say. Then when it's time for you to meet your maker, you won't be asking me or God, why this is happening to you.

"I believe in giving a person a chance in life. You believe in screwing up people, unsuspecting people. You believe in killing, maiming, and torturing people for no damned reason at all.

"Are you aware of how many people are on the strip and in the hotels on New Year's Eve? Are you aware of how many people are going to burn to death, be crushed to death, suffocate, or just blown up? No, you don't, and you just don't give a damn.

"Sucker, I'm giving you something they are not getting; a reason and also the method of your death. I have told you a lot and now I'm going to tell you one more thing. Your stupid ass is going to die in a hail of gunfire and it's not going to be mine! Your so-call partners and fellow police officers will do it for me!

"I promised myself, I wouldn't kill you, but if you keep pushing my buttons with that stupid ass shit coming from your mouth, your death will come a lot sooner than you think!"

With this all said, Jamie starts to feel better and calms down enough to ask McCulley the question that has been nagging him for a long while now, "Now, since I got you talking, tell me what you are going to gain by killing hundreds of people?"

McCulley's anger is rising fast now. The slurs didn't have effect on him before, but the threats of death and the thing that Jamie said about his fellow police officers killing him was starting to get to him. *Who the hell does this nigger think he is? He doesn't know shit my friends would never kill me. This asshole is in a world of trouble if he thinks they would ever turn on me. They would shoot Ramirez for even delivering the message.*

Shit, this nigger better hope he is far out of the country after he releases me. There won't be a safe place for him anywhere in this country. But what the hell is all this shit about killing everyone? Has this guy lost his mind? He doesn't have enough facts to make me look bad. This sucker has to try to make up lies and shit. This asshole is going to pay for this, if it is the last thing I do. If I'm going to die over some lying ass shit like this, I'm going to choke the life out of that black son of a bitch before I do!

McCulley tries to struggle to his feet so that he can get to Jamie, but the chain and the lack of use in one of his legs restricts him. "First off, you tell me how in the hell do you know I have anything to do with bombing any hotels?"

Jamie walks over, pushes McCulley back into his chair and collars him, pointing his finger in his face. "I told you once, and I am going to tell you again! I have tape recordings, as a matter of fact; I have 1,700 minutes of tape. That's 120 hours of listening to you and your friends. And pal, you better believe I haven't gone through all the bullshit on a whim.

"I got your ass and twelve other cops. If, and that is if, and when I go to prison, you're going to be in the next cell...and I got a real strong feeling I'm going to be lot safer than you're going to be!

"From my experience in prison, a white guy has about sixty days before he becomes somebody's bitch. And with what you're going to be charged with you may not even survive prison. Now answer my question punk!"

McCulley sits back in his chair and can't believe what is happening to him. "Like I told you before, I haven't got anything to do with no bombing. Those guys are only bullshitting; they're not going to blow up anything. They just want to get a little notoriety. They want people to know they exist and they want their politics known."

Dumbfounded, Jamie looks at McCulley. "My god McCulley, these people are for real! Man, you are dumber than I thought. They are for real! On several occasions, they held meetings and you were not there. The things they want to do are not to scare anyone. They plan on killing people...a lot of people. Now, you sit here talking about me going to jail–Buddy, you have no idea what kind of people you're dealing with. You will be the one going to jail because you are guilty by association. You are part of this conspiracy."

Still trying to maintain his macho image, McCulley sits up and looking worried about the prospect of going to prison. "Give me another drink," he demands anxiously.

Jamie leaves the room to fetch another drink and takes a shot for himself. Bringing back the drink to McCulley, Jamie can't help but think that maybe he is starting to crack McCulley's armor. The talk of bombings and prison, have started to elicit the responses that Jamie wants.

"Here you go, sport." Jamie gives McCulley his drink and looks at Ramirez who is slowly nodding away. He then returns to his seat to finish his story. "Hey Ramirez, are you with us?"

After hearing the sentence pronounced, Jamie and Billie stood motionless before being led out of the courtroom. They were placed in a holding cell where they stood and looked at each other and began to laugh out loud.

Then Billie looked at Jamie with a big grin on his face. "I got a joint. We may as well smoke it. If we don't, they are going to take it away. What can they do? Arrest us?" So they lit the joint and laid back and smoked it.

After several hours, they were transferred to the county jail where they were stripped searched and told to put on bright-orange overalls. They were then taken to a room with two beds and kept segregated from the rest of the jail population. They remained isolated there for two days.

Boarding the bus to Jackson State Prison was something Jamie only used to tease prisoners about when he worked in the lock-up at the city jail. The guards would tell the prisoners *"The only thing that's going to beat you to prison is the headlights on the bus."* And sure enough, he found himself sitting at the front of the bus, watching the headlights shine down the road.

The first and most humiliating thing Jamie and Billie had to deal with was stripping naked, bending over, and spreading their cheeks to have their anus and rectum inspected.

They received their prison garb and were assigned their cells. Because they were ex-cops, they were again segregated from everyone else for their own protection.

In their cellblock, roaches crawled over the walls and floors. The insects looked at Jamie as though he were invading on private property. No matter how much he brushed them off his bed, they quickly returned in full force.

The rats were more brazen than the roaches. He was afraid to go to sleep for fear they would begin to nibble on him. As time passed, Jamie began to hear female voices, and he felt good to have someone of the opposite sex to talk to–but he seemed to have forgotten he was in men's prison.

The female voices turned out to be homosexuals. Jamie was locked up in the same cellblock with these jokers for one week and then he was moved to another cellblock with everyone else.

He was on continual lock-down because of who he was. He was only allowed out of his cell two hours a day with other prisoners who were being protected or who were rich. Each morning and evening, for one hour Jamie was allowed in the exercise yard. Jamie and Billie saw each other twice a day. It gave Jamie some comfort to know Billie was there.

At the end of their thirty days during which they were transferred from one cellblock to another, the prisoners were relocated either to a camp or the Detroit House of Correction (DHOCO).

Names were called out for people to leave and Jamie heard them call Billie's name. Jamie began packing, but for naught, because he was not leaving. Then the fear really set in; he was totally alone now. He fell back into his bed and began crying and praying.

It took about three days before he got over his fear. He finally received a letter from Billie telling him where he was. They sent Billie to the Detroit House of Correction, and Jamie was hoping they would send him there also. For the next thirty days, Jamie did nothing but wait. Billie would write Jamie, telling him he was looking for him to transfer there soon.

Finally, Jamie's papers arrived for his transfer, but to his dismay, it was not to DHOCO. Instead, they sent him eight hundred miles away to the Upper Peninsula of Michigan. He was now too far to receive any visitors; he was more alone now than ever before. He felt the mayor was not content with just locking him up, but had arranged for him to be so far away, that it would be almost impossible for him to receive visitors.

The stay was miserable and every waking moment was consumed with the thought of going home.

With no friends to keep him company in prison, Jamie spent most of his time watching out for him. He may have been over eight hundred miles away from where he used to work, but somehow word about him being a cop leaked out. Everyday was a struggle.

There aren't too many people in prison that are hated more than cops. Child molesters and rapists were the lowest on the totem pole, but police officers on the wrong side of the bars weren't too far behind.

Being black helped Jamie out a bit while locked up. In prison, there is often a sharp division between the races: Blacks against Whites and Hispanics against Blacks and Whites. If you didn't belong to a gang, you generally didn't last long. Even people that weren't racists on the outside world learned really fast to fake it in the joint. The first rule of prison living was to cover your ass at any cost.

Many white males that may have been the most laid-back, unbigoted people on the outside were overnight converts to the Aryan Nation. The same was true for blacks and Hispanics; it wasn't about politics–it was about survival.

156

Being black helped Jamie out a bit, being a cop however, almost cost him his life. Jamie never knew who leaked it out, if it was an inmate from transfer, or perhaps some guard, but the moment people knew he was a cop, everything changed. It no longer mattered if he were black, white or purple; Jamie was a marked man. No longer having the protection of the black faction of the prison, Jamie had to fend for himself against not only the Aryans, but also the other prisoners of color that thought he was a sell-out. To top it all off, the guards weren't too much help either. From their point of view, Jamie was a bit of a curiosity; just what the hell was a cop doing in prison anyway?

The only thing that saved Jamie through the months was his will to live. When people are faced in certain "life or death" situations, it is customary that they either want to run or fight. Jamie was a fighter; and besides, he had nowhere to run.

Fights began breaking out and Jamie always seemed be in the middle of them. No matter who was fighting or how many they were, he always seemed to come out on top.

On top, in prison terms, meant he came out alive and with few injuries. Jamie quickly learned how to make a blackjack out of soap and an old sock. He also learned how to make friends with people who didn't care that he was a former cop.

Trading away anything he could, Jamie bought friendship. He may have had a strong will to live, but even that was not enough in prison. It never hurts to have people watching your back, and Jamie was willing to sacrifice for this. It was through sacrifice, skill, determination, and a lot of luck that Jamie made it through his time in the joint.

At the end of three months, Jamie was finally released on parole and sent to a halfway house in Detroit. He was allowed to return to work, but he had to report back to the halfway house at 10:00 p.m. each night.

The time came to meet his parole officer. Jamie went to his office and sat in the waiting room. His appointment was at 2:00 p.m. but 5:00 p.m. rolled around and they still hadn't called him.

He approached the receptionist and asked what was the delay and she told him to have a seat and they will be with him soon. Another half hour passed and then Jamie was called into the office.

As he walked in, he saw three men standing across the room. Then the door closed behind him. Before he could do anything, he was attacked by the four men and beaten to the floor. They picked him up and placed him in a chair and began to interrogate him about who he was and who sent him and who he was after. They hurled question after question at him.

What was Jamie doing there? Why was he transferred to that place? Who sent him? Did he work alone?

The men tried pumping him for information in between bouts of beating him. They never beat him enough to do any major damage or leave obvious signs on his body, but they did inflict enough pain to make it known that they knew what they were doing.

Jamie was clueless as to why he was being beaten. Who sent him? Those crooked officials–that's who! He wanted to tell them that. He wanted to tell them all to screw themselves that he was sent to jail wrongly. Why the hell were they beating him now? What had he done to them? Jamie could not think of any reason why all of this was happening…and then it clicked: he finally realized they thought he had been sent there to set them up.

Jamie assured them they were dead wrong about this and that he had really been arrested and sent to prison on trumped-up charges.

The men told Jamie that they had looked at his records, and there was no way he should have been sent to prison. The most he should have received was a suspension.

After talking at length with Jamie, they finally got the complete picture of Jamie's problem with the mayor. He was told to continue reporting to the parole officer as per instructions, and sent on his way without so much as an apology for the way he had been mistreated.

As time went on, Jamie began to feel he could no longer go on, because of all that had happened to him over the past four years.

Jamie began going to a psychiatrist, whose aim in life was to keep Jamie supplied with drugs.

Jamie didn't feel he was accomplishing anything, so he consulted a psychologist who helped him deal with his problems better than the psychiatrist had.

Jamie found out because of all the things that happened to him, he was probably developing ulcers. He went to a medical doctor who treated him and along with the psychologist, they all became good friends.

As time went on, Jamie couldn't seem to get anywhere in his life. He would come home tired from work, but it wasn't just work that made him exhausted. He was tired all the time. He was tired and never wanted to do anything. Not that there was much for him to do, but even at home, he would barely have enough energy to fall asleep in front of the televison. And when he did sleep there were nightmares.

The nightmares were the worst. He had dreams about his life before prison; about his family, his kids and his wife.   Normally, Jamie loved dreaming about them, but in his nightmares his world was hell. His kids and wife hated him in his nightmares and were always doing things to hurt him.

Sometimes his dreams were worse than others–and sometimes his family loved him in his dreams; but he always woke up to an empty bed. Then there were the dreams that he had about prison life–about the fights and all the near misses he had had–only in his dreams he never escaped and he never came out on top.

The psychologist began to help him with all of this. Basically, Jamie learned that he suffered from clinical depression and that he had a heavily bruised psyche. It would require a lot of healing for him to even begin to feel like his old self.

One day, while getting ready for work, Jamie received a call from his parole officer. He wanted him to come to his office immediately. So, Jamie finished dressing and went to see him.

This time, he was greeted warmly at the door by his parole officer and they went directly into the office. The parole officer looked at Jamie and said bluntly, "Somebody is going to kill you; you shouldn't be in the streets. Always have someone with you and don't stand by your windows."

He told Jamie he didn't know who wanted him dead, but he knew that whoever it was, they wanted it badly. He also told Jamie that because of his probation he couldn't leave Detroit until October, and that he would have to be really careful.

After that meeting, Jamie became quite paranoid. He didn't go out at night or see friends. He became a recluse in his own home. Then he started receiving phone calls; when he answered, the person on the other end would hang up. He also received threatening letters, in which the message was put together with letters cut from the newspaper.

One day, after arriving home from work, he noticed several of his windows shattered from what appeared to be gunshots. He didn't report it to the police, but he did notify some police officers to watch out for him.

Eventually he was laid off from General Motors because of the plant closing, so he would do odd jobs in the community until he could relocate to Las Vegas. He was very suspicious and protective of himself and he trusted no one. With no friends around and no one to talk to but family members, the time passed agonizingly slowly. He used this time to get closer to his family, not knowing when he would see them again.

Finally, the time arrived for him to leave. There was a tearful good-bye and he drove off to make Las Vegas his new home.

He left behind memories of the people who helped him through his trying times–people whom he would always carry in his heart. Jamie held these memories like a child would hold onto a teddy bear. Whenever things looked darkest, he would often sit and take time and remember that there were people out there who cared for him. There were people that show love for other human beings other than themselves.

But there were times that these same thoughts would tear him apart. There may be people in the world that cared about him, but they were a distant past–just shadows in Jamie's mind.

There were times when his mind would turn the love by the people in his past into something different–something twisted. There were times that some part of Jamie–some part of him that was not completely healed–would torture him with things that he knew he might never have again. At such times, he seemed to take perverse pleasure in thinking about the hurt he could inflict on those who had hurt him so badly.

But time heals all wounds, and time was one thing Jamie had a lot of...or so he thought.

JIMMY CULLORS/JOSEPH SZEWEZYK

chapter

7

THE PARTNERSHIP

The distant flashback ends for Jamie and he is brought abruptly back to the present. McCulley is barely paying attention to Jamie's story and Ramirez seems to be nodding off, or lost in a world of her own.

McCulley seizes the lapse in Jamie's story as his cue to talk.

"Okay, Jamie. You gave us a very touching story, and just to please you, I will say I feel sorry for you, but that still doesn't mean I give a damn. You were a felon, you are a felon, and you will continue to be a felon. You have shown me you didn't know the difference between right and wrong and you don't respect authority. Now, you are holding two police officers against their will. Tell me how the hell you are going to get out of that?"

Jamie pauses before he responds to McCulley. Just how was he going to get out of this? Things are going as planned, but even the most careful and well-laid plans may fail. A lot of Jamie's friends never believed in luck or fate, but Jamie has been around too long to blow things like those off. What if it was not his time to pull this off? What if something out of his control happens? Jamie tries to stifle these thoughts and turns his attention towards McCulley.

"Well, McCulley, I was hoping I could get to you about your wrong doing, but I guess I couldn't. You white guys are a hellva lot smarter than we are. I should have realized I was out of my league when I kidnapped you and your partner. Speaking of partner, look at her, she's knocked out. How much of that did she drink?" Jamie says motioning to the passed out Ramirez.

McCulley looks over at Ramirez. There lays his partner, passed out due to alcohol and drug consumption. Being such a small person, it didn't take long for the mixture Jamie was giving her to take effect. The alcohol acted as a depressant on her system which also served to kill the taste of the pills Jamie had been slipping into her drink; no knockout combination greater than nighttime allergy medication with a liquor chaser. Ramirez would be okay once she wakes up and Jamie added in his mind, she wouldn't have a runny nose.

Jamie addressed McCulley again, "Look McCulley, I have two kids in prison because of you. You were smart enough to trap them and set them up. I know I'm dealing with a pro."

McCulley is taken back by this statement. It is the first thing Jamie said all night that he agrees with.

"You're damn right... I am the best. You know your kids were easy to set-up. I really wanted to get them because they were my way of letting the community know you don't mess with Officer McCulley, because if you do, he will jam you up. I got respect in the neighborhood. When I come down the street, the kids disappear from the corner. When I want information, I get it quick. I get respect; I get those black nitwits to bow down to me.

"Your sons came into the neighborhood from 'Deee-troit' acting like their shit don't stink. I tried to warn them. I tried to let them know they were under my rules... but no, they had to continue to file complaints against me. And now I find out that I missed the main 'nitwit' who was doing all that filing. You brainless nitwit, believe you me I'm going to get your ass."

McCulley pauses, trying to remember the specific case of Jamie's sons.

"Now as far as your sons are concerned, they caused a stir in the neighborhood and a few other niggers decided they wanted to file complaints, too. Well, I got their asses, too. I showed that neighborhood not to jerk me around. If it hadn't been for them I wouldn't have the opportunity to flex my muscles. Boy... and flex is what I did. Just like you, I took my time and got everything together. I confiscated enough drugs in the neighborhood to put forty people in jail; but I used it to put twelve suckers behind bars–twelve suckers who were making my life miserable.

"Now, for the next twenty years, their lives are going to be miserable. For the next twenty years, they will remember they screwed with the wrong cop, and the people in the neighborhood will think twice before trying to make trouble for me. They now know that filing a complaint won't do a damn thing but get them locked up."

Lifting his glass as if he were making a toast, McCulley says smilingly.

"Here's to you Jamie, my boy. You and your sons are the greatest; I could never have done it without you."

Then McCulley sits back and laughs to himself. *All of this for two niggers... man, this Jamie guy is screwed in the head. Did*
him a favor anyway his sons would have ended up dead or on crack if it weren't for me. At least in jail they wouldn't be homeless crack heads.

Jamie cuts into McCulley's thoughts, "Just like I said McCulley, you are real smart. I guess the guys you hang out with are just as smart as you are; making all those plans to blow up buildings and kill people."

McCulley looks up at Jamie. *Kill people? Is he for real? We never planned on killing anyone. This guy is half baked... all of this wrong information... leave it up to some black piece of shit to not get his facts straight; no wonder he was kicked off the force.*

"No, Jamie like I said, they aren't going to kill anybody. We just want to make a little money. We figure if we tell them we're going to blow up their hotels, they will pay us not to. You know it's like... well, you know..." McCulley edges Jamie for the words.

Jamie picks up on where everything is going, "Yeah, kidnapping held for ransom–just like what I'm doing to you. So now, we're in the same club. Ha!"

McCulley's eyes narrow. *This punk thinks he is in the same club as I am? He can't even be in the same room without my permission. Lucky that's all this guy is...just lucky.*

"Same club my ass," McCulley says out loud. "We're in two very separate clubs. My club gets away; your club gets caught. Nobody is going to tie us to the bomb threats. Jeff and Jack have a plan where Steve and all the boys on the strip will pay us, and then we go on our merry way."

This is what Jamie was working for. Finally McCulley was starting to give the information more freely. Finally Jamie could start reeling his line in and see what he caught. The only question for Jamie now is if the fish were a minnow, or was this catch a Northern Pike.

"Hey McCulley, do you honestly think that Steve and the boys are going to pay you a dime? If they pay you, they will be paying every jackass that comes along and demands money. Have you ever thought of that?

Look McCulley, open your eyes. Better yet, I have something I want you to hear. Maybe after you listen to a few tapes, your ass will come back to earth. These tapes I have were recorded at the motel on Boulder Highway. As I told you before, I have a few hours of listening pleasure just for you. Let me set it up for you."

Jamie starts to pace the room as McCulley listens with interest for the first time. Seeing that he finally has McCulley's attention, Jamie takes a breath. *Time to see what I caught...* he thinks to himself as he begins the story.

"Now on August 21, 1999 at 8:00 p.m., you were at work doing what you do best, protecting the Black community. Meanwhile, your friends were having a special meeting just for the elite of the group. Present at this meeting was your friend and good buddy, James Witherspoon. Then there was everyone else. The only person missing was you. Now, listen carefully." Jamie walks into the bedroom and returns with a box containing a tape recorder and ten tapes.

McCulley sits up in his chair as though he was going to open Christmas presents. Jamie places the recorder on the coffee table and begins to give McCulley a brief run-down of what's going on.

Jamie rented a room in the motel next door to the Longhorn Palace. He learned from his many visits to the bar that Jack Riviera was the leader of the group, and they used the motel to sell and distribute methamphetamines. They also used the room to hold meetings.

Jamie decided the best way to find out what was going on inside the room would be to get the room next door and bug the meeting room. So he went to the Spy Shop and purchased various listening devices and cameras. A microphone was placed outside the apartment to pick-up any activities going on outside and another would be placed through the wall to hear what was going on inside. He also purchased a VHS camera, tape and extension cords. Then he had to figure out how to get into their room.

The bar itself was on the corner of Clarence and Boulder Highway. It was approximately 50 yards long, running north-south and about 10 yards in depth. The back door was on the south end of the building facing the motel, which created easy access from the bar to the motel. Jamie needed the room next door to theirs, so he waited 12 hours until the room was vacant and went to the motel office and requested that room.

The room was well situated and from information obtained from the hotel clerk, it was identical to the adjacent room, only the layout was reversed.

When he entered the room, he canvassed the place, noticing the bed was in the middle of the room, with a nightstand on either side of the bed with a lamp atop each one. A dresser approximately 6 feet long faced the bed from the opposite wall with a large mirror in the middle. To the right of the door is a large table with a large lamp in the middle and two armchairs on either side of the table.

On the back wall straight back from the front door, was a large mirror with a double sink beneath it, and to the right, was the bathroom. The room itself was colored in beige with dark brown drapes and dark carpets. If the door and drapes remained closed you would never know the time of day.

Jamie began his surveillance by making sure he knew whenever there was someone in the room.

He drilled a small hole over the top of the door jam; just large enough to insert a small pencil-sized cable and small enough that it would not be noticed. At the end of the cable was a camera, which was hooked up to a monitor. He watched the monitor for three days and established a time when no one would be in the apartment. That time was the next day before 8:00 a.m.

At that time, Jamie drilled another small hole in the ceiling line right above the bed. He hurried before the maid arrived so she would change the bedding and gets rid of the dust from the drilling before the occupants returned. After drilling the hole, Jamie pushed the cable through and looked around the room. It was situated just like the clerk had said. He then pulled the cable flush to the hole and was able to see the entire room, except for either side of the bed, where he placed two more cameras on the seam of the floor.

After setting up the cameras, Jamie viewed the monitor and saw he had four quadrants. One quadrant covered the outside of the room and the other three quadrants were on the inside of the room. He then drilled a hole beneath the bed, where he slid a microphone through the hole and pushed it to the center of the bed. Now he had his eyes and ears and for several months, he sat in his room leaving only when the room next door was empty or when he went to the bar to purchase drugs. He was never seen entering or leaving the room and was very cautious that-that side of the building was free of pedestrian traffic.

When the room was occupied, Jamie saw a lot of illegal activities, including robberies, homosexual activities; gang rapes, and drugs trafficking. None of that interested him but he knew he could use this additional criminal activity against the police officers involved.

McCulley was seldom there when these activities took place because he worked the swing shift, but they did arrange for McCulley to be there when they had their group meetings.

On one occasion McCulley was purposely left out of the meeting so they could get more detailed and intense with their plans to blow-up the four hotels. On this day, fourteen people were present and they were not open for the business of selling drugs. Present were:

> James Burg - police officer
> Jeff Newsom - police officer
> James Witherspoon - police officer
> Mark Wilcox - police officer
> Shorty Watson - drug runner
> Jack Watts Riviera – boss/owner of the bar
> Matt Peterson - police officer
> John Beasley - police officer
> Wilson Owens - police officer
> Dave Gardner - police officer
> Donald Sharp - police officer
> James Orr - police officer
> Keith Stenstrom - police officer
> Glenn McDonald - construction worker

They all sat around smoking marijuana and drinking Jack Daniels, when the topic emerged about how they were going to get away with their scheme. Putting down the bottle of Jack Daniels, the room got quiet as if everyone knew what was on the others' mind. Just how were they going to pull all of this off? The group stared at each other for a while until someone broke the silence.

"Hey Jack, we have been over and over this method we're going to use to get in and out of those hotels, but you ain't never said how the hell we gonna get outta Las Vegas."

Two other men looked each other in the eyes and read that they were thinking the same thing.

Heads nodded and utterances of agreement were pronounced in the room. The man everyone seemed to be talking to wasn't paying much attention to his colleagues.

Instead he seemed more interested in watching how the smoke from his cigarette rolled around in the stale room light.

"Yeah, Jack, that's been bothering me too. I have no intentions of staying in this town when we do this thing. These cops will shoot us first and ask questions later."

Then everybody joins in the general clamor until the lone man sitting in the corner silenced them, James Witherspoon, McCulley's best friend.

"Why don't you all shut up and think," he demanded.

This man has sat down and thought up all these plans... a sure way of getting a little recognition around the country for us, and you think he is going to let us get caught? "Look, none of us is Tim McVeigh, and none of us is going to jail, but the one who is not here is the one who will play that role."

Everyone looks around the room. McCulley is conspicuously absent. McCulley always seemed to be missing when they talked about the "big picture" of the whole plan. Not a single one of the group could remember a time when McCulley was present for an entire conversation about their plan. Everyone thought it was just timing, everyone just passed it off as unimportant... until now.

"You mean to tell me we are going to stick this whole thing on 'Chew?'" asked Officer Orr, who was just putting down another shot of Jack Daniels.

Witherspoon looked around at the group. He couldn't believe that nobody had thought of this before. Well, he hadn't wanted anyone to catch on too fast; it appears his plan has worked.

"Why not," he asked. "He's the most logical person-he has no friends here; nobody likes him."

The others were still a little wary on this subject. Why was McCulley's only friend setting him up?

Was this some sort of trick, or joke? He couldn't possibly be serious... or could he?

"But, he's your friend. If you're not his friend, why the hell did you bring him around us for?" Orr asked again.

Witherspoon stood from his seat in the corner and approached the main group sitting around the room. He didn't intend to get up, but this seemed like the best way to get his point across to everyone at once; to get it across and to make sure he was understood clearly.

His words were flat and without emotion,

"He ain't anybody's friend. We needed a fall-guy, and he fits the bill."

"You mean to tell me that we have been sitting around here with that asshole putting up with his shit because we thought he was your friend, and you don't even like the jerk?"

"That's right," Witherspoon acknowledged, "we needed a sucker and I chose him. Nobody would miss him. Nobody would be surprised if he did some shit like this."

"His mama don't like him and neither does his brothers and sisters, and he dam sure won't be missed on the department. I feel we have to use him as a fall guy because he would probably spill the beans if he gets caught."

"What's going to stop him from spilling the beans when they catch up with him," someone asked.

Witherspoon smiled a bit before he answering, "Well, I wouldn't worry about that too much, because he is going to die during the explosion."

The others in the group didn't seem to comprehend everything at once. The reality of the plan was just starting to sink in for some of them. The bombing of the hotels was always talked about, but up until now–until they talked about McCulley dying to cover their own asses, no one really gave the whole situation much thought. They were simply waiting to cross that bridge when they came to it. But now with Witterspoon seemingly having everything planned out; things started to become real to everyone. Witherspoon took the silence in the group as an opportunity to pass along the next phase of their plan.

"Before I tell you any more, let Jack explain to you what's going to take place."

Jack got up and started to go to a pile of papers he had in a folder. He moved like he had rehearsed the whole situation... because he had. Witherspoon and Jack had planned everything out from the beginning. They knew tonight would be the night to set their plan into action–not just part of the plan, but the whole thing. It was time to see which in their group was for real, and who had to be eliminated.

"First off, James pass these papers around. This paper I am passing around contains the oath of our union. I want you all to look them over then we're going to recite it out loud. If you don't want to abide by the rules and regulations mentioned in this oath, you may leave now. If you choose to stay, you will only be allowed to leave in a body bag."

Everyone looked at each other uneasily, but not one got up to leave. So Jack had everyone recite the oath out loud.

"Everyone raise your right hand and repeat after me. I... 'Write your name in the blank.'

"Being a member of Fascists Supreme, do solemnly swear to uphold the principles, philosophies and ideologies of this organization.

"It is our sworn intent and purpose to antagonize, persecute and destroy, if necessary, all the inferior races in the United States of America, including, but not necessarily limited to: gooks, spics and greasers, niggers and nigger-lovers and kikes and all other enemies of our country and our race.

"We will arm ourselves as necessary to do battle with any force that is sent against us in an attempt to destroy our organization, our country, or our way of life.

"As a member of this prestigious organization, we are willing to give our lives for the noble cause of White Supremacy. We are the most powerful race in the world and will go to any length to establish our rightful place in the world.

"As a sworn member of this proud organization, I understand and affirm that I am a member for life, and that renouncing my membership is not an option.

"I hereby swear my allegiance to Fascists Supreme and its duly elected officers. I will bear true faith and allegiance to them and the principles of this organization. I will obey their orders without question. And I swear to take the secrets I learn here to my grave. I acknowledge that the penalty for violating this oath will be death. I take this oath freely and without any purpose of evasion whatsoever, so help me God."

The members of the circle looked at each other. Some of them were in awe-struck; some were wondering if they really were ready to take this final irrevocable step, but none voiced their opinion. As far as they were concerned, the time for voicing opinions was gone by the time they stole the explosives. Jack looked at the group with satisfaction.

"Good," he said, "that's good. Now back to McCulley. None of you sorry, sons of bitches have been doing your homework. We needed someone who is good with explosives, and this sorry ass y'all been talking about is just that person. He was an explosive expert in the Army before he got into the military police. He really knows his stuff; that's why he's here.

"He's going to handle this operation all by himself...that is as far as the cops are concerned. He has already been to Kentucky and obtained dynamite to add with the dynamite we stole from that rock quarry in Arizona. We have enough to blow-up ten hotels.

"The dynamite is hidden in a cave out in the desert where he has been going for the last few months' settings up the charges. No one else has touched the stuff. His prints are all over everything.

"Because you are all cops, come Christmas Day of this year, 2001, you will each carry ten charges and begin placing them in strategic locations throughout the hotels you are assigned to. And because you are cops, nobody will stop you. McCulley has decided on the locations for the charges.

"These charges will not knock the buildings down, but they will cause a lot of damage and trap people inside."

Jack pauses for a second to take a drag off his cigarette; "All of you will wear surgical gloves before you place the charges, all of you, that is, except McCulley.

"The hotels, that will receive the charges, are the Venetian, M.G.M, Mirage, and Caesar's Palace. That's where the largest concentration of people will be.

"On December 31, 2002, McCulley will be notified that something has gone wrong with his charges and will be sent back to check them. He will be carrying an extra charge, which will be set to blow at 10:45 p.m. He will be alone.

In the confusion, the remainder of the bombs will go off as scheduled, creating more death and destruction. As far as McCulley is concerned, all the charges will be set for 12:00 a.m., January 1, 2003. McCulley will die with the charge in his procession. When the FBI and ATF investigate, they will find evidence pointing to McCulley and to McCulley alone.

"You see, we have learned our mistakes from Tim McVeigh. No one is to act any differently toward McCulley, and no one is to let him know what's going on. If I find out any of you violated my rules, you will die and your death will be something no one would want. It will be very slow and hideous. You will be chopped up one limb at a time. Are there any questions?"

Jamie turns off the recorder and looks at McCulley who is white as a sheet. McCulley shivers a little and looks back at Jamie. *Is everything on that tape true? Is that how it really went down?* McCulley's mind raced with possible answers. *Maybe it was all a set up by Jamie. Maybe Jamie was some greedy bastard that wanted in on the cut from the motel.* But, those voices, they were his friends voices, he was pretty sure of that.

McCulley tries to think of all the times he had with James Witherspoon, was there something odd about him?

He needs time to think, but time was something neither he nor Jamie had a lot of.

Seeing the look of confusion and slight fear on McCulley's face, Jamie tries to push the issue,

"Okay Mr. McCulley, how do you feel now? Still think your friends are your friends? Do you think they have your interest at heart? From listening to this tape, I get the impression that no matter where you turn somebody's trying to punk you out. And from what I can see, you're faced with three of the worst options a man can face: death, death, or the rest of your life in prison.

If I were you, I would take what I am offering you because death can come quick. If you want to defend your buddies, twenty years or so takes a while to go by...and who knows, after you've been cornholed enough times in the joint, you may want to change your name from Clarence McCulley to Clarissa McCulley."

"How do I know those tapes are real?" McCulley snaps. "How do I know those are the people you mentioned?"

Jamie looks into McCulley's face. *This guy is for real! He isn't trying to be a smart-ass anymore.*

He really is grasping at straws to explain all of this in any other possible way but the truth.

Jamie feels a strange connection between himself and McCulley, but for that brief moment in time, Jamie sympathizes with the hapless officer. It isn't everyday that your world comes crashing down on top of you. It had all happened to Jamie before, and now McCulley is feeling the weight on his shoulders.

"Look McCulley, don't be stupid. You recognize the voices and you know what they're talking about."

McCulley thought about this for a moment. *Jamie is right; the tapes do sound a lot like my friends. It's all something they would say too.* But no matter how much evidence one part of his brain grasps that his friends were trying to set him up, McCulley's other half still resist it— still trying to find other explanations.

"Man, you went through a lot of trouble to set all this stuff up. How do I know you didn't fake the tapes?"

Though McCulley tries to put up a confident front, Jamie sees through him as if he were a piece of cellophane. All of the possible questions McCulley might have for Jamie, all the possible denials; Jamie is prepared for the questions and denials, in fact, he counted on them.

"I'll tell you what, you stick with your sorry story it doesn't matter to me. But I will remind you, there are such things as, voiceprints, and they will prove these people are who I say they are. And on top of that, I have videotapes."

Jamie looks over at McCulley and starts to speak slowly, making sure each word sinks into the officer's head, "In the meantime, you will be dead. You will die working with them, or you will die by the hands of your friends, or my plan will fail and you will spend the rest of your life in prison. So now, you have the big picture. Your life ain't worth a damn. How do you feel now?"

McCulley begins to squirm in his seat. The alcohol and the ketamine that Jamie has given him are having an effect on his body. He isn't completely numb at this time, but he is nowhere near the condition he needs to be in to actually use his limbs effectively. Jamie likened the sight of McCulley squirming in his chair to that of a fish that has just jumped out of the water...so close to regaining control of his element, yet so impossibly far away.

Turning his head from McCulley, Jamie does a visual check on Ramirez. "Look at Ramirez sleeping like a baby. She doesn't have the slightest idea what's going on, but she is going to be the messenger and the savior of thousands of lives."

McCulley looked over at the limp body that lies bundled in the chair next to him. There sleeps his partner, her face devoid of expression with her chest moving up and down rhythmically. She looks peaceful to McCulley–so peaceful and fragile. How can someone as fragile as that make it out of this situation and stay alive long enough to save people while he, as tough as he is, would probably end up dead?

"What do you mean? How is she going to save anyone?"

"Well, I guess it doesn't matter if I tell you this because you won't be around. Ramirez is going to be in charge of all the evidence against you and your buddies. You see if there are fifteen of you renegade idiots, there are probably another twenty turncoat cops who will protect you scums. I don't trust any of you, but I have to trust somebody. Somebody has to get my kids and those other guys out of jail, and somebody has to expose your little group. Before me, I have one person and from what I have found out about Ramirez, she fits the bill."

Jamie's last words pull McCulley's attention from Ramirez. McCulley is about to say something when he hesitates. Something was happening inside of his body. Something big is building up and he can feel it like a crescendo.

A white light flashes in front of McCulley's eyes and he was shaken to his core by something that hits from deep within. He jerks as if stricken by a physical blow. It was all becoming clear to him, for the first time, McCulley starts to see with his eyes open. He reviews all that has gone on with his group of friends, adding in everything that Jamie has been talking about, along with tapes. Everything is becoming clear to him.

Recovering alcoholics call it 'hitting rock bottom,' a moment of clarity in which the person can shake off the haze long enough to see just how bad their situation really is. For Officer McCulley, his moment has just arrived.

"Look, I didn't know they were doing all that! You got to believe me! Jamie, I could help you. I could expose everyone and everything. I will go to court and testify against everyone and admit to the setups. I can help you. With what I just heard, do you think that I am going down for these assholes!"

Now it is Jamie's turn to play cat, "McCulley, I have sat here with you for over twelve hours and you have done nothing but talk about 'niggers' and badmouth everyone who isn't of white persuasion. You have yet to impress me in any way. I wouldn't trust you as far as I could throw you."

Now highly intoxicated, McCulley is beginning to realize that he has underestimated Jamie. He has come to the realization that Jamie holds his life in his hands and the world is against him. He has no where to turn, and it's pissing him off.

With a spiteful look in his eyes, McCulley's darker side replies to Jamie, "Fuck you nigger. You can't use that tape if you are dead. My friends probably knew your filthy ass was listening in on them. All of this bullshit you're doing is just to see me squirm. Well, I'm done squirming. If you wanted a bitch, you should have picked Ramirez.

"I know you probably think I am an asshole. Well, who cares what you think? All the tapes and shit are nothing. You can shove them straight up your ass. The only person going to prison here is you. That is if you don't die first.

"Even if you don't die, you really think a little bitch like you will last long in prison? Not with the enemies you've made. I can assure you that we will let you live long enough to see your kids die of an 'unfortunate accident' right before you follow them a few weeks later by wasting away in the hole... just another nigger checking out."

Jamie looks amazed at McCulley. Here it was all in black and white and McCulley still couldn't believe it. Jamie stands firm because he knows McCulley is weakening,

"Number one, I'm not going to die. Number two, I'm not going to prison. I have been over every detail with a fine-toothcomb. It's going to be close, but I'm going to get away. Someone has to be my diversion and guess who that someone is: *you*! Because you know so much and you know how you're going to be exposed, you have to die... I can't trust you enough to let you to live.

"You would probably kill Ramirez just to protect yourself, and everything I have worked for over the years will have been in vain and I will have the U.S. government hunting me down. No, you must be eliminated. You must die so others can live.

"Understand I have never in my life purposely set out to kill or have anyone killed, but you changed that in me. You are responsible for the person who stands before you. There is nothing you can say or do to change that. As you can see, it is written in the cards. Your life ends here."

The words are now beginning to take effect on McCulley, but Jamie's cool composition has even more of a control over the officer. The fear is now consuming his entire body, but the liquid courage that he has been consuming is winning the battle.

"Look Jamie, I will do anything! I will keep my word. My mother hated me. My brothers and my sisters hated me. I had no friends. The closest person to me was my father and he's dead. In school, I was a bully until one day; half the school jumped on me and put me in the hospital. Nobody liked me. I never had a girlfriend; I never married...

"Is that the shit you want me to say? You must be joking. You are the one that is running out of time. Sooner or later the police will arrive and when they come knocking on that door, there isn't going to be a bullshit trick in the world you can pull to keep them back.

"Just think, you'll die, Ramirez won't be any wiser and I will go free. Best of all, I get front row seats to the whole thing."

Jamie, not feeling any of the sympathy that crept up on him before, continues to taunt McCulley. *Bullshit, McCulley; you've said nothing but bullshit. I can see the fear in your drunken stupid little eyes, I've got you, I finally got you. But how far can I take this; can I get everything I want from this sucker in time? I'll just have to push a little further to find out.*

Jamie's mother always used to say, "You can't make an omelet without breaking a few eggs," but now Jamie was trying to do just that: McCulley was no good to him, or his sons, if he was too broken.

"Funny you should mention your family, McCulley, because I know all about them. What, are you surprised? I was tracking and back tracking your ass for a very long time. Mother's a nice lady you know..."

McCulley shoots up at this part from Jamie, "My mother? How the hell do you know her?"

Jamie sits back with a slight interest in the change of McCulley's outer tone. *Mention what an asshole he is and nothing happens. Bring up his mother and he is mine. Funny, even the biggest and baddest racists are someone's kid. It's time to let McCulley in on a little secret.*

"McCulley, you sent my children, my family, my life, into a hell hole because you were just that big of a bastard to do it. You didn't give a shit about what happened to anyone. After digging deep into your life, I decided to hold an insurance policy, just in case. You see, McCulley, you aren't the only one in this room able to screw up someone's family. You took my kids, so I took someone related to you."

Jamie stops to check to see if he has McCulley's attention. For the first time he finds McCulley at a loss for words. Satisfied that he finally has McCulley's complete and undivided attention, Jamie decides to give a window into his plan.

"You see, McCulley, if you would have stayed in contact with your mother, you might have known she has been feeling a little ill lately. At least that is what her neighbors will tell you. In fact, if you should ask them, they would probably tell you she left in a medical response vehicle a few days ago. Maybe if you kept the questioning up, one of them might recall the lone driver a black male, beard with glasses.

You see McCulley, you need me now. You need me to make it out of this alive and fine. If I don't make it, your mother doesn't make it either. I don't want to hurt anyone, but if I am dead already, then what difference does it make to me?"

McCulley barely even heard the words come from Jamie's mouth. He was in trouble and he knew it. *My mother...that guy took my mother. What the hell is going on, too many drinks, I can't seem to think clearly anymore. I hate this asshole, I want him dead, but I need to help him now? I need to help him or my mother will die? Why should I care? She never did anything for me. But, I care. I do care. I need to talk some sense to Jamie, he needs to understand. It wasn't my fault; I don't want to kill anyone either.*

It was suppose to be a money scam-harmless, just go in, set the casinos up and get the money. Nobody is supposed to get hurt. But now, I realize that my so-called friends were lying to me all along. Money was never the issue-killing people for a political statement was.

Now faced with the possibility of his life ending, McCulley tries to plead with his executioner.

"Jamie, all my life I have pushed people around. I thought I was invincible. Everyone was afraid of me. I don't know what happened to me. I do know I wasn't like this when my father was alive. I turned into this monster after his death. I spent a lot of time with him. We used to do things together.

"After he died, nobody was there for me so I guess I decided to take the world on by myself. I never thought I would need anyone. I never thought I would be in so much trouble. I needed some friends, so I found James. He turned out to be just like me and so did his friends. I was in a world of my own and I didn't need anyone anymore. I found my friends. I wasn't like this before I met them... I didn't hate anyone... I treated everybody the same. They taught me to hate and I did it to fit in. I couldn't mess up a good thing because they were all I had.

"Now I find out they intend to use me and it makes me feel like the fool I am. If I could, I would apologize to everyone I know I've hurt. I just need that time. I need to do something to correct the wrong I have done. Please Jamie, give me that chance!"

The words coming out of the officer's mouth ring true. Jamie doesn't need to question this.

With all the background checking that Jamie has carried out on McCulley, he knows that what McCulley is saying is as true as if it were Jamie himself speaking the words. The problem now facing Jamie is knowing when to push on and when to back off.

If he pushes too much, McCulley might crack completely, but if he doesn't push enough, McCulley might still have a venomous attitude towards him. Jamie needs McCulley to be his rattler, but he doesn't need to be bitten by him. With this in mind, Jamie decides to push on.

"McCulley, I am quite sure you have been through a lot of trials in your career. So, I know you have seen people blame other people or other things for their actions. Now you're doing it. Now you want me to believe that you screwed a few hundred lives around just because your father died? McCulley, kiss my ass! You are not going to cop out on that bullshit. I don't want to hear it. Your words don't mean shit to me!"

Jamie holds his breath for a bit. *Maybe I pushed too far on him? He's just sitting there now, not saying a damn word. Well, either I pushed him too hard or I didn't... no use worrying about it now. What is done is done; we'll just have to see how this redneck responds.*

"Hey, I am not trying to cop out on anything. I just don't want to die. All my life I lived for myself. I screwed up I know this. You have my mother, Jamie. You have something I can't replace in my life. I don't want to kill anyone; I never wanted to kill anyone. I know I've been a real asshole, but give me a break. Just let her go free and maybe we can talk about this stuff."

Jamie now begins to show his sympathetic heart. McCulley has suffered enough, the snake is charmed and Jamie doesn't dare to push him too much more.

Pretending like he didn't expect any of this to happen, Jamie lets a small sigh of relief out before he responds to McCulley, "You know I find it very hard to do anything for a scum like you. You don't give a damn about anyone else, but the moment your ass is in a sling, you're pleading for help. Well, I have news for you... I can't help you. The name of the game is self-preservation. You're my out and without you I'm looking at an untold amount of time behind bars with my kids.

"Against my better judgment, I'll listen to what your ass has to say. You see I'm not like you. When a sucker like you begs I can't help but feel for him. I used to help people who were down in life. I can actually pat myself on my back and say that what I taught them actually turned them around and they became productive members of society.

"You, I would say, are not even a challenge. And only because people like you, change your mind when you are in trouble! But, I'm not here to give you a lesson on life! This is not a classroom and you are not my pupil."

This is it. What McCulley says next will indicate to Jamie if he has truly been successful at his ploy or not. Jamie begins to wonder if he had read McCulley correctly when McCulley starts to speak. By the tone of McCulley's voice, Jamie knows he has judged the situation correctly.

"Look Jamie, I would be willing to be a pupil. I would do anything you say. I need some help; I need some guidance. I have never had anyone to help me or care enough to help me. I know something bad is facing me and I don't have the guts to face it alone. I don't know what to do to get out of this, but I am willing to do anything." *And as soon as I get the chance, you are one dead nigger,* McCulley finishes in his mind.

Anything! That word echoes through Jamie's mind. *Looks like I reeled in a Northern Pike,* Jamie exult to himself. With 'anything' dancing around in his head, Jamie goes in for the kill.

"It's a shame to have a full-grown man in your predicament. I know I could ask you to do anything right now and you would probably do it, but again I am not that type of person to take advantage of the situation the way you would."

Jamie stops to look at McCulley with a bit of sadness on his face, "And the way things are now, I would hate to see you die, as pitiful as you are. And on top of everything, it's too late to come up with something else."

McCulley, now sensing an opening, sighs with relief and stares at Jamie.

"I have an idea!" he announces.

"What? What is it?"

"I could go with you."

That stops Jamie in his tracks. Go with me? That isn't the response Jamie is expecting, but it might do, if Jamie could work the answer a bit more. Just how serious was McCulley with his answer? There was only one way to find out.

"You are out of your mind! Remember you are the prisoner. What do you wanna do, become Patty Hearst? You trying to pull that Stockholm syndrome shit on me? I have seen a lot of bullshit on TV, but this is real life. I'm not to taking your sorry ass nowhere."

Jamie pauses for a second and shakes his head. He hadn't exactly planned McCulley responding like he did, but perhaps he could still use this to his advantage. Jamie needed time to think. Just then McCulley resumes pleading with him, giving Jamie's mind the time it needs.

"Jamie, just listen to me! If I stay here, I will go to prison like you. Besides, you have my mother and I need you alive to keep her safe. I won't let you down!"

Made sense. That's all that Jamie's mind could think of. Everything McCulley is saying makes sense. Jamie admits to himself that he would be acting the same exact way if the roles were reversed.

Man, when faced with danger, had two options, fight or flight. Sometimes it was better to choose flight and live another day. Jamie knows this is what McCulley is choosing. McCulley still could end up in prison-or dead-if he goes with Jamie, but there is at least a chance of everyone getting out of this situation in one piece. But does McCulley really deserve this chance at life?

"Wait a minute sucker. If it weren't for you, I wouldn't be in this shit."

McCulley scrambles for an answer, "I know Jamie, but I can help. I'll put a confession on tape that will get your kids out of prison. I will also confess to the other false charges on the other prisoners and get them released also. I will tell what I know about the bombing. Like I said, I will do anything.

"This is the first break I ever had in my life. Please, I'm begging you to let me go with you. I will follow all of your orders and if nothing else, you will be able to trust me. I won't pull any tricks, I promise. If I do anything stupid, you can kill me. Then I know I will deserve it. Please give me a chance to redeem myself. I need someone to trust me and you seem to be my only hope."

The words ring across Jamie's ears, he turns his back to McCulley and smiles. These are the words of someone that lost all hope and Jamie knows it. McCulley is Jamie's slave, he could do just about anything he wants with McCulley, as long as he shows the promise of McCulley having the chance to live another day. Jamie has his snake, and now the snake knows if it wants to stay alive, he has to depend on Jamie.

Jamie turns back to face McCulley, "I don't know about this. I have everything worked out for only one person. I never figured or imagined to be involved with the person I kidnapped."

McCulley catches a glimpse of something in Jamie's eyes, but cannot tell what exactly he sees. It was almost as if Jamie was expecting him to act like this. McCulley dismisses the thought and tries to appeal to Jamie's sensitive side. "Look Jamie, you talk about the person that you are...giving and caring about people. Why not give me that opportunity to be one of those people you have turned around!"

Jamie shakes his head as if he were in deep thought. McCulley starts sweating even more while waiting for Jamie to answer him. The sweat is starting to pour into his eyes, and the residue from the hair gel McCulley uses blends with it, causing his eyes to sting and tear. Blinking away the pain, McCulley focuses on Jamie's eyes again.

The look he had seen before is back, this time his mind starts to place it. The look in Jamie's eyes is identical to the one a cat has when playing with a mouse it has caught. McCulley subconscious mind begins pulling up information to the conscious part of the brain. Then Jamie snaps McCulley out of his concentration.

"Okay, I will think about it, but remember you won't be the only one dying if you cross me. Your mother will meet you in hell too. In the meantime, have another drink; it looks like you need it."

Jamie gets up and goes to the back bedroom and returns shortly with some blank tapes, paper and pen.

When Jamie returns to the room, he finds McCulley staring out into space, shaking back and forth. McCulley is covered in moisture; it is impossible to tell how much from the water Jamie poured on him and how much is due to the heavy perspiring that he has been doing ever since the officer experienced his moment of sobriety.

"Okay McCulley, I'm going to take a chance just to get this shit over with. I'll take you with me, but first let's get with the tapes." Jamie approaches McCulley while loading a tape recorder with a blank tape. "I want you to tell how you incriminated twelve guys and just in case you don't remember their names, I have a list. Here is the tape recorder...now, for victim number one."

Jamie sets the tape recorder and hands the microphone to McCulley. While McCulley talks, Jamie writes down the incidents he describes.

Jamie starts McCulley off with the first name, "James Willie Nelson-Arrested and convicted on the charge of Sale of Cocaine."

"James Nelson," McCulley intones, "was a kid in the neighborhood who continued to harass me. He would stone my car and run and he sold crack on the corner of "D" Street and Bonanza.

"One day, I was really pissed off and just wanted to hassle this jerk. I saw him from a block away and decided this was the day he was going to leave the streets of Las Vegas.

"I always keep a bag of confiscated rocks in my briefcase and I decided to use them. I parked my car and walked around the block and through the alley; just close enough to him where I knew he couldn't get away.

"I hid behind some bushes and when he walked pass me, I jumped out and wrestled him to the ground and pulled out my bag of rock cocaine and held it in his face. I arrested him for possession with intent to sale. He was found guilty and was sentenced to ten to twenty years."

"Kenneth Patrick!"

"Kenneth Patrick was a "Wanna Be". He terrorized the community, committing small time crimes just to get recognition.

"I stopped him one day while he was hanging out with his "Homies". He snatched away from me and spit in my face and ran. I couldn't catch him and when I returned to my vehicle, everyone was standing around laughing at me. I promised myself that I would get him.

"Three days later, I saw him on the corner and called my partner to meet me, but he was to go on the opposite side of him to make sure he wouldn't get away.

"I got one of my junkie snitches to take a bag of rock cocaine I had with me, and give it to Kenneth. As soon as Kenneth had the bag in his possession, my partner and I rushed him, grabbed him and the bag and charged him with "Possession with Intent to Sell Cocaine", he received five to ten years."

"James Doolittle!"

"James Doolittle was another smart mouth and a faggot. I just didn't like him at all. His thing was running and telling everyone I was around. I didn't need anyone informing on me. So one day I located a stolen car and figured I would put it on him just to teach him a lesson.

"So again, I got one of my stoolies to do my dirty work. I picked this certain stoolie because he gave me some misinformation. His name was Fred Willis. He is on your list also, I guess."

Jamie looks up from his note taking; "Yeah you're right."

"So, I gave Fred a rock to smoke and told him to get James to give him a "blow job" in the vehicle.

"When they were both in the car, with James behind the wheel, my partner and I rode down on them and busted them for "Possession of a Stolen Motor Vehicle". I was not familiar with their arrest record, but both were in and out of jail for several felonies and this time they received five to ten years for being habitual."

"Lumas Taylor!"

"Lumas Taylor was a Black Activist. He was always in the community preaching hatred against the Whites. I just didn't like him for that.

"I took a gun from a junkie who was trying to sell it to me. He said he found it in the alley. I had no reason to doubt him so I gave him two rocks for it.

"I ran the serial numbers and found out it had been used in a homicide and decided to use it to put Lumas away.

"Lumas had a studio apartment on Washington Ave. So one night when he was not home, I climbed in through a window into his apartment and planted the gun.

"After a period of days, I reported to Homicide that three people (junkies) knew who killed William James; they got a warrant and searched Lumas' apartment and found the gun.

"I gave the three junkies a pound of coke to testify against Lumas and say that they saw Lumas do the shooting. He was found guilty and sentenced to ten to twenty years in prison."

"Maurice Taylor!"

"Maurice Taylor-oh he was an easy one. His problem was he wanted to go straight. He had a lot of problems early in life and finally got a job, a wife and a child, but he still hung around with the wrong crowd.

"This particular day, I just wanted to screw somebody Black. I had been irritated all day by Black people.

"A run came out about a shooting and I received the run and made it there just as Maurice was driving away.

"My partner and I stopped the car questioned him, and we saw a gun lying on the back seat. We arrested him and charged him as the shooter.

"The test on the gun came back positive as the gun used in the shooting, but we later found out that the real shooter had thrown the gun into the car, unbeknownst to Maurice, and the shooter left town.

"The witness to the shooting was also forced to leave town by my partner and me and we threatened four other guys in order to get them to testify against Maurice. Maurice received seven and a half years to fifteen years for Second Degree Murder."

"Jesus Mendoza!"

"Jesus Mendoza. He was a gang banger and I felt he was involved in a lot of the crime in the neighborhood. He also was an easy one to set up.

"When it came to B and E's, we always felt that Jesus was involved. So, we arranged to have a house broken into and leaked the news to Jesus. Sure enough, Jesus appeared on the scene looking into the broken window.

"As soon as his head disappeared into the house, we appeared and arrested him for B and E. He received two and a half to five years for Breaking and Entering. This was his second offense."

"Terry White, Lawrence Wilson, and Joseph Phillips."

"Terry, Larry, and Joe...sounds like the Three Stooges. At any rate, these three were my stoolies and they lied to me about a drug buy and they were also "drug runners". These guys went to prison legally... I didn't have to set them up.

"I knew when they made their drug pick up. So, I informed Narcotics, and they caught them red-handed with four pounds of Coke. They were charged with Delivery with Intent to Sell. They received Ten to Twenty years."

McCulley stops at this point and looks over at Jamie. With a deep breath, McCulley finishes his confession with the people Jamie wants to hear the most about, "Your sons on the other hand, Marvin and Jamie Collins–I paid a junkie a couple of times to say he purchased coke from your sons' home.

"When the raid came down, I assisted and went into the back bedroom, opened the window, and retrieved a bag of coke I had placed outside the window just before the raid.

"They received ten to twenty for Possession with Intent to Sell. All nine of these men were railroaded into prison. If I hadn't done what I had, none of these men would have been locked up today.

"I am sorry for what I have done and I am terribly sorry for all the pain I've caused for the innocent people involved.

"If I could, I would take back all the things I have done, but since that can't happen, I am trying to make amends now by admitting to the fact that all nine of the guys mentioned were deliberately framed by me, Clarence McCulley.

"I am not being forced to admit to anything and I am making this statement on my own free will.

"The second part to this confession has to do with the bombing of the Mirage, MGM, Venetian, and Caesars' Palace hotels in the city of Las Vegas.

"Involved are fifteen people including myself:

John Beasley	Glenn McDonald
Dave Garner	James Orr
Jeff Newsome	Wilson Owens
Matt Peterson	Jack Riviera
Donald Sharp	Keith Stenstrom
James Witherspoon	Mark Wilcox
Shorty Watson	James Burg

"We all have conspired to blow up the above mentioned hotels. Until today, my understanding of the whole situation was that the supposedly bombings were going to be a hoax. The plot was to take place as follows:

"Myself, Donald Sharp, Mark Wilcox, and James Burg were to walk into our assigned hotels, each carrying ten bundles of six sticks of dynamite which are to be placed in strategic locations around the outer perimeter of each building.

"Each bundle will have a timer, which is supposed to be set at twelve o'clock midnight on New Year's Eve."

"We were to leave each location and meet up back at the bar on Boulder Highway. At that time, all fifteen of us are to be together when each hotel is to be called and appraised of the situation. We figured this would result in mass hysteria.

At that time, over 750,000 people are expected to be on the strip and our bombs would really cause some problems. But according to our plan, the bombs would really turn out to be flares. We were planning to use the panic and confusion to extort money from the casinos and to publicize our concerns about the plight of the White men in America; about how we're slowly losing our rights, jobs, and dignity to other races.

"Today, I found out real dynamite is to be used, not flares, and that I was to die in one of the explosions as a "martyr" to our cause. I am not giving this confession because of threats or fear for my life. I have not been made any promises or talked with any police officials pertaining to these matters.

"I am making this confession solely on the basis that I do not wish to hurt anyone and because the information that was presented to me was false. People–a lot of people–were going to die and I was going to be betrayed by my so-called friends and accomplices. I do wish to cooperate with the authorities and will supply all and any information necessary to place the individuals involved behind bars."

McCulley looks at Jamie. His mouth is dry from all the talking he did in the recorder. Emotionally spent and physically exhausted, the only thing McCulley wants to do now is put the whole situation behind him as far as he can.

"Okay Jamie, how's that? Do you have enough information now? Will that convince you I'm for real?"

Jamie stands up and gathers all the papers together and rewinds the tape as he replies to McCulley, "No, not quite. There's still the matter of you being alive and my escape."

McCulley whips his head around to face Jamie, "Wait a minute, you can't do that. You said if I gave you a confession you would allow me to live and you said I could go with you."

Jamie cuts McCulley off, "Relax McCulley, I know what I said, but we have a few things to work out.

"First, if you live and are not in custody, your friends may call off the bombings and in order to make a good case... we have to have intent. We have to have the ways and means; we have to have solid proof so they will never get out of prison.

"Second, in the beginning, your demise was going to be my diversion. Now that you're going with me, I have to figure out something else. So, help me think. We don't have much time. I feel the most important thing is figuring out how to fake your death."

8

THE IMPOSSIBLE ESCAPE

McCulley laughs, but the tremor in his voice gives away the seriousness of the situation. "I don't like this shit. I'm tired of listening to you talk about my death. Why do I have to die at all? Why don't we just leave here while we have a chance?

"We could leave Ramirez tied up and give her the instructions and the tapes. Later, when we are away from the authorities, we could contact the prosecutor's office and explain what's going on. Maybe later we can arrange my death so the plot can continue and the bad guys can get caught."

McCulley stares intently at Jamie. *I don't want to die, he thinks...not now, not like this. Get gunned down by my ex-friends to hell with that. The least Jamie can do is give me a sporting chance.*

"You make it sound so easy. All we have to do is pack up and leave...like no one will be looking for us. I have diversions, but none of that would cover our asses if we did that. We would just be common criminals with nothing accomplished. Don't forget the money from the bank. We'd just be plain old bank robbers."

McCulley blinks as he picks up on a word, "What do you mean 'we'?"

Jamie tries to hide a smile as he sees McCulley's eyes become wide. It seems that the worse things get, the funnier they become to him. Laughter and being able to understand the joke of being a human is the only thing that separates us from the animals.

Jamie is learning this now, with two police officers hostage, a robbery, and the incident with the guard's wife, and his own kids being locked up.

"Jamie is trying his best to not just break up laughing. If you told him this would be the situation ten years ago, he would have laughed in your face and thought you were stoned.

"Now, faced with that very reality, he feels like laughing, but in his own face. Jamie nods his head at McCulley, "If you leave with me it becomes 'we,' bro'."

McCulley just stares at Jamie. *This man is serious, he is going to let me walk out with him, but if I do, then what? I'll be blamed for everything he has done; they'll really be looking to cook my ass then.*

Still, what choice do I have? I either go with this sucker's plan or I get gunned down as a decoy. Looks like we'll have to be partners for now… for now.

"So, if *we* don't leave now, what are *we* going to do? *We* can't just sit here. McCulley says with more than a hint of urgency in his voice.

"Well, I got what I came for, plus some added baggage. I guess we may as well leave."

"Where were you headed anyway?" McCulley asks Jamie.

Jamie looks at McCulley for a second before he responds with a huff, "That's none of your business until we get there. Just because you made a few confessions, that doesn't mean I'm going to spill my guts to you. Just be patient. As a matter of fact…wait, what's that?"

"What, what are you talking about?" McCulley asks.

The sound of squealing car tires heard in front of the house draws Jamie's attention. Jamie puts a hand up to shush McCulley. "Be quiet and listen. I hear cars… let me look out the window. Well I'll be damned! They're here."

"What, who's here?"

"Your buddies…now sit down and shut up. It looks like I have to go back to my original plan."

Jamie takes another peek out the window; "I'll be damned. It looks like the whole police department is out there."

"I thought you had everything covered. How did they know you were here," asks McCulley in a screeching tone.

Jamie turns his attention away from the window and back to McCulley, "You're a cop, think. It was probably the neighbors or someone who saw me. Everything is all right, they just got here a few hours earlier than I expected.

"It's early in the morning and dark. I can use the darkness for our escape. That makes it a little better.

"If you are for real about what you said, now you have the opportunity to prove it. Here have another drink. I have to think a bit." Jamie hands the bottle to McCulley and begins to pace the floor.

McCulley manages to bring the bottle to his mouth. As he takes a drink, something creeps into his mind: *according to plan?*
This has to be the dumbest sucker alive if being discovered and having the place surrounded by the entire police force is 'according to plan'. McCulley takes another drink from the bottle–*dumbest, or the most dangerous.*

"So, everything is going according to plan, huh?"

"Yes. The only problem is that I was going to call the police, but they came instead. Call...yeah. That's what I will do. Where is the phone? Oh, here it is...911"

Jamie dials and paces the room, waiting for the 911 operator to pick up the line. Everything will have to go smoothly on the phone or all is lost. Jamie's biggest fear right now isn't the cops outside; it's the 911 operator. If she doesn't believe his story, or take him seriously, the plan won't work. If the plan doesn't work, then Jamie knows his sons will never see light of day, and he won't get to either.

The voice on the other end greets Jamie, "911– where is your problem?"

"Yes ma'am, I have a message for you to deliver."

The voice sounds irritated at this comment, "Sir, this is an emergency line. If you want to deliver a message, you have dialed the wrong number."

Jamie, expecting something like this to happen cuts to the chase, "Shut up lady and listen. Right now, the police have surrounded my house. Tell them not to attempt entry or there will be two dead cops in here."

"Sir, what is…?"

Jamie hangs up the phone in the middle of the operator's reply.

"What did she say?" McCulley asks.

"Nothing really… in a minute or so, that phone is going to ring. So, get ready–that's when the shit is going to hit the fan."

Dead cops? He just said two dead cops? McCulley's mind is racing. *What the hell. I don't want to die– he said Ramirez would live from the start. Has this guy lost his mind? I thought we had a deal!*

"What do you mean? Are you for real about the two dead cops?"

Jamie doesn't even give McCulley a glance, "No fool, but they don't know that. I just said that to buy some time."

"Some time for what? Do you want to fill me in on what's going to happen?"

Now Jamie finally looks over at McCulley, "Okay, like I said you now have the opportunity to prove yourself. We are going to go through with my original plan. So here it is…but first we have to prepare you."

"What do you mean prepare me?" McCulley does not like what he hears.

"Just hold on, I have something for you to wear." Jamie runs into the bedroom again and returns with some civilian clothes: a shirt, pants, and a skullcap. "Here put this on."

McCulley tries to move his arms but is stopped by his bonds, "Now, how in the hell am I going to change clothes if I'm chained to this pole?"

Before Jamie can answer the phone rings, "Wait a minute, the phone is ringing." Jamie picks up the phone, "Hello, can I help you?"

The voice on the other end is stern, a bit too stern–almost to the point of abusive, "Okay, young man, this is Sheriff Kerns of the Metropolitan Police Department. I want you to surrender my officers and come out with your hands up. The house is totally surrounded. There is no way you can get away."

Jamie frowns, "Is that all you have to say Sheriff?" I'm disappointed."

"No. We want all of this to end peacefully and we don't want anyone hurt."

Jamie cuts the man off, "Up until now, everything was okay. Now, it looks as though I'm pushed into a corner. You back off and I'll let you know who is going to surrender."

"Look Mr. Collins, we know who you are, where you come from, and what you did for a living. Now, if you are having a problem, maybe we can help you."

"Yeah, help me the way you helped my kids. They were innocent and you helped them into a cell in Indian Springs. No telling what you may do to me–and I am guilty of something."

There is a brief pause at the other end of the phone; "Is that what this is all about...your children?"

"Yes, it is. My children were framed by this police officer I have in here, and nothing was done about it. So I decided to take matters into my own hands. I want my sons released from prison right now and I want justice–and not 'field adjudication,' either...for myself."

The sheriff's voice becomes more reasonable, "Look Jamie, if you give yourself up, we will try and resolve the matter peacefully. But then there is the matter of money stolen from the bank. You will have to answer for that."

Jamie cuts the sheriff off again, "Look Sheriff, the money is mine and my family for all the problems your corrupt officers caused us, so you can forget it. Sheriff, before we go any further with this bullshit conversation, I want you to know I'm not going to give up, you're not getting the money and if you try to force your way in, I will kill these two cops."

Jamie looks at the windows. "If you could see the windows here, you would notice they all have steel sliding shutters. So you can't shoot in any tear gas or stun grenades, plus there are booby traps set all around the house. So until I am ready to come out, you just sit and rest. Have a nice day." Jamie hangs up the phone and turns to McCulley.

"Okay Jamie, what now," McCulley asks, a little shell shocked from the way Jamie handled the conversation with the sheriff.

"Go ahead and start changing clothes and leave your bulletproof vest on. You're going to need it."

"Need it? Need what? What do you mean I'm going to need my vest?"

"Like I said McCulley, you are the diversion and on top of it, this is the way you're going to prove yourself to me. Jamie drops down on one knee to come level with McCulley's eyes, "If you are planning to pull some shit, I will have one opportunity to put a bullet in the back of your head."

McCulley holds his breath as Jamie finishes his statement, "If you're on the level, you will probably end up with a broken rib or two. Either way, you're going out that door with me or without me."

"Okay, explain to me how I'm going to be your diversion and how the hell are we going to get out of here."

"First off, I have to get the ketamine and give Ramirez another dose before she wakes up. This way, she will remain unconscious through the rest of this ordeal."

Jamie goes into the kitchen, prepares another dose of the drug for Ramirez and returns and places it over her nose and mouth. "Okay, now that's done, turn on the TV, maybe they will have something on about us."

Jamie heads into the back bedroom with the tape recorder and all the tapes. He places all but one of tapes in a green duffel bag. That one is inserted into the recorder, which is then placed atop a box.

He runs a wire around the door, over the ceiling and back to the floor, where it is connected to the pull pin of a police stun grenade that is tied to a chair nailed to the floor. Jamie then sheds his clothes and puts on police riot gear and a helmet.

Jamie goes to the closet and brings out a mannequin, and dresses it and places it in the chair. He fetches a red can containing gasoline, opens it and pours the contents around the room.

Then he turns on the tape recorder, leaves the room and closes the door. He enters another room where he sits down and writes a letter for Ramirez. The letter is an important element of Jamie's plan and he hopes he has made enough of an impression on Ramirez where she will follow his instructions.

Dear Ramirez,

In the past few months we have spent time together. Not enough to really trust each other, but enough that I hope you have developed a little understanding of me.

I told you that I have to give you a lot of responsibility and I know you can handle it.

But understand this responsibility is not to be taken lightly. There are many lives at stake and you have to handle things the way you see fit. I just hope you will think about all the things that have happened over the last few hours and come to a conclusion in my favor. If not, all the things I have planned will have been for nothing.

In a few days, I will call you at your home to give you the location of a green duffel bag, which contains a number of recordings, pictures and video film of McCulley's friends plotting to blow up several hotels. The duffel bag will also contain a tape recording of McCulley's confession of how he railroaded my sons and nine other men into prison.

I need you to locate an F.B.I. agent you can trust and share this information with him. You and the agent will decide together how to handle this "explosive" situation. Ha-Ha... pun intended!

Please, Ramirez, under no circumstances are you to divulge any information with the Sheriff's office. Information will leak to the newspapers and everything will be for nil. Please explain to the FBI that I will not give up the information unless my sons are released, and the $757,000 belongs to me to compensate me for my trouble.

PLEASE HELP ME

JAMIE C.

After completing the letter, Jamie returns to the living room. McCulley has everything on that Jamie gave him to wear. Things aren't perfectly adjusted and McCulley looks like a half dressed tourist that has been drinking too much in the desert sun. Jamie decides that he will just have to make due with the way McCulley looks. This isn't a fashion show; it's a hostage situation.

"So my clothes fit pretty well on you."

McCulley looks over himself and replies "Yeah, they would fit better if you take this chain off." He looks at Jamie and sees that Jamie changed out of civilian clothes and put on some police gear.

The gear looks familiar to McCulley and he knows why. *That's my stuff! He took my extra gear and suited up! This guy is crazy...*McCulley's train of thought is broken by the television.

"We have some late breaking news: The police have a barricaded gunman at 6116 Fawn Circle. That's in the area of Jones Boulevard and 95 Expressway.

The suspect barricaded inside is believed to be holding the missing police officers hostage, but as of this time no demands have been made.

We now have conformation: the two missing police officers are in the house. It's unknown whether or not they are injured. At this time, we have no ID on the suspect."

The news broadcast is also being seen at the Indian Springs State Prison. Jamie's sons are alerted to the broadcast, which gets the prison staff a little excited.

Something is happening on the outside. It was rumored something was going down soon–something big– and now the people on the inside were learning that it was for real.

A father of two of the inmates was supposed to do something that would help spring them and a few others from jail. Things like this didn't happen often and the prison started to buzz with the news. Two inmates in particular were astounded by what they are hearing.

"Hey Jamie, Marvin...turn on your TVs' I think what you have been waiting for is on now. Get the rest of the guys' attention they need to hear this."

Jamie, Marvin and a few of their friends gathered around their televisions in their cells. The news is on, but not at its regular time. Something is important enough to break the station's schedule to air a live report.

"Marvin, daddy robbed a bank and kidnapped McCulley. He's doing what he said he would do."

Marvin just stares at the television without replying to Jamie Jr. All the prisoners with television sets are viewing the news and begin hurling their barbs at the two young men. None of their remarks get through to the boys, however. They are too absorbed in what the television is reveling about their father's new way of bringing about justice.

"Yeah, man, yo'daddy is one crazy sucker," exclaims one inmate.

"This will be a first for me. I have been in prison for ten years and never seen a whole family locked up at one time. I guess we can make room for him in Clarence's cell. He'll be leaving soon." jokes another.

"Come on Willie; he may get us out of here. Why don't you have a little confidence?"

"Awe man, to hell wit you! How the hell do you think that man is going to get us out of here by committing more crimes than all of us together?"

"Look man, why don't you two be quiet so we can hear what's going on, another inmate yells. "We won't know anything unless we hear what's going on in the world."

The twelve men sit and watch the news, hoping that what Jamie was doing, will get them out of prison. In their minds they aren't in prison any more. They are completely lost in what is going on in the television sets. The tension begins to ease and many sigh in relief and then hold their breath. The television news flash is giving them something that many never thought they would see or know again–hope.

The newscast continues:

"We have learned that the house was rented to a single man only a month ago. We have talked to neighbors, but no one seems to know him. They say that most of the time he's not home. They have never seen him have any visitors; they feel he is a loner of some sort.

We just received information that the suspect also fits the description of the man wanted for questioning in the hold up of the security guard at the bank on Spring Mountain and Valley View. And he appears to be the same man who broke in to the home of the security guard and tied up his wife.

It seems as if this man is on a one-man crime spree. So far, we have him wanted for kidnapping the security guard's wife, robbing a bank, and now kidnapping and holding two Metro Police Officers.

"Is there any word about the officers held in the home, John?"

"No Doug, but we do know that contact has been made with the suspect and that he refuses to give himself up.

"We also understand that the suspect says his sons were framed by the police officers he is holding captive.

We are unsure as to what the suspect's intentions are and we don't understand what he hopes to gain by robbing the bank and holding and kidnapping so many people, but it looks like the suspect may be holding the police officers in exchange for his sons.

"Doug as you can see, the house seems to be well fortified. We are unable to see any movement inside the home because of the metal shutters.

It seems that the suspect was well prepared for the arrival of the police, but still we can't understand what he hopes to accomplish. There is no way for escape as you notice the house is totally surrounded and the only way for the suspect to get out unharmed is to surrender".

"John has anyone surfaced who knows the suspect?"

"No Doug, at this moment, the suspect is a total stranger, but I am quite sure that when the telecast is seen, someone in Las Vegas will come forth who recognizes him."

"Okay, John we will return to you shortly as the situation develops.

"Again, we repeat the two missing police officers have been located. They are being held at a location on the Westside of Las Vegas. It is believed the gunman is holding the police officers; he feels were responsible for framing his two sons who have been sentenced to prison.

"We are unsure whether the police officers have been injured or if they are still alive.

"The house in which the two officers are being held is well fortified as though the gunman had planned this ordeal over a period of time. It has also come to our attention, that the gunman is a suspect in the robbery of the security guard at Valley View and Spring Mountain earlier this week and for the kidnapping of the security guard's wife.

"Just a minute, we have something else coming in from John. John, what's going on now?"

"Well Doug, we are going to be speaking shortly to a well-known acquaintance of the suspect. We just received information that an old friend of his lives very close by. We are going to be leaving here and will report back to you in a few minutes."

"Okay John, keep us updated on the events of this major crime spree.

"Again, we have another example of a vigilante taking matters into his own hands and committing crimes of his own to rectify what he perceives as an injustice against him.

"Carla Simmons is downtown at Police Headquarters speaking with Community Information Sergeant Jack Carson. Carla, go ahead.

"Doug, we're at Police Headquarters with Sergeant Jack Carson of Community Information. Sergeant Carson, would you please give us a little insight on the two Police Officers being held captive by the gunman who states these officers are responsible for framing his sons?"

"Ms Simmons, here at Metro, we stand behind our officers. Each one was chosen because he or she met our high standards.

Officers Ramirez and McCulley are of high quality and graduated at the top of their classes. The training they received would help them maintain order and peace in the community, not wage war on undesirables.

We, at Metro feel that the suspect is at his wits' end and is using whatever means he can to obtain the release of his sons.

His sons were found guilty in a court of law and were judged by their peers. We are satisfied with those findings and do not doubt our fellow police officers."

"Sergeant Carson, we have information that Officer McCulley had several run-ins with the people in his area and that several complaints were made against Officer McCulley. Can you explain?"

"That doesn't have anything to do with the price of tea in China. Our officers receive complaints daily from the public; that only proves to us that they are doing their jobs."

"So, if an officer receives a complaint several times from the same individual, that doesn't raise your eyebrows? Could the suspect be telling the truth?"

"We investigate every civilian complaint to its fullest and if anything comes up to show that the officer

was in the wrong, he will be disciplined, and we found no problem with Officer McCulley or his partner, Officer Ramirez or they would not be on the force today."

"Okay Doug, that's all the information we have. This is Carla Simmons reporting live from Police Headquarters."

"Thanks Carla. Now, we are going back to John who is reporting live from the home of Rena Taylor, a long time friend of the suspect."

"Ms Taylor, can you tell me how long you have known the suspect and who he is?"

"It's been about six years, and at one time we were pretty close."

"Close, you mean boyfriend and girlfriend?"

"Yes, that's correct."

McCulley looks over at Jamie and back at the woman on the television set. *She isn't half-bad; I wonder how Jamie got her? I wonder what else about Jamie there is that I don't know.*

"Hey Jamie, you mean to tell me that was a woman of yours?"

"Yeah, me and Rena were pretty cool at one time. Now we are just good friends. Now hold your questions. I want to hear what she has to say." The two turn their attention back to the newscast.

"And how long was that relationship?"

"It lasted about a year."

"Could you describe for our listening audience what type of person he was?"

"Jamie and I spent a lot of time together and we cared for each other so much. So much we remained friends after our break-up."

Rena's voice seemed a bit distant at this point.

"Do you think the officers inside have anything to worry about?"

Rena snaps her mind back into the moment, *"First off, I do not appreciate you coming into my home asking me personal questions, but I decided to cooperate just to get you off my back. So when I answer this question, there will be no more and if you come around my home again, there won't be any questions and answers.*

"No, the police officers don't have anything to worry about. I doubt Jamie would hurt anyone, but understand that Jamie's sons are in jail because of that asshole, McCulley and guess what? So is my son.

"So, if Jamie crosses that line and does harm to McCulley, you can best to believe the bastard deserves it. Don't stop here just to ask questions about Jaime go through the community and ask questions about Officer McCulley. You'll be surprised with the answers you get there.

"Another thing, if Jamie should do harm to McCulley, he will be doing the community a big favor. Jamie, if you are watching, I love you and take care. Good bye Mr. Newsman.

" Ma'am hold on, you said Jamie. What's his last name?

The reporter turns to the camera in time to see Rena slam the door in his face. Trying to play everything off on live television, the reporter closes with a deliberate misinterpretation of what Rena has said.

"Well Doug that was the suspect's ex-girlfriend and from what she says, Jamie, as she calls him, can be unpredictable and potentially dangerous."

"Thanks John, please keep us informed of the events as they develop. Well, that ends our special news report. Stay tuned to Channel 7 EyeWitness News for further details. Now we return you to your regular scheduled program.

As a commercial appears about a new diet drink that promises instant weight loss and more energy, McCulley sits back into his chair and whistles thoughtfully at an image in his mind.

"So, Ms Taylor is your ex-girlfriend? Not bad."

"That was several years ago, and as she said, we're good friends now."

Just friends, Jamie thinks. *How many times have I thought about her through these years? How many times I*

*wanted to change things, but couldn't? 'Just friends'
doesn't do any justice. That was a term reserved for
women that didn't want to be intimate with someone, but
didn't want to hurt their feelings.*

What Jamie and Rena had was beyond that. Jamie
sighed a bit as the vision of Rena danced through his head.
*What we had was beyond that, but what now? What can
happen now that I am in this situation?*

McCulley breaks the silence; "My uniform fits you
well."

Jamie snaps out of his thoughts, "I know I'm glad
you had it in the trunk of your vehicle. When I was doing
my investigation of you, I found out that you belonged to
Tactical Section and that fell right into my plan. You had
the black combat uniform, shotgun, the M16, and to aid in
our escape, smoke bombs."

Jamie then turns around to model the gear, "Now
that I'm fully dressed, how do I look? Can you recognize
me when I pull this visor down?"

"No, not really, but what are you going to do in that
uniform?"

"Let me put it this way, it's my way out."

"And I have to wear civilian clothes? That's a little
backwards. I'm beginning not to like this." McCulley says
with a bit of anxiety in his voice.

Jamie looks at McCulley with a slight grin, "Well
McCulley, if you weren't such an asshole, you wouldn't be
in this situation. Believe you me, this is the only thing I
could come up with to get us both out of here. Plus, it
helps prove your loyalty to me."

Jamie gets in McCulley's face and tries to
emphasis the importance and sincerity of his next words,
"Understand this, both of us are going to put our lives on
the line. Both of us can be killed or spend the rest of our
lives in prison. I would much rather die in front of this
house than to be locked up. So, now is the moment of
truth. Are you going to go through with this, or are you
going to give yourself up and risk the life of your mother?"

McCulley, seeing he has no other options, responds to Jamie, "I'm with you Jamie, let's do it."

McCulley tries to struggle with the clothes that he has placed on himself. He isn't getting much ground though. *I look like a damned vagrant. How the hell does he expect me to dress myself chained to this pole? Why doesn't he help me out? I swear that sucker is enjoying all of this.*

As if he could read McCulley's mind, Jamie goes over and unlocks his prisoner. "Okay, here are the keys. Take those handcuffs off and finish dressing."

McCulley makes quick work of the lock and finishes dressing, "Okay, Jamie, now what?"

Jamie goes to the rear of his chair and brings out two wooden arm braces with straps shaped like the letter "L" and sits them in front of McCulley, "Sit down; I have some braces for you to put on."

McCulley looks at the wooden braces in Jamie's hands, "What kind of braces?"

McCulley's mouth drops open. *So much for my sporting chance...what the hell is all of this? They won't know if I am an officer or a criminal coming out like this—not to mention that I have civilian clothes on. Those guys out there will think I am armed and shoot me dead in a second.*

"Are you out of your mind? Those suckers will kill me."

"Okay, then you're going to prison."

"Look Jamie, I know I said I would do this, but man I'm going to die out there." McCulley is pleading his case to his captor.

"No you're not. That's the purpose of the smoke bombs and your bulletproof vest. The worst, like I said, is a broken rib or two. I will be there to help and make sure you don't die. Believe me; we both will leave here together."

"Jesus, Jamie! They'll blow me full of holes. That vest ain't gonna protect me from a headshot. I will feel a lot better if we took away the main reason they would continue to shoot me–those braces. I don't need them to have more then one chance or reason to blow me away. Either you get rid of the braces or you can shoot me now!"

"Okay McCulley, you win. That was the old plan you were supposed to die. Now that you are coming along with me, we do have to keep you alive. Forget the braces."

McCulley breaths a sigh of relief and quickly pulls off the braces and they both give in, "Okay Jamie, we've come this far, now I am ready to go all the way. I am depending on you. Please don't let me down."

Jamie tries to comfort McCulley. "McCulley, we're going to make it, we're going to get out together. Just be patient and do as I say and we will make it."

Jamie looks over at McCulley and checks his watch. *No time, no time for foolishness now. We have to get a move on; everything has to get going.*
"Sit here for a few minutes; I have to set things up in the back room. Another news report is about to come on. Watch it and keep me up to date."

The two men advert their attention to the television set. The news reporter is back on with an update of the situation. His studio hair looks a bit out of place, almost if he had to go on before the make-up artist could get a full hold of the situation. Trying to be professional, the anchorman doesn't let his looks get in his way of reporting the news. This was something big; this could possibly make or break his career.

"Good morning, I'm Douglas Wayne reporting to you from Channel 7 Studios. There is a tense hostage situation at 6116 Fawn Circle, where a gunman who is also wanted for the robbery of an armored car security officer and the kidnapping of the guard's wife is holding two Metro Police Officers captive.

"It's unknown at this time if any harm has come to the police officers or if an attempt has been made by the police to enter the building. We have our reporter on the street, John Wiggs at the scene.

"John, are you there? Are there any new developments since our last broadcast?"

John Wiggs looks into the camera on cue, *"No, Doug, there has been very little contact with the people inside and the phone goes unanswered. Right now it's not known if anyone is alive, but we do hope nothing tragic has happened. Right now, we're going to speak with the Sheriff.*

John makes his way over to where the Sheriff Kerns is standing, *"Sheriff, can you elaborate on what's happening and what's being done to get the police officers out safely?"*

The Sheriff reacts to the question and gives a brief statement, "Right now, John, all we can do is wait. I am sure the officers are safe because Mr. Collins is planning to use them as a bargaining tool. We've had the house checked out and there is no way we can insert tear gas. So, we will sit and wait and see what develops."

Wiggs pushes on with his questions, *"Sheriff, have you gotten anymore information on the suspect?"*

"All we know at this time is that the suspect is a resident of Las Vegas and that's all.

"Sheriff Kerns, we appreciate your comments and we know you have to get back to the situation at hand."

Wiggs finishes his words with the Sheriff and goes over to where another Channel 7-*crew* member is motioning toward him.

"Doug, we have a person here who states she is a good friend of Jamie Collins. Her name is Anita Goin. Ms Goin, we understand that you are an acquaintance of Mr. Collins.

McCulley draws Jamie's attention again to the TV, "Hey Jamie, I think you had better come in here and listen to this. It's another one of your bitches; I mean one of your female friends."

"Yes, I am his beautician. It's been about two or three weeks since I have seen him. I just want you to know he's not a killer; he's a kind, gentle, man. I am well aware

of what's going through his mind and I am only here to try and convince him this is not the way to set things straight.

Jamie, if you are looking at the news, I want you to know that no matter what happens, I am still in your corner. Just please don't let this end in your death. I will be there for you. That's all I have to say. I am not going to answer any more questions. Thank you.

Just like the other interview with Rena Taylor, the woman walks out of the camera's sight without even looking back. The reporter has no choice but to try to play this off again. It seems like it will be a long day for the news crew at Channel 7.

"There you are Doug, a plea from a friend. It seems that Mr. Collins has quite a few friends in and out of town, but that still doesn't change what he has done. There still aren't any changes in the situation, Doug. We will keep you posted. This is John Wiggs, reporting live from Channel7 News.

McCulley leans back in his chair. "Hey Jamie, who is she?"

Jamie responds in a way that makes McCulley think he wasn't really paying attention to the words as they came out, "She's just another friend. She cuts my hair. That reminds me. I have to call her before I leave town."

McCulley sits back and lets a small chuckle slip. *What the hell does this guy think, he's just going to waltz out of here and be totally free? Getting out of here alive is just one part of a very big plan that is needed to be taken care of. Hell, if we get out alive, we are going to be on the run for most of our lives. There is no way that we can stay here long enough to make casual phone calls.*

"Oh, somehow we're going to get past a hundred cops and a couple hundred people," McCulley retorts, "and during our escape, you're going to stop and make a phone call. Yeah right!"

"Don't worry; we'll be long gone when I do that. Everything is ready in the back. We have ten minutes before we're on our way."

Then McCulley suddenly begins to shake. The crescendo of fear that has been building up just broke through the floodgates.

Ten minutes? I can't do this; I'm going to die! I don't want to die! What choice do I have, if I stay in here, I'll die, if I go with Jamie, I'll probably die too. Why did it all have to come down to this, why was I such an asshole all my life? I wasn't like this before, what the hell was I thinking?

Now this is it, in the time that is less than it takes to bake a pizza, I'm going to go out and be the distraction for Jamie. Distraction my ass, I'm going to be shot to ribbons out there. I know it; those guys don't play around. They will suspect something is up and then I'm a dead man. Shoot first, ask questions later. Shit, I'm a dead man, a walking dead man.

"Man, I'm about to lose control of my body. The fear has never been so strong I can't stop shaking." McCulley stammers out.

Jamie tries to calm him down. "Be cool McCulley, I know this is not Hollywood... I wish we had whatever they use to become super heroes, but I guess we have to rely on plain, old adrenaline."

McCulley's face comes alive with a sudden inspiration, "Hey Jamie, I got something that may help. I have some cocaine in my pocket."

Jamie gives McCulley a stunned look, "McCulley, the last thing I need now is some cocaine. Why don't you keep that stuff in your pocket and let's get ready to get out of here."

"Jamie, I'm the one who's going to face a hail of gunfire. I think the last thing you can do is allow me to fix myself up so I don't feel it."

"Listen, McCulley, I am letting you take this chance to prove yourself to me. This is for your ass and your mother's ass. You might want to be sober for this; besides, I don't trust your ass enough to have you coked up on me."

Jamie picks up the letter he wrote Ramirez and walks over to her. He stands over Ramirez, trying to decide where to put the letter so she could find it, *I wonder if I put this note in her shirt pocket will she find it or should I put it in her shoe? Why not put it in her front pocket. When she gets out of here that will probably be the first place she puts her hands.*

"Okay, good idea, now for the phone call."

"You and those damn phone calls! Who the hell are you calling?"

Jamie smiles at McCulley while dialing the phone, "Your boss, who else."

"911, what is your problem?"

"This is Jamie Collins; would you please have the Sheriff give me a call? Just tell him, I'm the one in the house he has surrounded."

Jamie hangs up the phone and walks over to the CD player and puts on a disk.

"One more thing, I have to put on a song I want to hear while we are on our way out. It's James Brown's 'THE BIG PAYBACK'."

Then the phone rings, Jamie goes over to pick it up, "That's it, you ready to "rock and roll"?"

McCulley looks nervous and pleads for a hit of coke, "Wait, one blow."

Jamie shakes his head as he answers the phone, "You and that damn coke. Hold on while I answer the phone." Jamie puts the receiver to his head, "Sheriff?"

"Yes." responds the voice on the other end.

"Have you ever seen the movie 'Butch Cassidy and the Sundance Kid'," asks Jamie with a smile on his face.

The Sheriff's reply is a bit puzzled, "Yes, I have."

"Picture the ending." Jamie hangs up the phone, looks at McCulley and hopes that he is ready, "Time to get going, Butch."

McCulley's eyes start to narrow as he accepts his destiny, "Yeah, time to go…"

Jamie goes over the plan with McCulley, "When I open the door, I am going to roll this smoke bomb. You walk out and start yelling, 'Don't shoot, it's me McCulley."

Jamie takes a deep breath, looks at McCulley while he takes out two smoke grenades and slowly opens the front door. As the door opens, he pulls the pin on the grenade and tosses it on the porch and rolls out on the porch, followed by McCulley, "Ready? Go!"

McCulley rushes out the door through the smoke. The smoke stings his eyes but he doesn't stop, "Don't shoot, it's me, McCulley!" he screams desperately. "Don't shoot, it's..."

McCulley runs out of the house and into the smoke, three shots meet him in his chest. His forward motion came to a quick stop when the bullets strike the bulletproof vest. The pain was agonizing and McCulley lets out a loud screech that pierces Jamie's heart. Jamie watches as McCulley hits the ground.

Jamie made his way toward McCulley, as he held his prep radio close to his mouth, and begins to yell, "Command Post One-stop shooting! It's McCulley! Police Officer down! Police Officer down! This is Scout Alpha-13. I'm on the porch. The man who came out is Officer McCulley. Hold your fire! Hold your fire!"

chapter

9

THE CHASE

"Okay you got to help me," Jamie says nervously to McCulley. "I'm going to attempt to carry you to the emergency wagon."

He struggles to lift McCulley as other officers run toward them.

"It's okay. I got him," he yells to the approaching officers. "He'll be all right. The perp is in the house, barricaded in the back room. The officers that went in will need back-up."

"How's McCulley? And where is Ramirez?" inquires an officer.

"He took a few in the chest. It seems like he may have a few broken ribs. He had his vest on. I guess Ramirez is still in the house."

Just as Jamie gets McCulley to his feet, the sheriff approaches him. "Just a minute Officer, before you go anywhere. As soon as you get this man to the hospital, I want you to report to my office. Who told you to go on that porch? You were ordered to surround the building and watch for movements, not go inside."

"Sir, I wasn't going inside. I just wanted a prime position, and if I hadn't been on the porch, our own men might have killed Officer McCulley."

The sheriff shakes his head, "We'll deal with that later; get McCulley to the hospital."

"Yes sir."

Jamie smiles to himself, grabs McCulley by his belt and starts walking to the E.M.S. van, "Wow, that was close," he mutters under his breath.

The paramedics meet Jamie and lay McCulley on a gurney, strap him in and then lift him up into the back of the van.

"Get us to UMC in a hurry," Jamie orders. "This officer has been shot three times in the chest."

One of the paramedics quickly removes McCulley's shirt to reveal three large purplish-black bruises where the bullets had struck. The other technician takes the patient's vital signs.

Crackling comes over the prep radios as voices try to get in touch with the Sheriff.

"Command Mobil One, we're inside the house. We have Ramirez. She seems to be okay, but suspect gave her some kind of drug. She's unconscious but appears to be breathing normally."

"Any sign of the suspect?"

"No sir, we think he is locked in the rear room. As a matter of fact, sir, we know he's in there. He's yelling through the door."

Another EMS team enters the house and removes Ramirez on a gurney. The police are in the house hovering around and hugging the walls of the hallway as they listen to Jamie's voice come through the door, shouting, "Get back, you're not taking me alive."

Then two shots ring out. The officers hearing the shots, kick open the door, which causes an incendiary grenade to explode, setting the room on fire.

"Sheriff, two gunshots just came from inside the room... we're going in."

"Sir, we kicked the door in and some kind of device was set off, causing an explosion, which set the room on fire. We're going to need the fire department right away."

"Everybody out of the house, the flames are going to engulf the house." responds the sheriff trying to react to the situation.

While the police are simultaneously talking to a machine and now fighting a fire, Jamie and McCulley are riding away listening to everything on the prep radio, "McCulley, how are you doing?"

"He'll be all right," responds the medic riding in the back with them. "From the looks of it, there are some broken ribs. You won't be running around too much for a while, Officer. You're going to have to rest for about six weeks until your ribs heal. It's going to hurt like hell, but they'll give you something for the pain."

Jamie smiles, "You see McCulley; I told you so. Now everything else is downhill. When we get to the hospital, you go in and I will get the car. Make sure you get something for the pain."

Jamie removes his helmet and leans back against the wall of the truck and addresses the paramedic who is securing McCulley's head to the stretcher, "What's your name?"

"It's Clarence."

"Well Clarence, could you give me a few of those elastic bands? I just like to keep them handy because you'll never know when you need them. Thanks a lot."

Jamie then leans over to McCulley and whispers in his ear, "These are for you while we are on the road. Okay? We're pulling up to the hospital now. Remember, keep your clothes in sight and be ready to go. They will have that fire out in a few minutes and find a mannequin instead of a human body."

"We're here. You go out first Officer, so we can get the gurney out."

Jamie gets out and watches the paramedics unload McCulley from the vehicle. Several hospital staff members meet the arriving party. A lead nurse addresses the situation.

"How bad is he?" The nurse asks as they rush McCulley inside.

The two paramedics accompany McCulley, pushing the gurney as Jamie brings up the front.

"Multiple gun shot wounds to the chest. No penetration. He was lucky to be wearing his vest. There appear to be some broken ribs and possible internal bruising," replies one of the paramedics as they rush McCulley through the hospital doors.

"His vital signs are all stable."

The group rushes past a few doors as McCulley gets a view of the ceilings. Running through a set of doors, the nurse keeps in contact with McCulley, "Officer can you tell me your name?"

McCulley tries to stare up at her. *Is she kidding? My name?* "Listen, I took shots to the chest not the head, lady."

The nurse shrugs off the comment, "Your name sir."

"McCulley, my damn name is McCulley."

They rush McCulley into the Emergency Room, where Jamie is told he has to stand outside. The last thing Jamie sees is a doctor rushing towards the table where McCulley has been put on for examination.

Back at the house, the Fire Department has gotten the fire under control and the police are standing by to see what they will find in the house, "Sir, the fire is just about out now. If he is still in there, we're going to have a large piece of toasted flesh to deal with."

Ramirez is finally coming around in the EMS van and the sheriff is anxious to speak to her.

"Sheriff, Ramirez has regained consciousness. Do you want to talk to her?"

"Yes, I do. Where is she?"

"She's over in the wagon, Sir."

"Good." The sheriff says, heading towards the ambulance.

Ramirez is sitting on the edge of the gurney, holding her head and sporting a blood pressure cuff. A medic seems to be jotting down notes about her condition as the sheriff approaches.

"Ramirez, how are you doing? Are you all right?" The sheriff says as he puts a leg up onto the vehicle.

Ramirez looks up at the sheriff in a haze, "Yes Sir, but my head is kicking my ass. What happened? What's going on?"

"That's what I want to know. You smell like a distillery."

"Sir, I don't remember a thing. All I know is I woke up inside of this EMT wagon. Maybe after a few hours, things will come back to me, and I could answer your questions. Right now, I'm not worth a dime to anyone, including myself." Ramirez answers dully through her pain and confusion.

"Okay, we're going to have you transported to the hospital to have you checked out, and tomorrow I want you to report personally to my office."

Ramirez feigns a salute, "Yes Sir, I think the best thing for me now is sleep."

Jamie leaves the hospital and starts walking at a brisk pace around the emergency entrance and out onto Shadow Lane. He crosses Charleston Boulevard and heads to the Mini storage.

He's carrying all the tapes in a duffel bag and runs pass the storage office without being seen. He punches in his code and the gate opens. With bag and helmet in hand, Jamie runs to his unit, reaches the door, unlocks the gate and pushes it up. He gazes at the squad car and everything is just as he left it.

Jamie opens the trunk and retrieves two bags from the trunk-one filled with clothes, and the other with money. He places the bags in the back seat of the squad car, gets in, backs the vehicle out and drives away leaving the door open.

He again punches in his code at the gate and pulls out onto Charleston Boulevard and drives back to Shadow Lane, makes a left turn and then goes back to the emergency entrance. He parks the vehicle right at the door and runs inside, passing the guard on duty.

The guard is more attentive towards the nurse he is talking to than watching his post. He glances up at Jamie passing him. The guard says nothing to Jamie, since he is still in his police gear and turns back to the nurse...

"Excuse me," Jamie says to the guard, "I'll be right out. I have to pick-up my partner."

"Okay sir, take your time."

Jamie runs down the corridor looking for McCulley's room. He tries to peek in each room but is having little luck finding him.

How the hell am I supposed to find anyone in this damn madhouse? I hope he is out of the emergency room by now; it's going to be a long day if he isn't. If he's not out, I'm going to have to ditch him, can't have anything slowing me up... not now. There's a nurse; I'll ask her where his room is.

Jamie approaches the nurse that helped McCulley in, "Excuse me, which room is Officer McCulley in?"

The nurse points down the hall, "He's in Bay One. They just wrapped him up. The x-rays came back and all he has are a few broken ribs. You can go in and see him if you like."

"Okay, thank you."

Jamie frantically walks through the emergency room, passing injured people, people crying and some moaning. Finally he locates McCulley off by himself, lying in the bed staring at the ceiling.

"There you are! Come on man... put your clothes on!"

McCulley looks over at Jamie, "Man this shit hurts, I can barely move."

"You had better move and take the pain or you will have a long time in prison to recuperate."

"Okay Jamie, take it easy," McCulley says as he winces in pain.

"Where are your shoes?"

"Under the bed, I think."

Jamie reaches under McCulley's bed, "Oh, here they are. Give me your foot."

While Jamie is helping McCulley get dressed, a doctor comes up, "Excuse me Officers, what are you doing?"

"I'm getting dressed, so we can leave."

Jamie covers up McCulley's mistake, "He's not leaving; he just wants to walk around."

McCulley catches on, "Yeah, I want to move around a little bit. I don't like hospitals. I need some air."

The doctor looks at McCulley a bit concerned but gives in, "Okay, but don't go far. I'll be calling on you shortly."

Jamie waves at the doctor with a smile on his face, "Okay, Doc. We'll be in the lobby."

"McCulley, can you make it?" Jamie whispers. "The car is parked outside the lobby."

"Sure, let's go."

Jamie helps McCulley to his feet and they start down the hallway, "A little faster pace, please, McCulley. There's the door... just a few more feet."

Back at the house, the fire is finally extinguished. An officer approaches the sheriff and requests his presence inside the house. "Sheriff, I think you had better come here, sir."

"What is it?"

"I need you to take a look at this sir."

The sheriff looks over at the officer and then to a group of reporters, "It had better be something important, I have all these reporters waiting to interview me."

The officer and the sheriff walk into the burned-out house. They make their way back to the room, where Jamie was supposed to be, "In the back room sir, over in the chair."

The sheriff doesn't give the chair more than a glance, "Yeah, I can see. The stupid jerk committed suicide and set himself on fire."

"Sir, look at the body," the officer says patiently.

The sheriff walks over to the body and takes a long hard stare, "It's a damn mannequin!"

The officer maintains his patience with the sheriff, "We know sir. Somehow the suspect got out and got away, sir."

The sheriff feeling that he has been made a fool of, kicks the wall as he tries to figure out just how Jamie could have escaped. Then a revelation comes to him, and he begins to yell on his radio as he runs out of the building,

"That's him, the guy that was taking McCulley to the hospital. Call the hospital and tell them to hold McCulley and the man with him, and get some officers to the hospital, now! Lt. Wilson, contact Air One and get them airborne. Tell them we need them in the area of UMC, ASAP!"

"Yes, sir."

Now all the officers at the scene are frustrated and angry. The few officers who are no longer needed at the crime scene race away, heading toward the hospital, hoping that Jamie is still there.

At this time, Jamie and McCulley are in the patrol car with their hearts racing, but feeling secure nevertheless.

"All set McCulley? Let's get the hell out of here. We got to hit that expressway quick. Get those clothes in the back seat, and put them on, and be quick about it. We're heading out to Primm.

I figure they won't know about us in this police vehicle for about ten minutes. When you get dressed, you'll have to drive to give me an opportunity to change."

McCulley pauses to give Jamie a look of astonishment, "Man, how long did it take you to dream up all this shit? The escape still has me dumbfounded. I wouldn't have thought of it in a million years. When we get to wherever we're going, we're going to have a long talk."

Jamie glances at McCulley, "In answer to your question, it took two years. Two years of anger, frustration, and desperation. Are you almost dressed? We're approaching the Henderson turn off, now. We don't have that much further to go. Hurry up man!"

"Okay, when you reach the Sloan exit, pull over, but while I'm driving, my chest is going to be kicking my ass. Did you bring those pills for the pain?"

"Yeah, look in that bag on the floor in the side pocket."

McCulley exclaims in total amazement, "Well, I'll be damned! Look at all this money!"

"Don't bother the cash, that's what we have to live on. So, leave it alone."

McCulley still goes through the money, "Is this the money from the bank? How much is it?"

"Yes, it is and as far as I know, it's about $757,000. Now get your ass out of the bag and get dressed."

"Man, that's almost a million dollars, and it's ours!"

"Right now, it's mine!"

McCulley shoots Jamie a questioning glance, "What do you mean it's yours. I got shot just to get us to this point, so I know half of the bag is mine!"

Jamie nods, "You got shot because of the shit you pull on innocent people, so put the money away! We still have a long way to go. Remember, right now, we are being chased."

"Chased? Where are the chasers?"

"Look McCulley, you're going to have to smarten up a little. Have you been listening to the radio?"

"Well, not exactly. Between trying to change clothes and this excruciating pain, I have not paid attention to the radio."

Jamie cuts McCulley short, "At any rate, they have all cars, plus a helicopter-all of 'em out looking for us! Right now, they are at the UMC Hospital! Listen!"

Jamie turns the radio up so McCulley can hear.

"Air one to radio: We are over UMC Hospital. Is there a description?"

"Air one: Right now, we're looking for two males; one is Metro Police Officer who was shot in the chest at the house on 6116 Fawn Circle Avenue. He has chest injuries and broken ribs, so there is no possibility he will be mobile."

"The Officer's name is McCulley, Clarence. He's a White male, six feet two, 250 pounds, with blond hair. He is dressed in civilian clothes. The second man is a Black male, six feet, light complexion with dimples, short black hair and glasses. He is dressed in Metro's riot gear with helmet."

"It is unknown whether Police Officer McCulley is a prisoner or not. He had opportunities to expose the

perpetrator, but did not do so.   Both were last seen getting into an EMT wagon and taken to UMC Hospital."

"Air one: check."

"Radio, 7-Charlie-14."

"Go ahead, 7Charlie-14."

"Yes radio, we just received information that the two subjects in question left the hospital in a marked Metro Police car. Right now, there are so many police vehicles here, they could blend right in."

"Do we have a number on the Metro car?"

"Negative, Radio."

"Check, 7-Charlie-14. Attention. All cars be on the lookout for a salt-and-pepper team in a marked Metro police car. Their twenty is unknown."

"You hear that McCulley? Here, I'm pulling over so you can drive. I have to get out of these clothes."

Jamie pulls the car over at the Sloan exit and climbs in the back seat, but has to get back out to assist McCulley get behind the wheel, "Okay, now go... go! When you get to Whiskey Pete's, pull into a space in the lot!"

"Then what?"

"Just wait and see." Jamie says as he rests his head against the passenger window.

Meanwhile, another News Bulletin is broadcast over the TV.

"This is another Channel 7 News bulletin. We are interrupting your regularly scheduled program to bring you an update on today's exciting hostage situation, which began earlier this morning on Fawn Circle on the West Side of Las Vegas.

"We have John Wiggs on the scene. John, can you update us on what has happened so far?"

"Doug, it's been truly an amazing day. It seems like something out of the movies. This house we are standing in front of was occupied by an armed suspect who was holding two Metro Police Officers captive. Notice, I said occupied. Somehow, even though the house was

surrounded by more than fifty police officers, the suspect escaped with one of his hostages."

"The scenario goes this way Doug. At approximately 6:00 a.m., today the suspect called the sheriff and asked, 'Do you know how Butch Cassidy and Sundance Kid ended?' The sheriff replied 'yes'.

"About five minutes later, the front door opened; a smoke bomb was tossed from the inside of the house and a figure rushed out. The figure was shot at least three times in the chest, but no bullet took effect because the figure was wearing a bulletproof vest.

"Now, get this Doug, the figure was Police Officer Clarence McCulley, the kidnapped police officer came out of the building in the mist of a smoke bomb and the officers outside felt the subject was armed and opened fire.

It is not known why he emerged from the building in this manner. The injured officer was rushed to the hospital with another officer in tow. The suspect then barricaded himself in a back bedroom and two shots were heard, and when the officers tried to enter the room, they saw that the suspect had set the room on fire."

"Doug, that's not the end of the story. When the fire department was called and the fire was extinguished, they discovered that the body inside was a mannequin.

"The police now feel that the person who escorted Officer McCulley to the hospital was the suspect dressed as a police officer. Police are at this moment searching the UMC area to ascertain if the police officer with Officer McCulley is, in fact, the suspect being sought".

"John, can the police explain how the suspect gained access to a police uniform, and how he managed to get past the police without being detected?"

"Doug, the only thing we can say is that the suspect is a very smart individual. He's always one step ahead of Metro, but the Sheriff has assured us that the suspect, one Jamie Collins will be caught."

"John, what about the other police officer, Dolores Ramirez?"

"Well Doug, Officer Ramirez seems to have been knocked out with some type of drug and for most of the time, she was unconscious. She's sitting in the ambulance now; they will be transporting her to UMC in just a few minutes."

"The Sheriff says Ramirez is coherent, but just a little dizzy because she is coming down from the drug the suspect injected her with.

"Also, at this time, Ramirez can not give us any insight on what went on in the house. We're hoping we will get more information later on in the day."

"One more thing Doug, there was no evidence of the missing bank loot in the home, and from speaking with the Sheriff, the police officer who left with McCulley was carrying a large bag."

"Okay John, we're going to have to leave you for the moment. We have Cheryl Quincy at UMC Hospital. Cheryl, go ahead."

"Doug, again it looks like Metro is only footsteps behind the suspect, Jamie Collins. The reports we have are that the suspect left this hospital 15 minutes earlier in a marked Metro Police vehicle.

At the present time, the direction he took is unknown but the suspect has Police Officer McCulley with him and our sources within the hospital report that McCulley didn't look like he was force to accompany the suspect.

"People were unaware of what was taking place and did not pay that much attention to the two individuals. Doug, they could be anywhere in the city by now, and because they are driving a marked vehicle, that makes just about every police vehicle suspicious.

"Cheryl, just what is the Sheriff doing about the situation?"

"As of this moment Doug, we have no answers to any of your questions. We will just have to wait and see what the sheriff does."

"Cheryl, stand by. We have John with the Sheriff now."

"John, what do you have?"

"Doug, the Sheriff is here with us and we're going to pose that question to him. Sheriff, we know the suspect escaped in one of your marked cars, what are you going to do now?"

"Since our suspect has one of our vehicles and has access to our communication, I've decided to have all vehicles stop-no motion whatsoever-and each vehicle is to report to location. All three of our helicopters Air 1, 2, and 3, will patrol from the air."

"Now, the suspect has no choice, but to abandon the vehicle if he wants to escape. That will give us a better chance of apprehending him."

"Won't that put the general public at risk?"

"No, I doubt it. You see the suspect seems to have his plan already mapped out and by doing what I just said, the suspect might have to ditch the vehicle before he wants to."

"I understand, Sheriff. Is there any more news about Officer Ramirez?"

"Not at the moment, other than the fact that she was just transported to UMC. We have not gained anymore information from her at this time."

The sheriff starts to turn away from the camera, "Now, I have a job to do. If you have any more questions, please contact me at my office tomorrow when I can properly answer your questions".

"Okay, thank you, Sheriff Kerns."

"There you have it Doug. Things are just really heated and uncertain around here and I feel we won't be able to get any more information at this time."

"Okay John, are you staying at the scene?"

"Yes Doug, I'll be here in case of new developments."

"That was John Wiggs at the scene on Fawn Circle. We will now rejoin Cheryl at UMC."

"Doug, the EMT's have just taken Officer Ramirez into the hospital and from what I could see, she looked all right. She was talking and was very much in control of her

faculties. No one is allowed into the hospital at this moment, so we are going to have to wait until we get an update on the condition of Officer Ramirez."

"Okay, John and Cheryl, we want to thank you for your information and keep us informed on the events."

"That was our report on the suspect and the police officers. Stay tuned to our station for more information."

****

Jamie and McCulley finally reach Whiskey Pete's. Their fear is a little settled now, somewhat, but their flight to freedom is long from over.

"McCulley, pull in right there, and come on; we have got to hurry and get away from this vehicle. I got the bags, now try and get to the Tram and cross over to The Prima Donna. After that, walk over to the lottery store, I will meet you there."

McCulley grabs Jamie, "What are you going to be doing in the meantime?"

"Number one, they are going to be looking for a Black man and a White man together. Number two; I have to create a diversion. Now go ahead, I will see you in a few minutes, and try not to show the pain you're in."

"Okay, I will see you later."

McCulley limps away slowly to the Tram. He finds it very difficult to run or even to walk fast. The more his lungs work, the more pain they cause.

He enters Whiskey Pete's and climbs up the stairs to the Tram where he has to wait for it to arrive. He then takes the opportunity to sit down and rest, trying not to call attention to his pain. There are several couples also waiting for their ride, while their children are restless and running around.

The Tram finally arrives and McCulley finds it difficult to get up. One of the fathers offers his assistance and gets McCulley to his feet. McCulley struggles to the Tram and sits down.

"Are you all right?"

"Yes, I am. I am just a little sore from a car accident. I broke my ribs."

"What happened to your nose? Did the accident just happen?"

"Sir, I don't want to be rude, but will you leave me alone."

The man sees McCulley's turn in anger and becomes frightened. "Okay...okay...I'm sorry."

The man gets up and goes back to his family. The family huddles together, whispering about McCulley. McCulley leans back in his seat and closes his eyes. Before he could get any relief, the Tram arrives at its stop.

Again McCulley struggles to get up, only this time without the man's help, who walks off the Tram while looking back at the injured officer.

McCulley is finally on his feet and exits the Tram and walks down the steps at the Prima Donna Hotel.

It's a long walk for him, passing the gambling tables and slot machines. He walks through the new shopping center past the busy shoppers who seem to be watching him as he walks painfully by.

He finally gets outside and sees the Lottery Store, which is about 250 yards away. He leans against the building breathing in short shallow pants and wonders to himself, how he's going to make it.

After wading through the parking lot, McCulley reaches the store and sits on the ground next to the building and waits for Jamie.

Jamie in turn, gathers together the three duffel bags and a large piece of cardboard and turns on the lights of the police vehicle and quickly walks away, not noticing a man scrunched down in his car trying to hide. Instead of Jamie riding the Tram, he walks across the parking lot to the Interstate.

Jamie walks about two hundred yards on the southbound side of the Interstate. Stopping directly across the Interstate from the Lottery Store, he pulls out the large piece of cardboard, unfolds it and lays it on the ground in plain view. On the cardboard it reads 'TO L.A.'. Jamie then sits on the ground and waits until the traffic is clear and gets up and runs across the Interstate.

On the other side, Jamie has to walk another two hundred yards to get to the store. As he approaches, he can see McCulley sitting on the ground leaning on the building asleep. He walks up to McCulley and kicks him on the bottom of his feet, "Now, how are you doing? I see you made it all right."

McCulley stares at Jamie's shoes, "Yeah, I did. Now, what are we going to do?"

"We're going to hitch a ride to Vegas."

McCulley looks up at Jamie and slowly gets up and leans back on the building and stares at Jamie, "Back to Vegas? Are you nuts?"

Jamie smiles, "That's one place they won't be looking for us and right now every road going out of Vegas is going to be watched, and they will probably set up road blocks."

"So, I guess we are going to walk?"

"No, watch this." Jamie looks around and sees a middle-aged black man coming out of the store looking at his lottery tickets, strolling to his car, "Excuse me, sir. Look, my car broke down across the street at Whiskey Pete's and I need to get back to Vegas. I wonder if I paid you two hundred dollars, would you give us a lift to the C.A.T. terminal in downtown Las Vegas?"

The man looks up at the sound of the money offered, "Fo' two hundred dollars, I'll take you to yo' house."

"No, that's all right. Downtown will be just fine."

The man starts to take the deal but stops, "But first, I hope you ain't gonna rob me or anything or you're not runnin' from the police or nothin' like that?"

"No. It's just like I told you, my car broke down and I need a ride for me and my friend."

The man begins to hesitate and Jimmy reaches into one of his bags and pulls out two hundred dollars and begins to wave it at him.

"Okay, blood, come on. Let's go."

When the man agrees to give Jamie and McCulley a ride, more information concerning their escape is being broadcasted over the police radio.

"Air One, come in."

"This is Air One radio."

"We just received a call from a citizen, stating that there is a marked police unit parked with the motor running at Whiskey Pete's parking lot at Primm. You want to head that way and check out the vehicle. NHP will also meet you at the scene."

"Ten-four. Air One ten-seventeen that twenty."

Jaime walks to the car with the man and the man opens the trunk and tells Jamie to put his bags in. Then Jamie goes and gets McCulley, who is now in excruciating pain. They walk to the car and climb in.

When McCulley gets into the car he lays back and closes his eyes, revealing two nostrils filled with dried blood. Jamie searches in the pockets of McCulley and finds the pain pills. He takes two pills out and hands them to McCulley, "Here, take these pills; they will make you feel better."

"I don't have anything to drink. I can't take any pills without something to drink."

"Here young man, you can have my coke. I got half a can left."

Jamie takes the can from the man, "Thanks Mister. Here McCulley, drink this."

"Okay," McCulley pops the pills into his mouth and chases them with the coke and lies back again.

Jamie senses the man is worried about why McCulley is so beat up, "Well, to tell you the truth, our car didn't break down. We had an accident on the Interstate and went into a ditch. My partner struck his face and chest on the dashboard. I think some of his ribs are broken."

"Maybe I should drop you off at UMC."

"No...no... that won't be necessary. We have someone meeting us at the C.A.T. Terminal Downtown. We can make it from there."

The man shrugs, "Well, I just wanted to make sure you got yo' money's worth."

"It's nice of you to be so thoughtful sir, I'm sure you will get repaid for your kindness. Maybe you will hit the lottery."

"I'm not concerned about hitting the lottery. I probably will never do that. Playing the Lotto twice a week just helps me make it through life. It helps me to dream and forget about the bad things going on around us.

People should learn to take things in stride. Look at that fella who kidnapped those cops. He just done gone and gave up his life for some no good kids. I know he don't think they gonna let 'em go. If he does, he's a bigger fool than I am."

Just as he finishes the sentence, three squad cars and a helicopter speed by going in the opposite direction.

Jamie and McCulley both sit up and watch the police pass, knowing exactly how far the police are behind them. Seeing the helicopter was even more frightening. Jamie looks at McCulley and in a downward motion; he moves his hand, telling McCulley to calm down.

The man is still rambling on about the kidnappings; oblivious to the fact his passengers are the ones the police are looking for.

The car is traveling at the maximum speed limit and Jamie wants him to move a little faster, knowing that in a few minutes, every cop in the area will be at Whiskey Pete's and then heading for L.A.

He also knows it's only going to take a few minutes before they realize that Jamie and McCulley are not headed for L.A., and they will start blocking the roads going back to Las Vegas. So Jamie figures out a way to make the man go faster.

"Excuse me, but what year is this car?"

"It's a 1978 Firebird; I've had it for ten years. I'm the second owner and nobody drives it but me," The man replies patting the dashboard.

"Have you ever driven it fast?"

"No, not really. I don't want to push it too hard. This car has to last me for a while."

Jamie pushes on, "But you have to blow out the carbon build up every now and then don't you?"

"I guess you are right, but where do I do that. They have speed limits you know. I can't afford a ticket."

Jamie laughs, "Have you been looking or listening in the last ten minutes. Nine police cars have passed us at a very high rate of speed in the opposite direction, evidently there is something going on back there. The last thing you have to worry about is a ticket. Come on; let's see how fast this buggy can go. Go ahead; put the pedal to the medal."

With a sly grin, the man puts his foot down, "Okay, here we go. Wow, this sucker hit a hundred really fast."

"Yeah, look at the black cloud of smoke it left behind. If I were you, I would keep this speed all the way to Las Vegas. That's about forty miles. It should really clean out all that carbon."

Trying to keep the sound of his excitement down, the man replies to Jamie, "You're right, I've been wanting to do this for quite some time."

Now, Jamie and McCulley have gained some needed time. They need to get to Las Vegas before the police start blocking traffic heading north. As they are heading north on the Interstate 15, the activities of the police are intensifying.

****

"Air One".

"Air One, go ahead."

"Air One, what is your twenty?"

"We've landed in the parking lot of Whiskey Pete's and we have located the patrol car. We also have police vehicles from NHP, CHP, and Metro, radio. Request you hold up any other vehicles heading in this direction until we find out which direction the subject took from here. We have one person here who states, he saw a Black male exiting the vehicle. Will advise further after we talk with him.

"Check, Air one".

"All units southbound on Interstate 15. Hold your present twenty until further notice. Do not head for Whiskey Pete's. We are code at that twenty."

The scene around the stolen vehicle is hectic, while Air One interviews the witness. Air one guides the witness to one side to question him away from everyone else, "Excuse me sir, would you mind stepping over here with me."

An old man in his sixties approaches the police officer, smiling and pushing his glasses up on his nose. Bubbly and happy to supply information, he almost trips over the cane he uses to help support himself while he is walking. As the officer is questioning him, he continually holds up his finger, trying to interrupt the questioning.

"Sure why not?"

"Okay, you said you saw a Black man leaving the police vehicle?"

"Yes. Yes, I did. I thought it was rather peculiar that this man should be getting out of a police car, especially out of the back seat. I thought he was a prisoner escaping, so I laid low so he wouldn't see me."

"What did you see after that sir?"

"Well, I watched a lot of 'America's Most Wanted' and I learned to get a full description of the person and what he is doing. So I watched him very carefully. He got out of the car and he had three bags with him."

"What kind of bags?"

"Gym bags or army duffel bags, I'm not sure, but I do know one was heavy, one was medium, and one was light."

The officer looks a bit dubious, "Sir, how could you tell the weight of the bags if you were in your car?"

"It was just the way he handled them. For the first one, he used two hands to put it on his shoulder; the second one he slung over his shoulder with less effort, and the third one he carried in his left hand." The witness said with pride, as if he expected the reply.

"Okay, what did he do afterwards?"

He goes to the driver's side of the vehicle and reaches in and turns on the lights."

"Why did he do that sir?"

The man looked a bit confused for a moment, "I don't know, but he walks away in a hurry."

"Which way did he go?"

"He walked up toward the southbound Interstate."

"He walked away carrying three bags toward the southbound Interstate?" asked the officer.

"Oh yeah, he also had a piece of cardboard, which may have been a sign."

"Did you see him get into a car?"

"No, no I didn't. I saw him walk up to the interstate and then my wife called me. I turned to see what she wanted and looked back and he was gone."

"You didn't see him get into a car?"

"No. You can't see any cars on the Interstate from here, as a matter of fact; I wouldn't have been able to see him after he got to the Interstate if I had watched him from here."

"Okay sir, would you tell me what he looks like?"

"Sure that's easy; I wrote it down. I told you I watch 'America's Most Wanted'. I noticed his face first, he was a light skinned colored boy; must have been 30-40 years old with short hair, I guess. I couldn't tell much because he had a Detroit Tigers hat on. You know, I know it's a tiger's hat, cause I'm a baseball fan. I got a cap from every baseball team."

"Okay mister..."

"That's Samuels," the man interjected.

"What's that?"

"Samuels...Samuels is my last name."

"Okay Mr. Samuels, is there anything else?"

"Yeah. He had dark glasses...you know sunglasses, clean-shaven except for a mustache and he had them things in his face. You know holes in the jaws."

"Dimples?"

"Yeah, dimples. He was wearing a blue jacket with a bulldog on the back, and blue jeans and gym shoes... white."

"Is there anything else you can remember? Wait a minute."

As they were talking, another officer approaches. The officer giving the interview turns to the man walking towards them, "Hey Fred, Mr. Samuels here says he saw the suspect walk up that hill toward the Interstate. Go up there and see if you can find anything."

"Okay Walt, I'll be right back."

Walt turns his attention back to Mr. Samuels, "Now Mr. Samuels, is there anything else you can remember about the suspect?"

"No not really, but if there is anything else I can do, I will be more than happy to help. By the way, who is he and what did he do? With all these cops around here, he must have killed somebody."

"No not yet, we just need to talk with him."

"Yeah, just like a cop, to keep everything to yourself." Mr. Samuels said with appointment, after all, he did to help them.

"Mr. Samuels, before you leave, we're going to need your address so we can contact you in case we need more information."

"I live in Idaho... me and my wife are on vacation. We are on our way to California. Now, if you gonna put us up in one of your fancy hotels and feed us we will be more than happy to stay."

Just then, the officer returns from the Interstate, "Hey Walt, Look what I found, a sign that reads 'TO LA'.

"Mr. Samuels, is this the piece of cardboard you seen the suspect with?"

Samuels looks at the sign intensely, "Wait a minute, turn it over."

The officer turns the board over and shows Mr. Samuels.

"Yeah that's it! That's what I saw under his arm."

"Two more questions Mr. Samuels. Was there a White man with him?"

"No, he was by himself," Samuels answers without hesitation.

The officer reaches into his pocket and pulls out a picture of Jamie and shows it to Mr. Samuels, "Is this a picture of the man you saw?"

"Sure is. I would recognize him anywhere."

"Hold on a minute Mr. Samuels. I have to call my dispatcher. Air One to Radio."

"Go ahead Air One."

"Radio, we have an eyewitness description of the suspect; it appears to be our 407 and 427 suspect, Jamie Collins, but he is no longer wearing a police uniform. He's dressed in civilian clothes with a Detroit Tiger's Baseball Cap, sunglasses, a blue jacket with a bulldog on the back, blue jeans and white gym shoes, and he is carrying three duffel bags. The suspect was alone and there was no sign of Officer McCulley. He may have hitched a ride to California, probably the LA area. We have a sign he used to request a ride."

"Air One, how long ago was the suspect last seen?"
"Ten-twelve, Radio."

The officer turns back to Samuels, "Mr. Samuels, how much time has passed since you last saw our man?"

The man looks off into the sun as if it could tell the answers, "Oh, I would say it has been a half-hour to 45 minutes by now."

The officer goes back to his radio, *"Air One to Radio."*

"Go ahead Air One."

"It's been approximately one half hour to 45 minutes since the suspect was last seen."

"Check, Air One. Your call is ten-forty-nine to the Bakersfield, California exit. Ten-eighty-seven the California Highway Patrol on the line. They are setting up a roadblock in that area and be on the lookout for anyone straying off the interstate.   Direct your witness to the Supervisor on your twenty."

"Ten-four, Radio. Air one out".   The officer puts down the hand held radio and stares towards California.

chapter

10 THE MASQUERADE

Jamie and McCulley have successfully diverted the police and are now pulling up to the C.A.T. Terminal in downtown Las Vegas. They look around the bus terminal to make sure it is okay for them to enter. Jamie double-checks the area for anything that could cause a problem.

Just a rent-a-cop over here. Nothing to be worried about. All the real cops are half way to the Nevada-California border by now. Calm down, Jamie, calm down. We made it, now we just have to get out of Dodge.

"Okay Clyde, thanks for the ride; and don't spend that money in one place." Jamie says getting out of the car.

"Don't worry; I will put it to good use. Especially since my old lady don't know about it. Y'all take it easy." Clyde waves good-bye to the two fugitives and pulls out of the bus lane after Jamie and McCulley remove their belongings from the car and trunk. The two sit down at the bus terminal and watch Clyde drive away.

McCulley looks over at Jamie while holding his ribs in pain; "We're really going to take a C.A.T. bus?"

"Hell no, McCulley! I just said that, so the guy wouldn't be too suspicious. What did you want me to say to him, 'gee, mister, could you give us a ride to the transit bus terminal so we could escape the police force looking for us?' "

McCulley glares over at Jamie, "Listen, I'm in some pain right now and don't really need all of your shit! So if we aren't going to take the bus, why the hell are we here?"

In answer, Jamie gets up and walks towards the Post Office, "First things first, McCulley. We need to see what your buddies are up to."

As they approach the Post Office, Jamie pulls out the hand held police radio he stole from the squad car, and turns it back on as he takes a seat on the steps.

By this time, the pills were taking affect, and McCulley's pain has subsided significantly, although he stills feels some discomfort. At least, he manages to sit on the steps and brace himself against the wall. Then the crackling of the radio intrudes into their awareness once again.

All units on Interstate 15 be on the lookout for 427-suspect, Jamie Collins, a light complexioned black, male, fifty years old, six feet tall and two hundred and twenty pounds. Suspect is wearing a blue Detroit Tigers baseball cap, sunglasses, and blue jacket with a bulldog on the back, blue jeans, and white gym shoes.

Suspect is said to be carrying three duffel bags and was last seen hitching a ride to LA. At last sighting, the suspect was alone. He is considered armed and extremely dangerous. Handle ten-zero.

After hearing the broadcast, Jamie immediately stands and starts looking around while taking off his hat and throwing it into the shrubbery and also discarding his jacket. He turns to McCulley with fear in his eyes, "Shit! We had better hurry and get out of this town. It won't be long before they have us on TV."

McCulley looks worriedly at Jamie, "Okay Jamie, I'm with you, but how the hell are we going to leave?"

Jamie stops for a second. *Just how the hell are we going to get out of here? Come on McCulley think. Damn it! They are going to be looking for me wearing those clothes, I already took them off, and that takes care of that problem. But if they had half a brain, they would also be on the look out for a black and white male walking together.*

We need to get out of here fast, but with McCulley moving slower than my grandmother, there is no way we can out run anyone if we needed to. I'm going to have to ditch the sucker if I want to get out alive; he just cannot come with me. Unless... unless we break apart. Then we would be just a white guy with a limp and a black man walking downtown.

Nothing would connect us, and we would blend in perfectly.

"Look, we have to separate." responds Jamie as he articulates his thoughts.

McCulley looks at him distrustfully, "What the hell do you mean, separate?"

"We're going over to the Greyhound Bus Terminal, but we can't be seen together. Since you are slower than I am you trail me and I will meet you there... and don't take all day. I have to purchase tickets." Jamie explains, using his best comforting voice.

McCulley sighs and gets himself ready to move again, "Okay, let's go."

Jamie takes off and with every step he leaves McCulley further behind. The only thing he can't seem to leave behind is the sinking feeling in his stomach. His stomach starts to knot with the thought of him getting caught by the police.

Jamie passes one block, then the next. On his way crossing the street, he encounters two Metro bicycle patrolmen. Jamie trying not to look suspicious, Jamie waits patiently for the signal to change.

"I guess that guy got away, I don't know how the hell he got out from a building surrounded by SWAT officers, though," one of the bike cops comments to his companion.

"Just between you and me," responds his partner, "I figure all of this is just some sort of media bullshit. There is no way we are that screwed up to let this guy walk out free. He had to have friends helping him out. I hear there is some sort of black gang behind all of this shit."

While the two bike officers discuss the situation, Jamie is doing his best to remain calm. His heart is beating in his ears, as the 'Don't Walk.' the crosswalk is still lit in the traffic signal.

Shit! How long is this light going to last? I don't think I can take more of these two talking like this? If any of them had a brain or a good description, they would have nailed my ass by now.

Jamie's worries start to subside, when the crosswalk sign finally changes and the bike cops pass him by. Jamie reaches Fremont Street and crosses while blending into the crowd.

In the middle of the crowd while crossing the busy intersection, Jamie turns his head in time to see McCulley hobbling toward him. McCulley doesn't know Jamie is watching him, but Jamie still isn't sure of McCulley's loyalty.

He feels if McCulley was going to defect, there was no time like the present. Then he reflects, *maybe he will do anything for friendship. Well, that has to be seen and proven.*

In the meantime, the thoughts are on getting out of town…the last leg of the big adventure. He can't come this far and get caught at this point. Jamie continues up Fremont Street, stopping every now and then to watch McCulley, passing old hotels such as the Horseshoe, 4Queens, and finally stopping to rest at the Golden Nugget.

McCulley tries to make the best time he can, but his ribs are killing him and every step is torture. It is to the point where he doesn't dare breathe out of sync, or the pain would overwhelm him.

Damn, he thinks, *I wish I could just take a minute to rest. What am I thinking about? Rest? Shit, it would hurt if I rested anyways. I hate this shit, I feel like I am ninety years old with my ribs like this.*

Where the hell is Jamie now? If I lose him, I am screwed. He better not ditch me; I don't know what the hell I would do if he lost me. I'd really be screwed then…like I am not screwed enough as it is.

Jamie watches McCulley as he stops and rests in front of the Glitter Gough. Jamie can see that the pain of six broken ribs was taking its toll on McCulley's body. As he watches McCulley, he notices how well McCulley blends in the crowd. He could almost be mistaken for a homeless person.

Now, McCulley resumes his trek and gets within a block of Jamie. Jamie reaches Main Street and crosses over to the entrance of the Greyhound Bus Terminal.

Jamie looks out the window of the terminal and he can see McCulley struggling down the street.

After standing for a few minutes, McCulley enters the terminal and Jamie motions for him to go to the restroom. They both enter the restroom separately and Jamie hurriedly pushes McCulley into a stall.

McCulley bends over placing his hands on his knees for support, trying to look up at Jamie, he breathes out, "Man, I'm whipped. I can't wait to get somewhere and sit down."

Jamie doesn't seem to notice as he responds, "Well, you will have your wish in a few minutes. We have thirty minutes before our bus leaves, but first we have to make some changes. Let me stand on this toilet, so no one will see four feet in a stall. Now I'll open my little bag of tricks."

As Jamie opens up his bag, McCulley tries to take a peek, "What's in there?"

Rummaging through the bag, Jamie answers McCulley without looking up, "Make-up, so we won't be recognized. Hold still so I can put some glue on your face."

Jamie turns to McCulley with a bottle of make-up glue in his hands. He smears glue on McCulley's face and then takes out some facial hair and neatly pats it on his face. Next came some black shoe polish, just a little to make McCulley look grubby. Jamie messes up his hair and puts sunglasses on him. Next, Jamie does the same to himself and then peeps out of the stall to see if anyone is around.

"Okay McCulley, let's go, I have to purchase the tickets and lock up this bag."

"You're going to lock up the money?"

"No fool, the tapes; I have to leave them for Ramirez. Come on, you carry this bag. I'll keep the money."

Jamie and McCulley walk out of the restroom separately. Jamie stops at the lockers and places the bag containing the tapes into one of them. He slides a quarter into the slot and the key ejects in return. Then he locks the locker, puts the key into his pocket and walks over to the ticket line.

****

In the meantime, the lucky two-hundred-dollar man, who drove Jamie and McCulley to the C.A.T. depot, was at Circuit City on Sahara and Decatur, purchasing a brand new VCR. He looks around and can't seem to make a decision, even though he is limited with only two hundred dollars.

Seeing the man is looking a bit lost, an employee comes to help him out, "Excuse me sir; but can I help you?"

"Yes, I would like to have this VCR please."

The employee nods in approval as if the man just purchased a bottle of wine, "Yes sir, this model is our best seller. We also have a three-year warranty, and a special bonus, they come in a variety of colors."

The man shakes his head looking over the VCR, "No, black will be all right."

Walking towards the register, the employee tries to enhance his commission, "Sir, we also have a special on our TV's over here.

Just as the salesman points out the television sets, a news bulletin airs, which not only grabs the man's attention, but also nearly floors him.

"Good afternoon, we are interrupting our regularly scheduled program with an update of today's events involving Jamie Collins.

"Again this elusive fugitive has escaped the nets of the Metro Police Department. For those of you who are not familiar with the trail of terror unleashed by Mr. Collins, here is Douglas Wayne to give us an update.

"*The camera cuts to the on-the-scene reporter,* "*Thanks John, Well two days ago, Jamie Collins entered the home of Gladys Figson under false pretenses and tied her to a toilet in her bathroom.*

"*He forced her to make a tape recorded message instructing her husband, Clyde Figson, who is an armored car guard for Armored Protection Company, to give Mr. Collins the money he was collecting.*

"*Collins escaped that scene with seven hundred and fifty thousand dollars in cash. Some hours later, he called 911 and asked for the police to come out and investigate a prowler. When the officers arrived, he somehow overpowered them, kidnapped them and moved them to another location on Fawn Circle, where they were held for one day.*

"*SWAT teams eventually surrounded the house, and again the suspect escaped, this time with one of the officers, Clarence McCulley. Officer McCulley was injured in a shootout at the house, and was apparently taken to the UMC emergency department by the suspect, who was dressed in police riot gear.*

"*Collins managed to elude the police again and escaped in one of their marked patrol cars. The injured officer, Clarence McCulley, is also missing from the hospital, and his role in all of this is unclear at this time.*"

The reporter pauses for the producer to get the still images to match his report, the transaction is almost unnoticeable, unless you were looking for the pause, you would never notice it.

"*The stolen police vehicle was located at Whiskey Pete's Casino in Primm. Mr. Collins was positively identified leaving that area hitching to Los Angeles. There are roadblocks set up as far as Bakersfield, California. But as of this airing, no one has seen either the suspect of Officer McCulley.*"

The screen splits to show both men at the same time, "*Doug, I am quite sure that Collins is not wearing the police uniform he was in when he escaped the home on Fawn Circle in Las Vegas.*"

*"That is correct John, when Collins escaped from
the house and from the hospital, he was wearing a police
uniform and riot gear.*

*"The eyewitness who saw him abandoning the
police vehicle, said he was wearing a Detroit Tiger
Baseball cap, a blue jacket with a bulldog on the back,
sunglasses, blue jeans, and white gym shoes and he was
carrying three duffel bags."*

Upon hearing the description and seeing Jamie's
picture, Clyde dashes out of the store, into the parking lot,
and begins to walk around in circles, slapping himself in
the head and stomping the ground calling himself stupid.
People walking by slow down and stare, wondering what
was his problem.

"What am I to do? He says aloud. "Boy, am I
stupid. That sucker lied to me." He continues pacing as
people walk by, "I got to tell somebody…but then again,
maybe I shouldn't. He gave me two hundred dollars.
That's part of the money he stole. If I tell the police, they
will want the money back. What am I going to do?"

Suddenly he stops pacing as an idea comes to his
mind, "I know, 'Secret Witness'. That's it-I'll call Secret
Witness, that way I can keep the money. What if he kills
someone?"

The man runs to his car, drives across the street to
the AM-PM convenience store, goes straight to the phone
and dials directory assistance.

"Directory assistance, what city please," comes the
automated response.

"Las Vegas. Give me the number to Secret
Witness."

"One moment, sir." The man waits a moment
while the computer processes his request, "That number is
555-1234."

"Okay, thank you." Clyde says as an automatic
response to the machine. He hangs up the phone and dials
the number while repeating it like a mantra.

"Secret Witness…can I help you?"

"Yes ma'am. I have some information on someone wanted in a kidnapping and armed robbery. Do I have to give my name?"

"Sir, if you don't give your name and there is a reward, you won't be able to collect."

Clyde thinks for a moment and decides that the reward wouldn't be enough, "Right now, there is no reward for this individual and if there was, I don't want it."

"Okay sir, what is the name of the person you have information on?"

"Well ma'am, it's that fellow Jamie Collins. I picked him up at the Prima Donna, along with a white guy– I think maybe the missing cop, and I drove them to the C.A.T. Bus Terminal in downtown Las Vegas."

"Sir, this is important information; can you hold on for a minute?"

Clyde starts to panic and hangs up in a hurry; he feels they may want to talk him into coming to the police station. He then gets back into his car and drives home, feeling relief, knowing he told someone of Jamie Collins' whereabouts.

Jamie is at the Greyhound bus terminal trying to purchase tickets. The line snakes around the cramped terminal and Jamie tries to stand patiently.

He knows that soon, the whole city will be looking for him. The line moves slowly as there seems to be a hold up in front. Apparently, a customer has a problem with the bus schedule and wants the company to change their route to satisfy her needs.

"That's bullshit, that's what that is. I have money, you want money? I have it. I just need to get home to San Diego."

"Ma'am, I apologize, but there are no more buses to San Diego tonight. Our next departure for that city isn't until tomorrow at 9:00 a.m."

"How the hell am I supposed to get home? Just get one of those buses that you aren't using. I need to get home, don't you understand English?"

The worker behind the desk can feel the temperature rise about ten degrees as the irate and drunken customer continues to abuse her. "Listen, there is nothing I can do about this; if you want the scheduled changed, you are going to have to contact the main office. And I don't have to listen to your profanity. If you don't stop right now I'll call Metro and have you arrested."

The woman demanding a ticket flies off in a huff, "You are damn right, I will contact them, and then you'll be fired! You'll see...you don't know who I am! I'll have your job!" The woman storms off, shoving her way through a crowd of people.

Jamie is the next in line and tries to make things easy for the clerk, "Have your job, huh? Yeah! Right! She's out of her mind. I'd rather look at your face, then to look at hers any day. Did you get a look at that face, and what about that mouth? I've smelled toilet bowls that were fresher than that woman's breath."

The clerk starts to laugh with Jamie, feeling more relaxed, "How can I help you sir?"

"Two tickets to Tucson, Arizona, please."
"Two tickets, that comes to $94.73."

Jamie pulls out a few twenty-dollar bills and hands them over to the clerk. The clerk checks the bills to make sure they are real and hands over the tickets, "Here you are sir and thank you for traveling Greyhound. The bus leaves pretty soon though, so you might want to hurry. If you need to put any big baggage on board, the tag line is to your left."

Jamie accepts the two tickets with a smile and looks around for McCulley, who was standing outside leaning on the building. Jamie walks out to where McCulley is standing. Before Jamie can speak, four police cars pull to a screeching halt in front of the terminal and eight officers ran past Jamie and McCulley into the terminal.

The pulses of both men were pounding so hard, they are afraid they can be heard by anyone passing by.

Jamie looks in the station and sees the officers are at the gates of each of the departing buses.

He turns and looks at McCulley, who is leaning on the building cursing; "Shit...Shit...Shit...What the hell are we going to do now? We can't get on the bus and if they are looking for us down here, they are looking for us all over town. Why don't we just turn ourselves in? I can't take anymore of this shit. I'm in pain and my heart is about to jump through my chest."

Jamie speaks to McCulley in a muffled voice, "Look, I told you to be cool. I told you its going to be close, so don't freak out on me now. Here, turn sideways so they can see us from the inside and take a drink from this bottle."

"I don't want a drink? Just get us the hell out of here, now!"

Jamie won't take no for an answer, "Look, the drink is to put alcohol on your breath, and its' also to calm you down enough to get you on the bus. They can't recognize you. I want you to walk on that bus, just like you walked over here from the C.A.T. Terminal. Now, take a big drink and head for the bus! But wait a minute...let me give you a little spray of this."

McCulley looks at the spray bottle in Jamie's hand, "What is that?"

Jamie shows a small grin, "Just wait and smell," he says.

Jamie reaches inside his bag, pulls out a spray bottle and sprays McCulley twice. McCulley's face turns red instantly and his nose wrinkles up, "Damn man, what the hell is that? That stuff smells worse then shit!"

"It's skunk oil. Now, walk slowly toward the bus. I will see you inside."

McCulley, now smelling like a skunk, walks nervously towards the bus, at Gate 6. The police are checking each male who gets on, and McCulley is sixth in line. While standing in line, the people in front of McCulley turn back and look at him, smelling the foul odor penetrating their nostrils.

As McCulley starts to get on the bus, the police approach him. By now the odor is quite strong and instead of the police even questioning him, they retreat and allow him to board the coach unmolested.

As soon as McCulley enters the bus, Jamie runs with a limp calling for his so-called friend, who is already boarded, "Hey Willie, wait for me...hey Willie." As soon as Jamie gets to the bus, the police stop him, "Excuse me officers; I got to get on the bus with my friend."

The cop starts to question Jamie, when he breathes the stench coming from him, "Ah man, it's another one of those stinky bums."

The senior officer takes a step back, "Let his ass by. He's about to make me sick."

Jamie looks at both officers, "Thank you, officer. Is there a problem I should be concerned about?"

"Yeah, getting your ass whipped if you don't get away from me."

With a frightened look on his face, Jamie turns up the bus steps, "Okay sir, you don't have to be so mean!"

Jamie gets on the bus and heads toward the rear, when he is sure the police officers can't see him, he lets out a small sigh and joins McCulley. They begin to laugh together, paying no attention to the people staring at them from six rows away.

****

While Jamie and McCulley make their escape, Ramirez is trying to recuperate from her recent ordeal. Barely making it to bed the night before, she is curled up in her blankets with one pillow under her head, and one over it. Her bedroom is quiet and the blinds are blocking the sun. Tossing around in her bed, Ramirez is suffering from nightmares, an after effect of the ketamine.

Chasing...chasing... Someone is chasing me, but who? I can't see. I can't outrun whatever it is chasing me either. Damn it. I can't escape.

She spots an opening in some trees overhead. She launches herself up towards the trees, trying to fly for extra height. *I'm going to make it. It won't ever find me up here...No! It can't be!*

Something has a hold of me, I can't get out. I can't get out! Who is it, I still can't see! Leave me alone, leave me alone. LEAVE ME ALONE!

The alarm rings, snapping Ramirez out of her nightmare. She reaches over and turns it off; it's 7:00 a.m. Lying in bed, she tries to forget her dream, and instead thinks about the events that transpired the day before.

She wonders what she is going to tell the sheriff. How is she going to convince him, that the majority of the time she wasn't awake?

One question after another, rushes into her mind like a hurricane. *What happened to Jamie and McCulley? Why would they leave together? What did they discuss? They were at each other's throats. So, what transpired while I was out of it?*

These questions continue to bombard her imagination as she drags herself out of the bed. She stumbles a bit as she makes her way to the shower. The warmth of the water sent a sensation through her body that caused her to breathe a momentary sigh of relief. She sits in a curled position, allowing the warm water to beat out the tension of the last two days, as she tries to both forget and remember her experience with Jamie.

After showering, she begins to get dressed and prepares for a meeting she doesn't want to attend. A meeting, that's going to send her mind into overdrive. What will be the questions...and the answers?

After getting ready, Ramirez heads into the kitchen and prepares some toast and coffee, but the image of Jamie continues to haunt her.

That man must really love his children or they are truly innocent. One way or another, the truth is going to come out.

If only I could get that type of love from someone. This man seems to have a heart that can reach out and really touch someone. I know he had me in his arms. I know he felt me close to him. It would really be heaven to wake up and find someone like him close to me everyday.

Stop, stop it right now, he's a felon, he kidnapped me. What am I thinking; I can't have a man like that in my life? What kind of life would that be? Wait a minute...that man can change, and change instantly.

She recalls Jamie's anger when he hit McCulley in the face with the shotgun, and then a daunting memory hits her.

He wants me to help him. I am supposed to contact the FBI about something; but what is it? How can I help him? He committed crimes, and I am a police officer, what am I going to do? Make myself look like a full-fledged fool protecting someone who's violated my rights as a citizen? I can't do that. I won't.

On top of it, how am I going to sway the FBI? They have no feelings. They want a conviction...they want my Jamie in jail.

What am I saying? What do I mean my Jamie? How can I help him? I don't know what to do. As well prepared as Jamie was, I know he didn't just disappear without giving me something to go to the FBI with.

The toast pops up in the toaster, when the doorbell rings. Ramirez looks back at the clock to make sure it was still in the morning hours.

It's too early for anyone she knows to come over. No salesmen would be out either. Who the hell can that be this time of morning?

Ramirez walks over to the door and looks through the peephole and sees several reporters waiting for her to answer the door.

The thought of facing a group of reporters was not the way she wanted to begin her day. So she walks back away from the door, and hopes they would leave.

But the thought of Jamie continues to plaque her. She remembered him from the gym and how he looked. Tall and trim...he had dropped his gym bag and the contents had fallen out on the floor. She walked over and helped gather his things, and remembers that he was still sweating from his workout. The T-shirt he had on was wet with perspiration and he eluded a sweet musty odor.

She had noticed that his hands were big and manicured, but yet rough like one that had work with his hands. No wedding band?

Was he married? His smile caught her attention, which quickly focused on his face... a boyish-looking face, except that his moustache said he was older then he appeared. He had been very thankful for her help.

The next time she remembers seeing him, was when her and Willis were at the restaurant. He remembered her and walked over to the table and again thanked her.

If memory serves her right, he had on a beige Armani suit, and he wore it well. His walk was sultry without the arrogance of most men who think they are looking good. She was sure he did think that, but it didn't show.

Ramirez also remembers how the ladies looked and stared at him as he walked past them. Even the men noticed him. If only she hadn't been with Willis... maybe....

What am I thinking? I sound like some love struck high school girl. Why am I thinking of this son of a bitch like this? My life was fine until he walked into it. Why did I have to meet him under these circumstances? He's a perfect man, perfect criminal, and a criminal that wants my help, which could cost me my job. Who's going to pay my bills? Bills nothing, I could go to jail!

She glances at her watch and sees it is 8:00 a.m., time for her to leave. I have to get going, those reporters better be gone soon. I'll wait 'til 8:30; maybe they'll be gone by then. If not, I will just back out of the garage without stopping and if they get in the way, then so what. They shouldn't be on my property anyway. Damn vultures.

As the thoughts of her trying to get out of the house race through her head, she casually strolls into the bedroom kicking the clothes she wore the night before out of the way. For some strange reason she kicks her shirt the hardest and it flies into the air and lands in front of her, discarding the contents of the pocket. A folded piece of paper unfamiliar to her grabs her attention. She looks at the paper, wondering what it is, and notices it is a letter for her. She sits down on the floor and begins to read.

I knew that asshole didn't leave me hanging. I knew he had to give me some type of information. I knew it...I knew it! He did leave me something.

I am not to tell the sheriff anything that went on. He wants me to wait until I hear from him. How in the hell am I going to do that? Who the hell does he think I am? I have to write a report. I have to tell everything I know. If I don't, that means I will be falsifying an official document.

This man is in deep shit and now he wants to bring me down. Why me? I can't handle this shit. I can barely remember what went on. I don't have that much to tell the sheriff, anyway! I need to think of something though.

Come on girl, think. If you go in today, you will have to make out a report. If you have to make a report, you are either going to rat Jamie out or falsify the report. I can't go in. That's it, I just can't go in.

Can't go in? And do what, stay home all day with my head under the blanket? They'll come looking for me. I have to go in, but I have to make them not think of the report... not just yet. Somehow, I have to make them forget about the report, or at least figure a way around giving a totally accurate one that won't be lying on my part.

Yes, I just need more time to think this over. Maybe Jamie needs my help like he says. Maybe.

Look girl, you have been through a lot in the past three days and you have found yourself thinking about someone you don't even know. Ask yourself, why you would help a stranger.

He robbed a bank, but what if what he says is actually true about McCulley setting up his kids. That would justify him robbing the bank, right? Saves time in court.

Another thing, what about those innocent people who would die in the bombing, what if that's the truth. And he is going to give me those recordings and videotapes, right? That would prove he is telling the truth.

Dolores girl, the man has been involved with this shit for over two years. Either he is telling the truth, or he is just a basket case. Which is it?

Ramirez goes over the letter in her hand and remembers the things that happened while she was tied up.

She recalls the stories and how she felt. Jamie made her feel like she could make a difference, like the first time in her life, she could matter. It was all up to her, all up to her and the amount of trust she was willing to give to a man that she barely knows but somehow trusts.

Okay Jamie, for now, I'll go along with this, but boy you better be on the up and up. I'm putting not only my ass on the line, but my career as well all for you. You better have something good.

After reading the letter, Ramirez gathers up her keys and purse and goes through the kitchen and into the garage.

Remembering what's outside, she gets into her car, starts it up and puts it in gear. She has no intentions of stopping for anyone; just as expected the garage door opens slowly; there the reporters are waiting just like vultures.

Ramirez guns her motor and out she goes, forcing the reporters to dodge the huge piece of metal moving backwards at a high rate of speed.

She was now in the street and on her way to a barrage of questions.

JIMMY CULLORS/JOSEPH SZEWEZYK

chapter

11 RELIEF

The Sheriff's office was just as busy as the front of Ramirez's home, but the Sheriff remained in his inner office. He was not ready for reporters either...not until he hears from Ramirez. His frustration was showing as he yells through the door, "Is she here yet?"

Over the intercom his secretary replies, "No sir, she hasn't arrived. Sir, can I bring you a cup of coffee?"

Meanwhile, Ramirez is trying to filter her way through the crowd of reporters outside of the building and then she is recognized. The crowd gathers closer to her vehicle as she moves ahead at two miles an hour, heading for the garage. She finally makes it through and the police close ranks on the crowd, as Ramirez makes her way to a parking spot.

When Ramirez exits her vehicle, she is met by a police officer that directs her to the Sheriff's private elevator.

On the way up, the thoughts of what to say to the sheriff still rings in her mind. She knows she has to tell him something, but suddenly the door opens and she enters the sheriff's inner office, where the secretary greets her.

"How are you doing Officer Ramirez? I am so glad to see that you made it through your ordeal. I have some coffee for you, and the Sheriff is waiting to see you. Follow me," the secretary says, offering Ramirez a cup of coffee.

Ramirez follows the secretary into the sheriff's office shaking at the knees. She has never had to all out lie the way she is going to, but to help serve justice; she knows she has to see this thing through.

Entering the door, the secretary drops off a cup of coffee for the sheriff and leaves while giving Ramirez a sympathetic look. Ramirez straightens her posture as she waits to be addressed by the sheriff. Her heart is beating rapidly as the sweat begins to form in her palms. Placing her hands behind her back, Officer Ramirez stands at attention, thankful that the stance hides her hands.

The sheriff looks her over silently. He is a bit unsure of himself and where to start with her. The silence only lasts for seconds, but it seems like an eternity for Ramirez.

Taking a sip of coffee, the sheriff breaks the silence, "First, I want you to explain to me, how in the hell did you and your partner allow yourselves to be kidnapped?"

Ramirez is a bit taken back from the sheriff's offensive attitude, but tries to respond calmly, "Well first off sir, we didn't allow it to happen. We were very cautious and we weren't expecting to get ambushed."

"Officer Ramirez, how in the hell could you not expect something may be amiss when that same apartment you went to was the apartment of two people your partner helped put in prison?"

"Sir, I was not aware of who the apartment belonged to."

The sheriff's face starts to turn red at Ramirez's answer, "You mean to tell me that you and your partner never discussed that house and it's on your beat."

"That's correct, sir."

The sheriff shakes his head in disbelief, "What kind of relationship do you and your partner have? You're supposed to know everything about your partner and he is supposed to know the same about you. Now that we know you both went into a possible dangerous situation nonchalantly, tell me how Mr. Collins got the drop on you."

"Well sir, I followed McCulley into the house after Mr. Collins opened the door. We both were walking in, when the door slammed, and Mr. Collins had a 12-gauge shotgun pointed at us. We didn't have an opportunity to react, and he ordered us to the floor." Ramirez pauses as she remembers the first moments of her capture. "He then had me disarm McCulley and myself and ordered me to toss the guns to the other side of the room. He took my handcuffs and had me handcuff McCulley. Then he handcuffed me. After handcuffing us, he injected us, with some kind of drug. The next thing we know, we were at a new location chained to a pole."

"Did he tell you why he was doing this?"

"Yes, he said McCulley was responsible for framing his sons and putting them in prison and that he was going to keep us there until McCulley confessed."

"Did McCulley finally confess to this?"

"Yes, he did."

"During the time you were held prisoner, did you hear anything else?"

"Sir, I was unconscious most of the time we were held captive. I don't know what else transpired."

This was not the answer that the sheriff wanted to hear, "What do you mean, you don't know what transpired? You were there! And how did he get McCulley to confess to framing his sons?"

Ramirez silently bites her tongue realizing that she let out more information that she wanted to, "Sir, to be perfectly honest, I don't know. That was one of those times I was unconscious."

"Why were you unconscious?"

"Sir, I can only think because of lack of sleep and possibly being drugged."

"Drugged?"

"Yes sir, Jamie–I mean, Mr. Collins gave us each an injection of something, which knocked us out. He had everything prepared and planned as though we were going to spend a lot of time there. Everything he had done was planned well in advance. That's why we were caught off guard–he was waiting for us."

"Ramirez, I notice you continually refer to the suspect as 'Jamie'. How close did you get to know him?"

"Sir, he talked a lot about his life, and after spending so much time with him, I feel as though I know him. He is a person you could learn to like in a very short time."

"Okay Ramirez, how do you like a person who kidnaps a woman; ties her to a toilet; feeds her and then robs her husband of $757,000?"

"Well sir, remember he did the same to me, except I don't have a husband to rob. I'm not going to say I like what he did, but I will tell you this, I understand what he is going through.

"The money he stole, he feels it is owed to him. He says he filed a lawsuit against the people of Las Vegas for allowing people like McCulley to become law enforcement officer and to recover the expenses he incurred during his investigation, but decided to settle out of court for the amount of money taken from the bank."

The sheriff begins to become even more agitated at Ramirez's responses, "So now, you're telling me, you approve of the robbery?"

Ramirez tries her best to cover herself, "No sir, I'm not saying that. I'm saying I understand."

"You said something earlier about McCulley confessing to framing Mr. Collins' sons."

"Sir, I uh, uh, well I meant that Mr. Collins wanted McCulley to confess. I'm not sure if he did or not because the next thing I remember; Officers were waking me up.

"What he wanted McCulley to confess to, I don't know. I'm really not sure," Ramirez starts to falter while telling this part of her story, so she quickly changes the emphasis, "What I do know is that, we were chained to a pole."

"During all this time, what was the suspect doing?"

"Sir, he spent a lot of time talking about himself and his times on the police department in Detroit. He was trying to drive home a point about partnership, and how partners can screw each other."

"Was he referring to you and McCulley?"

"Yes sir, he was. He pointed out how much we didn't know about each other. And he also pointed out to McCulley, how treacherous his friends are. I didn't quite understand where he was going with this conversation, but I got the feeling that most of the conversation was directed at McCulley."

Sheriff Kerns rests a hand on his desk, trying to level his face with Ramirez's, "Ramirez, you want me to believe that all the suspect did was talk about his life? What kind of shit is that?"

"Sir, as I stated earlier, for the most part of the ordeal, I was unconscious."

"Ramirez, I need to hear more. There has to be more. No one in their right mind does something like this just to tell you about his life and give you a philosophy on how partners should be with each other!"

Sheriff Kerns says as he slams his fist against the top of his desk. The force of the blow makes the coffee cup jump like a marionette.

The outburst startles Ramirez and she responds by talking faster, "Sir, I'm quite sure that things got quite interesting after I was out, but I could tell he was leading up to something. And because McCulley won't sit still long enough to listen, the suspect shoved the butt of a shotgun in his face.

"I am trying to remember as much as I can, but the time I was awake was early in our kidnapping. I was awake long enough to eat some chili and three drinks, which I believed were spiked."

Red at the face, the sheriff stops and issues her a warning, "Ramirez, I suggest you take a little time and evaluate what happened in that house. If you continue on the road you are traveling today, you are going to talk your way out of a job.

"Now, before you say anything else to me, I suggest you contact your union and an attorney. As of this moment, I am ordering you not to speak to anyone concerning what happened in that house until I have you back here for more questioning. You are now placed on administrative leave until further notice."

The sheriff starts to sit back down at his desk when he points at the door for Ramirez; "You may leave now, but remember what I said."

Ramirez breathes a sigh of relief and quickly exits the office. She rushes down to the garage and heads to her car, and in a matter of minutes, you could hear the tires squealing as she heads for the FBI Building on Charleston and 10th Street.

Ramirez is totally consumed with guilt and can hardly wait to unload. She needs to talk with someone fast, before she talks her way off a job or into worse trouble. She can't understand why she is protecting Jamie. It's like he has his arm in her back and controlling her every move.

She wishes she could remember more, but everything is still a blur. What happened in that house? I wish I could remember.

Then her thoughts are directed towards another man. She remembers she has not contacted Willis. He will want to see her, but she totally disregards him for the time being, because she has her job to save and some innocent people to get out of jail.

She spots the FBI Building and hopes that she can get an investigator who understands. Even against her better judgment, she still has the welfare of Jamie on her mind.

She parks her car and heads up the stairs of a building she passes on a daily basis, never knowing that one day she would be entering it to save hundreds of lives.

A locked door and an intercom system meet her. She depresses the button and waits for a response. A female's voice answers her buzz, "State your business please."

"My name is Dolores Ramirez with the Metropolitan Police Department of Clark County. I need to speak to the Special Agent in Charge, please."

"That would be Damen Clark; do you have an appointment?"

"No I don't; but I have to see him right away."

"Hold on a moment. I will check to see if he is busy." Ramirez waits patiently and the voice returns on the intercom, "He says he is quite busy right now; could you return in an hour?"

"I guess if you don't give me any choice, but would you please do me a favor and give him a note. It is of vital importance that he reads it!"

"Yes, sure...hold on; I will buzz you in."

The door buzzer vibrates the door with a loud noise and Ramirez pulls the door to her. As she enters, she rambles through her purse looking for paper and a pen to write the note. In the note to the Special Agent in Charge she writes:

> *Mr. Damen Clark,*
> *There is going to be a bombing of four major hotels in Las Vegas, and I know who's going to do it!*
> Officer Ramirez

She folds the paper and places it in a discarded coin envelope found on the floor. The inner door opens and an arm reaches out for the note.

"Would you see to it that he gets this? I will wait."

"Okay ma'am, have a seat."

A husky voice startles her. Ramirez peeks in the slot in the door and sees only his eyes. She takes a seat, grabs a magazine and begins to survey the dreary room, which is colored in a lime green, and finished with four metal chairs and a table with *Life* and *Time* Magazines sprawled over the top.

Again, her thoughts drift toward Jamie; she wonders if he is all right. It seems really odd for her to continue to have thoughts about someone who held her captive, but she knows it's only because he made such a major impact on her life.

Nothing so exciting has ever happened in her life. She liked the way Jamie handled himself. He seemed so complacent and yet so desperate. Ramirez's thoughts were interrupted, when the door swings open and the eyes she had only seen through a slot in the wall, turned into a burly bald black man.

"Come this way," he instructs her. "Agent Clark would like to see you now."

Ramirez gets up and walks pass the guard with her petite body, and stares upward at him as though he was a giant. She had never seen anyone as huge as this man. His head barely fits under the doorframe. She walks down the hall toward an arm that extends out of the doorway and then a head appears.

"This way…so you're one of those Police Officers I've been hearing about over the last few days."

Special Agent Damen Clark had been following the ordeal with the police officers. He hadn't expected to meet up with the officers, at least not yet. Now here was this small petite woman, who seemed like she couldn't hold her own, let alone be a cop… possibly violating police protocol.

"I guess you can say that; my name is Officer Dolores Ramirez."

"Come in Officer Ramirez; have a seat. Shouldn't you be downtown filling out paperwork?"

"I was, but the sheriff advised me I should obtain an attorney and notify my union representative; but before I do anything, I need your help."

Agent Clark looks over at the woman in front of him and tries to assess the situation. *She is the woman from the newscasts, but why is she here? This doesn't make any sense; the sheriff must have wanted to see her right away– why would she be in my office? Her superiors cannot know about this. There would be no need for them to send her here.*

The reports did say something about a missing officer, but wouldn't that be an Internal Affairs project? I have enough things on my hands without making sure the police in this city don't go bad. But that bomb threat, maybe that has to do with the officer that is missing. Only one way to find out.

"My help?"

"Yes sir."

"Before you go any further, do you know by coming here and giving me any information on whatever it is without first turning it over to your commanding officer, you may be putting your job on the line?"

"Yes sir, I am well aware of what I am doing; but there is no other way for me to handle this because there are other police officers involved... other officers who may kill me or get away with the crimes they are about to commit. I don't know who to trust or believe in the precinct. I need someone that is not on the inside and objective!" Ramirez pleads at the agent.

"Okay, how can I help you?"

"Well sir, it's a long story. I hope you have the time."

"I have been keeping up with this case ever since it began; because I knew we would eventually get involved ever since I found out your captor robbed the armored truck. You have my undivided attention. Fill me in," Assures Agent Clark.

"Well sir, I don't have all the information, I am waiting for a phone call."

Agent Clark looks a bit puzzled, "A phone call?"

"Yes, a phone call from Jamie Collins."

"Jamie Collins, the guy who kidnapped you? Why would he be calling you?"

"Sir, let me start from the beginning. The money Jamie took was a way of suing the Clark County Government for hiring rogue officers like McCulley."

"Officer McCulley?"

"Yes, Officer McCulley is involved with twelve other Police Officers and several civilians who are plotting to blow up four hotels in Las Vegas on New Year's Eve in the year of 2003." Ramirez explains, then continues, "Now sir, if you don't mind, would you please not interrupt me. This is hard enough for me as it is."

"Okay Officer, go ahead." Clark says as he rests against the back of his chair with a pad and paper in his hands for any notes he might need to make during her statement.

Ramirez drifts back to the time when Jamie held her and her partner captive. She goes through each scene like someone looking at a storybook they have read before. She knows everything that has happened and tries to skip to all the good parts. Once she becomes confident in her mind that she knows what to say to the FBI agent, she starts her story.

"Like I said, the money from the bank is an informal way of Jamie suing the County for allowing McCulley and his friends to become Police Officers. He also wants restitution for anguish caused by the arrest and conviction of his two sons, who were admittedly framed by McCulley.

"While in the process of investigating McCulley, Jamie uncovered an elaborate scheme created by twelve other Police Officers and civilians to blow up four hotels in Las Vegas. These men belong to a racist group, whose ideas consist of world domination by the white race. These men want to cause as much damage as possible to human life and property, just to bring recognition to their cause.

"Right now sir that's all the information I have. That's why I am waiting for the phone call from Jamie. He has more information pertaining to who's involved and everything else you want to know.

"He asked me not to discuss the matters at hand with Metro because we don't know who else may be involved. That's why I withheld so much information from the sheriff–we don't want the plot exposed before we got you involved."

The agent stared out at Ramirez for a second, and then went back to scribbling in his notebook. Ramirez didn't know if he believed her story or not.

Maybe he won't believe a word I said. I wouldn't blame him. What proof do I have of anything that happened? Just my word against...against what? Nobody is even speaking out for anything else. It's just my word, hell, if I were him; I wouldn't believe my story either.

What if he does believe me though? Will he act on it, or just send me to jail? Jamie, why did you put me in this position? I didn't ask for any of this. I told him before that I wasn't strong enough to do these things! Why...

Agent Clark, who has completed taking his notes, cuts off Ramirez's thoughts. "So getting me involved is going to help in what way?"

"Number one; it will put the real criminals away and possibly save many lives. Number two; it will help to get Jamie's kids released from prison."

Clark nods his head, "And what does Jamie get out of the deal?"

Ramirez thinks for a moment, "Well, I would assume he wants immunity."

The tension in the office increases as each second ticks by. Ramirez now feels that she might have been better off just telling the Sheriff everything, instead of going through all of this with the FBI.

How can I know that he, a total stranger, can be trusted? What if the FBI is in on it too? Then what? I'll end up dead, plain and simple.

Stop it girl, you need to be positive about this. Not everyone is crooked in this world; someone has to be out there to help you.

"When is this so called phone call supposed to take place?" asks Agent Clark.

Ramirez looks up at the clock, "Well, it has been 14 hours since Jamie escaped from the house. I would imagine anytime soon."

"Well that doesn't give us much time."

"Time for what?" Ramirez asks Clark, who is now writing something else in his book.

"Time to tap your phone and find out where he is," Clark responds without so much as a glance at Ramirez.

This gets Ramirez's attention, "Tap the phone? Why? Jamie is going to supply you with information to help save lives and you want to tap my phone. When you find out where he is what are you going to do? Arrest him?"

"Yes, I would think so," Clark responds flatly.

"Look sir, this man has gone through a lot of trouble to get to where he is now. I am quite sure he didn't set all this up to get arrested. Isn't there another way to handle this?"

Ramirez's mind starts to race. *Shit, what have I done? Have I just given Jamie up to the Feds? What will become of him? I didn't want any of this to happen. Damn it all.*

I never wanted any of this shit to happen, and now it looks like I am helping them capture the one person I care about. Care about? Why the hell did I just think that?

I need to remain focused on this issue, not on any school girl feelings I might or might not have for someone I hardly even know.

"Officer Ramirez, just how do you expect me to handle this? The man is wanted for four kidnappings and bank robbery. What do you propose that I do? Go and kiss his hand and say thank you for a job well done! Are you crazy? Is that why you came down here...to plead his case? As a matter of fact, what type of relationship do you have with this man?"

Without thinking, Ramirez stands up and goes to the defense of Jamie and then sits back into the chair, surprised at herself. "The only relationship I have with the suspect is the fact that he held me captive. I don't know him other than what he has told me, but I do think giving him an opportunity to talk, without the threat of jail is something he really deserves.

"He has risked his life to try and save his children—children he obviously loves dearly. Not to mention the fact of exposing the plot to exterminate thousands of people who will die because of some idiots who want notoriety. I think you should do more than kiss his hand; I think you should kiss his ass. Oh! Excuse me sir."

Ramirez finishes while putting a hand over her mouth, as if she could catch the last few words before they hit Clark's ears.

Agent Clark raises an eyebrow at Ramirez, "My, my young lady, did I hit a nerve? I think you should sit back and evaluate yourself. You are walking on some very thin ice here. If you continue on this route, you're subject to lose your job."

"Look sir, I made a promise to an individual that I hardly know. I feel I am a good judge of character. No way would I be putting myself in so much jeopardy unless I knew I was right.

"I know Jamie committed some serious crimes, but I also know he is doing much more than that. I know he spent a lot of time gathering evidence you had no idea existed. I know he put himself in harms way for quite sometime in order to get that evidence.

"I also know that how he has helped, should be weighed against what he has violated. You have the ability to convert all the things Jamie has done wrong into something positive and give him a break."

The agent looks at Ramirez as though he wants to chew her up and spit her out. He turns away from her and stands up looks out the window and smiles, "Ramirez, what do you want me to do?"

"Let's just wait until Jamie calls, and see what he has to say; then go from there. I want to play this until the end.   Understand this, Jamie has been involved in this over two years, and from what I can see, he is very level headed.

He planned everything, even his get away. Remember he got away from a house that was not only surrounded by police officers, but the news media and hundreds of spectators. I also feel that when he calls, you still won't know his exact location. He is not a dummy."

The words hit Clark as if he finally sees something that was invisible before.

Two years in the planning?   This wasn't just something Collins did on a whim.   This man had everything planned out; he wasn't in it just for the money. If that were the case, he'd be long gone by now.

Revenge? McCulley might be guilty in Collins' eyes but, if it were just revenge he wanted, he could have killed McCulley a long time ago. Why the big show? What was worth all of this? What was worth his ass, what would Collins risk his life for? Maybe Ramirez is right, maybe this Collins guy is on the up and up. We'll see though; we'll see.

Agent Clark breaks from his thoughts, "I'll tell you what, Officer Ramirez; I will do as you ask and not trace the phone, but I will record the conversation, and then I will decide where we go from there. Deal?"

Ramirez perks up at this part of the conversation, finally, a break, "Okay, I agree."

"Sit there for a minute Officer Ramirez. I'll be right back."

Agent Clark leaves the room and crosses the hall into the office of Special Agent Ralph Phillips. "Ralph, I have a case I want you to work on."

"Sure thing, what is it?"

Agent Clark sits on the edge of Ralph's desk, "Have you heard about the two police officers that were kidnapped?"

"Yes sir, I have."

"Well, I have one of them outside now... Officer Dolores Ramirez. When you finish what you are doing, I want you to go over to her home and wait for a phone call, but that's only after you set up a recorder to record the conversation.

"After you do that, you, Officer Ramirez, and I will have another conversation. Another thing, I need you to put a trace on the phones of Rena Taylor and Anitra Clark before you go to Officer Ramirez's home.

"I feel the suspect responsible for this little crime wave, will be contacting one or both of these women. These women are close friends of the suspect.

"After you have completed all these things, bring Ramirez back here and we will go from there."

"Okay Sir, I have everything covered. I will get back with you as soon as everything is complete."

After talking with Agent Phillips, Clark returns to Officer Ramirez.

"Since we have a problem with security leaks in your department, I am going to assign an agent to you who has only been in Las Vegas for two days. He has been with the agency for 15 years now, so you won't have to worry about inexperience. I will send him out to your home and you are to go directly there and wait for his arrival."

Ramirez gets up from her chair and shakes Clark's hand on the way out, thanking him for his time. She starts off back home to get everything ready for the agent's arrival and Jamie's phone call.

Slipping back into her place was a bit tricky, since there were still reporters camped out in front of her door. Using an old trick she learned while coming home too late after curfew. Ramirez parked her car a few blocks down the street and hopped the fence to her neighbor's back yard. Climbing over another fence she finally lands in her own property.

Ramirez looks up at her bedroom window and is relieved that it is still open. She pops the screen off the window and slides inside of her house.

Once safely in her house, she relaxes on the couch, knowing the reporters outside are clueless to her arrival.

Now, I just have to sit back and wait for the agent, or Jamie's phone call. Hope he calls; I'm pretty screwed without it.

Ramirez goes off in her mind and reviews everything that has happened; slowly she begins to lose her fight with sleep and fades off into a peaceful slumber.

The Greyhound bus pulls in its stop in Tucson, Arizona. People are rushing to get off, trying desperately to pull fresh air into their lungs. Mutterings about how good it is to smell the sweet air is heard amongst the 75 travelers, who are scurrying to get their luggage before the fowl odor follows them.

Inside, the bus driver checks to make sure no one is left. Reluctantly, he walks toward the rear of the bus and covers his mouth and nose as he pulls down the two blankets used to contain the fowl odors reeking from the two men who are stretched across the rear seats.

"Hey...Hey... you two."

No response so the driver kicks the seats and finally McCulley wakes up, "Okay man! I'm awake! You got my attention!"

"Wake your friend and get the hell off my bus. Y'all smell like hell."

McCulley pokes Jamie for a bit, "Hey Jamie, wake up! I think we're at our destination."

"Where are we?" Jamie asks while his eyes are still closed.

The bus driver answers for McCulley, "You're in Tucson. Get your stuff together and get off."

"Okay man, we're leaving!" McCulley says a bit annoyed at the driver by this time.

"Damn McCulley, you stink." Jamie laughs as he gets his bag and walks down the aisle.

"Yeah sucker, you smell just like me.'

"We got to find some place to clean up." Jamie says and stops before he exits the bus, "Sir, is there a shower or something in the terminal?"

"There aren't any shower facilities, but there is a sink and running water. I think both of you should use it," replies the bus driver, as he tries to scoot the two off the bus.

"Okay man, we got the hint." McCulley retorts.

"Come on McCulley; let's go so this man can have his bus back."

Jamie and McCulley exit the bus looking like two homeless people carrying two bags. McCulley's chest is now feeling a little better, but still hurts.

They walk pass angry glances and murmuring from the crowd toward the awaiting restroom. As soon as they enter the restroom, the few men inside, hold their noses and rush out.

Jamie looks at McCulley and wipes his forehead, as though he were removing sweat and he starts peeling off his clothes, and McCulley follows suit. Both men are now standing at the sinks, dressed in nothing but their underwear, frantically scrubbing their faces and the rest of their bodies.

After scrubbing, shaving and removing false hair and changing clothes, emerging from the restroom are two very different looking men...this time carrying one bag. The smelly grubby clothes are placed in a bag and thrown into a trash can.

"Okay McCulley, how do you feel?"

"I'm still in pain, but it's a lot better than yesterday." McCulley says, while testing out his ability to breathe.

"Come on I have to make a phone call."

"Who you gonna call? Oh never mind, I know. It's that chick from the TV, right?" razzes McCulley.

"Yeah, you're right. Come on."

Jamie walks over to the phones, followed by McCulley who's looking around and holding his chest. He drops a few quarters in the phone and dials the number.

"Hello?"

"Anita?"

"Yes."

"This is me?"

There is a pause from the other side of the phone, then, "Oh baby, I'm so glad to hear from you. Are you all right?"

"Yes, I am."

"Boy you better not get caught; these cops around here are pissed at you."

"Well, I have no intentions of getting caught. I just wanted to say thank you for sticking up for me."

"Sure baby, anytime."

"Well, I have to go, just in case they have your phone tapped."

"Jamie, take care of yourself and stay in touch."

"I will. Be good."

Jamie stands with the receiver in his hand staring at the wall while McCulley seems to be walking with less difficulty and makes his way towards Jamie, a bit easier than he did in Las Vegas.

"Okay, did you take care of your business?"

"Yes, I did. Put your sunglasses on and hail a cab. I will meet you outside. I have to make one more call."

Jamie drops his money into the phone coin slot and dials another number.

"Hello."

"Hey Rena; I can't talk long, but be good and thanks a lot. I will call again soon. I will show you my gratitude."

"Jamie, Jamie....Wait!"

Jamie doesn't wait for her to talk. He hangs up the phone, while Rena is calling out his name. He then picks up his bag and leaves the terminal and meets McCulley, who is patiently waiting in a cab.

"Where to," asks the cabbie

"Take us to U-Store-It Mini Storage on Mills Road."

"You know that's quite a ways away?"

"Yes I do, here's $50.00 to start the ride." Jamie says as he hands over some cash to the driver.

McCulley leans over to Jamie and whispers, "Where are we going now?"

Jamie seems annoyed by McCulley's question, "I told you, you would know when we get there and not before, so sit back, take a couple of pills and relax."

"Whatever you say, I see you're in a good mood." McCulley says a bit offended.

Jamie sighs, "McCulley, I'm just thinking about a few things so if you don't mind, I'm not in the mood for talking."

Jamie is now lost in a world of his own. He is now a fugitive and he is terrified with the thought of Ramirez not being able to keep her end of the deal. Then his thoughts drift towards... his sons.

On the day of their verdict was handed down, Jamie went to their apartment to pick them up. He was in good spirits and felt everything would be all right. He knocked on the door and a loud, heavy voice yelled back.

"Who is it?"

"It's me; it's your father. Open up!" The door was unlocked and slightly ajar. Jamie pushed the door open and he saw Marvin, his oldest son walking back to the couch with his pajamas on.

"Why aren't you dressed? You got two hours before you are due to be in court."

"I'm not going!"

"What do you mean you're not going?"

"Daddy, I said I am not going. I don't want to go to jail. Especially for something I didn't do."

"Son, you have to go, and how do you know you're going to jail?"

"Daddy, look at all the bullshit evidence they planted against us. They want us in jail and that's what they will get. I am scared daddy. I didn't want to be like you. I don't want to go to jail for something I didn't do and I am not going."

Jamie walked over to comfort his son, "Marvin, no one is going to lock you up. You are innocent. I know it, you know it, God knows it and so does the jury. They are not going to lock you up."

Marvin pushes away from his father, "Dad, I listened to you when you said to file a complaint against that cop. I listened to you when you said, I had nothing to worry about, I listened to you a lot and where has it gotten me? I'm not listening any more. And they can all kiss my ass."

"Look, I don't care what has happened; you're going to court. You're going to see what they have to say. You're not going to become a fugitive, running and hiding, afraid of your own shadow. You are going to do as I say or I will kick your ass and drag you down there myself."

Marvin's eyes started to tear as he shot an answer back at his dad, "Yeah that's your answer? Kick my ass? Well, go right ahead and do it. You're the big bad daddy. Go ahead and kick my ass, then what? Nothing! I am tired of all this bullshit. I have been a good son, I have been a model citizen and where has it gotten me? I'm screwed and you helped them screw me. I wish I were dead, because that's what I will be when they send me to jail."

"Son, I want you to know this is just as hard for me. I don't want to take you there and watch them put you away, but I don't want some over zealous cop to put a bullet in your ass either." Jamie said as he tried to rationalize with Marvin.

The yelling disturbed Jamie Jr., who was also still in the bed. He came into the living room right in the middle of the argument, "Hey, what's up! What's all the yelling about? What's going on?"

"I see you're not ready either! I hope you're not full of the same shit as your brother!"

Jamie Jr. looked groggily at his father, "What are you talking about?"

"Your brother says he's not going to court. I hope you didn't have the same thing for breakfast?"

Jamie Jr. shook his head, "I have every intention of going, but I don't want to. I feel they are going to find us guilty and send us to prison. Daddy, I don't want to go. I didn't do anything."

Now it was Jamie Jr's turn to start crying. He turned away from his father so his dad would not see his tears. Jamie looked at his sons and saw how frightened they both were. Hell, he was frightened too, but he needed to be strong for them. Whatever went down that day in court, Jamie knew that he would see his sons again, even if he had to break them out himself.

"Jamie shut up! Daddy is not going to listen to you–he's Mister Justice himself. Follow the rules, do what they say, and then let them screw you."

"Marvin, first off, I don't care what the circumstances are… if one more curse word comes out of your mouth…"

"Yeah…Yeah… You're going to kick my ass."

"Marvin be cool. Why are you so against daddy? He didn't do anything to you."

Marvin's head was spinning with emotion. He really didn't know why he hated his dad so much. All he knew is that his life went from perfect to messed up. He was about to go to jail he knew it. Why didn't the others see it too? There was no way they were going to get off.

The cops want him and his brother behind bars; they wouldn't stop at the court system. Marvin almost hoped for jail–if he did get free, the cops would just kill him anyway.

Why did this all happen? Why couldn't his father have just let well enough alone?

"If he had kept himself out of our business, we wouldn't be in this shit. File a complaint for what? So that asshole cop could frame us?"

Jamie had enough of his son's talk, "Okay, go ahead and blame me. Go ahead. I will accept all responsibility for whatever happens to you; but understand one thing; it won't stop there.

"I will not rest until your case is settled. I mean settled properly and the right people punished. I will not let this rest, even if it kills me. I refuse to let anything happen to the both of you.

"I know it's hard, but for now let's see this through. Let's see what's going to happen. We don't know if you're going to jail. We just have to follow the rules until there is no other alternative. I promise you both one thing, if you are found guilty and sent to prison, you will not be there long. You will get out, even if I have to kill someone in the process."

Jamie stops and embraces both of his sons, "I love you both and both of you have made me a proud father. Now, I'm asking you to trust me one more time! Don't give up on me!"

Marvin was pacing the floor, not knowing to run or to do what his father was asking him to do. He had always listened to him, but now he was terrified, terrified of being locked up.

He kept shaking his head back and forth as the tears rolled down his face. *Run, just run,* is what his mind kept saying, but in his heart he knew what his dad was saying was right. He would have to run for the rest of his life, looking over his shoulder...and what about his brother? He couldn't let him go to prison alone.

Jamie Jr. didn't know how to help Marvin. He was just as afraid as Marvin was, but he wasn't about to run. His dad always faced up to his problems, and he was going to do the same. He walked over to Marvin and hugged his brother with all his might. Together, they were going to see this through. Marvin looks at him and knew what he had to do.

Both brothers looked at their father, the man they trusted and believed in. All three of them stood holding onto each other with tears streaming down their faces.

The silence of their bond was strong. There wasn't anything that would come between them, not even the bars of a prison. Once more, they looked at each other, and they knew it was time to go. Both brothers walked to their rooms to get dressed, still afraid, but with the faith and strength that their father would not let them down.

The thoughts of that day and how it turned out, weighed heavy on Jamie's mind. And here he was with McCulley...working with the man who had railroaded his sons into prison.

Fighting off the desire to kill McCulley was the hardest thing he had to do in his life. While following McCulley and tracing his roots, Jamie came across opportunity after opportunity to kill him, but he knew that wouldn't solve anything. He would wind up in prison along with his kids... not to mention the death penalty.

The sound of the cabby's voice broke Jamie's concentration, but doesn't stop the contempt he feels for McCulley, as he stares at him.

Jamie's heart rate has risen and his anger is more prevalent than ever, but he realizes that the situation had changed and McCulley is working with him as planned.

Jamie begins to smile as he stared at McCulley, because he knows that if nothing else, he finally has McCulley where he wants him. McCulley was a part of the robbery, whether he wants to be or not, and if they get caught, McCulley will be in prison with Jamie and all the other people he put there. The plan was signed, sealed and delivered. There was no way he can get out.

Ramirez was drugged and can't tell what transpired and McCulley's fingerprints were all over the rental car. Now, all that was left was to tell McCulley of his involvement, which Jamie felt was going to be sheer pleasure.

"We're here...your fare is $97.20. You owe me $47.20."

Jamie reaches into his pockets for the fare, "Okay, young man. Here is fifty and a twenty dollar tip. You have a nice day." After paying the fare, Jamie reaches over and wakes up McCulley, who seems to have fallen into a deep sleep. "Hey...hey McCulley...wake up, we're here."

McCulley stretches and rubs his eyes, "What...what."

"We're here. Come on and get out."

Jamie exits the cab, stands and stretches, as he absorbs the fresh air and looks around the too–familiar surroundings.

Things haven't changed at all in the four days since he left the area. The old man's truck is parked in the same spot, the area is just as desolate as ever and the building, which holds the office, was still holding its own.

"Why the hell did we come here?"

"There's something I have to pick up."

"What?"

Jamie starts to walk away from McCulley before answering, "Don't worry just follow me."

JIMMY CULLORS/JOSEPH SZEWEZYK

chapter

12 PEACE OF MIND

Jamie walks into the overcast building to find the old man asleep in his La-Z-Boy and his wife rocking in her rocker crocheting.

Without much effort, the lady peeps over her glasses and yells at her husband, "Tom....Tom...Wake up."

The old man stirs, but doesn't open his eyes, "Yea... whatcha want?"

His wife points towards Jamie, "That colored man is back. I guess he came back fer his truck."

The old man turns his head around to see Jamie standing there patiently. Without even the slightest thought of getting up to see what Jamie wants, the old man decides to help Jamie without actually doing anything.

"Hey young'un', how ya doin? Thought it would be aw'ile fo' ah sees ya again. Have a sit down, take a load off yo' feet."

"No, that's quite all right. I just need to get my truck and get out of here."

"Thare ya go again...allus in a hurry. Y'all city folk jes' never gonna learn are ya? One day ya gonna wake up dead cause of all that hurrin'...Then what ya gonna do? Now I gotta git outta mah comfortable chair, to wait on ya.

"Who dat you got witch ya? "Somebody ya picked up from one of thar bar fights? He sho' look bad."

The man raises his voice to McCulley, "Hey younin'...yo wanna piece o' meat fo them eyes of yourn. It'll stop the swelling' and stop 'me from getting any darker."

McCulley, realizing how pitiful he must look tries to hide his face and declines the help of the old man, "Thanks a lot but I think I can make it without putting anything on my face."

McCulley turns his back while Jamie tries to get the old man's attention again.

Two of the crabbiest people in the world, and I had to bring them together.

Jamie puts himself in the old man's line of vision, "He'll be alright, but I believe you owe me money. I paid you for a month and my truck was stored here for four days."

The man loses interest in McCulley and now looks at Jamie oddly, "Now youngin' ya gonna make me havta think. Cain't you jes' leave it here fo the rest o' the month, and we kin call it even?"

Jamie shakes his head, "No old man, I need my truck, but I will go one step further. I will just take my truck and you can keep the money you owe me. How's that?"

The old man throws his head back in the chair and begins to rub his chin as through he had to think about the offer.

I wonder if I can get mo money from this man? Ah know these city foke like to spend money jes' to make a impression. "Hey youngin', you think you might wanta add a lil' bit to that cause ya know I kept a eye out fo' yo' propity?"

"No old man, that's all you get. As a matter of fact I bet you got an old mattress full of money somewhere don't you?"

"If'n I do youngin', you ain't gonna know 'bout it, but that offer o' yours sounds good ta me youngin'.

"I jes' loves yo city foke, an' the way y'all spends money. Not like mah Anna and me. We save o'var money an' use it wisely. We don't spend it on thangs we don't need.

"Look at that telly-vision. We done had tha' fo goin on thirty years, an' it jes' as good when mah son brun' it to us.

"We caints gets channels in too good, but tha' causin da cable company done moved in, and mess wit da reg'lar channels.

"We ain't gonna bent o'er to them, we gonna keep doin' what we been doin' and save our money fo a rainy day. We don't need no cable. Ain't nothin' on telly-vision noways, but bad news. Maybe one day, when we saves enough money, we can git to that big city you come from 'Las Vegas'."

Jamie is barely paying attention to the man rambling on— instead his thoughts are on making sure everything goes smoothly.

They may have escaped the Las Vegas Metro, but they were not free and clear quite yet. There was still much to be done before Jamie would feel safe.

"Where's the restroom?"

The old man points to the far corner, "O'er thar in th' corner. Thar's a strang hangin down in the middle of the room. Pull it and th' light will come on."

Jamie turns and heads off to the restroom, but then stops to ask something of the old man, "By the way, do you have an envelope?"

The man digs behind a stack of papers and produces an aged envelope that may have been white at one time, but is now yellow with coffee stains and age. "Here ya go youngin'."

Jamie takes a look at the envelope and goes off into the restroom. While Jamie is in the restroom, McCulley wanders around, surveying the area. He doesn't wander too far—the pain in his ribs has become active again. Clenching his teeth, McCulley lets out a stifled breath, as the old man looks him over.

What the hell is this guy looking at? Where did Jamie go? An envelope in the bathroom, why the hell would anyone need that?

The old man ignores McCulley's anti-social body language, "Why don't ya sit down youngin'? Ya look like ya in pain."

McCulley looks over at the old man, "Well, I guess I will." With a few slow steps, McCulley makes his way over to the chair, where he sits and tries not to move his chest too much.

"What's wrong wit ya? Ya keep holdin' yo chest?"

"I was in a car accident and broke six ribs." McCulley said between breaths.

"My, tha' musta really smart." observes the old man.

"Well it only hurts when I laugh or breathe hard."

"Where y'all headed?"

Just as McCulley begins to answer the old man's question, Jamie emerges from the restroom, "Hey old man, I've been thinking; you've been so nice to me, I guess the least I can do is return the favor."

"What do yo mean youngin'?"

"Well, it's like this–while I was in Las Vegas I made a little money. I want you and your wife to share in my good fortune–I figure, since you helped us out in the Korean War–and I am quite sure you've helped a lot of other people–I'm going to help you.

You can go and get a new TV, have cable installed, go on a little trip to Las Vegas and have money left over, maybe buy some new clothes."

McCulley's eyes start to widen, but the old man doesn't notice. All he notices is that someone just offered to give him a great deal of money just because they were feeling nice that day.

What doze this boy wont from me? Maybe he loss his mind; city folk do that now an' again. But whut if he don't go nuts, does he have da money? As long as he has da money, why should ah care what be goin' on wit him?

"What are ya saying boy?"

"I said–here take this, have a nice life–and you and your wife enjoy yourselves, but do not tell anyone where the money came from, agreed?"

The old man shakes his head in agreement and takes the envelope–opens it and sees an untold amount of hundred dollar bills staring him in the face. He jumps around, grabbing his wife and dancing in a circle.

While they are celebrating, Jamie and McCulley leave the office quietly and walk out to the storage unit.

"How much money did you give him?"

"Five Thousand Dollars."

McCulley's veins pop in his neck, "Five Thousand Dollars? You gave that redneck five thousand dollars?"

Jamie shoots a glance at McCulley, "Yes, I did. I just wanted to make someone happy."

McCulley scuffs at Jamie's response, "You sure did–listen to that old man scream. It sounds like he's outside."

Jamie nods, "He is loud."

As McCulley turns around, he could see the old man and his wife running towards their truck. Neither one has ran so fast in years.

The old man is so excited, he is in the truck and has it started and moving before his wife could pull her right leg in and close the door. In a matter of seconds, the only trace of the couple was a cloud of dust from the gravel on the road as they headed for town.

Jamie turns smiling, and continues walking toward the unit. McCulley walks while turning in circles, looking at the dilapidated buildings and sagebrush growing around them.

"Why the hell would anyone want to leave their belongings in this dump? If a good storm comes along, it will wipe out everything. I wouldn't leave my dog here. As a matter of fact, what kind of truck do you have parked here? It must be a hunk of junk."

Jamie pauses at the door before he answers McCulley, "I will do you a favor and let you make up your own mind. Here we are."

McCulley peeps into the cracks of the unit and sees the red Nissan Frontier and smiles.

"Okay man, we got some wheels. Thanks a lot, I thought we would be traveling in a hunk of shit, but we got a brand new dusty truck. Hurry up man, so I can sit down and rest my ass."

"Okay just relax; I have to unlock the door." Jamie states as he goes for the lock.

McCulley lurches past Jamie, "Aww man, to hell with that shit, watch this."

McCulley takes a swift kick to the door and they both had to jump back to avoid being hit by the doors falling to the ground.

McCulley turns around, expecting to see Jamie astonished by his feat of strength, but instead Jamie has a look of disappointment, "Damn man, now you are causing work for me. I have to move this shit out of the way, so we can get the truck out, but since you kicked the door, you will help me move it. So get to work."

McCulley tries to pick a piece up, but immediately clutches his chest, "Man, I can't move that stuff–my chest is already killing me."

"You should have thought of that before you kicked the damned thing down. That's what I don't like about you. You don't think...you act! That's why you're in so much trouble. You never think!"

McCulley reacts as though he was hit with a sudden thought and walks away and leans on the storage unit, "Speaking of thinking, I have been thinking, about all this shit. I don't think I'm in as much trouble as you say I am. All they have on me is, I lied and had a few people locked up."

Jamie looks up from moving the debris, "Hey asshole! Don't forget about your friends, they will probably kill you because you know too much."

McCulley shrugs, "Ah, I can get around that. All we have to do is arrest them at the same time and my problems are over."

Jamie stops to look straight at McCulley, "Well Mr. McCulley, I have some bad news for you. You, my friend, are also implicated in an armored car robbery."

"I'm not concerned about that either because I didn't do it!"

"I don't think anyone is going to believe you."

"Why not, I wasn't there and the only reason I'm with you is because you made me think my life wouldn't be worth a damn if I stayed. I could tell them the truth; they will believe me and help me get the other guys who are planning to blow the hotels."

Jamie can hardly control himself from laughing out loud at McCulley. This is the moment he has been waiting for, "Well, smart-ass, how in the hell are you going to explain your fingerprints in the get away car?"

McCulley stops for a minute. *Fingerprints? What the hell is Jamie talking about? I was never in that damned car. He's just trying to scare me, that's all. Well, I don't find this very funny and the shit is going to end soon.*

"What fingerprints? I was never in that car."

Jamie smiles again, "I beg to differ Mr. McCulley. How do you think you got to the other house? Also, on the day of the robbery, you hadn't started work yet. You had plenty of time to participate and get to work.

"You see I wanted you to know how it felt to be framed, just the way you framed all those other guys. You will be charged and you will go to jail.

"You see; everything all the way to this point was planned. I kidnapped you, and I placed you in the get away car. I pointed out all of your illegal friends; convinced you that you were in trouble and I exposed your get away not only on national TV, but also to the sheriff at the house.

"Then there are the doctors and nurses and police officers at the hospital, all the people on the tram. How about the man who drove us back to town? At the bus station the other police officers and last the lonely old man and his wife.

"All of them will testify that you put up no effort to get away. No one saw me hold a gun on you! You have no one to testify on your behalf, so where does that leave you? In prison with me, and all the people you framed, and don't forget about your mother!"

As Jamie completed what he was saying to McCulley, he bends over to remove parts of the door. McCulley stares at him for a while. The pain in McCulley's chest starts to subside the anger pushes all other feelings aside in McCulley.

That son of a bitch. He framed me! I should kill him for it right now, that little bastard! He wants help picking up boards? I'll give him help.

McCulley picks up a board and with all of his might he slams the board across Jamie's back, knocking him to the ground. McCulley then hits Jamie several more times with the board and kicks him in the stomach, turning Jamie on his back. The enraged officer has burning anger in his eyes and kicks Jamie again only this time in his face, causing blood to gush from Jamie's nose.

Jamie trying to defend himself rolls over and tries desperately to get to his feet, but with every movement a blow from the board meets him.

The board finally breaks from McCulley's last blow and Jamie takes his opportunity to get to his feet. Rushing McCulley with a head blow to the chest; both men fall to the ground in agony. Moans and groans were heard for a few minutes and then they roll over laughing at each other.

Jamie looks over at McCulley, his face is bleeding and he is holding his chest.

Well, I knew there would be hell to pay when I told McCulley. Damn, I wish those boards weren't around though. Well, we got all the hostilities out of the way now; things should be a bit smoother.

Jamie starts to laugh at this last thought.

Funny when smooth means "just a man hunt".

"Man your face looks like mine!" McCulley says as he laughs at Jamie's face.

"I think you broke my nose!"

"Doesn't that pain feel good? You can feel it all the way to your feet. Not to mention your back. How's it doing?"

"Man, you didn't have to go there." Jamie says rubbing his back.

"Yeah sure! I'm not supposed to do anything to you after you framed me?"

"That's right, you didn't give anyone else an opportunity to do it to you. So you only got what you deserve!"

"Well now that I am implicated in the robbery, I want my share of the money! If I calculated right, you owe me $378,500! And I want it now!"

"Man, you're having problems holding yourself up, much less carrying all that money."

"You let me worry about that. Now, give me my money!"

Jamie starts to give in on McCulley's request, "Okay! Okay! Tell you what, let's get the hell out of here and you can count it out while we are on the road."

Both the men drag their battered bodies off the ground. They struggle moving the door to allow them to back the truck out of the storage unit.

After backing the truck out, Jamie loads the other bags into the rear of the vehicle. He puts the bag of money into the vehicle with them and drives out of the storage area.

While McCulley is getting excited about seeing so much money, Jamie picks up his cell phone to call Ramirez.

Ramirez you had better be home or a lot of people are not going to have a happy New Year

Ramirez has finally settled in to her house. The reporters around her home are starting to lose interest in staking out her house. They don't leave her area completely, but they aren't perched outside of her door anymore, either. Several of the smaller news crews are congregating around their vans and having lunch, just waiting Ramirez to reappear.

In the modestly kept home, Ramirez walks around, trying to keep busy cleaning all the nooks and crannies in the home, while a stranger sits in her recliner, snoring and occasionally waking up to watch the TV watching him.

The blaring sound of Sally Jesse Rafael was broken by the sound of the doorbell. Ramirez feels it is probably some news reporters and refused to answer the door. The ringing persisted and then the knocking starts; finally Ramirez's name is called. Ramirez goes to the door and peeps through the peephole and sees it was her boyfriend Willis.

She turns and leans against the door and rolls her eyes. She knows this is not the time for a visit from him; she doesn't feel like answering any questions, but she opens the door anyway to try and get him to leave.

"Hello Willis, how are you doing? Why didn't you call before you came over?" Ramirez says, trying to hide the annoyance in her voice.

"Look Dolores, open the door and let me in, I need to speak with you! For the last few days I haven't done anything but worry about you. Let me in so I can talk with you and see how you are doing. My mother and all of our friends are asking me questions I can't answer! I need some answers for myself!"

"Look Willis, I'm sorry, but not today. I am in the middle of something and it needs my undivided attention."

Willis doesn't seem to hear anything Ramirez is saying, "NO! I'm coming in right now! I want to know what's going on and I want to see my woman!"

With a hard push, Willis opens the door, pushing Ramirez back. He enters the house, looking around and finally sets his eyes on Agent Phillips sitting in the recliner relaxing.

"So, this is why you wouldn't let me in. You have someone else entertaining you."

Willis walks past Ramirez and heads straight for Agent Phillips, "Who are you and what are you doing here?"

Agent Phillips looks warily up a Willis, "Well sir, I would very much like to answer all of your questions, but I can't. I will give you my name though–its' Ralph Phillips."

Willis turns towards Ramirez, his head whipping around so fast, she fears he might have broken his neck, "Dolores, who is this guy, and why is he lounging around here as though he lives here? Is this your new man? Is this why you haven't been in touch with me?"

Ramirez tries to get a grip on the situation, "Look Willis, there are a lot of things going on in my life at the present, and I don't have time to explain them. You're just going to have to trust me."

Ramirez looks at Willis, with a small twinkle of authority in her eyes. She has been pushed around a lot in the past, but that stops now.

I can't allow myself to be bullied like this; too many people are counting on me. Either Willis sees things are better left off for today, or he doesn't. His feelings are too small right now to take in consideration, a few thousand people's lives count on me now, and I won't have some jealous fool ruin everything.

"Trust you? You've been kidnapped, held hostage and when you get out of the jam, you don't even call me! Then, I come over to your house; a strange man is sitting around here watching TV and you're cleaning. And you can't explain to me what's going on!"

Willis starts to pace the room as he screams at Ramirez, "Yet, you want me to trust you! I don't know if I can do that. My mother told me to watch out for you and maybe she was right. You don't love me; you're only using me to get next to my mother's money!"

Right in the middle of the conversation, the phone rings and automatically Ramirez tunes out Willis and turns to the phone. Agent Phillips and Ramirez look at each other while Willis rambles on about trust. Ramirez immediately grabs Willis by the arm and leads him to the door.

"Come on Willis, you have to leave."

Willis puts on the brakes and uses his weight to stop Ramirez from dragging him out of the house. "I am not going anywhere!"

Ramirez opens the door and asks Willis again to leave, but he refuses. Agent Phillips runs toward Willis and pushes him out the door and slams and locks it, while Ramirez runs to the phone.

"Hello?"

"Hello? Is that you, Ramirez?"

"Yes, this is she." Ramirez breathes a sigh of relief; she recognizes the voice, "Jamie is that you?"

"Yes it is. How is everything going?"

An unexplained feeling of relief comes over Ramirez as she hears Jamie's voice. She pays no attention to Willis, who still standing outside, shouting her name and beating on the door. She absorbs the sound of Jamie's voice, disregarding what was said.

"Hello! Ramirez! Are you there?"

Ramirez snaps back into the moment, "Oh...Oh yes...Yes Jamie, I'm here. I am so glad to hear from you. Are you all right?"

"Yes. I'm doing just fine. Did you do what I asked?"

"Yes I did. As a matter of fact the agent is here now." Ramirez says as she looks towards Agent Phillips, as if Jamie could see him over the phone.

Jamie breathes a sigh of relief when he hears that the agent is there. Good, she got the FBI involved and they believed her enough to send someone over to wait for this phone call. Now, I just have to see if the FBI wants to cooperate with me or not. I sure hope they do, there isn't a lot of time for hardball.

"Okay, that's good. I knew you could do it. Now go into the bedroom, and pick up the extension and give the phone to the agent."

Ramirez hands Agent Phillips the phone and runs into the bedroom. From the bedroom, Ramirez nervously listens to the conversation between Phillips and Jamie.

Agent Phillips has the phone, and on the other end, a cheery greeting was heard. Phillips tries to concentrate on what Jamie is saying but also the tone that Jamie uses.

For a man on the run from the law, this guy sure seems happy, like he just won the lottery or something. The only lottery this outlaw won is the 'free stay at the federal pen' lotto.

Jamie's words break Phillips thoughts, "How are you doing Agent Phillips?

"So you're the famous Jamie Collins? Or shall I say, infamous?"

"If you want to put it that way...yes I am. Either way, I'm still the same person."

Ramirez interrupts the conversation, giving Phillips the opportunity to know that she is listening, "I'm on the phone Jamie, now can we get some answers? And where is this so called evidence?" Ramirez says trying to rush Jamie into solving her curiosity.

"Ok Ramirez, just hold on a minute. What have you told the Sheriff?" Jamie asks, going back to the matter at hand.

"Nothing much, I didn't have too much to say. Remember I was out cold for most of that ordeal."

"Yeah I remember. I hope you're all right."

Ramirez's mind goes back to the time where Jamie held her and McCulley prisoner. She can't help but to think of his plight and all of the things he planned and the time it must have taken. He did all of this for his children, a love like that was something Ramirez didn't see often in her life. If only...

"I am all right. Well Mr. Agent, what do you know so far?" Jamie asks turning the emphasis back on Agent Phillips.

"Actually, quite a bit. You robbed an armored truck, you kidnapped three people, you stole a police vehicle and equipment, you committed arson, and you are a fleeing felon. Need I say more?"

Phillips waits on the phone for Jamie's response.

I am quite aware of the fact that this guy knows we're going to be tapping his phone call. I wonder why he is spending so much time on the line. It's as though he wants us to know his location. I wander what he has up his sleeve. Sounding all smug because he thinks he got away with everything, well he's got another thing coming.

"Okay I will admit those things happened, but what about what I have uncovered?" Jamie offers.

"Tell you what, if you give yourself up, we will take that into consideration." Agent Phillips replies flatly.

Jamie stifles a laugh, "Nope it doesn't work like that. I have too much at stake to give up. You have to come up with something better. Like immunity!"

Immunity? Who does this guy think he is? The only immunity he is going to get is the cluster shots he'll receive before they lock him up for three or four life terms at Chateau Enculer.

"Now you don't expect us to just give you immunity because you ask for it? Who the hell do you think you are?"

There is a silence in the room as the tension between the two men continues to build up. Both men want justice, but neither can decide the definition of that word.

"Like I said at the beginning of this conversation, I am Jamie Collins and I am not going to settle for anything less than what I ask for.

"I also have two more demands; one: my sons and the other men who have been railroaded by Officer McCulley are to get another trial, only this time a fair one.

"My last demand is that I keep the money for all the expenses I incurred, doing your job of discovering corrupt cops and a plot to destroy four hotels on a certain date, and possibly killing thousands of people. I know the information I have is worth more than the lousy $757,000.00 I took from the bank."

The response from Agent Phillips is slow and Jamie wonders about the agent. A lot is hanging on this man's ability to think on his feet.

This guy probably won't go for everything, but he better at least try to do something, or this is going to be one hell of a long negotiation. If people weren't so damn blinded by their own code of honor, this would take only seconds to get across. Wonder if Mr. Phillips will conclude that people's lives might be worth more than a few hundred thousand dollars.

"Well, first Mr. Collins I can't give you an okay on your demands. That has to come from a higher authority. Secondly, your demands would be better handled, if you give yourself up so we could discuss this matter in person.

Agent Phillips seems to be proud of his last statement. *This will make him come in and deal with us if he wants a deal at all. All of this bomb-shit looks like bullshit anyway. How the hell could any terrorist group get that strong and involve another law enforcement agency without anyone else knowing.*

This guy is full of shit, and as soon as he agrees to come in, that's when everyone will know how much shit this guy is really full of.

Instead of offering himself up, Jamie snaps at the agent, "What the hell did I just tell you? I am not going to do that. I am not going to sit in anybody's cell and wait for nothing. If my demands aren't met, I will keep my mouth shut and watch the whole thing unfold on CNN."

Jamie starts to sigh mentally. He knew this wouldn't be easy, but this joker makes McCulley look levelheaded. A game of chess. With thousands of people's lives at stake, this bureaucratic jackass still makes it into a game of chess. Bet he memorized the FBI handbook on this thing, and is reading it to me line for line.

"Mr. Collins, if you withhold all the information you have and people die you will be just as guilty as those who did the bombings!"

"Look at it from my point of view—so will you and the FBI. Now I'll tell you what. I will give you until this time tomorrow to talk to me sensibly or I will disappear.

You go and talk to whoever you have to talk to and explain to them I have a list of thirteen people, names and addresses and the plot on tapes, plus a confession from Officer McCulley vindicating all the prisoners who are held illegally in prison.

I am willing to turn over the information to you when and only when, my sons and the other men are granted a new trial and I can keep the money and not be prosecuted. No one was physically harmed and thousands of people will be glad that my accomplices and me saved their lives."

Phillips is a bit stunned at this last bit of information from Jamie. *What did he just say? Accomplices? He can't be talking about McCulley, can he?*

"Accomplishes? Are you saying that McCulley was in on this with you?"

"Let's just say, he was an unwilling accomplice."

Jamie senses that the conversation has gone on long enough.

If the FBI were doing a trace, they would have me pretty well located by now; besides, Phillips has enough on his mind to think about. Everything I wanted to let him know, bit by bit, they know now. At least, everything I wanted them to know for now.

"Ramirez, are you still there?"

Ramirez's voice pipes over the other end, "Yes, I heard everything."

"Good, you are going to be the middleman; I will not deal with anyone if you're not involved. It is important to me that everything goes the way I planned it. We don't have too much time and I want to make sure everyone involved gets caught and punished."

Phillips hears this and goes ballistic.

What the hell does this man think? He can do all of these crimes and just walk away? He won't get away; I won't let him. He is guilty of more things, than just someone that may or may not be planning to blow a building up. That isn't even a proven point yet, for all we know this guy is just scared and now trying to talk out of his ass to cut a deal. No way. This won't go down like this.

"Collins, you want the FBI to arrest people who you point out, but let you go free? Let me tell you something! This is not Hollywood; this is real life. The thought of vindicating you makes my skin crawl. To me, you're just as guilty as the ones you're trying to get arrested."

Jamie smiles at his end of the phone.

Good, I have Agent Phillips' attention now. He is thinking about everything I said. He may not believe everything I said, but he is thinking about it. Now, just play it cool, Jamie. Give them what you want to give them and nothing more. Time to play some mind games with Phillips.

"Mr. Agent, I am through talking with you, you get back to your boss and deliver my message. Bye! Ramirez you take it real easy, and look under your mattress, I have something there for you. I took the liberty to visit your home one-day while you were working. Bye, Loi Du Talion."

Ramirez hangs up the phone and starts to stomp over to where Jamie directed her.

He was in my house! He planned all of this! This guy was in my house long before everything went down! Why the hell did he do that? How dare he come into MY house and go through MY belongings! Agggggghh! I can't believe he did that. This better be pretty damn important, to break into my house and go under my bed. He was in my bedroom! I can't believe it!

As Ramirez's thoughts start to tear her apart, her body does a like-wise job of her bedroom. The room that was recently cleaned is now in shambles as Ramirez goes out on a destructive path towards her bed.

This better be worth it, Jamie. This better be worth it.

Jamie cuts off the phone and lays it on the seat and begins to breathe heavily. McCulley, who is still amazed by the amount of money he has in his procession mumbles to Jamie, "Man, the more I'm around you, the more I see your balls changing colors."

Jamie looks at McCulley for a minute before responding. *What in the hell is this guy talking about? Something about a guy talking about my balls just doesn't rub me right, McCulley better do some fast explaining.*

"What the hell are you talking about?"

"I mean, when I first got to know you, your balls were just big and flesh colored, then they got big and black like bowling balls. Next they turned to brass and now after that phone call, I would say your balls are made of steel.

Did you forget who you were talking to? Do you realize you don't threaten or give the FBI the 'old Tomato?' Your ass is never going to get out of prison. Your ass is going to have a cell by itself. The next time you see daylight, your grandchildren will have married children.

"Sometimes, I just wonder what the hell you're thinking. Sometimes, I figure you're just a man on a suicide run."

The words hit Jamie like a ton of bricks.

'Suicide run.' Is that what I am on? I don't want to die anymore than the next man; I just want my sons out of prison. I told them, they wouldn't stay there as long as I was breathing, but what if McCulley is right?

Am I losing sight of the big goal? Maybe I need to back off, but if I back off, my sons won't be free. Screw this. My sons come first, second and last. I'll do anything for them, even die.

"McCulley, you don't know what love can make you do. You don't know what it's like to be part of a family, much less have a family of your own.

"I love my mother, my siblings and my children. I promised my boys that come hook or crook, they're not going to spend too much time behind bars. I promised them that if I don't get them out of jail, it's because I died.

"So far, everything has worked just the way I planned it. Now that I have so many other people involved, I don't know what's going to happen.

"I know I am prepared to die, I just hope you are in the same frame of mind because if you're not, you're in for a long ride. I know of at least twelve people who will lie, cheat and steal to get at your ass and eventually they will kill you.

McCulley looks hurt at Jamie's words. He starts to think about everything that has happened to him, not only recently, but in his distant past also.

I've been an asshole most of my life. Maybe Jamie is right, maybe I don't know what it is like to have a family that cares for me, or friends that really like me. I have done some really shitty things in the past and I know one thing, I may not have a family or friends to do these things for, but I do owe it to someone. I owe it to myself to get my life back on track. Back to where it could have gone, instead of where it was going until now.

I was always selfish and afraid. No more. I won't be either anymore, I am going to right everything I put wrong. Then and only then can I live with myself, then I can move on. If I die, I die. We all have to go sometime. I rather die on my feet doing something that I believe in, than on my knees like a dog.

"Look Jamie, we have spent the last several days together and in that short time, I have learned one thing. If you bend over long enough, sooner or later somebody is going to come by and screw you.

"I have been an asshole most of my life and in those last few days I allowed you to point out to me fourteen suckers who took advantage of the fact that I was bent over and they screwed me.

"You also pointed out that, I somehow managed to screw myself. But what really hurt was, you stood by and watched all these people go through my ass and when I was down and out and couldn't take any more screwing, you screwed me again.

"But you took me in and you've done more for me by forcing me to take a look at my life. Something a father would do for his sons. I know you hate me for what I have done to your kids, and I hope to hell that I can make it up to you and them.

"Now, I am at the point where I am on your side all the way. If I have to die then so be it because this time, I am doing the screwing." McCulley laughs, "Screw the FBI, screw the sheriff, screw my friends, and screw the bank. Most importantly, screw the bank."

McCulley and Jamie laugh as they look over at the bag of money. McCulley looks over at Jamie's face and sees what it is really about. *Money? It isn't about the money. Screw the money too.* McCulley picks up the bag of money and looks over at Jamie. Looking back into the bag, McCulley laughs and throws the bag across the cab.

"Screw the money too. Right now I'm going to live and for once in my life I'm going to do something right, something I truly believe in. I'm going to get those men out of jail. I'm going to help get those guys who are trying to destroy the lives of others. And, I am going to spend the rest of my life protecting my ass and enjoying my life. Enjoying my life in... Yea, that's right; you're supposed to be telling me where we are going, so spill the beans. Where are we going?"

Jamie watches as McCulley makes an amazing transformation from the selfish piece of trash he once was, to this creature sitting before him now.

McCulley may not have it all together, but this guy is really trying. I believe he really won't be a bad person after all maybe we'll even become friends. Friends with the man that put my sons in prison...? That's fate for you. Fickle and funny.

"Okay McCulley, I guess I can tell you now. We're going to South America."

McCulley's eyes widen and his jaw drops a bit, "South America? South America is a continent. What damn country in South America?"

"Have you ever heard of Guyana?"

"No, I haven't. Is that an island or something?"

"No. It's a country in South America. Have you ever heard of Reverend Jim Jones?"

McCulley shakes his head, "No I haven't... I never been too much of a religious man."

Jamie lets out a brief laugh at this, "Well, neither was Jim Jones. You see, McCulley, the dear reverend had a commune in this country with a few hundred Americans.

"He convinced them to come with him because of some problems with the U.S Government or something, I'm not sure. But after awhile, he felt threatened and talked everyone into committing suicide. Those who didn't commit suicide, he had them killed. That's the country, we are going to."

McCulley listens to Jamie's explanation, as if Jamie was saying they were about to live in a lion's den.

Has this guy lost his mind? Cult, shit? Why the hell, we go to a horrible place like that? We have all this money, what the hell are we doing going to some haunted cult country mass-murdering suicide shit hole of a place like that?

"Why the hell do we want to go there?"

"Because they do not have an extradition treaty with the United States and it's a nice cheap country to retire in. For $500.00 a month, you can live like a king. That's a little more then five years apiece, of relaxation. Not counting any monies we may accumulate, or if we don't blow any."

Five hundred dollars a month, you can live like a king. *Screw the people that died there, that sounds like a good deal to me. With all of this money, we would be emperors over this palace.*

King McCulley the First! How about that shit. Damn, Jamie has thought about everything. He really did his homework; he really thinks we can pull this off. Guess this isn't a suicide run after all.

"What haven't you thought of?" McCulley asks in astonishment.

"I didn't think of how to keep you from bugging me when we get settled in Guyana." Jamie says through a smile.

McCulley shakes his head and gives Jamie a smile of his own, "Yeah, very funny. Get to driving."

As Jamie and McCulley were having their conversation, Agent Phillips and Ramirez look over what Jamie had left them.

They stand in the middle of Ramirez's bedroom; the room looks as if a hurricane went through it. One did, Hurricane Dolores slammed through the once clean room, turning it into the mess the two were standing in now.

Ramirez's anger had subsided for the moment, as she found that Jamie really did have a good reason to go through her house.

"Look at this!"

"What is it?" asks Phillips while trying to look at the objects in Ramirez's hands.

"It's a cassette tape and a picture." Ramirez says, as she looks over the picture.

Phillips snatches the picture from Ramirez and stares at it and to his surprise a bit of recognition covers his face. "I know this guy, we grew up together, and his name is James Witherspoon."

Ramirez was shocked, "What? You know this guy? He's one of McCulley's cohorts, and I think he is in on this plot."

Agent Phillips looks over at the picture again.

No, no way. Collins is full of shit. I know it now; no way can James be a part of all this shit. Collins is full of shit, and so is Ramirez.

Why the hell would one of my friends, no my best friend, think of doing any of this shit? I know him better than I know myself sometimes. There has to be a mistake, a mistake or this is all just an act to get to me.

"You're full of shit. I was supposed to meet with him in a few days. We are best friends."

Ramirez doesn't pay much attention to Phillips, "Let's listen to the tape and see what else Jamie has for us."

Agent Phillips nods his head.

Fine, we'll listen to the damn tape. Then you'll see; you'll all see how full of shit your precious Jamie really is. You'll see that my friend is innocent! I'm going to have to add defamation of character to this asshole's list of crimes. James will have a field day with this in civil court.

Ramirez takes the tape and places it in the player and the first voice to come on was that of Jamie.

"Well Ramirez, I see you found the tape. I thought it would be nice if you had something to bargain with. What you have is a photo of James Witherspoon. As you know he is one of Las Vegas' finest, but by his dress and what he is saying on the tape is another story.

I'm supplying you with this information so the FBI will know I do have the evidence I mentioned. If they can come to some type of agreement with me, I will give them all the tapes and pictures they need. So here is two minutes of an asshole."

The tape goes silent for a minute as both people stare intently at the tape recorder. Just when Ramirez begins to think that the tape was bad, or perhaps incomplete, more voices come over the recording. The voices are a bit unclear to Ramirez, but Phillips picks up on the first one immediately.

"Hey Watts, do you think we can trust the rest of those guys?"

"What are you worried about James. I have them under control. They will do whatever they are told"

"Watts, we haven't blown up anything yet. These suckers might freak out after they hear a thousand people are dead."

"Tell you what. I will use one of them as an example. How about Shorty? I will accuse him of something stupid and chop him up in pieces, just like I said I would, right in front of them. If that doesn't put the fear of God into them, then nothing will."

"Okay Watts, I think that will work. Maybe then I can go on and not worry about being busted."

The voices stop and static is heard on the tape for a moment. Agent Phillips can't help but to keep staring at the tape. *James? It can't be. Not the James I know. This still has to be bullshit, but it was on the tape. Need to have this tape analyzed, see if it is for real. No, I know it is for real, that was James' voice. I would know it from anywhere. But what the hell is he getting himself into?*

Jamie's voice comes back over the recorder; *"There you go Ramirez. Now you have Mr. Witherspoon speaking about death, and when Mr. Watson shows up dead, you will know who did it.*

"By now I will have spoken with the FBI Agent and if I figured out things right. We didn't come to any conclusion. So I will be in touch again and maybe by then I can tell you where to find the rest of the evidence. Have a lovely day, Loi Du Talion."

The tape goes blank and Ramirez shuts the player off. *That was certainly worth him coming into my house. Phillips has to know that Jamie is for real now, he just has to.*

"Well Phillips, what do you have to say now? And get that stupid look off your face."

Phillips stares blankly at Ramirez for a bit.

Stupid look on my face? Screw you, bitch. I just found out that my friend, my best friend, might be part of a terrorist plot? Not even a small part, but planning to kill people to get a point across? Screw you, screw Collins, and screw all of this shit. It's all bullshit. Screw this tape; the tape doesn't prove a damn thing.

"Ramirez, James is a good friend of mine. I have spent the last five years trying to get transferred to Las Vegas, just so we could hang out. We spent a lot of time on the phone making plans, and now I find out that my best friend is part of a terrorist group. You're all full of shit!"

Ramirez steps back from Phillips. "Yeah, I'm full of shit. So is the tape, huh, Mr. FBI? What a thick skulled asshole! Of all the people in the FBI, I have to get stuck with you. How's the water, Phillips? See the Pyramids yet?"

"What the hell are you talking about, Ramirez?"

"Well, since you were in denial, I thought you saw the rest of the sights too! You see it's like this little buddy. I have met Mr. Witherspoon, and he is just like he presents himself on that tape. He is everything that Jamie says McCulley is, and that's your friend."

Phillips is taken back. "Who do you think you are? Talking about my friend like this? Denial? I'll give you denial, you little bitch, you're in love with Jamie. It's plain to anyone that spends a moment with you. That is why you are doing all of this, because you love Jamie. Maybe you are in on the whole thing. Yes, that's it, your just trying to set me up, dumb broad."

"The things that you said to Jamie on the phone you really meant them, didn't you? You have already formed your opinion of him and you haven't even met him. But you have a friend you have known all your life and you think he is the best thing to come along, next to fresh air."

Phillips pauses to catch Ramirez's eyes, "My analysis of that conversation is that we are dealing with a real maniac. We're going to have to get him off the streets. I don't know who he thinks he's dealing with. He must have been watching too much TV."

Ramirez's sees Phillips' words as a ploy to make her upset.

This guy just doesn't get it. People are about to die, and instead of getting the information from Jamie that can save thousands of lives, he is willing to sell everyone up the river because if he does take the information, he might have to deal with the fact that his friend is an asshole.

Boy I feel like I am in one of those soap operas like "The Young and the Restless." Everybody knows everybody; everybody is in love with everybody.

"I see you have already formed your opinion of Jamie. How can you do that without even taking the opportunity to get to know him?

"Agent Phillips, don't get me wrong, but there is a lot more here than meets the eye." Ramirez sighs as she continues, "I'm going to make a long story short. The time I spent with him, I didn't look at the crimes he committed; I looked at the reasons why. He explained to me how much he loved his children and what he had done for them over the years.

"I listened very intensely. I felt the love and I also felt how he would do anything to vindicate his children. Especially, since he knew his kids were framed and have proof.

"Agent Phillips, are you aware of all the innocent men and women, who ended up in prison because another person wanted to make a name for himself, because another person has a heart of lead.

"Jamie Collins was a law enforcement officer for a number of years and is well aware of the consequences of his actions. To show you how much he believes in his convictions, I know he will die for them.

"Now in the process of gathering evidence to prove the innocence of his children, Jamie came across a plot that would obviously destroy thousands of lives. Not to mention, the lives of the surviving relatives.

"Remember the Oklahoma bombings, and all the lives that were sacrificed? The bombings on the Strip at four hotels would make that bombing look like a 4th of July celebration, compared to all the devastation it would create if it goes off like planned.

"Jamie is a thinking man. He knows that the FBI wouldn't let this happen and he doesn't want it to happen. It's a chess game; each side has to give a little in order to win. Jamie has made his moves. He contracted himself out to you and collected his money for his services.

Even though this was an unorthodox way of doing it, he completed the job. He has the names and addresses of everyone involved the time and dates of this plot, the location of where the explosives are stored, and their method of operation.

"In turn, he is asking for the release of his sons and to keep the money. I feel he rightfully deserves what he asks for because he risked his life and not to mention the expenditures he incurred during his investigation."

Phillips listens to Ramirez, but really doesn't hear a word she says.

There she goes, defending a no good for nothing jerk. If she loves Jamie so much, what is she doing here?

"Officer Ramirez, the man we just put out of your house–who is he?"

Ramirez's face begins to redden, "What does my personal life have to do with this case? Are you a complete jerk! I can't deal with this much longer, I swear if you keep this shit up, I'll just punch your lights out! Not even McCulley was this bad! And not that it's any of your business but he's my boyfriend! What does he have to do with this?"

"You could fool me. I am under the impression that this criminal Jamie Collins is the one you are in love with. I think you should have a drink, talk to your parents, talk to a doctor or maybe even go into your bathroom and beat the hell out of yourself. Better yet, go into your bathroom and lock the door, stay in there for a while and when you come out stay the hell away from men. Because woman, you are gone. Look at me. You are a Police Officer. Do you understand, a Police Officer?"

Phillips begins to see that his monotone voice and constant egging on of Ramirez, is getting somewhere.

She is already turning red, probably about to explode at any minute. When she does, maybe she will see how wrong she is by sticking up for Collins. She is our only witness and he has her under his spell.

"Look you jerk; I don't need the likes of you to tell me who or what I am…"

Ramirez starts as her fist clenches. Agent Phillips senses the body posturing change immediately.

Good, I am getting to her. A few more cracks like this and she will fall nicely. Then, maybe we can get something accomplished. "You are a Police Officer..." repeats Phillips in his monotone voice.

Ramirez is on the verge of cracking by this time. The blood vessels in her eyes feel like they are about to explode, and her nails dug into her flesh as she clenched her fist.

Who does he think he is? He isn't going to get away with it; maybe he is part of that asshole's plot too?"

"Don't tell me what I'm, you..."

Agent Phillips cuts Ramirez off, "Your purpose in life is to protect the citizens of Las Vegas; against aggressive people such as your Jamie Collins. He has committed some serious crimes; it is your duty to arrest and detain any criminal who violates the laws of society. Seemly, Mr. Collins has swayed you to the point of becoming an accessory after the fact."

Ramirez is about to take a swing at Phillips, when she stops and starts laughing at Phillips, "Wait a minute, you're just doing all of this shit to get to me. You don't like the fact that your best buddy is planning to kill people. You couldn't handle that fact and that is why you're trying to get me to break.

"Worse than a bully that just got beat up, you think you can take me on? Maybe you could get to the old Dolores Ramirez, but I am not her anymore. So screw you!

"I'm glad you said that, you asshole. You've forgotten the predicament you're in. The second in charge of this terrorist group is your best buddy. Before you start judging me, maybe you had better check out yourself. You are in the same boat with me, you son of a bitch. How are you going to explain that you were given information and didn't do anything about it? How are you going to explain that you jerk?"

Agent Phillips is starting to lose ground on Ramirez.

Shit, leave me alone. Dumb chick; stop trying to grill me on my friends.

It's Jamie Collins that did all the crimes, the only thing my friend is guilty of so far, is being on a tape. Maybe this will shut her mouth.

"Has the sheriff mentioned anything to you about the thin ice you're walking on," threatens Agent Phillips.

"Yes he has, but my role in this is that of a mediator. Jamie wants to go through me to make sure that things go ahead as planned without him getting arrested." Ramirez says as a come back.

Phillips looks at Ramirez. *Damn it, no point trying to beat her ass. Shit, I lost my cool; I've lost my cool. Just need some time to think, and can't do that if she and I are at each other's throats.*

"How are you going to assure him of this when you're to arrest him as soon as you are able?"

"Well Agent Phillips, I don't intend to be anywhere close enough to arrest him. My main objective is to fulfill a promise."

"And that promise is what?"

"To get in contact with you and make sure you get the necessary information to end this whole situation."

Agent Phillips tries to end the argument, "Officer Ramirez, I need you to answer this question. If the situation arises where you are face to face with your captor, will you arrest him? Never mind, you don't have to answer; your face told me the whole story. Come on put on whatever it is you wear when you leave the house. We have to meet the S.A.C."

Agent Phillips starts to get up to head for the door. Ramirez stops him.

Maybe I will arrest Jamie if I have to maybe I won't, but what about this jerk? Will he arrest his friend if he has the chance? I doubt it.

"Before I think about leaving, I will put that very same question to you. Will you arrest Mr. Witherspoon?"

Phillips chews on his lower lip and looks at Officer Ramirez with sadness in his eyes, "Yes, I would. Now let's go."

As the two plan to get the next phase of the investigation going, Damen Clark is waiting in his office for any information that may shed some light on this new case. Sitting in his chair, Damen looks up at the clock.

Just where the hell is that stuff I asked for an hour ago! I can't believe that Collins didn't call a damn person for this long. He had to check in with someone, he just had to. If I get up from this chair and catch one of my boys messing around while I am waiting for them to bring me the news in my office, their ass best get out of town, before I use it for a heavy bag.

Damen's thoughts are interrupted by a knock on his door. An agent pops his head in through the door as he knocks, "Sir, we have the information you requested on those three wiretaps."

Clark looks up at the Agent with the papers, "Thanks Matt, fill me in."

"Okay sir, the call to Rena Taylor took place in or around the area of Tucson, AZ. We also have the same information about Anita Goin. The calls were quick and to the point. He was aware that there was a possibility of the phones being taped."

Matt looks over a few scattered papers and picks up the piece that he was scanning for, "On the third tap sir, at Officer Ramirez' home the conversation lasted long enough to get a good fix on his cell phone. He was approximately fifty miles outside of Tucson AZ. Sir. When the conversation ended, he was twenty-five miles further south. It seems that by now, our boy is in Mexico."

Clark ponders all of this information. *Mexico? Why the hell would someone go to Mexico? They can't get away there, there is no where to run in Mexico. They'll be found. They'll be found, and they better pray it is someone working for us that find them too. Fugitives don't find it too easy to live in Mexico, especially an out of place one like Collins.*

"Well, we got him now. Matt, get in touch with our contacts in Mexico and see what they can do about tracking down our boy leaving the U.S. by way of Arizona. Also, tell them not to do anything until we get back to them. I have decided to play this thing out to the hilt."

Matt leaves the room as Clark sits back in his chair, rocking it while staring out at the ceiling. "Yes, play this out. Soon, we'll see how this ends, very soon. Mr. Collins, for your sake, I hope you are on the up and up about this terrorist stuff. You better be or you will wish that you burned in that fire, that I can promise you."

JIMMY CULLORS/JOSEPH SZEWEZYK

chapter

13 THE TRAIL

Clark is sitting in his chair reviewing the transcripts from the telephone calls that Jamie placed. *Hmmm, two women and Ramirez. But how much can we trust Ramirez? She was his prisoner and we know she was drugged; what if she starts to feel sympathy for him.*

It is only normal for hostages to start to feel something, some sort of bond towards their captors. I need to know where Officer Ramirez stands; I need her as a cop.

An agent interrupts Clark, as he starts to get lost in his thoughts, "Sir, the local sheriff in Tucson wants you to give him a call. He didn't give any specifics, just that you should call. Now that we have our subject in the Tucson area, I have a real strong feeling it has something to do with him. Here's the number."

Clark takes the number from the agent and grins, "Thanks a lot Matt."

Taking the phone in his hand, Clark begins to dial for the Sheriff in Arizona. *This could be interesting. I know Jamie and McCulley were last in Arizona, maybe this sheriff picked them up for speeding. Now that would be funny, poor guy gets away from everything but a broken tail light or some crazy shit like that..*

The ringing stops as a voice picks up, "Hello, Pima County Sheriff's Office, may I help you?"

"Yes, this is Special Agent in Charge Damen Clark of the Las Vegas Branch of the FBI; I need to speak to Sheriff Hearns."

"Oh good sir, he is waiting for your call, just a minute."

Clark waits for his call to be transferred. *For a small town, there sure are a lot of transfers in that sheriff's office. Hold? I was put on hold? What the hell is the matter with these people? Aunt Bea burnt her pie or something?*

"Hello. This is Sheriff Hearns."

"Yes this is Damen Clark from the..."

"FBI, Yeah I know. I have some information that may help you in the apprehension of one your fleeing felons...a colored boy by the name of Jamie Collins. That name is familiar ain't it?"

"Yes Sheriff it is. What type of information do you have?" Clark says, trying to keep Hearns on track.

"Well sir, an elderly couple by the name of Ed and Ella Banks came in here waving a poster I had received from the Internet and had it circulated around town. Saying they done spent some time wit him."

"Are they sure it was Mr. Collins?"

"Yeah...they said he come out to thar place of business twice...one time about a few days ago, and again, today. He said they talked fo' awhile but didn't think anythin' about him."

"What was the purpose of Mr. Collins coming to their place of business?"

"He parked his truck there for a few days and came back and got it. I s'pose it was after he committed those crimes in Vegas. He needed a get away car."

"Did Mr. Banks give a description of the vehicle?"

"Yes he did. It was one of them Nissan Frontiers; you know, the one on the commercials that drives through water n' rough roads, then slides into a garage backwards."

Clarks rolls his eyes, "Yea... Yea...I know. Did he give you a license number?"

"He said the license number is written down at his place of business, but he would get it fo' us when he comes back. Oh, the truck is red."

Clark pauses in his note taking, "Comes back? Comes back from where?"

"Well, let me put it this away. Your gonna have an opportunity to talk to him yo' self. He an' his wife are headed to Las Vegas. He says he needs a vacation and decided to take one."

"How is he getting to Las Vegas?" Clark asks, trying to hide his anger that the sheriff let the witnesses get away.

"He's gonna drive that old beat up Chevy truck he got."

"What is the color, license number, and how long ago did he leave?"

"The truck is blue and he left here about an hour ago. I don't know what the plate number is."+

No of course you don't, Clark thinks before he responds to the sheriff, "Sheriff Hearns, you have been a great help. If you can think of anything else please call me. I really appreciate you calling us."

"It was a pleasure to help. If thar's anythin else I can do fo' you give me a quick call now, hear?"

"Okay Sheriff, thank you."

After hanging up the phone with the sheriff, Clark continues to scribble notes on the case for another minute before he shouts out of his door for the agent that brought him the news.

"Hey Matt, come here quickly."

Matt comes in with a quickness that suggests a certain young eagerness, "Yes sir?"

"Look, contact the F.B.I. office in Phoenix, Arizona, and let me talk to the S.A.C. there."

"Okay sir, right away."

Matt takes off to his desk to look up the requested phone number, while Clark remains in thought on the case. *We need some help picking up this old couple that Barney let go. I still can't believe that guy let them go without asking first. He may be a big fish where he is, but it's a small pond, Hearns; it's a small pond.*

A voice, over the intercom breaks Clark's concentration, "Sir, we have Agent Bains on the line."

"Okay Matt, thanks." Clark says, as he picks up the phone, "Hey Bam-Bam, this is Damen Clark; I haven't seen or heard from you since the Academy. I didn't know you made it to S.A.C."

"Yeah Damen, I been S.A.C. for awhile now, I think it was about a year and a half after you made it."

"Hey man, I'm sorry I haven't been in touch. I have been working my tail off ever since I came to Las Vegas. It seems all the criminal elements want to get caught out here in the desert."

"I know what you mean. I'm catching hell here also. What can I do for you?"

"Well, I am quite sure you have heard about what's been going on up here with the kidnapping of those police officers?"

"Yeah, I heard about it. Are you calling to tell me the man is now in my state?"

"Well, yes and no. He was in your state, before and after the crime, but now he is in Mexico."

"My god what do we have here, a seal. This guy is really slippery."

"I don't know what to call him, but in just a little while, I'm going to catch him in my net."

"So, you are on his trail?"

"Well, you can say that. You tell me, how far can a black and white guy go traveling through Mexico in a red truck?"

"I guess you are right Damen, they would stick out like sore thumbs."

Clark laughs at the thought, then tries to get back to the task at stake, "Look, Bam-Bam, the reason I'm calling is, because I need you to locate some witnesses in this case."

The voice over the phone sounds confused, "Witnesses? I would think all the witnesses are in Las Vegas."

"Well, Mr. Collins stored his get away vehicle in Tucson, and the people who own the storage unit, are on the way to Las Vegas to vacation. What I need you to do is try and locate them on the highway and follow them to the state line where we will be waiting."

"Well, that sounds easy enough. What kind of vehicle are they driving?"

"It's a beat up blue Chevy pick-up. Two elderly Caucasians occupy it. We have no license number, but you can run their names through your DMV and get that information."

"Their names are Ed and Ella Banks of Tucson, Arizona."

"Okay Damen, I will take care of it for you, but you know this starts a, 'You owe me' list."

"No problem, Bam-Bam, now that I know where you are. As a matter of fact, we can have dinner soon. I will contact you. Okay?"   "Sure Damen, I will be waiting for your call. Take it easy."

After hanging up with the FBI agent in Arizona, Clark goes back to take more notes on the case. *I need to have some people meet the Arizona agents when they get to the stateline. I don't want any mess-ups; these guys will be in custody from the beginning until they check out of our building. Where's Matt?*

"Hey Matt, come in here please?"

Obediently, Matt appears, "Yes sir."

"Look, I need you to assign two agents to go the state line of Nevada and Arizona to rendezvous with agents from Phoenix. I want them to follow a vehicle from that location, to whatever hotel they are going to stay at. After they are registered and into their room, I want them brought here. Okay?"

"Got it sir, and there is an Agent Nelson here from Washington, D.C."

Clark nods, "Good, show him in and tell Stella as soon as Agent Phillips and Officer Ramirez arrive, send them into my office."

"Okay sir, is there, anything else?"   Matt asks before he leaves to fulfill his assignments.

"Oh yeah, have you heard anything from our contact in Mexico?"

"Yes sir, we have. It is Hector Rodriguez, he's one of our best, and he should be calling you within the hour."

"Okay, Matt, keep me apprised, and send in Agent Nelson."

"He's on his way in, sir," Matt says, as he exits the office.

Immediately after Matt leaves, Agent Nelson comes into Clark's office. Nelson introduces himself to Clark, and they both look each other over for a bit until Clark breaks the ice.

"Good to see you, Agent Nelson."

"Good to be seen, Agent Clark," Nelson says as he takes Clark's hand in a handshake.

"So, what can you tell me about the case? I have read the files and have been briefed on the way here, but I want to hear it from your mouth."

Clark nods and starts the story as both agents have a seat. Clark retells the story of Jamie Collins and all of the crimes he has committed, as well as the difficulty both Metro and the FBI have had in trying to acquire him.

After catching Agent Nelson up on the situation, Clark gives a bit of his own assessment, "From my point of view Ron, it's only a matter of hours before we join all the pieces together." Clark goes on to explain, "We haven't spotted the suspect yet, but we aren't that far away. As you can see from the map here, we figure that Mr. Collins, will be traveling down Interstate 19 to get to Mexico and from there get into highway 45.

"The problem is, we don't know where he is heading, but we have a contact in Mexico, who is going to try and intercept Mr. Collins before he gets too far into Mexico and we lose him."

Nelson inquires on Clark's methods, "This contact... is not going to arrest him, is he?"

"No....No, from our information, we gathered on Mr. Collins and Officer McCulley, neither one has ever been to Mexico and if they have any sense, they will know they have to have a guide. Someone who can get them around, someone who knows the countryside and someone who could help them avoid the bandits.

"That's where our man comes in. He will take them wherever they want to go and report back to us. We will have him in our snare."

"Good plan, but what happens after that?"

Clark starts to lean in on Agent Nelson. The next few things that he is about to reveal are for Nelson's ears only. Nobody else knows about what is about to go down, and Clark is determined to leave it that way. The less everyone knows, the less chance of someone screwing up by accident.

"He doesn't know it, but Agent Phillips..." Before Clark can finish his statement, Ramirez and Phillips make their untimely entrance into Clark's office, "Oh, Agent Phillips and Officer Ramirez, come in and have a seat."

"How are you doing sir?" asks Agent Phillips.

"Fine, Officer Ramirez, how are you holding up?"

Ramirez shakes a bit, but regains her self-control; "I will make it sir. Right now, I just want this whole thing over with."

"It will be Officer Ramirez, have a seat." Clark says as he points towards two empty chairs in his office. "Agent Phillips and

Officer Ramirez, I want you both to meet Agent Ron Nelson of the Drug Enforcement Agency from Washington, D.C."

Agent Nelson gets up from his chair and greets the two newcomers with a firm handshake and a smile. To Ramirez, the smile seemed a bit odd, almost like a smile a shark might give before feeding.

"How are you doing sir, it is nice to meet you." Phillips says in introduction.

"Thank you, Agent Phillips. The feeling is mutual." Nelson then turns towards Ramirez, "Officer Ramirez, so, you were one of the officers who was held captive? I know it was a trying ordeal, but we will see what we can do to make amends." Ramirez manages a weak smile and tries not to give away any of her inner thoughts. *Trying ordeal? What does he know about what I went through? These guys are just out to get Jamie, and that's it. They aren't interested in me or the lives that Jamie is trying to save...trying ordeal, indeed. The only trying ordeal I have had recently was being stuck with this jerk Phillips. Now look at me, I'm surrounded by FBI assholes.*

Clark breaks the awkward silence by buzzing his intercom, "Okay, enough for the formalities, Stella has our other two guest arrived yet?"

"Yes sir, they are in the TV room, getting acquainted."

"Okay, make them as comfortable as possible and tell them, we will be right with them."

"Okay sir." comes Stella's voice in affirmation over the speaker box.

All eyes are on Clark now. The people gathered in his office, came together under his request. They are all wondering why, exactly, are they there and what is going to be required of them before they leave the office. Ramirez especially is worried about this. Out of the group, Ramirez is the only one that would rather be someplace else.

Anywhere, just anywhere but here. I'm already surrounded by assholes, now Clark is bringing in more? Can't wait.

"Now that most of the players are here, let's get the game started." Clark then turns his attention to someone passing by, "Ralph, do you have the tapes from the conversation?"

"Yes sir, here you are." Ralph says as he hands over the contents of a package to Agent Clark.

Clark takes the tapes and the manuscripts from Ralph, and passes them out to the other people in his office. Taking the tapes of the recorded phone conversations, Clarks goes over to the stereo in his office and pops the tapes in. He plays each tape while the others follow the dialogue by reading the corresponding transcripts. After the second tape, Clark shuts the stereo off.

"Now, would you mind catching us up as to what was said...oh never mind I forget we have our copy and we're updated on the conversation, Ramirez that was for you. Your phone calls were not only recorded, they were traced also." Clark said as he waves the unplayed tape of Ramirez's phone call with Jamie.

Ramirez looks at the tape and then it hits her. She was used! *He said he wouldn't tap the phone! Now he has all of these other people involved, even one from D.C. This was all a set up from the get-go.*

They don't give a shit about what I said, not what McCulley did or the fact that there are dangerous people out there getting ready to blow up the Strip and kill innocent people. They just wanted his ass and I was the bait. I should have known better!

"But you promised..." starts Ramirez.

Clark interrupts Ramirez, "Officer Ramirez, sit your stupid ass down and listen to what I have to say. Mr. Collins has committed some very serious crimes and we are not conducting this investigation the way you want it. You are a law enforcement officer and as a law enforcement officer you will conduct yourself as such. You will not tell me how to perform my duties; you will not tell me how to deal with Mr. Collins. You will follow orders."

Ramirez looks at Clark, as if he just slapped her across the face. For all purposes, he could have, her emotions were running ragged.

How dare he yell at me like this? I hate all of these people. This isn't about doing what is right, this is about who has more authority, or should I say, who's got the bigger balls. Men! Hombres son como niños. I hate this.

I don't want to do this anymore, not when I have to deal with childish men. But I need to keep myself together too many peoples lives depend on this!

"Stella get the sheriff on the line...the Sheriff of Clark County."

Ramirez is not pleased by Clark's call. *The Sheriff? Why is he calling him? Clark has lost his damn mind. I am not talking to the sheriff or telling him anything. I don't trust him. That's why I came to the FBI in the first place!*

Clark looks over to Ramirez and tries to set her mind on the right path, "Now Officer Ramirez, what I am about to do is get you away from your present..."

Clark is cut off, "Excuse me Sir, but I have Sheriff Kerns on the phone."

"Okay Stella, thanks."

"Hello? Sheriff Kerns?"

"Yes, this is he."

"This is Special Agent in Charge, Damen Clark of the Las Vegas Branch of the FBI. I am calling concerning one of your officers."

Ramirez holds her breath as she listens intently to the conversation. She strains trying to hear each and every word as it is mouthed over the telephone wires. *He can't be serious, calling the sheriff? What kind of power play is this guy trying to pull off? He'll blow the whole damn case.*

"I have an idea as to who it is, but go ahead." replies the sheriff.

"We have Officer Ramirez here in our office and I want you to know that she will be reporting to us for an unspecified amount of time. I just wanted to get your approval."

Ramirez's ears perk up at this last statement. *Reporting to them? He isn't turning me into the sheriff; he is getting the sheriff off my back. Good, I don't need that guy on my back all day long. But, why would they do this? What do they have to gain? Maybe I misjudged them.*

"Why sure, we will do whatever it takes to co-operate with the FBI. Plus you will be saving us some money."

"Sheriff Kerns are you planning on running for the Senate or something in the near future?"

"I don't know, but if I do, you will be the first to know. Why did you ask that question anyway?"

"I just got a strange feeling you are trying to save the taxpayers money, but to no avail, your officer will still be on your payroll."

Kerns sighs, "Well you can't blame a man for trying."

"Okay Sheriff, we will keep you abreast of the things going on around here, you will have a report within a week, good bye."

Clark hangs the phone up without even waiting to hear if Kerns had anything additional to say or not. *The situation with Ramirez is settled, almost settled that is. She may be his, in the eyes of law enforcement, but she still needs to cooperate under her own will. At least, she needs to think it is under her own will.*

"Okay Officer Ramirez, that takes care of you. You are now under my command and you will conduct yourself as such." Clark turns his attention to the whole room now, "Now all of you listen up.

"In light of the situation, we have decided to put together a task force, but first we have to iron out this giant wrinkle. The first thing we have to do is get Jamie Collins and Officer McCulley. We have located them. They are on their way to Mexico by way of Tucson."

Clark scans the room to see if this causes a commotion in anyone present. Nobody stirs at the words, not even Ramirez. Clark is uncertain, if Ramirez has no feelings towards him knowing where Jamie is, or if she is just still a bit too shocked to have her mind catch up with everything that is going on around her. Either way, Clark goes on with his speech.

"Phillips what do we have on the phone call from Jamie Collins?"

"Well Sir, the phone call was made and Mr. Collins and I had an interesting conversation."

Phillips begins to say something else but hesitates. *Do I tell him everything? So what if Collins and I got into it for a bit, not like the bastard didn't deserve it. Damn guy, thinks he can get away with his little crime spree and that we should all bow down and kiss his ass, just because he thinks he may have some dirt on one of my friends? Screw him.*

Clark notices the hesitation, "And...and...go on."

Phillips clears his throat, "Well sir, the conversation went off without a hitch..."Phillips begins to fail at the words he wants to say. He doesn't know where he wants to go with his story.

Damn, I can't just tell everyone about the conversation, especially since, I haven't figured everything out about James yet. Why the hell, did we all have to be called in so soon anyway? This is some pretty screwed up shit if you ask me.

"Stop with the bullshit Phillips. The conversation was garbage and you did nothing but run Collins away. You are the most non-professional professional I have ever met."

Phillips is a bit taken back from the verbal lashing, and stands stunned. Ramirez takes this time to snap out of her own self-induced shell.

"Garbage, just like you, Phillips. Why don't you tell the nice agent how you lost your temper at Collins and then badgered forever on something that had no bearing. Why don't you just tell him how you almost lost the whole deal due to your hot temper and dumb big mouth?"

"Hold on Ramirez. We have to have a little order in this meeting. I take it you and Phillips didn't get along well? But that doesn't matter. I want you both to understand one thing..."

Clark is once again interrupted by the buzz of his intercom, "Excuse me Sir, we have Hector Rodriquez of Mexico on the phone."

Clark sighs as he takes one last look at Officer Ramirez and Agent Phillips. *Damn, I need everyone on the same page, not fighting each other. I ask for agents and the Bureau sends me spoiled kids with temper tantrums. This is just great, not only do I have to make sure Ramirez plays along, but I have to get one of my own agents under control. All of this and Agent Nelson is here too. He must be laughing his ass off at this mess.*

"Okay Stella, I'm going to put him on the speaker." Clark says and waits for the familiar buzz of the speaker phone changing channels, "Hey Hector, how are you doing?"

The voice that comes over is laced with a heavy Mexican accent, "Estoy bueno, Damen. Look like I get a una casa from dis case, no?"

"Well, Hector, we will have to see about that. How many people you got working with you?"

"Only one, mí primo Frankie Gonzalez. You see how good he is, mí primo es excelente. Tambien, you know he got niños, got to feed them; he knows if he does good job, you pay him muy bueno."

"We will see about that when the case is over. Maybe one day I will get to talk to him before he starts working for me."

"Well, senor, he already working for you. Lo tengo en el two-way radio; he following your camion rojo."

This news catches the whole room off guard. Clark leans closer to the speakerphone. *Could it be possible? Could his informant already have the trail of Collins and McCulley? This was going better than I have ever thought it could. Maybe Hector will get a house out of this after all.*

"You found him? I mean, you are sure you have found them?"

"Si, soy seguro. No many sal y pimienta sets driving Mexico in un nuevo camion like this. We pick him up just before I call you. Mí primo meet me here and despues, I stop I got out of my camion and drive pass us. Mí primo follow him until I finish talking con usted. Now we see how good mí primo es."

Clark gives a wide smile at the good news...*finally, something going our way. Good, now all we have to do is reel these guys in. Its almost over, nobody got hurt yet, and it's almost over. Thank God.*

"Where are you, Hector?"

"Estamos en el village de Agua, Mexico. Aproxadamente 25 kilos entre Mexico."

"Look Hector, why don't you go after your cousin and call me when the red truck stops for the night."

"No worry, Señor Damen, your red truck esta en manos buenos.

Clark stares hard at the speakerphone. *Good hands? For Hector's sake they better be in good hands. These hands better be the no-fumble, always carry and catch and whatever else a football player needs to get the job done. If anyone messes up now I'll have all of their asses before the next siesta.*

"Okay Hector, but if your cousin loses my red truck, I am going to fire the both of you."

"No problema...no problema."

"Okay Hector, there are other people in the room I will introduce them. There is Officer Ramirez from the Las Vegas Police, Agent Ralph Phillips Las Vegas Branch of the FBI and Special Agent Ron Nelson of the DEA from Washington, DC."

"Washington huh? Jew must really want this guy. He must be bad vato, eh? How many people he kill?"

"He didn't kill anyone, but the crimes he committed are very serious."

"Ahh, I got chew. What chew want me do?"

"Hold that thought, Hector. Okay everyone, listen up. As you all heard, we have the suspects under surveillance right now and it looks like it is just a matter of time before we are ready to reel them in.

"Now, if everyone here can get along enough, we might just able to pull the fugitives in without a lot of blood shed."

Clark looks over the room to make sure he has everyone's attention, "We're going to work something out that will make everyone happy. I have you on the speakerphone so everyone can hear you and you can hear them. Okay?"

"Okay, no problemo, Señor Damen."

Clark walks over to where Ramirez and Agent Phillips are sitting. *Now I need to have these two jokers on the same page long enough for this operation to really go down smoothly. Collins may or may not be on the level about all this information on the bombings, but it will all mean shit if I can't get these two to work together.*

"Now back to you Ramirez and Phillips. We are involved in a very serious operation and we need the cooperation of the both of you. I want you to take your personal feelings and put them to the side. Ramirez I am speaking to you mainly."

Phillips starts to open his mouth, but no words come out. *I have to tell him, I have to tell him that my best friend may be in on this plot somehow too. If I don't, I know Ramirez will. Better off hearing it from me than her, might make things go down easier.*

"Sir, because of recent developments that last comment is going to have to be directed at the both of us."

Clark looks his agent over. *What the hell is Phillips talking about? How can he be in anything in Las Vegas? What was he here for, a day or two? Maybe Ramirez was right; maybe there is a reason for her and Phillips fighting.*

"What are you talking about?"

"Sir, before Ramirez interrupted us, I was about to tell you that I have now become personally involved."

Clark stops in his tracks on this comment. *Personally involved, now what? Each time we take a step forward on this damn case something always happens to have us take two steps   backwards. I feel like I'm doing the damn Waltz with these guys.*

"And how is that Agent Phillips? You have only been in this town two days. How can you be personally involved?"

Phillips looks at Clark and then over at the entire room. *Have to tell them sometime, I guess no time like the present. Hell, I'm sure James isn't involved in any of this. That's it, I'll just bring him up and then they'll check up on him and find he is doing nothing wrong. They'll see. They will all see.*

"Well sir, if you don't mind, I'm going to bend your ear for a few minutes. You see I was born and raised in Minneapolis, Minnesota and I had this friend, his name was James. The both of us wanted to get into law enforcement and we felt this way ever since we were around the age of ten.

"We were in the R.O.T.C. in high school together, just to get a little military experience, but James enlisted in the Army and I decided against it. I went on to study law and he became a military police officer.

"We stayed in touch with each other up until the last five years. I got married and he went on about his business.

"I later found out that he was a Las Vegas Police officer and I was divorced. We started communicating again and I told him that one day I would surprise him and come to Vegas. I never told him what I did for a living. I wanted to surprise him when I got here. Well, as you can see I have been quite busy with settling in and you assigned me to my first case."

Phillips pauses to catch his breath. His mouth is dry and his lips feel glued together, but he continues, "Well Sir, my first case involves my best friend. Mr. Collins left a picture and a cassette tape for our listening pleasure and the tape contains the voice of my friend James and another guy by the name of Watts. The picture is my friend." After listening to Phillips, Agent Clark runs his fingers through his hair and walks towards the window.

Involved, personally involved. Damn, this guy is Phillips' best friend. Two days, that's all he has been here for and he has already screwed up an investigation. This isn't the Waltz anymore; this is some sort of backward Fox trot.

I'm the woman, and these jerks are leading. How the hell would Collins know about Phillips' friends? Maybe it is just coincidence, if not, and Collins really did plan all of this. Clark sighs. Either way, this is going to be a long day.

"This shit throws another wrench into the fire. Did this son of a bitch know you knew this James character?"

"No sir, I doubt it. Remember I've only been here two days. I don't think he could have put that together."

Ramirez looks over at Phillips. *Don't think he could have put it together? Has this man not read the file on Jamie? Jamie didn't have anything happen he didn't want to. He planned this whole thing out, down to his escape. He knew things that nobody else would even think of. Better believe it, buddy, that Jamie knew about your shit.*

Ramirez now walks over to Phillips and gets into his face, "That's the problem with you Phillips, you are always underestimating Jamie. But at the rate everything has been going, I don't doubt if he knows there were any ties between Phillips and this James person."

Clark watches Officer Ramirez show the problems of Agent Phillips' thinking. *This girl really can be useful. Maybe her eyes are opened up enough now. I definitely need her to be an able law enforcement officer and not some lovesick puppy. Now, if I could only have Phillips open his damn eyes too. Looks like the man feels for this James guy like Ramirez does for Collins.*

"Ramirez I am beginning to like you, and understand your perception. You feel you have a knack of reading people, do you? Well tell me Mr. Collins' next move."

Ramirez backs off of Phillips and thinks for a minute. *What would Jamie's next move be? He has the money; he and McCulley made it to their escape vehicle. Where would he go in Mexico? What would he do? I don't think Mexico is the last stop for Jamie. He didn't plan all of this out only to be caught a few hundred miles away. No, he must be going south, or to a seaport, but where?*

"Sir, right now Mr. Collins is no different then any other criminal. He feels he is safe and he is on his way to an even safer place. This safer place was not discussed, but from what I have seen he is well prepared."

Clark absorbs Officer Ramirez's assessment of the situation. *He may be smart; he may have planned all of this out, but the way she talks about him. Maybe I am wrong; maybe her feelings for him are still going to get in her way. She sounded proud that he did all of this, well prepared. Well prepared for what? A shoot out? She needs to tell me more.*

"Prepared? Prepared for what Officer Ramirez…the demise of Jamie Collins or the demise of this case? Young lady, let me tell you one thing, you are not ready for anything. You think you know Mr. Collins but you don't.

In just the last few hours, I have gathered enough information on him it will make your head swim. I will admit one thing; he knows what he's doing. He hasn't shown himself to be dangerous and can talk his way out of trouble and his way into women's panties, so step back and look at the big picture. The man is a professional…"

Ramirez hears Jamie being described in such a different light. *All of this talk is crazy, Jamie is a professional, but he isn't a bad man. He is only doing this to save his kids and everyone else that McCulley put away wrongly.*

This isn't like we are dealing with some common criminal that does things only for his own greedy needs. Why can't anyone else see this?

"Yeah, a lot more professional than a few people I know." Ramirez says shooting a glance at Agent Phillips.

Clark catches the glance. He also catches Phillips rolling his eyes in response. *Yes, a lot more professional than some people. Ramirez seems to be on the level at times, but we will find out soon enough.*

What about Phillips though? His psyche report didn't mention any of this bullshit. 'Eager to work and willing to go that extra mile,' that's bullshit; more like holds evidence and throws tantrums.

"Okay Phillips, now it's your turn. I am going to give you an option. You can back out of this case now or you can stay for the duration. But I want you to know that because of your relationship with this individual, you would be vital to us."

Phillips looks away from Ramirez and directly into Clark. *Can I turn my friend in? Can I do that to James? If James broke the law, I would have no other choice. I don't think he is guilty, but if it is my job to bring him in, then I will do it.*

"Sir, there is no hesitation on my part. I was assigned to work on this case and here I will stay."

Clark nods his head. *Good...good, this is what I need from my workers. Phillips says he will work on this case, he better keep his word. If I ever find out that he isn't giving one hundred percent on this one because he might get his friend in trouble, then he is going to have a long time to catch up with his friend as his new cellmate.*

"That's what I wanted to hear."

While the show went on inside the room, Agent Nelson just followed the conversation in his chair. Hector also followed the whole thing over the speakerphone. Both were having doubts that with Ramirez and Phillips involved the way they were, that this case would be an easy one.

"Hey S.A.C., esta todo bieno? So much love I feel. Que pasa con cada uno; they seem so uptight?"

"Not to worry Hector, everything will work out okay."

The words going to Hector weren't comforting him too much. *Work out okay? They better work out okay? It's my ass on the line man. Nice for you to say they work out okay from the office, Damen. Everyone's a super hero from their armchair; meanwhile it's my ass that will get blown off in the field if everything isn't okay.*

"Sure, everything is okay, but how are we suppose to get together when Collins and McCulley are in Mexico?"

"Just relax Phillips; Agent Nelson will explain that to you. But we have some other business to take of first."

Clark hits his intercom again, "Stella will you have Ms. Taylor come in here please."

"Okay Sir."

After the intercom buzzes in static for a moment, Stella comes in while leading a woman into the office as well.

"Ms. Taylor is here for you, Agent Clark." Stella says as she ushers Ms. Taylor in and then disappears through the door again.

Clark goes to greet the woman, "Ms. Taylor come in and have a seat."

"Before you start asking me questions about Jamie, I want you to know I had nothing to do with the crimes he committed or that he was going to commit any crimes."

"Don't worry Ms. Taylor; we don't want any incriminating statements from you. All you are here for is to give us some idea as to the type of person he is."

"Okay that's easy. I met Jamie at a bar. He had just come in from a meeting. He was sitting at the bar alone when I walked in. It seemed like a matter of minutes before the bar was packed with women.

"The women took turns trying to talk to him because they knew he wasn't from the neighborhood. He was dressed in a tailored black suit and those pretty dimples just stuck out.

"He seemed like he didn't want to be bothered with them, but he talked to them anyway. He was really nice and bought several of them drinks. I was sitting at the other end of the bar surrounded by men and just like Jamie I didn't want to be bothered by them.

"It was karaoke night and we all were just having fun laughing at the people trying to sing. Jamie walked over to me and asked if I wanted to do something I would always remember for the rest of my life and that was to sing with him.

"Neither one of us could carry a tune, but he convinced me to do it anyway. We made fools of ourselves, but it turned out to be one of the most memorable nights of my life. He was a real gentleman, a man every woman would want.

"He finally walked me to my car and asked me to kiss him goodnight. I refused then he asked me to kiss him on the cheek. I agreed and proceeded to do so when at the last minute he turned his head and kissed me on the lips and before I knew it I slapped him."

Taylor stops to give herself a small laugh at this memory, "He didn't look surprised. It was as though he expected it.

"He smiled and said that one dimple really enjoyed that. Then he walked away after we exchanged phone numbers. Two days passed before I saw him again and for the next year we saw each other everyday.

"I moved in with him for several weeks, we did nothing but love each other. He was so sweet, caring and tender and cared about nothing but my needs.

"When he came home from work, I had his dinner ready and we ate and made love again. Those were some good old days._I wished they were still here, but just like every other good thing in my life the relationship ended with him just disappearing out of my life.

"I didn't hear from him again until the other day...almost a year later. His voice was just as sweet as ever and I started to melt just feeling the vibrations flow through my body.

"The last time I saw him I slapped him. I slapped him because he disappeared on me. Right now I would do anything to take that slap back. I realized I still loved him, he made my life whole. I really miss him.

"Now I guess I will never see him again, after all the trouble he's in now. I guess when you catch him; he will spend the rest of his life in prison. But if he does go, I will know he did the things he is accused of to help my son out of prison. Maurice Taylor is one of the men who was framed by McCulley and Maurice is my son."

Clark picks up on the part on her son. *There are more people Officer McCulley supposedly put into prison unjustly? I wonder if Collins really does know them all.*

"So one of the men he is speaking of is your son?"

"That's correct, he promised he would do everything he could to get my son out, and from what I can see I guess this is everything."

Ms. Taylor goes up to Agent Clark and puts his hand in her own while beginning to plead for Jamie, "Sir, I want you to know, Jamie doesn't have a mean bone in his body. He wouldn't hurt a soul. He was pushed into what he felt he had to do. When you catch him, don't kill him, he is a good man."

Clark takes the hands of the woman off of his own. He tries to do it in such a way not to make the woman more upset. *What kind of spell does this Collins have over people? It seems like he has the whole world fooled.*

This guy really has to stop; he is a danger to himself and everyone around him. Worse of all, nobody that he meets on the street will get the chance to know something is wrong, they all love him and would never suspect him of anything. The perfect criminal, Jamie is that damn next door neighbor that slices twenty kids up and then has his neighbors stand up for him on television. Gee, he was never mean to us. He seemed so nice. Bullshit.

"Okay Ms. Taylor that's all. You can go home now."

"I hope I was of some help and if I can do anything else, I will be available."

Stella enters the room and takes Ms. Taylor by the arm. Before she leaves the room, Stella turns around to see if Clark wants anything else.

"Stella, have Ms. Gray come in please."

"Okay sir, she's on her way." Stella says on the way out.

"Come in Ms. Gray, have a seat. No need to be nervous. We just want to ask you a few questions."

She cautiously goes towards the empty chair in the office, saying, "I didn't have anything to do with what Jamie did! We are just friends."

"How good of friends are you?"

"I'm his beautician."

"How long have you been his beautician?"

"A few years."

"How did you meet?"

She thinks for a moment before responding. "Well Jamie was a commercial window washer and I happened to see him one day while he was working. I passed him and he said thank you. I stopped and turned towards him because I didn't understand why he was thanking me.

"I said to him, thanks for what and he smiled with those dimples and said for making my day. I couldn't help but smile and walk away. A week went by before I saw him again. I would come to work everyday hoping I would see him then that day arrived.

"I was sitting in my car smoking and saw him. For some unknown reason, I started shaking as I walked towards him. I just wanted to see those dimples and hear that voice. We stood and talked for at least forty-five minutes. I told him everything about me and that I had just started working as a beautician.

"He promised me he would try and get me some customers. He got me a few and he also became one. He says he liked the way I cut his hair and would always give me a twenty-dollar bill.

"We have spent time together outside my shop if nothing else but to talk. To me, he seemed like a person who had a lot to give, but no one to give it to.

"I guess that's why he worked two jobs. He got to meet a lot of people at Treasure Island–that really_made him happy. If nothing else, I know Jamie is a real caring person. I know Jamie wouldn't hurt anyone unless he was pushed into that situation.

"If I could, I would do anything to get him out of this trouble, but I guess it is too late and I probably never see him again.

"You know something, I wanted so much to go to bed with him and he continually told me he couldn't because he didn't want to be just another man in my life. He said our friendship would last longer. I'm going to miss him, and I think I really love him. Don't hurt him please; give him a chance to redeem himself."

Clark backs off of the chair Gray is sitting in. *Better give her some room in case she wants to try to latch on like Taylor did. Seems like Collins has been busy playing Don Juan to the women of his neighborhood. Wonder how Ramirez is feeling right about now? She probably feels like she's just another egg that the hen tried to lay.*

"Ms. Gray, when was the last time you saw or spoke to Jamie?" Clark asks while already knowing the answer.

"Yesterday, he called me and spoke for about ten minutes if that much."

"What did your conversation consist of?"

"It wasn't that important; nothing that would interest you."

"Do you know where he is now?"

"No I don't." She shakes her head and staring at the floor.

"Do you love Jamie?"

Her head pops up at this question, "No I don't. Like I told you, he never gave me the opportunity to get that close to him."

"Okay Ms Gray that will be all. You can leave now."

Stella appears in the room and escorts Ms. Gray out like she did Ms. Taylor. When the pair walked out of the room, Clark shuts the office door.

"Okay everyone, you've heard from two women who are close to Mr. Collins. Now we will hear from one more. Officer Ramirez, you've heard all the things those women had to say about Mr. Collins, now what are your feelings?"

"It seems as though I've have known Jamie for ever and I truly agree with those women–he's charming. That seems to be his way with people, mostly women.

"I also agree that Jamie would not be doing any of those things unless he was provoked, and it took someone like McCulley to provoke him.

"Sir, I am glad you have thought about giving him a chance, a chance to prove that he is the type of person who needs a break."

Clark is almost amazed. *Jamie certainly has a way with the women. And it doesn't matter to them what he has done except that he is a kind, and charming person.*

He has a way of making each one feel special in their own way. What a real Don Juan. Collins may have good character witnesses, but if Officer Ramirez thinks I'm going to take it easy on a felon just because his friends like him, well she has another thing coming.

"Ramirez, don't jump your guns. Nobody has mentioned anything about a break. What I was trying to do was get a census on the man we are dealing with."

Clark leans over to the speakerphone while not taking his eyes off of Officer Ramirez. *Better check to see how things are south of the border. I want this guy, and I want him now.*

"Hector, are you still there?"

"Si, I can't wait to meet Mr. Collins. Es un hombre tan castigador. A real talker."

"Don't concern yourself about lessons; right now we have a situation we have to deal with. You get off the phone and find your cousin and don't lose this man. Everyone else sit back and get comfortable, we have a lot of work ahead of us."

JIMMY CULLORS/JOSEPH SZEWEZYK

Chapter

14 THE NET

Jamie and McCulley have stopped to rest from driving. Both men are a bit thin from travel and need to walk around for a bit. Jamie goes and checks his surroundings as McCulley goes into the bag and counts out the money. It's time for each to have their share; after all, McCulley has shown great remorse for what he has done. If he ever gets caught, it will not go so well for him.

"Okay Jamie, the money is split up now. Here's your half and I got mine. Of course you are five thousand short because of the money you gave the old man and his wife."

"No problem McCulley, I have more then I can use anyway. Are you happy now?"

"Sure, now let's get to this Guyana. How much further do we have to go anyway?"

Jamie looks over at McCulley. *How much further? Are you there yet? I'm hungry; I have to go potty. Damn guy sounds like Jamie Jr. on a road trip. How much further? Just one more country, McCulley, just one more country.*

"Let me put it this way McCulley, we have to cross the entire country of Mexico." Jamie answers McCulley as he goes for his road atlas, "According to my map, we will have to travel through nine states in Mexico; Sonora, Sinaloa, Aguascalientes, Jalisco, Oueretaro, Tlaxcala, Veracruz, Oaxaca, and Chiapas.

After Chiapas, we will be in Central America. And as you can tell, it will be quite a long drive, but first we will stop in Cananea. There, we will pick up a guide, who will lead us through Mexico."

"How far is Cananea?"

"About five miles, we will spend the night there and get an early start tomorrow."

"Yeah, that sounds like a real winner to me. I could use a bath and a change of clothes, maybe a little relaxation and maybe a drink or two without any chains to hold me down. Can this truck move any faster? I am tired of being confined."

Jamie smiles, yep, just like Jamie Jr., "Just be patience, we will be there fast enough."

As Jamie and McCulley trade remarks on travel, Hector and Frankie are watching every move. Unknown to either wanted man; they have been watched since they arrived in Mexico.

"Frankie responden, es Hestor." Hector said trying to reach his cousin Frankie over their two-way radio.

"Si, vaya a continuacion Hector, le oigo ruidoso y claro," Frankie responded while waiting for Hector to give him the update.

Loud and clear, Frankie has been listening to too many gringo's speak.

Frankie looks down the road to see if he can still spot the dust being blown up from Jamie's driving, "Si, Soy alrededor de un cuarto de un killo detras de Collins. Parece están dirigiendo a Cananea; que seria un buen lugar para pasar la noche."

Cananea? *Why would they pick that place to stay? Maybe this Collins doesn't know too much about Mexico?* "Que va a entrar en contacto con el bossman grande en America sobre sus planes?"

Frankie sighs. Y*eah, leave it up to me to contact the Americans. Not like I am not doing anything else right now.* "Si, los llamare cuando consigo a Cananaea, despues de que se coloquen adentro para la noche."

Hector thinks about the situation for a moment. *Well, we know where they are going to stay, no sense in following them. Frankie should get everything ready, make sure things go down the way we want. If we pull this off without a hitch, maybe we'll get a bonus.* "Okay ahora,

Frankie, quisiera que usted los pasara y conseguir un cuarto en el hotel para nosotros y cerciorarse de alli es un cuarto para ellos en un area donde estaria duro que se escapen."

Set it up so they don't escape? No shit, Hector. I thought I was going to let them have any room they wanted, maybe someplace public. Then, after I made their beds and brought them breakfast, we'd try to bring them in. Damn it, primo, this isn't my first day out, I know what to do.

"Okay Hector, ahora los estoy pasando. Parecen son absolutamente felices y sin un cuidado en el mundo Cananea es llanura derecha el camino que puedo verlo de aqui."

Smug as two bugs in a rug, eh? Well their rug is about to be set afire. "Estoy cerca de cinco kilometros fuera de ciudad que estare alli antes de que usted consiga a nuestro sitio. Consiga el cuarto seleccionado para ellos primero y cerciorese de que no son sospechosos cualquier cosa. Espera justa para mi en el pasill o despues que."

Play it cool Hector? Cool is my middle name, man. The transmission ends and radio silence is once again the rule. Everything is being set in Mexico. Things are starting to work as planned. Jamie and McCulley think they are getting away with it all; Hector and Frankie think they are about to have the drop on the fugitives. Only one plan will work out in the end.

****

As the plan to capture Jamie and McCulley starts in motion on the Mexican side, another phase of the plan begins in Las Vegas. This time it isn't Jamie vs. the FBI, rather the FBI working for Jamie by trying to investigate his claims.

"Phillips, we have a problem with your newfound old friend. Did you know what type of activities he was involved in, "asks Agent Clark?

"No sir, I haven't seen him in quite some time, but we have been talking in the last few years."

"And what did these conversations consist of? Clark asks while jotting more notes down.

"Mainly, talking about things we use to do...my marriage, his past life. You know same old stuff."

"He never mentioned anything about his present activities?"

"No sir, the only thing I know about him in Las Vegas is that he is a police officer and that he likes to go to Arizona to fish."

"Does he know you are a member of the FBI?"

"Sir, I didn't tell him. I wanted to surprise him when I got here. He could have gotten that information from my mother when he called there, but she never told me she mentioned it to him. I don't think he knows."

"Well, Ralph we are going to hope he doesn't know. Does he know you are in town?"

"Yes sir, I am supposed to meet with him in a few days."

Clark reflects on Phillips' answer. *A few days? This could work out, but we can't wait that long. We should have Collins and McCulley by then. I don't want anything to go wrong. If we get Collins and McCulley in a holding cell before we bust this crooked cop ring up, we could have some serious problems on our hands. They'll know we are on to them if they see McCulley go to jail.*

Stella's voice interrupts Clark's thought process, "Sir, I have Mr. Rodriquez on the phone."

"Okay Stella."Hello Hector, tell me some good news."

"Hola Damen, everything bien. Your hombre es in his room all tucked para la noche. Tighter than a bed bug. No worries with our side."

"Good work Hector, we are on our way. Keep your eyes on everything until we get there. Our arrival should be within the next two hours. Meet Agent Phillips at the airfield and he will have more information for you there."

"Si, Damen, no problema. Hector out."

As Hector signs off, Damen turns around to address the room. This is the moment he has been waiting for. It's time to reel the net in.

"Men and lady, we now have our seal in a cage. Ralph, you and four other agents, are assigned to pick up Mr. Collins. When you get there you are to let him know in no uncertain terms whom he was with, and from the conversation you had with him on the phone that assignment is right up your alley."

"I have a plane waiting at the Executive Terminal in McCarran Airport. Now get out of here and bring both of them back here in one piece. As a matter of fact, Phillips let's go into your office for a minute."

Phillips leads the way out of Clark's office and the two meet in his office. Clark shuts the door behind him, making sure that nobody will hear what transpires inside.

"Have a seat Ralph. I want you to really put some fear into the heart of Mr. Collins. He has gone too far with this vigilante type of law enforcement. Yes, he has a point, but there is a way to go about things other than the way he did it. I want this man to know that what he has just brought himself into is not something out of the movies."

Clark takes a deep breathe, and lets it out as a sigh, before he continues, "As for McCulley I don't think he is a victim. I have this gut feeling that he is into this up to his neck. I want them both treated the same. In other words, beat the shit of them both. Then tell them they have now completed basic training and they are going into action. Bring them back here in one piece and able to talk and move around."

"Sir, I don't think we will have any problems, and you will have Mr. Collins here in one piece."

"Ralph get out of here. And tell Ramirez to relax until you get back. I don't want her to leave here, show her the lounge and tell her to get comfortable."

"Okay sir, I'm on my way to the airport, I will be back as soon as possible."

Agent Phillips leaves his office in search of Ramirez. She is still sitting in the other meeting room and

JIMMY CULLORS/JOSEPH SZEWEZYK

is lost in her thoughts. Phillips approaches her and gently tries to break her from her daydream.

"Hey, sorry we got off on the wrong foot. Listen, come with me. I will show you to your quarters for the evening. This should be okay, and no reporters will bother you there."

Ramirez looks up at Phillips and answers while stretching, "I hope it is comfortable. I need a good nights sleep."

The two make their way down a maze of corridors, until they get to a sizable place with some furniture for Ramirez to rest on.

"Here you are, this is the lounge, make yourself comfortable."

"Don't I get any blankets?"

Phillips forgets he is trying to be nice with Ramirez, "Look Ramirez, this is not a hotel make the best of it."

"Phillips what's your problem? You have been acting like you are pissed at me ever since we left my house. You got something against me?"

"Fine, you want to hear the truth? No more bullshitting. Let me put it this way. I don't like you and I don't like your boyfriend. I wished I didn't have to work with you. I think you are a bitch. You think this is a game, and you call yourself a cop. You are a piece of shit and I think you should go to jail with your friends."

Ramirez has heard enough, "Are you about nothing? You're going to stand there and talk shit to me and you call yourself a FBI agent.

"You asshole, don't you ever approach me in that fashion and say anything negative to me again. If it happens, I will take that little dick of yours and snatch it off and stuff it down your throat.

"You are not jerking with any of your little girlfriends, who you impress, with your job. I am one who will kick your ass. Now get the hell out of here and do as you are told, you little pussy."

"Ramirez, we will finish this…"

"Phillips, get the hell out of here. Go, you damn wimp, get the hell out of my face!"

Phillips walks out of the room pointing and smiling at Ramirez and heads toward the awaiting vehicle and set out for the Executive Terminal at McCarran Airport. Upon their arrival, Phillips and his entourage were whisked to a private jet belonging to one of the major hotels that loaned it out because of a favor owed.

****

As the agents jetted off towards Jamie and McCulley, the two were blissfully unaware that anything was going wrong. They had checked into their hotel room and started to relax after a long drive.

The room was quiet except for the TV, which was showing the first version of King Kong in Spanish. Both Jamie and McCulley were engrossed in the movie while they drank Tequila and beer.

Several times you could hear McCulley laughing out loud over the movie and making comments about the style of acting.

Jamie keeps looking over at McCulley during his comments. *Damn fool, can't take him nowhere, always saying something about nothing. Well, I'll just have to soundproof his place when we get to Guyana.*

"McCulley, why don't you be quiet and watch the movie?"

"Man, I am quite sure you have seen this movie as much as I have, so sit back and enjoy it and drink some more tequila. Pass me the bottle"

"McCulley, look at King Kong, is there anything about him that reminds you of me?"

McCulley stares at the giant ape on the screen. How big and mighty he looks, even when dubbed in Spanish, the people know that the others are frightened of him. What the hell does this guy have in common with King Kong? McCulley snickers *must be the size of their balls.*

"Man what are you talking about? That thing is at least fifteen stories tall. You are not that tall."

"Yeah, ha...ha, you called me an ape awhile back, and I just want you to look at the ape and tell me if there is any resemblance."

"Look Jamie, I am sorry about the things I said about you. I wished there were something I could do to make amends, but there isn't, and on top of that I think you now have your revenge.

"You have me implicated in a hold-up I was nowhere around. You have me in a foreign country hiding from the law and you have tempted me with a little more then a quarter of a million dollars.

"Yeah, you got your revenge and screwed up my life also. I look at it this way. We are going to be together for some time and we have to get along a lot better than this.

"The past is going to haunt us for awhile, so we are going to have to come to some sort of a truce.

"I am sorry for what I did to your kids. I am sorry for what I did with the other men, but I am going to make amends. I told you I would testify to the fact that I was lying when all of them were arrested and sent to prison. What else do you want me to do?"

Jamie looks over McCulley. *Just where the hell am I going with all of this? Why am I still angry at McCulley? We beat the hell out of each other and everything should be cool between us now. The past is the past; I should let things lie where they are, but still...*

"McCulley, I know I'm wrong for bringing up what you called me and yes I agree with all what we called each other should be forgotten, but I am still pissed, because neither one of us would be sitting here in this room if you hadn't done what you did. But because of the friends, you have we may be able to get out of the trouble we are in."

McCulley tries to read Jamie, to see if he really means what he is saying. *Of course, he does. This guy means everything he says, almost like one of those old fashioned cowboys that say they would kick your ass before they did.*

"Now you're talking. I need to know how the hell that's going to work."

"It's like this; I have quite a few tape recordings of your friends plotting to do their thing. I have dates and time and their method of escape, and because of the nature of their crime, the feds may be a little lenient on us if we supply them with the information."

McCulley's eyes widen. *Lenient if we supply them with information? What the hell is all of this talk? Sounds like Captain Suicide is calling it quits? He better not screw me, not after all of this shit I've been through with him.*

"Wait a minute man, you sound as if you're about to give up!"

"No McCulley, that's not the case. You see, sooner or later, I have to start negotiations and I would rather it be sooner. But, we won't talk about it now, let's sit back and enjoy ourselves for a minute. We can talk about this tomorrow."

McCulley sighs and is put at semi-ease, "Okay Jamie, you're the boss. Cheers, let's get blasted."

Agent Damen Clark is in his office, trying to get as much done as he can in the limited time available. Already things are going fast and he needs to be certain they all go off without a hitch. A lot of lives dangle in the balance of how this case turns out, and Clark knows it.

"Stella, I need you to get Sheriff Kerns on the phone right away."

"Right away, sir," pipes Stella over the intercom.

Clark turns his attention to the other agent in his office, "Ron give me the package you brought from Washington."

"Here you are." Agent Nelson says as he hands over the package for Agent Clark.

Agent Clark takes the package and looks through it. Checking the contents like a schoolboy would check his backpack before school, Clark turns to Nelson with a seemingly satisfied look on his face.

"Boy, you guys are really thorough. Is there anything missing?"

"No Damen, everything is there and I want you to know, I'm only doing this because we are friends and I am helping another friend out."

Clark nods in understanding; "Do you do this often?"

Agent Nelson frowns, "No, I don't and hopefully I never will again."

"Why are you doing this? Putting your ass on the line like this?"

"Like I said, I'm helping a friend. He has done a lot for me in the past. I can't let things go along the way they are without doing something. In a way I think he knows I am his ace in the hole."

"Well, let's hope your friend doesn't take advantage of you." Agent Clark responds in a warning voice.

"He won't, I know him too well."

Clark goes to respond to Agent Nelson when Stella's voice breaks the conversation by intruding over the intercom.

"Sir, the sheriff is on the line."

"Thanks Stella, Hello Sheriff Kerns?"

"Yes it is."

"This is Damen Clark again. What do you have on your agenda for the rest of the day?"

"Well, as you know I am quite busy, and I may be tied up for the next several days. What can I do for you?"

"Well sheriff, I want you to cancel all of your appointments for the rest of the day and come to my office right away."

Silence came over the other end of the phone. Sheriff Kerns could not believe his ears. *Take the rest of the day off? What the hell, I can't do that, I have a million reporters buzzing at my door just waiting for the next scoop on the fugitives. Just brush them all off? What about the other things, like that drug dealer shooting I have to deal with today?*

"You got to be bullshitting. There's no way..."

"Sheriff, all of your problems will be solved when you get here."

"Are you telling me you have Jamie Collins?" The Sheriff asks with a tinge of excitement in his voice.

"No sheriff, that's not the case. What's going on here is highly confidential and cannot be discussed on the phone. I need you here in my office within the half-hour. Also, I don't want you to mention a word of our conversation to anyone or where you're going. Just leave right now and get here fast. And do not...I said do not bring anyone with you."

"Okay Agent Clark, I'm on my way."

Hanging up the phone, Clark turns back to Nelson, "Now Ron, I have the sheriff, you and me and the papers from Washington. We're all set except for briefing the sheriff. Now we wait."

****

The waiting was over for Agent Phillips and his team. Watching out the window of the jet, Phillips could see the buildings get larger. He could see the wear and tear on them. After looking at the condition of the airport, he doubted that it was on the map at all.

This place looks more like someone cut the grass in a straight line over here. How the hell is the pilot supposed to land?

Seeing that they weren't slowing down at all on their final approach, Phillips braces himself for impact.

The wheels of the private jet finally touched down in a remote airfield in a foreign country. At the end of the runway was a gold Chevrolet Bronco parked with a bearded man waving frantically.

The plane comes to a complete stop and the ramp opens and out steps five men dressed in dark suits. The bearded man walked up to the plane and introduced himself.

"You make it one piece? I'm Hector."

Phillips meets Hector halfway, "How are you doing Hector, I am Agent Phillips and these other agents are here to assist us. Do you have our suspects contained?"

"Si Phillips, they quite busy ahora. They got a bottle of Tequila, a couple of six packs of Tecate, and a dozen burritos. They settle in for night. Give them about una hora, they be drunk y dormido."

Phillips' team unloads the plane bringing along their belongings. Agent Phillips walks up at point with Hector. The two engage in conversation trying to catch each other up with any plans that may have surfaced since they spoke on the phone.

"Who's watching them, your cousin?"

"Yeah, mí primo, he cool. He put un agujero in the wall; can see very much. You ready?"

"Sure how far is it?"

"Nine, ten kilometers away, we be there fifteen twenty minutes. We have room next door and a few refrigerios, ahh, comida y cerveza for you…just in case."

The drive is pretty easy, as traffic is non-existent. Everyone seems to be tucked away in his or her home for the night. A few parties blare off in the distance, but nothing that bothers the Agents as they make their way to the hotel. Hector pulls in to the hotel entrance and parks close enough to the room to make the moving in easier.

"Hecho! That's the room they are staying in, alli. Ours is aqui, and there is the truck."

"Where is your cousin?"

"Frankie? He inside waiting and watching." Hector says then changes his tone to mock the FBI agent, "Just as instructed, sir."

The men stand and look at the building for a few seconds and then enter their motel room. On the inside they sit and discuss their strategy.

"Okay men, this is it. We know they are armed, but we have one advantage. They don't know we're here. The entire operation will take place quickly and smoothly. Frankie, give us the layout of the room."

Frankie takes out a rough drawing of the room next door. Everything is sketched out pretty accurately and the drawing itself amazes even Phillips.

"They're two beds in room; each bed is to the...the...como que dicen derecha, ahh... right. Bed on right of the door. On left is a dresser aproximadamente five feet long with a mirror and TV on it. There no exit."

"I see no weapons. If they do have any, they'll be in the bags just to the right of the door. They are drinking for two hours and have made many toast. Right now they passing out, should be sleep in minute."

"Thanks Frankie, this seems like it's going to be an easy arrest, but don't take any chances. There are six of us and two of them. They are intoxicated and sleepy.

"I want the door hit once, so Johnson, you and Williams hit it as hard as you can right at the knob. We don't want them to have a chance of waking and retrieving their weapons."

"After the door is open, Johnson, Williams and Evans you run to the furthest bed. Frankie, Hector and I will take the other bed. Frankie do you know who's in what bed?"

"El negro esta en la primera cama"

"Okay that's perfect. Now I don't want anyone dead, but I do want their asses whipped. We need to let them know who we are and the crimes they committed will not go unpunished. Does anyone have any questions?"

Agent Phillips looks over the room. Not one hand is raised, not one questioning face glances back. His men are ready for action; they are ready to strike. This is when Phillips will learn just how well his boys do in battle. It's all or nothing this time. If they succeed, then they will have their fugitives, if they fail...

"Okay men let's go, and remember when that door is hit, we all rush in at the same time and hit anything moving."

The men file out of the small motel room and line up approximately six feet from Jamie and McCulley's room.

Johnson and Williams are at the front with the battering ram with Evans right on their tail. Phillips, Hector and Frankie are next and everyone is waiting for the command.

With a loud bellow from the pits of his stomach Phillips gives the order: "Go...go...go..."

At the same time the other five men release growls as though they were on the line of a professional football team.

The door is hit and there was no resistance from the hinges. The door hit the dresser knocking the TV to the floor. Johnson, Williams and Evans found themselves having to dodge the door as it slides from the dresser. Evans dived over his two partners landing on the back of McCulley who was awakened by the noise.

In a matter of seconds, the six men rendered McCulley and Jamie unconscious. Their tired, intoxicated, battered bodies could not take any more damage and gave into superior authority.

To Jamie it seemed like months had passed before he feels the chill of the cold water covering his body and bringing him back to reality. Because the pain his body was in the blood running down his face and the bleariness in his eyes, he had no idea what reality was but managed to mumble a few words.

"Who the hell are you?'"

Phillips with a smirk on his face walks over to Jamie, grabs his hair, pulls his head back and repeats Jamie's favorite phase.

"Loi Du Talion"

Phillips then holds up a tape player and plays James Brown's "Big Pay Back"

A voice makes his way through the split lips of McCulley, "And here you come with the French shit. Speak English and tell me what it means, and turn that goddamn music off!"

Agent Phillips turns towards McCulley with an amused look on his face. *He can't be serious? He really has no idea what this is all about? Looks like I am going to have to teach this corn-fed boy some smarts.*

"McCulley, you mean to tell me you been through all this shit with Collins here and he didn't tell you what Loi Du Talion meant...some Partner. Well, I won't let you wonder any longer. It means 'The Law of Retaliation.' I just did it back to you."

McCulley shakes off the cobwebs in his head. He assesses the situation. *All right, looks like we are caught and some egghead asshole is giving me French lesson 101. Screw this; I've gotten out of tighter situations. When I get out of this one, that jerk's dead.*

"You're a real joker aren't you? I wished I had one minute with your ass. I would rip you apart, limb by limb. Even in the condition I'm in now. You are a jerk and that shotgun is your crutch. Has anyone ever told you, you are a pussy?"

Momentary, Phillips reverts back to the last conversation he had with Ramirez and then back to taking charge, "McCulley, shut that mouth up, and Collins, I need your attention also. I'm going to take you both on a little plane ride back to sunny Las Vegas, all compliments of the U.S government."

Jamie looks over at Phillips. He looks him up and down. *This guy was sent to get us? No way, no way did this guy nail us. This guy couldn't even nail his old lady without help from someone else.*

Jamie laughs openly to taunt Phillips, "So you're the posse? Are you the best they could send?"

"Look Collins, we caught you that's all that matters. We were good enough to do that. Hector; pull your truck around so we can get out of here before the *Federallies* get here. Come on men; get these two boys up and out of here. I will get the bags."

Phillips allows everyone to leave and gathers McCulley and Jamie's bags together and goes through them looking for weapons and comes across the money. He sits and fans the money and leans against the wall wishing the money were his and is interrupted by Hector.

"Hey Phillips, what about Collins truck?"

"Leave it here. If you want, my cousin could take it off…"

"Oh yeah, Hector we need you to bring the truck back to Vegas, that way you can get paid sooner."

Reluctantly, Hector agrees and everyone gets into the truck and head for the airfield. In a matter of twenty-five minutes, they were at the airfield loading on the plane for their trip back to Vegas.

Phillips relaxes back into his seat. His first assignment in Las Vegas is a success. *Now they have to give me the respect I deserve, even that wanna be cop, Ramirez. She'll see just how good I really am and just how much of a piece of shit, Jamie Collins is. Better call and check in at the office, make sure Agent Clark has the good news.*

Stella's voice once again appears in Clark's office, "Sir, we have Agent Phillips on the phone."

"Okay Stella, I got it. Go ahead Phillips, tell me you have our two packages all wrapped up."

"Yes sir, we do and we should be in Las Vegas in about two hours."

"You didn't damage the goods did you? And I hope you brought the money back also."

"Sir, except for a few leaks here and there, the package is in good condition, and as far as I can see the money is all here. We also have Hector bringing Collins truck. He should be in Vegas by tomorrow"

"Okay Phillips, good job. We will see you in a couple of hours."

Phillips hangs up the phone and stares out the window of the plane. *Soon, soon we will be back in Las Vegas. Maybe after we touch down, I can finally take a shower or something. All of this running around in the heat has me sweating like a dog.*

Still don't know what I am going to do about James though. What went wrong? What the hell went wrong with him? If I could just talk to him, just for a little while, I know I can learn everything from him, maybe even talk him out of any stupid shit before he does it. He's just confused, that's it, just confused.

Phillips tries to keep the conversation in his head, trying to see what he should do with Witherspoon, but sleep finally takes over the agent somewhere over Arizona.

The plane touches down at McCarran Airport in Las Vegas and an awaiting bus stands by with armed guards to escort the prisoners to the FBI headquarters on Charleston Blvd. The two prisoners exit the plane in handcuffs and shackles and shuffle their way to the bus.

Within twenty minutes, the bus was pulling into the FBI garage and another twenty minutes passed before they were finally in Damen Clark's office.

"Sir, our guests have arrived."

"Stella, show them in and get Ramirez, I need her in my office now."

"Okay sir."

Stella walks in while Collins and McCulley bring up the front of the party, the rest of the agents fall in behind them. As she finishes escorting the group to Clark's office, Stella leaves to search for Ramirez.

Clark gets up to greet his new guests, "My...my so this is the elusive Jamie Collins. Come in have a seat, you too McCulley."

Jamie and McCulley enter the room both of them swollen and bloody from their battle in Mexico.

Jamie surveys the room and notices one person who brought a smile to his heart. He didn't react; he just followed orders and sat like he was told. McCulley on the other hand saw the Sheriff and felt embarrassed and held his head low, but the sheriff acknowledged his presence.

"So this is how you represent the Las Vegas Police Department? Are you aware of the shame you brought down on us? You had better be glad there are laws because if there weren't, I would take you out back and shoot you myself. Sit your ass down!"

Following the sheriff's outburst, Ramirez walks into the room. Again the sheriff blurts out a remark. "Ramirez, so you couldn't trust me yuh? What kind of sheriff do you think I am? The things I want to say to you would only make me look less than the gentleman I am so I won't. Sit your ass down!"

Jamie, McCulley, and Ramirez were sitting side by side facing a table, where also sits Damen Clark, Ron Nelson, and Sheriff Kerns. For a moment, there was total silence until Damen Clark speaks.

"Stella, I do not want to be disturbed under any circumstances, understand?"

"Yes sir."

Damen now directs his attention to Jamie, "Mr. Collins, when I first heard about the bank robbery I said to myself, all I have to do is wait and this fool and the money will show up...oh, just a minute."

Damen stops his conversation and picks up the phone to speak to Stella, "Stella, do you have the money?"

"Yes sir, I do."

"Did you do as I requested?"

"Yes sir, I will be finished in a few minutes."

"Okay, I will let you know when I need it."

Jamie listens to Damen's conversation and wonders what he was going to do with the money. Then a thought goes through his mind. Maybe I have a deal.

Jamie looks at Ron Nelson and Nelson gives him a wink. At that moment, the weight of the earth was lifted off Jamie's back, and he drops his head in relief, and continues to listen to Damen.

"Now, as I was saying. I knew the money and the perpetrator would show soon. Then, I got the news that one of the security guards' wife was held hostage while they robbed her husband.

"I thought to myself, these guys are professionals and we may not see them again. So we staked out the bus station and airport, while the sheriff was checking the major highways leaving town.

"We were confident the perpetrator was confined to the city limits and again all we had to do was wait." Clark turns to McCulley, before he continues, "McCulley, when you and Ramirez were kidnapped, we didn't put two and two together until Jamie here opened his mouth.

"We didn't know who this Jamie Collins was until we put a face with a name and phones began to ring off the hooks. We got calls from City Cab Company, a Chinese restaurant, passengers on buses, and neighbors of the security guard. It seemed to be highly unusual for a man who is going to commit as many felonies as you did in one day to make himself so well known in the city.

"The sheriff and I worked long and hard on you Mr. Collins and we found out a lot about you, but we weren't satisfied. We figured there was more to your mad scheme than meets the eye.

"First, you came at us with the fact that your sons were wrongly accused and sent to prison along with eight other men. You also stated you have evidence that McCulley was the cop who railroaded these men. McCulley, look at me and tell me, is that the truth?"

McCulley looks up at Damen and responds, "Yes sir, it's the truth. I did railroad those men into prison."

Clark nods in approval, "Okay, now we have it straight from the horse's mouth. But we will get to that later." The agent turns back to Jamie, "Now Jamie, the sheriff was satisfied with that being the reason for your kidnapping the officers, but I wasn't. I was still puzzled as to why all the attention and why the money was taken."

"So with the help of Ramirez, all my questions were answered. I knew in my heart that you weren't some common criminal. I knew you have been involved in a lot more things than you let on. Ramirez and McCulley, did Mr. Collins tell you anything about his past?"

McCulley looks at Jamie as if he had been betrayed again and responded. "Yes, yes he did. He told us about him being a cop and going to prison. Is there something he omitted to tell us? Is there someone or some group he is involved with that helped him in his crime spree?"

"Relax McCulley, Mr. Collins here probably told you a lot about his life, but I am sure he didn't tell you about what I'm going to tell you. Nobody close to Mr.

Collins is aware of his activities. I will stop beating around the bush and let Agent Nelson have the floor. He's from Washington, DC, and works with the DEA.

McCulley and Ramirez are now sitting at attention staring at Jamie who still has his head down. They are both now wondering whom this guy is that they have spent the last three days with.

Ramirez's heart is beginning to beat faster and wants to know if she put her career on the line for nothing. "Are you going to tell us that Jamie is a drug smuggler, pusher, or something in that area?"

"On the contrary, Officer Ramirez let me finish. Did Mr. Collins tell you about his activities on the police department?"

"Yes he did, and he also told us he went to prison for those activities."

"Okay, now listen, Mr. Collins, or shall I say Jamie, was on the force in Detroit and involved in quite a bit of corruption, all the way to the top.

"We became involved with Jamie in 1979. He was sent to assist us on a drug raid and after the raid we talked a bit about the flow of narcotics in Detroit. He was a little perturbed about why we continued to bust the smaller dealers and the larger dealers went unharmed.

"We explained we had no control as to who we busted and we could bust the big guys if we had help.

"Jamie told us, he and his partners had information on several big dealers and would set them up for busts if we would respond.

"We agreed with Jamie's terms, and within a week, he called us to meet him. When we arrived at the location, Jamie pointed out a house right off one of the main streets in his precinct.

"We staked out the house, and made contact with the people inside. In a two-week period, we purchased over forty pounds of high-grade heroin and cocaine.

"The day finally came for us to make the raid, and we requested Jamie's presence. Our man went inside to make a buy and survey the house and within two minutes our man was thrown out of a second story window, handcuffed and landing on a picket fence.

Needless to say, we rushed the house and arrested all the occupants only after we handcuffed them and threw them out the window. I never saw so much anger being released in one person in all my life. When we rushed the house, Jamie and his partner knew they had to be first through the door and Jamie took the lead with no hesitation.

"I was third behind him and he was carrying a shotgun. Jamie and his partner didn't wait for the battering ram. They hit the doorknob with their feet and the door was opened with two kicks.

"When Jamie entered the home, two males were knocked unconscious by his shotgun and he went at as many as he could with his bare hands. We had to pull him off of them.

"Needless to say, we worked with Jamie and his partners on many occasions. A lot of times his partners didn't know that Jamie assisted us in our investigations.

"Jamie's downfall came when he helped us set up a dealer, who had a relative high in the city administration. We raided this guy and, of course, Jamie was in on the raid, but the dealer recognized him. Jamie had arrested him twice before for drug possession, but somehow this guy never received any jail time. After that raid, Jamie received death threats, his children were being threatened and his house was shot at a couple of times. Then he got arrested and charged with Breaking and Entering.

"We didn't interfere with the Detroit Police Departments investigation, but we did find out he was being set up, and the orders came from high up in the city administration.

"We continued our contact with Jamie because we wanted to help him and if worst came to worst he could help us.

"He was found guilty and sent to prison, but before he left, we made a deal with him. We were getting request from the Department of Corrections to try and stop the flow of drugs into the prison system. So we decided we needed someone on the inside.

Jamie had proven to us on many occasions, that he was the one for the job, we approached him. He agreed and went to prison working for the DEA.

"Jamie started at Jackson prison and we arranged for him to be transferred to eight prison camps all the way to the Upper Peninsula, one mile from Marquette Prison.

At the end of three months, Jamie had information on seventy-two prison guards, and when we busted them, we confiscated over one hundred pounds of cocaine and heroin. It was time we got Jamie out of the prison system and advised him it would be to his advantage to leave the city.

"Again, Jamie agreed and we set him up in Las Vegas along with one hundred and seventy-five thousand dollars for his services and one thousand dollars a week for one year until he was settled.

"Over the past fifteen years, Jamie has worked with us off and on. All it took was a phone call from me, and Jamie would go wherever we told him. His duties were to follow a load of drugs from their pick-up point to drop off point. Then return home. He would be paid handsomely anywhere from ten to fifteen thousand per trip depending on the amount of drugs.

"Now we are at this point. I've known Jamie quite well for over twenty years. When I heard about what was going on here, I had to come and help a friend."

Jamie looks up as Ron walks around the table and they meet with laughter and a hardy hug from each other. Jamie let out a sigh and the relief comes to his face. He can barely keep a smile from his face. *God, thank you. I knew you wouldn't let me down. I knew it, I knew what I was doing was right. Ron proves it. Now I have a friend, now they will listen, they have to.*

"Ron, I knew you would be here. I am sorry I went so far out on a limb, but I couldn't trust anyone and I wanted my kids out of jail. You do remember them, don't you?"

"Sure I do. I bet they are big as hell, aren't they?"

Jamie smiles in thought, "Yeah, both of them are bigger then me."

"Okay Ron, back to the matters at hand. Now that we got a brief history of Mr. Collins, we still have to clear up a lot of things here."

Clark turns to Jamie again, "Collins, tell me, what is the purpose of taking the money?"

"Well, it's like I told McCulley, Ramirez and 'Shotgun Phillips' over there. I had expenses and my expertise."

The sheriff, who at this point feels inadequate interrupts Jamie, "Excuse me, Mr. Collins we run a police department in this town. We are not some back woods department with two deputies. We are as equipped here in Las Vegas as you were in Detroit. If you had a problem with one of our officers, you could have reported him. We would have investigated and our internal affairs would have made sure McCulley got what he deserves."

Jamie looks at Kerns and laughs in his face, "Excuse me Sheriff Kerns, I don't know if you have checked with your Internal Affairs department, before you came here or if you checked with them when I kidnapped your officers, but I have made ten complaints against Officer McCulley. The only thing that happened was my sons were sent to prison. So don't tell me about your department. I followed all the rules and I got nothing.

"Your officer had free rein to do whatever he wanted to do. Did you know he has an entire community afraid of him? How do you feel knowing you have an officer who set-up ten people, possibly twelve to go to prison.

"If Officer McCulley could get away with this, I guarantee you there are others who are doing the same. What are you going to do about them? As a matter of fact, what are you going to do?"

"What do you mean what am I going to do? Do about what," asks Kerns in a confused tone?

Jamie turns his head away from Sheriff Kerns. *There is no way that this man could have read the files and still be asking these questions. Either he is a total incompetent fuck, or he is being left in the dark.* Jamie glances back at Kerns. *Then again, maybe this guy is both.* "Agent Clark, you mean to tell me you haven't told him about his officers?"

"That's right Collins. I was waiting for this meeting. I felt just like you. I was afraid of a leak."

The sheriff looks at Damen and questions him. *What the hell is going on? Why won't anyone tell me anything? I didn't get this badge out of a Cracker Jack box. I earned my badge with my blood and sweat.* "What the hell are you talking about afraid of a leak... a leak about what? Somebody had better start talking."

Jamie turns his attention back towards Kerns, and gets right into his face, "Sheriff, see how much goes on under your nose."

Agent Clark senses a lot of hostility in the room and sees Kerns squirm in his seat, "Sit down men, Sheriff this is where McCulley comes in. McCulley, you want the floor?"

McCulley looks at the sheriff and Ramirez and starts by apologizing. *Man, I can't believe how bad I treated everyone. Look at Ramirez; she went through all of this shit. Never thought the kid had it in her. Looks like we both went through a life change, I stopped thinking with my balls, and she grew a pair. She's going to make a fine cop, I just know it. She'll be everything that I wasn't.*

"First off, I would like to apologize to my partner for getting her involved in so much shit. Then I want to apologize to the sheriff, for being an embarrassment to the department for lying on innocent people."

McCulley turns and directs the rest to the sheriff, "Now, Sheriff, I am involved with twelve other officers who believed in a pure White race and are plotting to blow-up four hotels."

Sheriff Kerns looks over at McCulley. *This guy is cracked! There is no way in hell any of this could happen without me knowing,* "I don't believe it, you got to be kidding."

"No sir, I'm not. Jamie has the evidence."

Kerns looks over at Jamie who has a grin he'd like to wipe off his face, "Young man, you have evidence against twelve other officers, implicating them in a terrorist plot?"

Jamie rolls his eyes, "No sir, McCulley was talking about how I lucked my way into the winning recipe for chili. Haven't you been listening at all? I mean, being uninformed is one thing, but can you really be this dumb?"

Agent Clark steps in before the men can go any further, "Mr. Collins, may I remind you that you are a guest of the FBI here and you are still wanted for several crimes. Please just answer Sheriff Kerns without the smart mouth."

"Sorry. That's correct sir, I do have the evidence."

Kerns squirms in his seat again after Clark plays ref between him and Jamie, "And that's why you took the money.   You figured you would hire yourself out to the city and charge them $757,000. I don't know about Detroit, but around here, you don't just go around hiring yourself out without proper authority!"

Jamie now standing, raises his hand from his waist and points his finger at the sheriff, "That is correct Mr. Sheriff, I did just that.

Have you even taken the time to talk to the people you are suppose to protecting? Have you ever spoke to any retired police officers from other cities?   Have you ever taken the time to talk with anyone other than those politicians downtown or people with money?

If you get off your ass and come out into the public, you will see what type of police department you are running.   You will hear people and veterans of police departments tell you, you have a bunch of jerks running around here with badges and guns; now you have them with bombs.

"I don't claim to be Superman or Batman and I will honestly say I would have left them jerks alone on Boulder

Highway, if I didn't figure out a way to use them to get my sons out of jail."

Jamie leans in closer to Kerns' face now, "You should be ashamed to have men on your department who belong to a terrorist group. You should be happy I came along and discovered what they intend to do. Just imagine the Strip on fire and your cops causing it.

Just imagine the amount of deaths and injuries caused by your cops. You are damn right, I took $757,000. As payment for the job I have done. You should give me more.

I have one more thing to say to you and that is don't ever question what I have done and the methods used to complete the job. If you do, I may not be able to hold my temper."

Jamie finishes his accusations at Kerns when he turns to Agent Clark and adds, "Not that I mean any disrespect, Sir."

Jamie sits back in his chair and tries to calm down while they watch the sheriff stare at McCulley. Damen then breaks the silence.

"Well, I can see we have gotten off to a great start and it looks like all the dirty laundry is hanging out to dry. Now we need to get down to business. Jamie, where is this so called evidence of yours?"

Jamie points to his pocket. "Evidence? You want evidence, I have all the damn evidence you or *60 Minutes* needs to bust these guys. I didn't go through all this shit to fall on my face.   In my pocket, there is a key to a locker at the Greyhound Bus Terminal downtown. Inside you will find a duffel bag containing tapes and notepads."

"Phillips, get the keys and give them to Agent Sharp and tell him to go and pick-up everything in that locker and get right back here fast."

"Okay sir."

The sheriff directs a comment to Jamie. "I suppose this evidence has the list of all my officers involved in this plot?"

"Yes sir, it does; it not only has a list of names, but I also have photos, videotapes, audiotapes, and dates and times."

"You are quite thorough?"

"Yes sir, I was. I wanted to make sure I had a good bargaining tool."

McCulley decides to break his silence. "Now that everything is out in the open what happens next? Are we going to get off after giving up all this evidence? Evidence that will prevent an untold amount of people from dying—or are you going to be blind to all the corruption that has ran rampant in your department?"

Agent Clark looks over in McCulley's direction. *He must be at the end of his nerves. First kidnapped, then he thought he would die, he agrees to confess all the bad shit he has done, like some altar boy going to Confession. Now here he is, a few hours after he thought he was home free, locked up in a room full of people that literally have his life in their hands.*

"McCulley this has been a long day and it is going to get longer, so let's not try to rush things, and since I'm talking to you, I may as well ask you a few questions. How do you fit into this? What made you go along with Collins?"

"Guilt Sir, just plain old guilt. I also figured that if I went along with Jamie, I would have a better chance with you guys. I just couldn't see myself going down for blowing up anything.

Sir, I didn't know they were for real. I didn't know they were going to actually kill anyone. When I found out, I decided to do something about it, and that was to expose them and testify against them. I have made a lot of mistakes in my life and I can't change that, but I can change the person I was, to the person I would like to be, a better cop serving to protect innocent people that deserve a better way of life.

Hatred towards people that are different from me is not the answer. Just give the chance to prove myself to all of you, please!"

"Wise choice McCulley, I understand that you also admitted to Jamie your guilt in railroading those other men."

"That's correct sir. I am guilty on that count and I am willing to pay the price."

Clark reflects on McCulley's words for a moment, "Don't be so willing, you don't know what the price is yet. I want the three of you to know I..."

Phillips re-entering the room interrupts Damen, "Everything is taken care of sir."

"Okay Phillips. Now as I was saying, I want all three of you to know, I am really impressed with you. Two of you are facing some very serious charges and it will probably be a hundred years before either of you get out of prison. So I am open for suggestions. What should we do with you?"

Jamie couldn't resist his opportunity to try and get off, "Well sir, I have a suggestion. I think you should take all the information and let us go and call it a day. Or am I assuming too much."

Clark lets out a small sigh. This guy has a point, but he isn't going to get off so easy. He probably went through with the whole plot, knowing he would just give the information about the bombing up as a trade-off to get himself off free.

"Mr. Collins, I can understand all the things you have gone through over the last two years. I can also understand why you have the attitude you possess at the present. I will tell you one thing, if you continue looking at this situation as though it were a day at the park, I will make damn sure your life is a worse nightmare than what you are living now.

"You have disrupted quite a few lives because of your anger. You have got half the citizens hoping you survive your ordeal and we release your sons.

"Do you know or even care what would happen if you should win? Are you aware of the type of chaos you would cause around the country? People everywhere are going to try and take matters into their own hands, and then disregard the law or those that work for it.

"I am well aware that sometime in the near future, a day is going to come when everything man has ever stood for will come to an end. I don't want that day to come while I'm working in this capacity. I want to be home with my family, off the streets.

So as it stands right now, your ass is under arrest. And if it were in my power your ass would be dead now and all we have to do is sweep everything under the rug.

But one thing, you have done the community a big favor and we have to take that into consideration. So cut it out with all of your sarcastic remarks because we have to come to a middle ground."

Clark waits for Jamie to say something in return, but begins to think of why Jamie would go through such elaborate lengths to do things. *McCulley...why frame McCulley for assisting in the robbery. We know Collins acted alone, and we know that McCulley was good as dead to Jamie. Why take the time to frame a dead man?*

"Oh Jamie, if you don't mind, I have another question for you. Why did you try and frame McCulley? Don't deny this because I am not stupid."

"Well, I wasn't satisfied with McCulley just being another one of the gang, and on top of it, McCulley is a marked man. I didn't want him to die. That would have been too easy. I wanted him to go to prison along with the people he sent there. I felt his life would have been a lot harder to deal with."

Clark nods his head and takes some notes on the situation. *That explains why the set-up, but if he wanted McCulley in jail, why would he go through all of this trouble to make sure that neither him nor McCulley were caught. He had plenty of time to ditch McCulley; the witnesses often spoke of seeing just Collins and not Officer McCulley. Why would a man go through all the trouble to set someone up, only to risk his own ass trying to save the man he set-up?*

"In taking McCulley out of the country with you, what would you have accomplished?"

"He would be on the run with me and no one would have believed him if we got caught. I want to add something if I may."

"Go ahead."

"McCulley and I have had some serious conversations about his life and why his mind reacts the way it does. I grew to like him. I felt that if we were to get caught, he needed a chance, and so I made up my mind that I would tell the truth and try to help him out.

Another reason why I had a change of heart is because he showed to me that he does have feelings for human life and respect. It makes me very happy to say with a little assistance from you, he can be the best cop on your force."

Clark has had enough with the way things had been going. *What the hell does Collins think this is? Oprah? Oh, he sent my sons to prison, he is the devil, but now I understand and like him. What a load of shit.*

"Aw, cut the crap. I don't want to hear any of that bullshit. I want to know when did you think you were so smart that you thought you could take on the U.S. Government?"

"Sir, I did not set out to take on the government. As a matter of fact, I thought by now I would be dead or under arrest in a hospital.

"I am waiting to be paraded around town in front of national TV cameras in shackles and chains. So you can say to the public, a person doesn't get away with crimes in this country.

"I'm waiting for you to use as me an example, but I can go down knowing the fact that this time I committed a few crimes. Crimes that not only out smarted the local police, but got the FBI wondering what else can happen in this country and who else is plotting to commit mass murder.

"Sir, I am glad I did what I did. At least my sons will get another trial. At least they will get out of jail. I don't care what happens to me. My life is almost over anyway."

"Yes, you are truly a product of the sixties. Don't you understand all that revolution bullshit went out with bellbottoms?"

"Look I'm not a revolutionary, I am a father trying to protect his kids, and it just so happened I stumbled on some assholes threatening to kill a few thousand innocent people in the process.

"If it weren't for that fact, I probably wouldn't have gone as far as I did. I know that in order to balance out things, I had to have a bargaining tool. And my bargaining tool was McCulley and his friends.

"In the process, I just so happened to pick up another lost soul who needed my help. In helping him, we both came to the conclusion that there is something to that old saying 'Death before dishonor.

"Now you got me, you got the evidence, and you got the money. So, what are you going to do? If you are going to lock me up let's go and get this shit over with. If you are going to make a deal, take these damn chains off me and let's talk."

Jamie looks over at McCulley and thinks of all the time they spent together recently, all of the good things that McCulley has tried to do in his life recently, how he has tried to turn himself around and how McCulley went out for him even when it meant his own life.

"I want you to know McCulley and I are a package. If you make a deal, McCulley is part of it."

Clark looks at the pair. *Damn 'Odd Couple' is what we have here. A crooked cop and a straight criminal. Would never believe this shit in a million years.*

I can't believe how Collins still sticks up for McCulley. Even when the chips are down, Collins sticks up for what he thinks is right. I don't know whether I should admire him or send him off to jail.

"You know Collins; I really like your tenacity. I feel a lot of people would have given up by now. I guess that's what Ron saw in you."

Clark's mind travels back to all the stunts that Jamie pulled. How he eluded all attempts to find and capture him. He made the whole city of Las Vegas look like a fool and there was nothing we could do about it. We only got him because we lucked out when they went to Mexico, if it weren't for that, Collins would have gotten away with the robbery and everything, and we'd be left holding the check.

"Mr. Collins, I don't know what else to say to you other than the fact that you are an asshole. I honestly don't know what to do with you, but thank goodness there are other people involved to help make decisions.

"The sheriff over there is on my side. Just like he told McCulley, the same goes for you. He wants you dead. But just like you said, you brought along with you some bargaining tools. I will have to admit your bargaining tools are really powerful not to mention your friends."

At the word 'friends', Clark glances over to where Agent Nelson is sitting. This Collins' must really be something for Nelson to put his ass on the line for him. He better be right about Jamie, or we all are screwed.

"I want you to know there are the reasons why we have come to these conclusions. Your thoughtfulness of human life made us really think about a deal.

"From talking with Ron, you have continued to show that you are truly a caring man. I was never under the impression you were a dangerous man. Because you took too much time to make sure you didn't put anyone in a dangerous position.

"McCulley, other than the fact that you ate the butt of a shotgun, and Ramirez, the risk you took, and even jeopardized your career, that says a lot for your character."

The focus of discussion shifted quickly off of Jamie and unto Ramirez. Ramirez looked up as if startled.

"Risk...you have no idea what I felt. The fear that I might lose my life, being held hostage, my body paralyzed by some drug unknown to me, being told that one of us would not make it out alive and then chained to a damn pole.

"Yeah, I jeopardized a lot, but not just that, I was scared shitless. But all that didn't matter except to save the lives of all these innocent people and doing what I set out to do and that was to make a difference."

"Sir, we both were in fear for our lives, and McCulley even showed his by the way he ran his mouth," teased Ramirez.

McCulley takes the teasing gracefully and agrees, "I can honestly say, I didn't know what fear was until all this shit happened."

Agent Clark interjects, "Well let me say one thing. This guy who held you captive meant what he said about dying for a cause. He would have done just that if necessary."

Clark stares out into his office; he doesn't focus on any one person or object. *This man is smarter than these guys know. Better tell them what I've found out about Jamie and his plans. They won't believe it until they see it, hell; I don't even believe it at times.*

"You see I know Jamie and people like him. You think you are so smart. I want you to know you are not half as smart as me. McCulley and Ramirez, Mr. Collins over here didn't have the balls to kill either one of you. Mr. Collins would have ran around the world before shooting you, because neither one of you were a threat to him. If you had gotten the drop on him, he would have made you kill him."

Ramirez, I want you to examine the weapons over on the table that Mr. Collins had in his possession."

Before Ramirez could make it to the table to pick up the weapon, Stella's voice came across the intercom again, "Sir, Agent Sharp is back."

"Okay, have him come in."

Agent Sharp enters the room as instructed with the material that Clark sent him out to find. The entire surveillance package Jamie put together is inside, resting comfortably in its package.

"Sit the package on the table Sharp and you may stay. Okay Ramirez, do you recognize the weapons?"

"Yes I do. This is the 357 Magnum he kept in his belt, and this is the shotgun he hit McCulley with. It still has blood on it.""

Ramirez holds the weapons in her hands and goes over them like they were dead pieces of wood. Heavy and cumbersome, Ramirez wonders how Jamie could even wield these weapons, let alone hold someone hostage with them. She starts to think back to when she was his prisoner but Agent Clark's voice brings her back into the present.

"Okay Ramirez, look at the pistol. Pull back the hammer. What do you see?"

Ramirez does as told and then does a double take on the pistol, "Sir, there is no firing pin!"

"What about the shotgun?"

"The same sir, no firing pin."

Ramirez stays over by the weapons looking at them with a stunned glance. *He held us hostage with an oversized water pistol. He couldn't have killed us with these even if he wanted to. Jamie really put his trust in us.*

But how did he know we would react the way we did? Just how much time and effort did he put into all of this? All I know is that I am glad I am not the one to piss him off.

"Like I said, you can thank your friends. Boy, does he know you. Mr. Collins, it's nice to know that there are still people who will die for a good cause. It is nice to know that you would sooner die than go to prison.

"No matter how we looked at the situation we can't get around the fact of what you have done. So I am here to tell you Mr. Collins, we have all the evidence you gathered and the money you stole. We have you in custody and we are the FBI and because I don't like you, you are going to jail under heavy security and we are going to make sure you stay alive the whole twenty years."

At this point, McCulley attempts to stand as he yells in Jamie's defense. "You can't do that; you can't put him in jail after all he has done for you. This man deserves a break. He deserves to go free."

Jamie's head drops as he hears McCulley argue in his behalf. Tears begin to roll down his face as he looks up at Damen. "What about my sons? What's going to happen to them?"

"Right now your biggest concern is yourself. If everything goes all right, you may have a cell next to them."

McCulley interrupts again. "What about my testimony? I lied, they are innocent."

"McCulley as I told Jamie here, you had better be concerned about your own well being. I am not going to let some little two-bit punk come in this city and run it like it's a dictatorship. Now, you shut up before you dig your hole deeper than what it is."

McCulley looks at Jamie and begins to apologize. "Jamie I am sorry things didn't work out the way you planned them. I know you done the best you could, but don't worry you have shown me what friendship is and I won't quit until I get justice for you."

Jamie shakes his head, "Don't concern yourself. Just get your life together. I will be just fine."

As everyone watches Jamie and McCulley say their tearful good-byes. Ramirez has her head down and is crying. All of a sudden her tiny whimpers become loud sobs and she jumps from her seat and pulls out her service revolver and backs against the wall.

"Everybody put your hands up and don't move. That goes double for you Phillips. I would just love to blow your head off."

The room is in total silence now and everyone's attention is on Ramirez, "Phillips, get your ass over here and take these cuffs and chains off Jamie and McCulley, but first, drop your weapon on the floor and kick it over by me."

Phillips shaking now, knowing Ramirez will shoot him walks over to Jamie and McCulley and unlocks the handcuffs and chains.

"Lay your monkey ass on the floor or die where you're standing!"

The sheriff, being the farthest away uses this opportunity to try and reach for his weapon, but is spotted by Ron Nelson, "Watch out Ramirez, the sheriff is going for his weapon!"

Ramirez whips around to meet her former employer, "Hold it sheriff. I will blow your brains out. Take that gun out; drop it on the floor and slide it over here."

While the sheriff complies, Ron Nelson makes a suggestion, "Ramirez, it looks like you have your hands full, why don't you let me help you?"

Ramirez looks a bit unsure at this. She hadn't planned on everything being so difficult. *Hell, I didn't plan on any of this at all. What the hell am I doing? The right thing, girl, you are doing the right thing, but what about Agent Nelson? I don't know this guy from a hole in the ground.*

Jamie sees her doubt, "Go ahead Ramirez, you can trust him. I know him as well as he knows me."

That's all Ramirez needed to make up her mind, "Okay Agent Nelson, you go around and collect everyone's weapons." She turns away from him and looks at the others. "When he takes your weapon, get down on the floor."

Agent Nelson walks around the room collecting weapons from everyone in the room and now has eight people lying on the floor.

Jamie pauses to question Ramirez. "Ramirez, why are you doing this? You don't have to involve yourself in this. They know you didn't have anything to do with this. Why are you messing up your life?"

For once in her life, Ramirez knows that what she's doing is the right thing. Always playing it safe and looking the other way. Not this time, too many lives were at stake.

"Jamie, I believe in your cause and like I told you back at the house, I am tired of people walking on each other. This white shirt wearing asshole lied to me ever since I walked into his office. "First, he lied about the wiretaps, then he lied about no harm coming to you and now he is going to send you to prison even though you solved a major case for him. Forget him, forget the sheriff, and forget about this job because for all I know, they could be part of the whole scheme."

The sheriff mumbles from the floor. "Have you lost your mind? I'll see to it that your badge is stripped. Hell, you'll never see daylight again if you keep on this course. Woman, you picked an interesting time to grow a set of balls. Ramirez, we will forget this ever happened if you just put down that weapon."

Ramirez scoffs at Kerns in disbelief, "Sheriff, what kind of fool do you think I am? I know my job is gone. I know you will arrest me, so forget it."

Seeing that the sheriff can't convince Ramirez to give up, Agent Clark tries his hand.

"Ron what are you doing? Why are you helping? I just know you are not willing to throw away your career."

"Don't worry Damen; I got friends in high places. I'm not worried about myself. Remember me saying earlier that I came to help a friend? This is why I am here. I haven't forgotten the type of person you are. I know you're not the type to be trusted. So I came prepared."

Nelson reaches on his side and pulls out a radio, "Dog to cat."

The radio crackles in response, "This is cat, go ahead."

"We have the mice laying flat. Proceed with the plan."

"Okay dog, on the way. Cat out."

Jamie looks at Nelson and smiles. "I knew I could depend on you, but how the hell are we going to get out of here?"

"Don't worry Jamie; everything is going to be all right. This reminds me of the drug deal that went bad in L.A. last year, remember that, don't you?"

Jamie looks at him with a question on his face. Ron tries to explain in the short time he has, "Come on Jamie, remember...in L.A... remember?"

Jamie now shows a sign of recognition, "Oh, of course, now I remember."

Nelson smiles now, "I told you never to forget our busts. You'll never know when you have to recall something. McCulley, come on get up, you're going with us. I think I recall Jamie saying you and him were a package. Move those chairs around; we're going to have some company."

McCulley looks puzzled but follows orders. As McCulley finishes with the chairs, a knock on the door is heard.

"Ramirez, get the door and let everyone in."

Ramirez opens the door opens and a line of fifteen people file in with their hands on their heads, followed by four men with shotguns.

"Come on in ladies and gentlemen. All of you find yourselves a comfortable spot on the floor."

As the people file in the room, Jamie, McCulley and Ramirez and Agent Nelson found themselves standing by the door.

Nelson starts to direct traffic, "Jamie go over and snatch the phone out and check and see if anyone has a radio. I know the sheriff has one. Get it."

Jamie does what he is told and the eight people begin to remove themselves from the room.

"Okay everyone; let's get the hell out of here."

As they were leaving the room one by one, Damen is reaching for his ankle holster and pulls out his five shot 38 revolver.

Nelson stops to address Agent Clark one last time, but doesn't see the movement in the middle of the chaos that just erupted.

"Okay Damen, I'm sorry we had to mess up your little plan, but you know how life is. McCulley get the money. Jamie get the tapes"

After getting the money and the tapes, McCulley and Jamie head out the door, but Jamie froze when he hears Damen yell, "You may get away, but Jamie isn't."

Then three shots ring out, striking Jamie in the back, sending him and the tapes into the hallway. Nelson retaliated by firing two shots back, hitting Damen as he fell to the floor.

Nelson shakes his head with sorrow and rage, "Why did you have to shoot him? You have no idea what you have done!"

Nelson rushes out the room and grabs a rope from one of the other men and pulls the door shut. He then ties the rope on the doorknob and extends it across the hall and tied it to another door. They then scramble to pick up the tapes and Jamie.

"Here McCulley, take the tapes and money, you and Ramirez get downstairs, there is a van waiting for us."

Nelson and another agent pick-up Jamie and carry him to the waiting van. The door was slammed and the squealing tires were heard in the darkness.

Somewhere in Las Vegas, a television set is turned on to the late night showing of a murder mystery. An old man is watching the movie on his new television set and is really getting into it. He has watched the show every night it has been on and can recite most of the lines word for word. Just getting into the 'good parts', the man becomes irate when a news flash breaks his program.

"We interrupt your scheduled program to bring you a Special News Bulletin from the Channel 7 Studios. Here's Douglas Wayne, reporting." uttered an ominous voice introducing the flash bulletin.

The camera cuts to a man that has become familiar over the course of the incident with Jamie. He is one of the lead reporters for the special news team of Channel 7.

"Over night, there were some drastic and deadly turns in the saga of Jamie Collins. We have John Wiggs on the scene at the FBI Headquarters on Charleston Blvd. John can you hear us?"

"Yes Doug, we are at the scene of the FBI Headquarters on Charleston Blvd. where a tragic turn of events has taken place. Yesterday in the early evening,

Jamie Collins was found in Mexico and returned to the United States to this office in Las Vegas.

Everything is still a little confusing John, but to my understanding the suspect and Officer McCulley were in this office being interrogated, by Sheriff Kerns, Special Agent in Charge Damen Clark, and Special Agent Ron Nelson from the DEA.

We don't have any information as to what transpired in the meeting, but Police Officer Delores Ramirez pulled her gun and demanded the release of Jamie Collins and Officer McCulley. Everyone was made to lie on the floor while they made their way out.

"Doug, there was another accomplice to this escape. Agent Ron Nelson from the DEA. He assisted Ramirez in disarming everyone and as they were making their escape, Agent Damen Clark shot Jamie Collins in the back three times. Ron Nelson returned fire hitting Agent Clark in the back twice. He was rushed to UMC his condition is unknown at this time.

"Agent Nelson, Officers McCulley and Ramirez, and Jamie Collins have escaped to an unknown location. We have no idea if Jamie Collins is alive or not. All hospitals are covered Doug, he will have to turn up soon.

"Sheriff Kerns was unharmed and at this time he refuses to make any comment."

"John, is there any way you can get any more information from the other workers or agent in the building?"

"No Doug, they are not allowing anyone into the building and they are holding all employees for briefings. I look at it this way Doug, we are going to have a long wait before we get any answers about what took place in this now gloomy building. That is all I have right now Doug, but we will be here throughout the day to keep you informed.

"This is John Wiggs from Channel 7 Eyewitness news."

The regular program starts up again, but the old man isn't paying attention. He has cornered himself in his room after digging an old shotgun out of his closet. He knows the men on television. He has had contact with them, and he can't help the feeling that someone is watching him this very instant. That is the thought that keeps him up through the night, while he hugs the gun like it was his child that he never sees.

Watching him; eyes, watching him.

Made in the USA
Las Vegas, NV
23 June 2022